THE WONDER OF IT ALL

Also by Karla Clark

Between Courses: A Culinary Love Story
Knotted Pearls and Other Stories
Annie's Heaven
Everybody and Their Brother
You Be Mommy
You Be Daddy
Three Ways to Be Brave: A Trio of Stories
You Be Grandma
You Be Grandpa
The Phony Baloney of Greta Maloney
You Be Teacher
The Picture Book Author's Helper: Your Planner, Tracker & Guide
Color Me Prayerful
I Know Things

THE WONDER OF IT ALL

Karla Clark

Main Course Books

THE WONDER OF IT ALL
Copyright © 2025 by Karla Clark

Cover art by Roni Golan
Cover design by Clay Anderson

ISBN: 979-8-9903871-2-6 (hardcover)
Library of Congress Control Number: 2025922962

MainCourseBooks.com

For my family: then, now, and always.

Family is family, whether it's the one you start out with, the one you end up with, or the family you gain along the way. –Unknown

THE

WONDER
OF IT
ALL

Prologue

THIS IS LEO'S story.

But to understand Leo—truly understand him—you have to begin long before he was ever born. You have to trace the line of women who came before him, women who shaped him not just through blood, but through presence and absence, through love both given and withheld.

To understand Leo, you first need to know his mother, Camille, and his aunt, Rosie. And to understand those two sisters, you must go back further…to their mother, Stella Maris, a woman whose hold on her daughters would echo across generations.

So, yes, this is Leo's story. But before we get to Leo, let's begin with the women. And to understand the wonder of it all, we start where most stories begin: with someone wanting more than the life they were handed.

1.
rosie & camille

AUGUST FIFTH, NINETEEN sixty-two marked an important date in American history. On that day, Marilyn Monroe died from an apparent drug overdose, the South African government arrested Nelson Mandela, and astronomers discovered the first quasar in the sky. But to Camille and Rosie Quinlayne—five and eleven years old respectively—August 5th was just *Cleaning Day*. And on cleaning day, their mother, depending on the weather, either locked them out of the house right after breakfast until dinner, or confined them to the basement rec room. Stella Maris Quinlayne, a Joan Crawford lookalike, scoured her Rockford, Illinois, three-bedroom brick bungalow every day of the week, but on Saturdays, she practically tore it apart and rebuilt it. The four beds were stripped, the sheets were washed, dried, ironed, and returned to the beds, where hospital corners were strictly employed. Furniture was moved. Floors and walls scrubbed. Surfaces disinfected. Pantry items were faced and re-alphabetized.

In the summer, cleaning days were no problem as Rosie and Camille adored being outdoors, riding their bikes up and down their tree-lined street with the other neighbor kids. They played four-square in Kimmy's driveway and *Mother-May-I* in Maria's backyard. If they were thirsty, they drank from the garden hose; if they had to pee, they did their business behind the bushes at the back of their fenced-in yard. Now, before someone starts to think Stella Maris Quinlayne starved her children, it should be noted that, at noon, she would set out two paper plates on the back concrete steps, one containing a peanut butter and jelly sandwich, and the other, a butter and cheese sandwich with the crusts cut off. Sometimes she would add a few pretzels, a Red Delicious, or a handful of green grapes.

On this particularly hot August day, with the sun high in a lightly clouded, baby-blanket blue sky, Rosie had promised to build Camille a fort in the backyard, so they'd parked their bikes in the garage and rooted around for supplies.

Petite, brown-eyed Camille, who had just turned five, idolized her big sister. Rosie was the best person in the universe—smart, kind, but mostly, brave. Camille had seen Rosie withstand bullying from the pretty girls when they called her *Round-Round Rosie*.

Rosie found an old green army blanket on a shelf in the garage. "This'll work," she told Camille. Outside, she shook it out, slung it over the clothesline, and instructed Camille to fetch four bricks from the flower bed to secure it. Just as Rosie put the last brick in place, the back door opened and Stella Maris placed two paper plates on the stoop. The gesture always made Rosie feel like a damned dog.

"What are you two up to?" Stella Maris called out, her beehive hairdo wrapped up in a chiffon scarf.

Camille shouted, "Rosie's making me a castle!"

"Well, you better put everything back where you found it."

"We will, Mommy!" Camille assured her.

They brought their lunch inside the tent. Rosie unsnapped from her belt loop her cherished transistor radio—her combined Christmas/birthday present—and turned to find the least staticky station. She still couldn't believe her parents had bought it for her. "It costs more than a week's worth of groceries!" Stella Maris had complained. But Barry Quinlayne had a soft spot for his girls and told his wife that forty-nine ninety-five wouldn't put them in the poor house. Rosie had asked for this exact model: the 9v Admiral Super 7. It came with a brown leather case. Rosie was head over heels in love with Ricky Nelson. In just two years' time, Ricky Nelson would be replaced by the Beatles, but the summer of 1962 belonged to Ozzie and Harriet's son. She turned the dial and found the Beach Boys' "Surfin' Safari." Rosie was also head over heels in love with the Beach Boys.

Camille complained that the old army blanket smelled musty. Its dark green color absorbed the sun and raised the temperature inside the tent to a sweltering level. After a couple of bites of her sandwich, she set her plate down and told Rosie she needed an afternoon nap. She peeled off her top (being only five, she had no shame about her naked chest) and bunched it up to use as a pillow. "Tell me a story, Rosie," she said. She relaxed and her thumb found the comfort of her mouth.

Rosie, round-faced and what Grandmother Quinlayne called "pleasantly plump," said, "Two more bites and then I'll tell you a story about Carmelita and Rosita and their latest adventure in Mexico." But Camille had fallen asleep before Rosie finished her PB&J.

Flies accumulated around Camille's unfinished sandwich, so Rosie took the paper plates and threw them in the garbage can in the garage. She picked some dandelions, popped off their heads, and made a bracelet from their sticky stems. She couldn't bring herself to go back into the tent—it was just too hot—but she couldn't leave Camille alone either, so she lay in the grass outside the tent, head-to-head with her sister, and listened to Camille's soft breathing, and then happily, to Ricky Nelson singing "Teenage Idol" on her radio. Rosie watched the clouds float across the sky and remembered the day when she first realized that not everyone's mother locked her children out of the house.

"Fresh air is good for them," Stella Maris would tell their father to justify her ban. "John-O is outdoors all day and he doesn't complain. I can't have them underfoot while I'm cleaning." John-O (John Oliver) was the only son, the golden boy. At thirteen, he had his paper route and lawn-mowing jobs. He was saving up to buy a brand-new VW Beetle when he turned sixteen.

"Can't the girls help you?" their father asked, not comfortable at all with his wife's rigidity.

"Barry Quinlayne! You know they wouldn't do it right!"

Rosie drifted off into a gauzy, summery sleep, the breeze sashaying across her skin. She woke to Camille's shrill scream. "Rosie!"

Rosie darted up, her heart racing, shaking off the sun-drenched sleep. She found her shirtless little sister sitting up, holding her foot. "A bee stung me!" Bees terrified Camille ever since one of her classmates had an allergic reaction to a playground bee sting that sent her to the emergency room. Rosie took a look. The stinger protruded from the side of Camille's foot so she pinched it out with her fingers. This sent Camille over the edge, and she started wailing. Between her tears, she said, "Oh, no, Rosie! I just peed my pants!"

Rosie looked down and watched a splotch of Camille's light blue shorts turn a dark blue. Camille pulled at her hair. "Mommy is going to be so mad!"

"Mommy won't know," Rosie said. "Take off your shorts and undies. I'll wash them with the hose and lay them out in the sun. It's no big deal, Cammy."

Camille gingerly removed her shorts and undies and handed them to Rosie with a look of apology. She scooched over to the other end of the tent where the grass was dry. She wiped her eyes with her fists and sighed. Rosie the rescuer. Thank God for Rosie.

"Stay put," Rosie told her. She carried the soiled clothes with two fingers, laid them in the grass, and hosed them down with the garden hose. She squeezed them out and lay them in the sun to dry and then joined her naked sister back in the tent. The poor thing tried to hide her private parts with her shirt while holding her foot. "It's really thromping now," she said. Rosie, always resourceful, scraped up a bit of dirt from a bald patch in the lawn, spit into the palm of her hand, and made a little poultice to rub on the sting. Camille settled down once Rosie applied the "magic mud."

Camille lay back down, her damp, blond curls sticking to her forehead. She stretched her shirt to try to cover her private parts. But the shirt was small and if she covered her chest, her lower parts were exposed, and if she pulled it down to cover her lower parts, her chest was exposed. "Tell me a story, Rosie," Camille said, whimpering.

Rosie knew she shouldn't, but she did anyway. "One day, while Carmelita and Rosita were at school, their mean mommy fell down the stairs and died. Carmelita and Rosita were sad, but they moved to Brazil with their daddy, and lived on a ranch where they rode horses for the rest of their lives. They realized that you really didn't need a mother."

"I just hope Mom doesn't come out here," Camille said, opening her eyes and adjusting the shirt again.

"She won't," Rosie said.

"Promise me you won't tell her I peed my pants," Camille said.

"I promise."

"Rosie, can I please wear *your* shirt? I feel so naked-ed."

"Okay," Rosie said and peeled off her T-shirt, wishing for the millionth time that her mother would let her get a bra. Her little buds embarrassed her. All her friends had bras. But Stella Maris said, "Sheesh, those aren't breasts, that's just fat and fat doesn't need a bra. Fat needs to lose weight."

Little naked Camille gave her topless big sister a hug for always looking out for her, when, out of nowhere, Stella Maris appeared.

"What in the name of all that's holy are you two doing?" she said, her dark, Joan-Crawford eyebrows accusingly arched.

Camille darted up and dropped Rosie's shirt, exposing herself completely. "Nothing, Mommy!"

Stella Maris stood with her hands on her hips. "Rose Marie?"

Rosie sat there topless, holding her hands across her chest. "We made this tent, but it got so hot, we just wanted to cool off," Rosie said, trying to sound nonchalant.

"Lord almighty! This is shameful! Rosie, don't you understand how this looks? Someone could walk by and think you two were doing something…well…something sisters shouldn't do to each other."

Rosie cringed. She was only eleven, but she knew what her mother was insinuating. Her jaw dropped. Then her heart followed. How could her mother think such a terrible thing! Tears welled up in her eyes as she grabbed her T-shirt and covered her breasts—her little lumps of fat—for somehow, she knew her life would never be the same. Once Stella Maris got something in her head, it was stamped into her neurons forever.

That night, their father tucked the girls in and pretended he didn't know about the day's incident. But Barry was so transparent. After kissing each girl on the forehead, he told them how proud he was of them, that he was glad he had good daughters who obeyed their mother and who respected people and their own bodies for that matter. "Remember," he told them. "Our bodies are temples of God."

Rosie punched down her pillow and turned over on her side.

Camille whispered, "Thanks for not telling on me, Rosie."

"You're welcome," Rosie said.

Camille would never know the cost. That night, at eleven years old, Rosie started plotting her escape.

2.
rosie & alisha

WHERE SOME HIGH school graduates matriculated with dreams for the future, Rosie Quinlayne had *plans*. Solid plans. She was going to change the world. Her senior year, she had landed a sweet deal as an intern in the mayor's office. And even though she viewed organizational politics as a necessary evil, she knew she needed to learn about the inner workings of local government or she could never change the world. She had to do something about this crazy country and where it was going. The Vietnam War, civil rights, women's rights, and poverty. But what could she do in Rockford, Illinois? She needed to be where the action was—in Washington, D.C.

Once her internship ended, Rosie and her best friend Alisha Weller were escaping. The plan was to take Alisha's car, drive to D.C., and show up at Alisha's older brother's apartment at Georgetown University. Just show up at his door and go from there.

But before D.C., they were going to attend what was hyped up to be the event of a lifetime: *Woodstock—an Aquarian Exposition Music and Art Fair* somewhere in the state of New York. When Rosie and Alisha found out their hero, folk singer/activist Joan Baez, was performing, they decided nothing could stop them.

The year, 1969, had started with the election of Richard Nixon, who promised to restore law and order to the nation's cities and provide new leadership in the Vietnam war. "New leadership?!" Rosie would shout at the black and white television in the den. "How about ending the war, you jackass!" One of Rosie's biggest regrets in life was that she'd missed the chance to vote *against* Nixon and *for* Humphrey by just a couple of months. She begged her mom and dad to please, please, vote for Humphrey, but the Quinlaynes had been staunch Republicans for several generations and had no intentions of jumping parties. "I think Mr. Nixon will make a fine president," Stella Maris had said.

Stella Maris was none too happy about her daughter becoming one of those "hippie-dippies." The day she caught Rosie in her bedroom distressing a perfectly good pair of blue jeans with a square of sandpaper, was the day she knew she had failed as a mother. The day Rosie appeared at the dinner table in a gauzy blouse without a bra, was the day she knew she had failed as a human being.

"I don't understand this so-called hippie movement at all," Stella Maris said more than once at the dinner table. Barry Quinlayne, who was a believer in eating dinner in peace, said, "Let it be, Stell."

Stella Maris never let anything be. "Well, John-O didn't go all hippie-dippie."

John-O was not there to explain himself; John-O was studying mathematics at the University of Illinois. "John-O is lucky to be in college," Rosie said, "or else he would have been drafted and fighting in Vietnam, and then *you* would have turned into a hippie-dippie."

"What's a hippie-dippie?" Camille asked. Sweet, clueless Camille, twelve years old and still playing with Barbie dolls. Lately, Camille had watched the big sister she idolized grow sullen and rebellious. The two girls shared a bedroom all through their childhood, and although Rosie tried to shield Camille, who was only in the seventh grade when Rosie was a senior, from most of her angst, it certainly spilled over. Camille was so different— a little yellow raft floating down a river, going with the flow, sweet, calm, taking the world for what it was, depending on others to make it better. Rosie always knew the hardest thing about leaving home would be leaving Camille.

"Let it be, girls," Barry said.

"Well, I understand," Stella Maris said, "about being anti-war. *I* am anti-war."

Rosie said, "Anti-war and political activism are just a part of the movement. It's also about breaking away from the mainstream culture and the corrupt government. We believe that peace and love are the answer to all things."

"Peace and love? Ha!" Stella Maris snorted, as she plopped a spoonful of mashed potatoes onto Barry's plate. "Do peace and love put food on the table? Flower power. Pa-lease!"

"You don't get it and you never will," Rosie said.

On August 13th at precisely two a.m., Rosie tiptoed down the stairs with a sleeping bag, a suitcase, and a duffle bag. She drew back the drapes on the picture window in the living room and looked out into the moonlight. Her heart was about to jump out of her chest. At three minutes after two, Rosie spotted her best friend Alisha Weller's white Chevy Impala at the end of the street and watched the headlights blink on and off twice. It was happening! She grabbed her gear and closed the door behind her—no goodbyes or long explanations, just a handwritten note placed on Camille's nightstand that read: "Cammy, please don't hate me. I was suffocating. I love you and I will call you soon. —Ro"

They would drive 850 miles in Alisha's semi-roadworthy, gas-guzzling Chevy to a 600-acre dairy farm near Bethel, New York, to attend the festival called *Woodstock*. Alisha's cousin Becki, who lived in Allentown, Pennsylvania, had purchased tickets for them—three-day passes for eighteen dollars each. They would pick up Becki first and then make their way north to the concert.

Rosie simply *had* to get away from her mother. All her friends agreed that she had the absolute worst mother on the planet. You could not please the woman. When Rosie brought home straight A's, her mom celebrated with festive dinners. When she agreed, as a middle-schooler, to join a weight loss organization called T.O.P.S. (Take Off Pounds Sensibly), she was rewarded with a shopping spree at the J.C. Penney. But Stella Maris needed perfection and when Rosie's face broke out or she put on a few pounds or used slang or slept late or quit piano lessons or showed no interest in learning how to cook or sew or garden, then Stella Maris withheld love and attention.

Rosie was a pretty girl in an old-fashioned, silent movie-star way. Grandma Quinlayne always said Rosie reminded her of the actress Clara Bow with her expressive brown eyes and heart-shaped lips. (Rosie did in fact share the actress's plucky, tomboy charm and pert audacity.)

That one summer, the day in the tent with Camille, when Rosie was only eleven years old, she started counting the years, months, days until she could flee. Rosie's mother made her feel *dirty*. It began with that innocent incident in the tent, followed by getting caught kissing Joey Bowers on the back stoop when she was thirteen, and then, with Stella Maris's discovery of a very private and sophomoric entry in Rosie's diary about wanting to make love with Davy Jones. Stella Maris made a big stupid deal about it, not knowing that Davy Jones was not a classmate but in fact the heartthrob singer in band *The Monkees,* and not even being embarrassed about it or apologizing after she called school and demanded the name and phone number of Davy Jones's parents.

The last straw was during her senior year, when Rosie discovered that her mom had been tracking her periods for years.

"We're really doing this!" Alisha said when Rosie hopped in, after throwing her stuff in the back seat. The hardest part was over—the escape. Now it was time to be happy.

"We're going to change the world!" Rosie said. "But first, we're going to hang loose, catch some rays, and listen to some great music!"

"Woodstock, here we come!" Alisha howled as she put the car in drive. She hit the gas and laid on the horn as they drove away.

"What an exit!" Rosie said. She was beyond excited. Thanks to having a cultured best friend, she had been to some great concerts in high school. Alisha's parents were huge music fans and much hipper than her parents. Dr. Weller was a neurosurgeon and Mrs. Weller was a public defender. Stella

Maris couldn't possibly refuse Rosie when she requested permission to go to Chicago with Alisha and her family to see a "musical" (she avoided the words "rock concert"). She saw Paul Simon in 1966 at the Arie Crown Theater, Neil Diamond the next year at the Cheetah, and The Who in 1968 at The Electric Theatre. But nothing could top seeing (literally *seeing* because who could actually *hear* them?) the Beatles at the International Amphitheatre in Chicago. But Woodstock was going to be something else altogether!

They packed maps of Illinois, Indiana, Ohio, Pennsylvania, and New York. They had marked their route with a yellow marker and calculated the gas they'd need at thirty-five cents a gallon. Accounting for food/bathroom stops along the way, they estimated they could make the thirteen-hour trip to Allentown to pick up Becki in one day. But they didn't plan on getting lost. (Rosie blamed Alisha, who turned out to be a sucky highway driver, tending to hug the median strip, draft behind trucks, ignore on-rampers, and insist on taking "short-cuts.") Somewhere in Ohio, they drove for an hour and a half in the wrong direction. They argued about whose fault it was for another hour.

None of that could dampen Rosie's spirits though. She was free, finally free. She found herself taking deep, cleansing breaths. She knew it was audacious to appropriate such a powerful quote for her own selfish purposes, but she found herself reciting Martin Luther King, Jr.'s quote over and over in her head: "Free at last! Free at last! Thank God Almighty, I am free at last!" Free from Stella Maris's strangulating, manipulative domination. With the window down, she luxuriated in the wind whipping through her long brown hair and swore to herself she would never look back. No matter what lie ahead, this was the right decision. She tried not to picture Camille's sweet, sad face.

They ran out of gas in Allentown, Pennsylvania, five miles from Becki's house. Two guys helped them push the car to a gas station a few blocks from where they stalled. Alisha called Becki from the payphone to let her know they would be picking her up shortly, and that's when Becki informed Alisha that her boyfriend Xavier was coming along.

"I hate Xavier!" Alisha said, banging down the phone.

"You haven't even met him yet," Rosie said.

"I know. But I know he's a creep by some of the things Becki's told me. He's like nine years older than she is. No job, no prospects."

"We don't have to stick with them, do we? You said Becki's going camping after the concert, right? So, we can go our own way."

"Yeah, I guess. It puts a damper on things is all."

It was said that hippies were bohemians of a different stripe. Xavier Dunborrow was a *hippie* of a different stripe. He swaggered to the car, shirtless, in low cut jeans, a red bandana holding back a mess of dirty, curly, blond hair, and smelling like B.O. and Budweiser. He wasn't bad to look at, but he was hard to listen to: his voice had a sandpapery quality to it which made you want to clear your throat. And he never shut up. From Allentown to Monticello he enlightened the "chicks" about the different sub-categories of hippie-ism.

"You got your Old School Hippies. Thems the ones who started it all. They follow bands all over the country and live out of their cars. Then you got your Spiritual Hippies, your George Harrisons. They're all about auras and consciousness and in tune with the galaxy. You got your Activist Hippie, you know, the protestor with the peace sign, who is not unlike the Eco Activist Hippie. Same thing only doesn't eat meat. Then you got the Artsy Hippie. The colorful ones."

"What kind are you?" Rosie asked, turning her head around to the backseat where Xavier was sprawled out with Becki, a long-legged redhead with freckled face and arms, in his lap. (He called her *Beckles* due to her freckles.)

He threw his head back and laughed. "Ha! That's classic, man. I am the grooviest kind, the *Au Natural* Hippie."

Rosie smiled and nodded her head. He certainly *smelled* au natural. She turned around and rolled her eyes. Rosie knew that she and Alisha were not genuine hippies per se, but two young, idealists who wanted to make the world a kinder, more peaceful place.

The last hour of the trip seemed the longest since Xavier back-seat-pontificated on every subject under the sun. Rosie knew a windbag when she heard one. She mostly tuned him out until he started talking about the concert; then she listened in. He said it was supposed to have taken place in Woodstock, New York, but the local community objected to the number of people the concert would attract. "Then, they moved it to a town called Saugerties," Xavier explained, "but those townies didn't want a bunch of hippies invading their town either. Next on the list was a town called Wallkill, but just months before the festival, townspeople protested and put a kibosh on it. Finally, the organizers rented a dairy farm in Bethel. And that is where we're headed."

Alisha stopped for gas and they stocked up on snacks. Back on the highway they were surprised when, shortly after, the traffic snarled, and everything came to a complete stop. Xavier got out to investigate and returned saying, "This is the end of the line, chickadees. Townies don't want us here and they're making a human chain to block the road into Max Yasgur's farm. We'll have to walk the rest of the way."

"Just leave the car here?" Alisha said.

"Yeah, everyone's doing it," Xavier told her.

They grabbed their stuff and set on the path following thousands of other concertgoers, who had in fact abandoned their cars on Highway 17B. Rosie couldn't get over all the cars piled up on the road, parked willy-nilly and every which way. Would they ever find their car again?

It took the foursome about six hours to navigate eleven miles. The trek was an experience in and of itself as they passed cars, buses, and vans painted in cheerful primary colors and psychedelic patterns, and made friends along the way—chatting through the open windows of the stranded cars they passed, stopping to have a beer with some hippies in a van, smoking a joint with some guys in a station wagon, and listening to some guys jam on guitars. Becki piggy-backed on Xavier until he couldn't take it anymore and said, "Off Beckles," and bucked like a horse. Becki landed on her butt and called him a bastard, but soon she was back up getting a ride and kissing his head and neck.

It started to rain a couple of hours into the trek, and they arrived at the gates at about noon, wet and exhausted from lugging their stuff—sleeping bags, coolers, picnic basket, duffle bags. (They had no tent because they had planned on sleeping in the car.) Along the way they learned that due to the thousands of people who arrived a day early, the organizers decided to remove the fencing and ticket gates and make the concert free to all, to avoid any angry crowds and violence.

Rosie couldn't believe the crowds! She'd never seen this many people gathered in one place in her life! Mostly young, but some older, some children, all in various states of dress and undress. Her jaw dropped when she saw a hippie and a New York police trooper talking and laughing together—especially since the hippie guy was buck naked.

Yasgur's farm was beautiful, a bowl-shaped pasture surrounded by lush, green hills. Xavier led the way. "Wow, man. It's a true peace-out!" he said. "We gotta find us a primo spot." They zig-zagged around waves of people as they meandered through the area to get as close to the stage as possible. Rosie thought people would get pissed when they cut in line, but everyone was high on peace and love and camaraderie.

"Xavey, I have to pee!" Becki said. Music to Rosie's ears because she was about to burst as well.

"Damn it, Beckles, now you tell me."

It took an hour to find the Port-o-Sans. You could smell them before you saw them. Rosie held her breath and wondered what they would be like in two days. Once they had relieved themselves, they zigzagged back through the crowds, making their way closer to the stage area. Again, people welcomed them: "There's room for you. We can move over!" Was this a different planet, an alternate realm? A sense of magic adorned the air. Something else adorned the air too...the marijuana cloud that overhung the area like a canopy. Xavier found a spot he liked, and they laid out their sleeping bags and gear just as it started to rain again. Soon the ground around them transformed into a muddy mess. Rosie unzipped her sleeping bag so that she could sit on half and cover herself with the other half. Xavier and Becki proceeded to make out in the rain while Rosie and Alisha people-watched and waited for the first performer to start. There was word of delays. A guy sitting next to Rosie named Corky told her the traffic jam had grown to seventeen miles long and the New York Thruway was finally shut down. They were going to have to bring the talent in by helicopter.

The rain stopped just as abruptly as it had started, and the sun peaked out. People were chilling out...smoking joints, passing around bottles of wine, blowing bubbles, sliding in the mud, and playing their own music to pass the time before the concert got underway. Guys climbed and hung from the scaffolding of the sound tower, making Rosie nervous. "Either they or the tower is going to come down," she told Alisha.

Corky told Rosie the organizers had underestimated the crowds. "We're barely through the first day and they've already run out of food," he said. Rosie was glad for their snacks and the sandwiches and fresh fruit Becki had brought along. She and Alisha were munching on a sandwich, when a helicopter swooped low and dumped out bushel baskets of daisies onto the crowd. Rosie and Alisha each put a daisy in their hair. It was so unexpected and magical!

Finally, a little after five o'clock p.m., the first performer, Richie Havens, came to the stage and the festival officially began. Corky told Rosie that the band Sweetwater was supposed to play first, but they were stuck in traffic. Rosie and Alisha jammed to the music. Becki enjoyed herself atop Xavier's shoulders. After Richie Havens, Swami Satchidananda gave an invocation and led the thousands of people in a sacred chant and a moment of silence. After Swami, Sweetwater played. In between performers some guy got on stage and admonished the crowd not to partake of the brown acid. "It's your trip but we suggest you stay away from the brown acid." Corky told Rosie that people were tripping in the "freak out tents."

Rosie wasn't about to take any acid, but partake she did of the grass and hashish. No wonder, Rosie would tell people years later, there was no violence at Woodstock—everyone was stoned out of their minds! And you really didn't even have to partake; all you had to do was inhale the marijuana-infused air. It rendered the crowd—estimated to be in the hundreds of thousands, possibly a half million—who were laid out on the pasture turf, simply mellow.

Rosie, exhausted from the effort of just *getting* to the concert, fell asleep during Arlo Guthrie's set and awoke at about 3:30 a.m. to Joan Baez singing "Swing Low, Sweet Chariot," acapella, her soaring voice cutting through the night like a comet streaking through the sky. Rosie sat up and wept. When

Baez finished singing, only a smattering of applause twittered from the crowd, as most were asleep or zonked out on drugs. Baez must have been a bit unsettled because she asked, "Is anyone out there?" Rosie sprung up and shouted, "Yes, Joan! We're here! We love you!"

It was simply magic. Until it wasn't. In just a short time, Joan's soaring soprano was replaced by the sound of torrential rain, complete with flashes of lightning and claps of thunder. "We should have brought a damn tent," Alisha said, as the two girls huddled under their sleeping bags. A tent probably wouldn't have done much good anyway—everything was saturated, and the strong winds ripped some tents apart.

The bands stopped and started due to the rain, with the goal of avoiding electrocution. (Later they'd heard that members of the Grateful Dead kept getting electric shocks from their mikes.)

"This is a nightmare," Rosie said, astonished that what had started out as a consciousness-expanding, peace-making mass gathering was turning into something not unlike an unsanitary tent city. When the rain stopped, they were caked with mud. "Let's explore a bit," Xavier said, so they packed up their stuff and wandered around. They came upon a strange tableau of hippies and freaks putting to good use hundreds of issues of *Screw Magazine* by spreading them out on the muddy ground like a blanket. Off to the side they had built a campfire and were roasting hotdogs. "Peace and love. Join us, beautiful people!" a girl said. Rosie and the group didn't hesitate, thankful for the warmth of the fire and a tasty hotdog. Afterward, they lay themselves down on the magazines and slept fitfully through the night.

Saturday brought more wonderful music—from Santana, The Grateful Dead, Janis Joplin—but also more rain, a two-hour trip back and forth to the disgusting overflowing Port-O-Sans, and the horrific news that a young concertgoer, who'd been lying under a sleeping bag in a field, had been run over and killed by a guy driving a tractor.

By Saturday afternoon, their food supplies had run out. Xavier and Becki volunteered to go scavenge for food but they returned two hours later empty-handed, explaining that the last two concessions stands had been set on fire because some hippie was pissed at a vendor who'd increased the price of a damn hotdog from twenty-five cents to a buck. As if a food fairy godmother knew they were starving, somebody started handing out complimentary Styrofoam cups of granola. Rosie wolfed hers down as if she hadn't eaten in weeks. They listened to some music.

The emcee was back on stage—the same guy who had warned them not to take brown acid—making a stream of announcements: "Jerry Donaldson, your diabetes medicine is at the first aid tent." "We have a lost little girl up here who says her Mama's name is Emily." (Rosie was shocked and saddened at the dozens of times the emcee announced a lost child!) "Logan McConnell, call your mother ASAP, she's worried about you." "Karen, meet Paul at the staging area."

Rosie started to get restless. Alisha, on the other hand, got wasted. "Rosie, this is euphoria! Peace and love and the genuineness of our fellow man. We really can change the world!"

Rosie noticed Alisha was missing a shoe. Her own were mud-encrusted on the outside and squishy on the inside. "Leesh, where's your shoe?"

Alisha looked down at her foot. "Right there! On my foot!"

"But where's the other one?"

"Right there! There she is!" she said, pointing to the same shoe.

"No, Leesh. You only have one shoe."

"Well, of course, Rosie, I only have one foot."

Wasted! Rosie hoped the granola they'd eaten wasn't laced with something. About twenty minutes later, Alisha was shrieking that she'd lost a shoe. She forgot all about the shoe though when people started handing out sandwiches. Some townspeople had made thousands of sandwiches and delivered them by helicopter to the concertgoers. Peanut butter and jelly never tasted so good.

Late on Saturday night—it was Sunday morning by then—during Creedence Clearwater Revival's performance, the couple in front of them decided it was the perfect time to have sex—right then and there. Rosie said, "Let's get out of here."

They left the festival field, crossed Hurd Road, and hiked over to the Art and Craft Fair, all the while listening to Xavier go on and on about how mind-blowing *The Who* and *Janis Joplin* were, as if they weren't even at the concert at all. Rosie tuned him out. They checked out the Bindy Bazaar—an area where concertgoers sold or bartered their wares. Rosie bought a tie-dyed T-shirt while Alisha searched for a pair of shoes, any kind; but nobody was selling shoes. Rosie worried about Alisha's feet. They'd heard hundreds of concertgoers had suffered foot lacerations and punctures.

Xavier, bored and crabby now that the sun had come out and it was hot and muggy, said, "I've got a great idea." The girls followed him as he led them back across Hurd Road, then across West Shore Road, past the performer's pavilion to a lake on a chicken farm adjacent to Max Yasgur's farm. Dozens of kids were milling around the lake. Then a helicopter landed in the heliport and a couple of guys got out. They walked over to the lake—it was called Fillipini's Pond, after the chicken farmer, William Fillipini—stripped off their clothes and jumped in. Once they did, a huge crowd of kids followed suit. Xavier and Becki peeled off their muddy clothes and jumped in. "What the hell," Alisha said, removing her shirt. Rosie hesitated. She'd never been comfortable with her body, especially the size of her breasts: she was a busty girl. But she was hot and muddy, and inhibition won out. There! A first for everything! One day she would tell her grandkids, your old Nana skinny-dipped at Woodstock.

They splashed around for a good hour. When they had enough and decided to get out, Becki realized someone had stolen her clothes and her duffle bag. "Who would do such a thing? Stealing surely doesn't fit in with the whole peace and love stuff, does it now?" Becki said.

Luckily, Rosie had the tie-dyed T-shirt she'd just bought at the Bindy Bazaar, and Alisha had a pair of clean underwear from her duffle bag to offer. So now, Alisha was walking around shoeless, Becki, pants-less, and the group was tired and crabby. "Let's get out of here," Becki said, looking a little ridiculous. "I just want to go home."

"I'm with you," Alisha said.

Rosie nodded.

"What? No way!" Xavier said. "I'm not leaving until I see Hendrix." Jimmy Hendrix's performance had been delayed due to the weather. "And what about camping? You backin' out?"

Becki and Xavier started arguing and then right before God and all the hippies, he hit her. Actually, he *punched* her, in the face. Becki fell to the ground, hand to her cheek. Alisha and Rosie rushed to her. A guy nearby said, "Dude, that ain't right."

Rosie screamed at Xavier: "What is wrong with you?"

Xavier just stood there, frozen, saying nothing, flexing the fingers on his hitting hand. Finally, he moved toward Becki. "Beckles, babe, it was the drugs. Babe. Beckles, I'm sorry."

And stupid Becki let him embrace her. Stupid, stupid Becki. Something made Rosie think this wasn't the first time he'd hit her.

The bubble that was Woodstock magic popped. The communal sharing of positive emotions fueled by peace and love and beautiful music seemed to be a hoax. Max Yasgur's words, spoken from stage had rung so true: "You proved that a half million young people can get together and have three days of fun and music and nothing but fun and music and God bless you for it!" Now they seemed naive and empty.

Xavier helped Becki stand up. Her left cheek was red and beginning to swell and there was a small, bloody scratch near her temple—likely from the ring Xavier wore on his right hand. "She's fine. She's fine," he insisted.

"We need to get her to the medical tent," Rosie said.

"She's fine!" Xavier said.

"I'm fine," Becki repeated.

"Bullshit!" Alisha said. "We're going to the medical tent."

"You go, Beckles, and I'm splitting. I mean it," Xavier threatened.

"What?" Rosie said. "Tough guy afraid he'll get arrested?"

"Wait, what if I need stitches?" Becki said.

"You don't need no stitches," Xavier said.

"Take me to the medical tent," Becki said. "I don't want a scar."

"It's a scratch!" Xavier said. When the girls started to walk off, he yelled: "Bitches, all of yas." He threw down his sleeping bag, and said, "I'm outta here." And took off in the other direction.

Becki fell to the ground and started crying. Rosie and Alisha sat down on either side of her, and Alisha stroked her hair. "It's for the best, Beck. He's a loser," Alisha said. Rosie watched Xavier in the distance, sure the coward would turn back, but he sped up his pace and disappeared into the wooded area that surrounded the pond.

The three girls, still with one pants-less and one shoeless, and now all a bit bewildered and still dripping with Fillipini pond water, made their way to the pink-and-white-striped medical tent, just across from the performers' pavilion. On their way, they came across a little naked girl, who couldn't have been more than two or three, wandering aimlessly, crying, "Mumma! Mumma!" Rosie scooped her up and the child latched onto her like a tree frog. "There, there, honey. We'll find your mumma. What is wrong with people?" Rosie said.

At the medical tent, a young woman took the little girl from Rosie, saying, "Lordy, another one!" A nurse attended to Becki's head. No stitches were needed. The nice lady also found a pair of shorts for Becki and a pair of plastic sandals for Alisha.

The girls all agreed they wanted to leave, but decided it was getting too late now. The hike to the car would take hours, something they weren't looking forward to doing in the dark. Plus, they weren't the only ones who were irritable, spent, and ready to go home: thousands of tired and hungry people had started a mass exodus. Better to wait until morning.

They walked back to the main stage area. The place looked like a battlefield now. It was surprising to Rosie that the young activists who cared so much about peace and love seemed not to care a lick about the environment. They left behind soggy wet sleeping bags, newspapers, cardboard boxes, coolers, clothes, food wrappers, cans, bottles, broken chairs, and tents that had been knocked over and trampled on. Everything sunk into the mud. Since so many people had left, the girls were able to find a place close to the stage. But a downpour delayed the next performer and so the girls just lie in their soggy sleeping bags, biding their time. Rosie watched as the crew wrapped plastic wrap around their precious equipment. "Let's just go," she said.

"I was hoping someone would say that," Becki said.

"Me too," Alisha agreed. "Let's hit the bathrooms and get the hell out of here."

Everyone else had the same idea—hundreds of people waited in the bathroom line. Not too far from the Port-O-Sans there was a phone bank. Becki wanted to call her mom and suggested that Rosie and Alisha stay in line while she ran over to the pay phones to make her call. It was getting dark now and Rosie said, "Leesh, you go with Becki and I'll stay in line. Come right back here."

Rosie waited in line, wondering if she would ever be dry again. The girl in front of her was talking to herself, saying she had met an angel with a purple face and cotton candy hands. An ominous feeling planted itself in Rosie's chest. It was the first time since arriving that she was alone among the crowds.

About fifteen minutes later, someone pushed her out of line. Hard. From the back, so she didn't see it coming. The person grabbed her by the hair, covered her mouth, and dragged her into the wooded area behind the Port-O-Sans. She knew it was a man by his strength and the sound of his grunting. The man pushed her up against a tree. "You fucking bitch!" he spewed out.

Rosie couldn't see much through the rain, but she recognized the voice: Xavier!

"You turned her against me!" he accused, gripping Rosie by the arms and shaking her.

She screamed but he covered her mouth again.

"You're gonna pay, you whore!"

Rosie always thought she could fight off an attacker. She remembered the recommendation to kick him in the groin. She tried to knee Xavier, but he was too tall, and she was too short.

He laughed, taking his hand off her mouth to grip her better.

Rosie cried, "Please Xavier, please don't hurt me."

He slapped her face and then jammed his hand down the front of her pants. "Shut up! Shut up!" he warned. He grabbed at her crotch, scratching and tugging. She jumped from the shock and pain of it.

"Heeeeeeelp!"

He slapped her again. A stupid thought flashed through her mind: instead of telling her grandkids that she skinny-dipped at Woodstock, would she have to tell them she was raped?

"Please don't—"

He read her mind. "I'm no rapist, you skank. I'm just teaching you a lesson to mind your own fucking business." Then, unexpectedly, he leaned in and bit her neck. Hard. Like a damn vampire. Afterward he pushed her to the ground and ran off.

Rosie lay on the ground for a long time, engulfed in darkness. She wished to God she was on a bad trip. Maybe that hotdog she'd eaten earlier *was* laced with brown acid. She moaned. Sitting up, she realized how lucky she was that Xavier didn't rape her. Her crotch area burned and his bites had broken the skin; she could feel little jagged bumps of skin with her fingers. When she brought her fingers to her lips, she could taste blood. She turned her neck to the sky to let the rain rinse the blood and Xavier's evilness away. She closed her eyes, and out of nowhere, Stella Maris's disapproving face appeared, making her feel...*dirty*.

Defining moments. Moments in your life when you experience something that fundamentally changes you and urges you to make a pivotal decision. Those moments define a person—their perceptions, behaviors, and philosophies. Rosie Quinlayne, eighteen years old, wet and muddy, and now defiled by a brutish leach, picked herself up, brushed herself off, and vowed never to allow a man to take advantage of her again. NEVER! Disoriented, she started walking through the rain, in the direction of the concert music. Back at the Port-O-Sans, she stood in line, not far from her original place, until Alisha and Becki found her.

"Where were you? We've been looking for you everywhere!" Alisha asked, hugging Rosie.

"We were so worried!" said Becki, joining in on the hug.

Rosie pulled her long brown hair around and over her right shoulder to cover the bite marks on her neck. "I've been right here," she said, smiling.

3.
rosie & paul

SOMEWHERE IN THE recesses of her brain, Rosie remembered that a human bite could be more dangerous than an animal bite due to bacteria and viruses residing in the human mouth. Risk of infection was occupying her thoughts as she, Alisha, and Becki walked with their fellow concert-leavers along 17B. A dark, damp sky loomed above, but the steady stream of headlights—the cars inched along like snails—provided enough light to see at least your own two feet in front of you. They'd been walking for two hours and still had a few more to go.

Alisha and Becki were quiet which made it easy for Rosie's thoughts to morph from concern about mild infection to dread about sepsis and death. She worried that she hadn't been able to clean the wound properly, other than letting the rain rinse over it. She started to imagine how filthy Xavier's mouth likely was, not having brushed his teeth in days. Gross. Then she began obsessing about his dirty hands...what if she got a bladder or vaginal infection? Disgusting. She engaged in an internal argument with herself about whether she should tell Alisha and Becki about the whole sordid incident. Most of her didn't want to breathe a word of it to anyone, but she knew Becki needed to know what a horrific person Xavier really was.

"Hey, pretty ladies!" called out a bearded guy in a teal Cadillac Sedan. "Hop on the back if you want!"

"You're a lifesaver!" Alisha said. The girls climbed up onto the back of the car and lay back against the rear window.

"Thank God! My feet were killing me," Alisha said. "Don't get me wrong, I appreciate having shoes, but these are giving me blisters."

Rosie, wishing a blister were her only problem, wondered if this were her road to Damascus. She fell asleep wishing she'd never heard of a concert called Woodstock. She woke up when Alisha shook her arm. "Come on, Ro, let's go pee." Rosie rubbed her eyes and got her bearings. A gas station. Great, she could pee and get a look at her neck. The gas station's bathroom was a filthy one stall deal. After she relieved herself, she pulled her hair back and looked in the mirror. Arrrrgh! It looked as though a vampire had eaten her neck for lunch. She counted five teeth marks that had broken the skin and a few more indentations. The surrounding area was red and inflamed. She grabbed some paper towels and some soap from the dispenser and cleaned the area as best she could. She took a couple of deep breaths and smiled as she opened the door for Becki to take her turn. She treated herself to a candy bar, then climbed up on the back of the car for the last stretch of the trip.

When the girls walked into Becki's house all straggly and dirty, Becki's mother thought they'd been caught in a tornado. "Oh, good lord, what happened to your face?" Mrs. Peterson asked, pulling her daughter closer to get a better look. Alisha gave Rosie a look—Becki hadn't told them what she was going to tell her mother. Unlike Alisha and Rosie's parents, Becki's mom *knew* she was going to Woodstock and then camping—she wasn't pleased about it, but she knew all the same.

"Oh, Mom, we were packed in like sardines and someone stepped on my face while I was sleeping."

Mrs. Peterson, tall and freckly like her daughter, was just thankful that Becki was home safe. "And where is Xavier?"

"He ended up staying…"

"Well, go get cleaned up. I'll make you breakfast."

A hot shower was a beautiful thing. And who knew brushing your teeth could be sublime? Peacing-out and changing the world was great, but sitting in a loving mother's sunny kitchen, eating bacon, eggs, and toast, was just what Rosie needed. Afterward, the girls lay on lawn chairs on the back patio. Becki dragged the phone out from the kitchen and recounted all the wonderful things about the concert to her best friend. There—it had happened already: Woodstock the Aquarian Exposition would be forever romanticized, described in an idealized fashion by every attendee and all the awful parts would be minimized or even forgotten. Well, not for Rosie. For Rosie, Woodstock sucked. Woodstock was music, drugs, traffic, nudity, rain, mud, death, public fornication, skinny-dipping, trash, and sexual assault.

Alisha called her mother collect. Rosie could hear Mrs. Weller's high-pitched angry voice over the phone. "I'm sorry, Mom, I know you're still mad at me. Actually, I'm not coming home just yet...Rosie and I are heading to D.C. to see David."

Listening in, Rosie wondered why Alisha said "just yet" instead of "at all." Was she having second thoughts? Had Woodstock been *her* road to Damascus?

"Rosie's fine. I'm sure Mrs. Quinlayne is beside herself. Becki's fine too, although she broke up with her boyfriend."

"I did not!" Becki said, sitting up.

Alisha said, "Well, then her boyfriend broke up with her—"

"He did not!" Becki said. "He'll be back."

And those three little words were the impetus Rosie needed to share her story. Becki could *not* go back to that miserable sleaze.

When Alisha hung up, Rosie said, "You guys, I need to show you something. But you have to promise never to tell a soul. Promise me. No matter what. Swear it."

"I promise," said Alisha, her brow furrowed in concern.

"I promise," Becki said, looking at the backdoor to make sure they had total privacy.

Rosie pulled her hair away from her neck and listened to the gasps.

Rosie was right: Alisha was having second thoughts about D.C. "I'm so ashamed to tell you why," she whispered. Both lie awake on a lumpy mattress in the guest room. "You're going to hate me."

"I could never hate you."

"You'll think less of me."

"Out with it, Leesh."

"It's just that I don't think I am a hippie at heart. All those people, peace and love and all. I just didn't connect, Rosie. I don't want what they want—to live poor and barefoot and drugged-up. I mean I'm anti-war and all, and I want civil rights and equal rights and all; I just want to have shoes and running water while I fight for those things."

Rosie chuckled. She could guess what was coming next.

"And Mom said Daddy would write me out of the will if I don't go to college. See, now you hate me."

"Leesh, you dummy. I don't hate you. I can see where you're coming from. But you know I just have to get away from my mother."

"I know, and so here's Plan B. We go see my *other* brother."

"Charlie?"

"Not Charlie, you goof. He's twelve. I'm talking about Jeremy." Jeremy attended the University of Wisconsin in Madison.

"Interesting," said Rosie.

"I know, right? We can go to school *and* fight the good fight."

"My parents won't pay a dime for me to go to school."

"Maybe your dad will. We'll make it work! You get a job first and establish residency so you pay state tuition. You can live with me! I'll get a single dorm room and smuggle you in."

"Leesh—"

"Rosie, Madison makes more sense than D.C. Maybe we're not quite ready to go that far. Look what happened to you."

After Rosie had shown the girls her neck and recounted the awful attack, the girls pleaded with her to tell Becki's mom, to go to the doctor, to call the police, something! But Rosie refused to take any action. "I just want to put it behind me. I only ask one thing," she said looking at Becki. "That you will never talk to that loser again."

"I promise. Of course, I promise," Becki said, hugging Rosie.

Alisha said, "Madison will suit us. We're just nice, midwestern girls. Maybe we'd get eaten alive in D.C."

Rosie didn't want to admit it, but everything Alisha was saying felt right. Rosie herself had realized she was more of an activist than a hippie. The whole incident with Xavier had shaken her. Maybe it would be better to be away from home *closer* to home. Then they wouldn't be so far from Charlie and Camille.

Rosie nodded. "Let's sleep on it, okay?" Rosie turned over and closed her eyes, but she'd already made up her mind. She was going to become a Wisconsin cheese head. She wasn't about to tell her mother that though. At least not right away. Let her think she was far, far away.

In the morning, Becki's mom convinced Rosie to call home. As she dialed, she prayed Camille would pick up, but she heard her mother's nasal voice say hello. Rosie hesitated.

"Oh. It's you, isn't it?" her mother said.

Rosie started. How did she know?

Stella Maris read her mind. "Mothers just know."

"May I speak to Camille, please?"

"No, you may not. You have broken her heart. She's been moping around for weeks."

"Mom, I've been gone less than a week."

"And your father! All I hear is, 'Where did we go wrong?'"

"Tell Dad he didn't go wrong at all."

"What's that supposed to mean, that *I* went wrong?"

"Mom, my escape couldn't have come as a surprise."

"Your escape! As if we were holding you prisoner. We fed, clothed, and educated you—private school, no less. And now you're doing drugs with naked hippies at concerts. Alisha's mom told me everything. What are you up to? What's his name?"

"Whose name?"

"The hippie-dippie you ran away with? When's the due date?"

"Mom! There is no guy. No pregnancy. Alisha and I are headed to D.C."

"D.C.! So now the hippie wants to be a politician? One internship with the mayor and she's ready to run for governor."

Rosie shuddered. "Tell Camille I called. I'll try her again soon."

"I'll never forgive you for this, Rose Marie! I had to tell all my friends that you're spending the summer abroad."

"Great. I'll call you from Barcelona."

Plan B didn't work out exactly as Alisha had planned. Alisha obviously couldn't sneak Rosie into her dorm room—she was lucky to get student housing at all since she was late to the game. But Alisha's brother Jeremy had some friends who rented a house on Mifflin Street and one of the girls said Rosie could rent her oversized walk-in closet for cheap. You heard that right, Rosie slept in a closet. For a year. But she had access to everything else—kitchen, living room, television, phone, bathroom—so the arrangement worked out.

Madison suited her. There was so much to do when she could find the time or extra funds. There were concerts, symphonies, ballets, plays, films. And because the city was the state capitol and home to a world-renowned university, it was a hubbub of politics and academics. Rosie worked as a waitress during the day at the Dome Restaurant across the street from the state capitol building and took classes at night.

Madison was the opposite of Woodstock: peace and love were replaced by anger and protest. The UW campus had become a hotbed for anti-war sentiment. Rosie and Alisha wanted to join in the demonstrations but Alisha's brother Jeremy didn't want them getting involved. Last year he'd taken part in the Black Student Strike at the university and almost got himself killed. A cop hit him in the head with a billy club. He used the scar at the top right of his forehead as a reminder to his sister and Rosie that protesting was too dangerous, and, in the end, didn't change anything.

The girls got involved anyway. One Saturday night Rosie and Alisha grabbed a cab after a concert (Alisha had worn a new pair of Candie's sandals with four-inch heels and couldn't walk "three more steps!"). The driver started up a conversation with the girls, asking if they were interested in student activism and the anti-war movement.

"Oh yes," Rosie said to the back of his head. "We were at Woodstock." (There, see: even Rosie had succumbed to romanticizing Woodstock once she discovered the street cred it provided.)

The driver said, "Man, I wished I'd gone. Were there really a half million people?"

"At least," Alisha said.

"We skinny-dipped," Rosie said proudly.

"We've checked out a few protests," Alisha said, "but my brother got his head cracked open at the black protest in February and he's against us getting involved."

The driver shared how he too had had his head massaged with a billy stick. "Three years ago, UW students organized a sit-in to protest Dow Chemical Company's recruitment visit," he said. "Dow is the company that makes napalm and agent orange which are used in Vietnam. Napalm should be outlawed!" he said. "It's this nasty gel that burns people to death. Anyway, the protest got out of hand and police in riot gear threw tear gas right outside of classroom buildings forcing hundreds of us to flee. The police panicked and then they barricaded us in an area between two classroom buildings. We thought we would be dragged out and arrested but instead the cops started clubbing people with billy sticks. Dow Day made national news—it was the first time in American history that police had used such force on college students.

"That's awful," Rosie said.

"I don't like the violence," the driver said. "Hell, I was the treasurer of the UW chapter of the Student Nonviolent Coordinating Committee. It's the cops that bring the violence, not us." He chuckled. "Most of the time anyway. Now I'm actually an alderman. Finishing up graduate school, driving a cab, and trying to do what I can to stop this war...all while trying not to get my head bashed in again."

"An alderman?" Rosie said, peering around the seat to get a look at the driver. "How old are you anyway?"

"Twenty-four," he said and grinned. "The name's Paul Soglin. We could really use your help."

Rosie scanned the crowd of hundreds of students gathered on Library Mall, looking for Paul Soglin. Armed in winter coats, gloves, and boots, she and Alisha were ready for the mid-February weather—cloudy with a chance of flurries and a high of only twenty—and for their very first campus protest. The girls had attended a few meetings of the Students for a Democratic Society and learned that the movement focused on the ways the university had become complicit in the military-industrial complex. By 1964, UW had more government contracts than any other university in the country. The protests focused on three main "eye-sores"—as the student leaders called them—the ROTC building, Army Math, and the Selective Services offices. They also pushed back against companies that contributed to the war machine like Dow Chemical. Today's protest was against recruiters from General Electric, manufacturers of aircraft engines used in Vietnam.

Rosie spotted Paul's head of dark wavy hair and called out to him. He waved and made his way over to greet them. "Thanks for coming!" he said, grinning and a little out of breath. He handed them some leaflets that featured a drawing of a skeleton and the message for G.E. to get off campus. "We're going to march to the Engineering building," he told them, pointing west. "Remember what you learned." UW students were well-trained in civil disobedience, what was dubbed "protest prep." Rosie thought a person who wished to protest just showed up and marched, but she learned there were actually techniques of non-violent resistance. Paul had shown Rosie and Alisha how to go limp when they practiced mock arrests and how to curl into a fetal position to shield their head from a beating.

Rosie and Alisha walked behind Paul and some other boys, who carried hand-painted signs that said: "Warmaker-Strikebreaker. Smash G.E." (Tens of thousands of workers at G.E. had gone on strike even as Nixon insisted the strike would hurt the Vietnam war effort.) While Rosie walked, the cold February air assaulting her nostrils and rosing-up her already naturally rosy cheeks, two things happened: she developed a passionate commitment to social activism and a terrible crush on Paul Soglin. She couldn't believe that someone so young had come so far. He was elected two years ago to the Madison Common Council at the ripe old age of twenty-two. In 1968, he ran for city alderman on an anti-war platform and it was the students who gave him his overwhelming win. The students were excited to have someone on their side in City Hall. But...alas...he was married. She was crushed when she found out, suffering the same reaction many girls had when they found out John Lennon was married. It just couldn't be! But it was. Her name was Diane and she was pretty and nice. Damn her!

Soon Rosie found her entire lifestyle revolved around political activity. She worked at the Dome, attended her night classes, did a little studying, and looked forward to the next rally, march, or demonstration. One of the attractive features of the opposition movement was the fact that it was a popular social event. There was nothing more invigorating than a rally! Rosie could feel her heart rate increase whenever she joined hundreds of fellow students as they convened on Bascom Hill (the highest point on campus) or Library Mall, then marched to the Capitol, Sterling Hall, the Old Red Gym, or some other edifice that offended them in one way or another. Oh yes, she was all in, truly believing that the "Revolution" was right around the corner. Woodstock was a dream; this was the real work. Things were unfolding. Maybe her generation would see the end of the war, the collapse of capitalism, imperialism, and the military-industrial complex.

Rosie wished Stella Maris could see her when she was protesting. She was fierce! Because she was a spark plug, the female protesters were drawn to her. Rosie was the one who showed up to rallies with extra poster boards and markers to make signs. Rosie was the one to start up chants: *"Hell no, we won't go,"* *"One, two, three, four, we don't want your fucking war!"* and *"Girls say yes to boys who say no!"* It did disturb her that sometimes the men didn't take the female protesters seriously. One time at a meeting a guy told her to "Sit the hell down. Since you're not subject to the draft, you're not qualified to speak on the issue." Man, that pissed her off. When it happened again at another meeting, Rosie and dozens of other women got up and left the room. She almost joined one of the women's anti-war groups—Another Mother for Peace or Women for Peace—but Paul pulled her back and told her to ignore the sexist assholes. He teased, "You don't need a rectal thermometer to know who the assholes are."

When they weren't in school or protesting, Rosie and Alisha could be found belly up to the bar at either the Library Lounge (Paul's favorite hangout) or the Nitty Gritty. Rosie was hungry for all the anti-war stories and would sit glued to her stool as Paul described all he'd been through since arriving on campus in 1962. The guy had packed more life into eight years than Rosie could have imagined! He'd grown up in the Hyde Park neighborhood of Chicago and was active even in high school. His first campus protest was in 1963 when he joined a couple hundred students at a rally on the steps of Memorial Union to oppose the presence of U.S. military advisers who the students claimed were actively participating in the Vietnam War. In 1965 he along with some fellow students went door-to-door in some affluent Chicago suburbs with petitions calling for real estate agents to show and sell more homes to blacks. But the event that changed his life was Dow Day.

Paul had shared a little about the event that night in the cab, but now sitting at a barstool with a beer in one hand, a cigarette in the other, and his wife Diane engaged in a conversation with Alisha, he went into more detail. Rosie stared into his dark, heavy-lidded eyes as he explained how the U.S. was dumping hundreds of thousands of tons of napalm in Vietnam, burning and scarring soldiers and civilians. "It's obscene! It's like liquid fire—they put it in bombs and in flamethrowers." He shook his head.

"So, we'd been against Dow coming on campus for years, but 1967 was the turning point. We marched up Bascom Hill to the Commerce Building and then started with a sit-in, packing a hallway where a Dow recruiter was supposed to be stationed. The dean of students had drafted a set of guidelines for student protests. If any student obstructed university operations or interviews, they would invoke disciplinary measures like probation, suspension, or expulsion, so we were prepared to be arrested or expelled, but not beaten! The university ordered us to leave. We refused because our demands weren't being met, one of which was just to move the recruiting interviews off campus. So, they started clearing out the hallway and then the Madison police in full riot gear charged in, swinging their nightsticks. Chaos erupted. They were whacking kids in the head and on the legs and prodding their sticks into stomachs. Kids were screaming and bleeding and hysterical. I'll never forget that sound—it was gut-wrenching. Like hitting a watermelon with a baseball bat. Then suddenly the crowd in front of me disappeared and there was nothing between me and the rushing police. Four or five officers came toward me and I started backpedaling. I pulled the collar of my sheepskin coat over my head and it helped protect my head, but then they hit me right on the base of my spine. It was like an electric shock and instinctively my limbs just shot out. Then they went to work on my legs and head." His eyes grew glassy. He took a swig of beer. "That's when I heard my mother's voice: 'You're doing good stuff out there, but don't do anything stupid and get hurt.'"

"Did you go to the emergency room?" Rosie asked.

"Yeah, I needed stitches, but I was okay." He lit another cigarette. "This one girl, well the cops clubbed her in the abdomen so violently that it ruptured her uterus!"

Rosie gasped.

"But we were right back at it that night. We had a monster meeting of three thousand people on the Library Mall. The guy who had led us that day had escaped the police but was suspended by the university. That left a leadership void. I guess I just stepped in. And now I've helped with dozens of demonstrations."

Paul's wife peeked her head around and asked, "Rosie, is he boring you with protest stories?"

"Not at all," Rosie said. "I want to hear them."

"Tell her about the block party," Diane said.

The fabled Mifflin Street Block Party. In May of '69, Paul was alderman and his constituents in the eighth district (which was student-heavy), tried to have a block party without a permit. Lots of neighborhoods in Madison threw block parties without official sanction. Paul supported the students and the party grew to hundreds, with kids dancing in the streets. "The police arrived and shortly after I show up in my rusty red Triumph convertible," Paul said. "Top down, with my friend, an attorney, in the passenger seat. I'd heard there'd been some trouble, so I brought Mel with me to help students who had been arrested. So, I drive down the very street the cops are trying to open up."

Diane piped in, "I had to bail him out, but I hardly recognized him when they brought him out. The jailers cut his hair!"

"They did not," Rosie said.

"They did." Paul said. "Something usually reserved for prisoners. Anyway, I had to go to trial and I was found guilty of failing to lawfully obey a police officer. The charge of unlawful assembly was later dismissed."

Diane said, "He regards his arrest as a badge of honor."

Rosie took a sip of her beer. She was still hung up on the jailer cutting Paul's hair. "They didn't really cut your hair, did they?"

"They did."

"I'm fine, Dad," Rosie said, using the payphone at the Dome on her break. She had been in Madison almost a year to the date—it was August 24, 1970. She usually spoke to her father on Sunday nights, but he'd called the restaurant in a panic when he saw the morning news about a bombing at the university. "I wasn't there, Dad. It happened in the middle of the night. We had nothing to do with it! A graduate student was killed. It's so terrible! The poor guy was finishing up work at three in the morning before going on vacation with his family. No, they haven't caught anybody yet. I'll be careful. Dad, that is not what we do. We are just as stunned and scared as everybody else. Who would do such a thing? It's totally demented. We're not about violence; we're about peace. Okay. I know. Okay. I'm sorry if Mom thinks I'm going to end up in jail. That's her problem. I gotta go. I've got customers!"

She really did have customers, and a particularly important one at that—the mayor of Madison. The Dome Restaurant was a favorite among politicians due to its proximity to the capitol building. Over the past year, Rosie got to meet many, and got to know some, of the city and state's VIPs, including the mayor, city councilmen, policemen, state and U.S. senators and representatives, the university chancellor, and even the notorious governor, who periodically called out the National Guard during UW's anti-war and civil rights demonstrations.

"Morning, Rosie," the mayor said, taking a chair. "You heard the news?"

Rosie poured coffee and said, "It's just awful. That poor man."

"Three or four other people were injured. We're still piecing it together. There will probably be at least twelve of us this morning. Can we push a couple of these tables together?" The police chief and fire chief showed up, then the chancellor.

Rosie served the group and listened in. She had learned when to be invisible as a waitress and when it was acceptable to interact. Stella Maris would think it was pathetic that she had "stooped" to waitressing, but Rosie enjoyed the job. The tips were decent, with the added benefit of learning the ins and outs of Madison politics.

The governor of Wisconsin was threatening to send in the National Guard again if the mayor wasn't able to get things under control with the bombing and the unrest. The mayor couldn't believe there were no leads on who the hell did this. The fire chief reported that the bomber or bombers used a stolen van and filled it with close to two-thousand pounds of ammonium nitrate and fuel oil. "Shit," the fire chief said, "pieces of the van were found as far as three blocks away. One of my guys found a piece on top of an eight-story building. These guys *almost* knew what they were doing, but the idiots missed their mark."

"They were targeting the Army Mathematics Research Center," the police chief said. "Five minutes before the bomb detonated, police dispatch got a call." He read from a notebook: "*Okay, pigs, now listen and listen good. There's a bomb in the Math Research Building on the University campus. Clear the building. Get everyone out of there. Warn the hospital. This is no bullshit, man!*" University police were on their way when the bomb ripped through the building. They damaged twenty-six nearby buildings, killed an innocent father of three, injured four others, and you know what, they scarcely damaged the Math Center."

"I believe this is part of a nationwide conspiracy of radicals bent on destroying American society," the mayor said.

The police chief said, "Nixon thinks so, too. FBI's already on the scene. It's no secret the students had it out for the AMRC."

Rosie froze mid-pour and almost spilled coffee on one of the aldermen who had joined the group. *AMRC. AMRC.* That sounded familiar. Wait a minute… She left the table, put the coffee pot back on the burner, and came right back, saying to the group, "I think I have some information that might be important...about the bombing."

Well, that got everyone's attention.

"A couple of weeks ago my best friend and I were at the Nitty Gritty. There were these guys at the bar, and I wasn't eavesdropping, but my friend had gone to the bathroom and it was that awkward few minutes when you're sitting alone, and you just hear people talk. These four guys were talking protest talk and then I heard them say, more than once, *AMRC*."

"AMRC? They said that? Are you sure?" the police chief asked.

"Yes, because I wondered who or what that was. First, I thought they said 'Marcey' like the girl's name. But then I wondered if it was...not an acronym...what's the other word...?"

"An initialism?" the mayor said.

"Yes. Anyway, I wondered what it stood for. *American something something corporation*? Or *Advanced Manufacturing something something*? I don't know. I was just trying to occupy my mind until my friend got back. Then just now I heard you refer to it."

"It's the Army Mathematics Research Center, or *Army Math* as it's known," the police chief said.

"Of course," said Rosie, "I just never heard the center called the AMRC. But I know those guys said AMRC several times."

"Rosie, this is important. Do you think you could identify them?" the mayor said.

"I don't think so. The bar was dark. I never made eye contact."

"Anything? Hair color. Clothes..."

"It was more about what I heard than what I saw."

"Still, it will be helpful. We'll need you and your friend to come down and fill out a report."

"Of course."

Rosie waited on a few more customers and noticed the buzz in the restaurant was increasing. It was almost as if she were watching a detective show. Another alderman arrived and told the group he had heard from his sister, in Bellville, thirty miles away, who was awoken by the blast. There was a phone call for the police chief. He took the call and returned to report to the group that an employee of a fertilizer plant in Baraboo said he sold a kid, claiming to be a UW dropout working for a local farmer, ammonium nitrate in bulk. "It wasn't an unusual request," the chief said.

After her night class, Rosie met Alisha at the Nitty Gritty. "Just think," Alisha whispered as they grabbed stools at the bar, "those guys might have been mapping out their evil plot right here."

"It's so sinister," Rosie said.

"What did your boyfriend say when you told him?" Alisha teased, nudging Rosie with her elbow.

"He's not my boyfriend! And he wasn't home. Diane said he was at a meeting. But I guess the police hauled him and other student leaders in for questioning this afternoon. Everyone is spooked."

"You know what we need?" Alisha said. "We need bodyguards, or better yet, boyfriends."

"Who's got time?" Rosie said, but she knew Alisha knew it wasn't about time. It was about what Xavier had done to her. Here she was nineteen years old and she had almost zero experience with guys. In high school, she went out with groups of boy and girl friends and went to the important dances—homecoming and prom—but now the idea of boys made her very uncomfortable, especially after Woodstock.

"We'll make time." Alisha lifted her beer glass for a toast, then she turned serious. "Hey, Ro, I've been meaning to tell you something I don't really want to tell you."

Rosie had spilled some beer and was wiping it up with a napkin. She looked up. "What? Just tell me."

"Becki is back with Xavier."

"What? No!"

"Pathetic. I know, right?"

Rosie put her elbows on the bar and rested her head in her hands. "I just don't get women."

"She begged me not to tell you, but I couldn't keep it from you."

Rosie closed her eyes and shuddered a bit, trying not to picture Xavier in her mind.

Someone came up from behind and put his hands over Rosie's eyes.

Rosie said, "I know it's you, Jeremy. I know your smell!" She was grateful for the interruption.

Alisha's brother laughed and sat down next to her. "Thought I would find you two here. Just wanted to make sure you little anti-war protestors were all right. You didn't bomb any buildings, did you?"

"That's nothing to joke about!" Alisha told her brother about Rosie hearing the guys talk about the AMRC a couple of weeks ago.

"Shit, Rosie, you're like a key witness," Jeremy said.

Rosie rolled her eyes.

"Things are going to change, my friends, I'm telling you," Jeremy warned. "This is the end of your peace movement. Haven't I been telling you somebody was going to get killed?"

That weekend, Rosie and Alisha hung out at a party at a ramshackle, three-story house on Wilson Street where dozens of kids jammed into the three small apartments and spilled out onto the back porches. The temperature was still near ninety at eleven o'clock, the August humidity punching you in the face. Rosie and Alisha squeezed their way out to the back porch for some air. "This humidity makes my hair frizz," Rosie complained.

"And what's wrong with frizzy hair?" Alisha said running her fingers through her long, loose afro.

"You know what I mean." She said this and then she and Alisha watched in horror as a girl threw up on her own shoes. Rosie, gagging, and Alisha, laughing, high-tailed it out of there. They took the back steps down and were going to walk to the Nitty Gritty when someone from the third story porch called out Alisha's name. They looked up.

"It's Tony Apello!" Alisha said to Rosie, hugging her arm. "That guy I like from my Design Fundamentals class." Tony motioned that he would come down. Alisha squeezed Rosie's hand. "He's so handsome—dark, curly hair, brown eyes, and the whitest teeth." They watched as he took the back steps two at a time and sauntered over. Then, at the very moment Alisha was introducing Rosie to Tony, a red plastic cup of beer plummeted down on Rosie's head.

"What the hell?" she snorted, beer dripping down her face. Once she wiped the beer out of her eyes, she looked up. The perpetrator, a chubby guy with glasses, was waving and saying, "Sorry! Sorry!"

Tony said, "Ughh. My loser roommate, Benny."

In a minute, Benny appeared, guilty, and out of breath. He apologized profusely, even peeling off his T-shirt for Rosie to use to wipe herself off.

"Gross!" Rosie snapped. "I don't want your sweaty shirt." She waved her hands to shake off the beer.

"What can I do?" Benny asked, pulling his T-shirt back on. "I feel like a jerk."

"You are a jerk," Tony said.

"Be nice!" Alisha said. "I'm sure it was an accident. I've got tissues in my purse."

"No, really, what can I do?" Benny asked.

"Do you have a car?" Rosie asked, using the tissues to wipe her face and eyes. "Can you drive me home?"

"No, but I can walk you home."

"I'm not walking home with you," Rosie said. "I don't even know you. You could be the Sterling Hall bomber for all I know."

Tony laughed. "Benny's not the Sterling Hall bomber. He's okay. Just a little clumsy is all."

Rosie, being Rosie felt a little bad for the guy. Close up, he was actually sort of sweet with an earnest face, a generous nose, and John Lennon eyeglasses. She said, "Sorry I snapped. I was just…"

"Shocked. Surprised? Alarmed? Pissed? Irate? Incensed? Infuriated? Hot under the collar?"

Rosie just stared.

"Sorry," Benny said, jamming his hands in his pockets. "I'm a journalism major. Always searching for just the right words."

"I like *hot under the collar*. But no harm done. I was at Woodstock for god's sake and covered in mud for three days. Okay, I'll let you walk me home. Alisha, is that ok? Are you going to stay?"

"How about this?" Tony said. "How about Benny walks you home, you get cleaned up, and then you guys meet Alisha and me at…" He held out his hands to invite her response.

"The Nitty Gritty," Alisha said. "We were going there anyway."

Benny Steiner was a freshman at UW. "A nice Jewish boy from Winnetka, near Chicago," he told her as they walked up Wilson Street, after closing down the Nitty Gritty. His parents wanted him to attend the University of Chicago, their alma mater, but "the buildings scared the hell out of me."

"The buildings?" Rosie asked.

"Haven't you ever seen U of C's campus? Man! Most of the buildings are Gothic style. The stained-glass windows and clustered columns are nice but the ribbed vaults and flying buttresses, come on!"

Rosie didn't know what to say.

"My dad's an architect," was his explanation. "Anyway, you're walking around the campus and you're thinking any moment a bat or a gargoyle or a vampire is going to swoop down and bite your neck!"

Rosie stopped in her tracks and looked at this odd boy. The word *vampire* had become a trigger for her. As well as *bite* and *neck*. Of course, the poor guy had no way of knowing that…it was just weird.

"You okay?" Benny said. "Is this where you live?"

They were standing in front of a preschool. Rosie gestured at the sign with her hand and resumed walking.

"It could be cool to live in a preschool if you think about it," Benny said, running to catch up. "You would always have snacks. There'd be naps on those nice little mats. You'd have lots of books and toys. Preschool was great. I really shined in preschool. You still *like* yourself in preschool because you don't know enough yet not to. I had glasses. Didn't bother me. Nothing wrong with glasses…until you get to middle school. What's the part of your body you like the least?"

"Excuse me?"

"For me, I would have to say my chin. It's a weak chin. But did I know that as a preschooler? I did not."

"Okay, I'll play. I would have to say my feet."

"What's wrong with your feet?"

"Nothing is really wrong with them, they're just big. It runs in the family. All the Quinlaynes have big feet."

Benny reached for her arm to stop her, then looked down at her feet. "They're not big at all, just the right size. And what's a quinlayne?"

Rosie didn't answer, but she smiled. She walked quietly alongside of Benny. After Xavier, boys frightened her. Plus, she didn't think anyone was interested—she had rounded out again after putting on the "freshman fifteen." She'd stopped wearing halter tops or skirts, or anything remotely feminine, and refused to wear makeup because of animal experiments. She wore jeans and T-shirts. She wore sneakers or flats even though her mother always tried to tell her that high heels would make her feet look smaller. She often hid behind her long, brown hair. After Xavier, she really didn't want guys to notice her.

"What's a quinlayne?" Benny repeated.

"A Quinlayne is me. I'm Rosie Quinlayne."

"Nice to meet you Rosie Quinlayne with the beautiful feet!" Benny said, grinning.

Rosie smiled all the way home.

Rosie and Benjamin Steiner, the nice Jewish boy from Winnetka, had become a thing.

"You're a thing!" Alisha said when Rosie called to tell her about their first date. Rosie uncharacteristically gushed about Benny. "He's brilliant and corny and absolutely adorable!"

"Uhm, to whom am I speaking? Can you put Rose Quinlayne on the phone please? But really, I'm happy for you!"

Rosie was sure Leesh would have been happier if things had worked out between her and Benny's roommate Tony. Ever since they were kids, the best friends had dreamed of double dates and double weddings. Tony and Alisha had one date, but he never called her afterward, and she was heartbroken. Rosie wasn't so sure about Tony anyway. His macho-man attitude turned her off.

Rosie found herself on a real date for the first time in her life. Benny asked her out to a movie but nothing playing appealed to them, so they ended up going to the Henry Vilas Zoo where they were treated to the scene of two monkeys masturbating. They got the giggles, and from then on, their secret code was "MM" for monkeys masturbating.

He made her laugh. He was innocent, funny, and kind. This time when Benny walked her home, they held hands. And when he walked her to the doorstep, he clumsily kissed her. Rosie clumsily kissed him back.

4.
rosie & benny

BENNY LIVED WITH Tony and one other guy in a two-family on Doty. About a month into their relationship, Benny invited Rosie over to his place for pizza. She happily accepted but never imagined it would be for *homemade* pizza. And Caesar salad! Benny's roommate Carl, a tall, lanky guy with brown wavy hair and a ski-lift nose, was a clinical nutrition major whose dream it was to be a food chemist. He was always experimenting with new recipes. Benny teased, "I hit the jackpot in terms of roommates: Carl does all the cooking and Tony is never home."

The apartment itself was immaculate—far cleaner than her place with the girls. In the kitchen, they sat at a wobbly wooden table, set with placemats and cloth napkins. The silverware was in the right places. Stella Maris would have adored Carl.

Carl adored Rosie. When she told him that she slept in a walk-in closet and mostly lived on Campbell's soup and Ramen noodles, he winced and said she would just have to come for dinner more often. "Come on Wednesdays," he said. "I don't have class on Wednesday nights."

And so, it became a tradition. Wednesday nights at Benny's. Carl would make a delicious dinner and then the threesome would play Scrabble and drink whiskey. One night after dinner, Carl put on his jean jacket and said he had a meeting and wouldn't be able to play Scrabble. On his way out,

Rosie caught Carl winking at Benny. "I wasn't born yesterday," Rosie told Benny as she came around and sat in his lap.

Benny laughed. "Well I was! I've never been with a girl, Rosie. Carl thought maybe if we had some time alone…" He gently slipped Rosie off his lap and took her by the hand, leading her to his bedroom, where they lay on his twin bed with the Smiley Face bedspread and made shy, tentative love. Rosie never felt so happy.

One night in mid-October, after a scrumptious dinner of chili and cornbread, Carl was pouring shots of whiskey when Tony sauntered in. It was the first time Rosie had seen him in months. Apparently, he'd sparred with his girlfriend at the Nitty Gritty. "She said I was shit-faced," he said, "which I am, but that never seemed to matter before." He was good and drunk. He sat down at the table, and after wolfing down a big bowl of chili and a couple of bottles of soda, he seemed to sober up a little. "Let's play some cards, why don't we!" he blurted out.

"We play Scrabble on Wednesdays," Carl said, even though they hadn't played in seven or eight Wednesdays.

Tony said, "Scrabble's lame. Hey, Rosie, you play poker?"

"Texas Hold 'Em or Five Card Draw?" Rosie said, trying to sound clever, even though a clever player she was not.

"Strip," he said, flashing the white teeth that had blindsided Alisha.

"Aw, come on, Tony," Benny said. "No way."

"Carl, clear this stuff away, will you?" Tony said. Rosie felt bad when Carl jumped up as commanded and cleared away Tony's plate. "And grab a deck of cards from that kitchen drawer, while you're up." Carl handed Tony the cards and then wiped the table down with a dishcloth. "You're game, right, Rosie?" Tony said. He shook the cards into his hand and began shuffling.

"No, she's not game," Benny said. "We're not game."

Rosie saw the smug look on Tony's face. She had experienced that kind of look from boys before. Something inside her wanted to prove to stupid men like Tony that women were equal in value and ability.

"I am *too* game," Rosie said, looking Tony straight in the eye. Carl sat down. He looked nervous. Rosie wondered how these two nice guys ended up living with a guy like Tony.

"We'll play the quick version," Tony said as he motioned to Carl to cut the deck. "Each player shows their best five-card hand. The player with the best hand doesn't take off any clothing, while the three losers do. Glasses and jewelry don't count."

The only jewelry Rosie wore was her POW bracelet, engraved with the name *Lt. Col. Jerry Lowings*. She did a quick inventory of her attire: a turtleneck sweater, jeans, belt, bra, underwear, socks, and shoes. Nine items. Surely enough to escape full-on nudity.

"Rosie," Benny said, "we don't have to."

"Aww, Benny-boy," Tony taunted. "It'll be fun."

"Rosie, he'll play until someone is naked," Benny warned.

"For god's sake," Rosie said, feeling her whiskey and sitting up straighter in her chair, "I skinny-dipped at fucking Woodstock."

Fast-forward and Rosie, three shots in and several hands later, sat at the table in her white bra and mint green bikini panties. In her hands—five really crappy cards. The thought racing through her head: *How the hell do I get out of this?* Maybe she could *pretend* to wriggle out of her underwear while staying seated and no one would see a thing. Tony would call her out for cheating. She laid out her cards and groaned.

"Okay," Benny said, pounding his fist on the table. "We are stopping. Rosie, go put your clothes on and I'll walk you home."

Rosie let out a sigh of relief.

"Oh, no you don't!" Tony said, leaping from his chair. "Fair is fair. She said she skinny-dipped at fucking Woodstock for god's sake."

Benny gave Tony a dirty look and rose from his chair. He gathered up Rosie's clothes, handed them to her and said, "Go ahead, Rosie. You can use the bathroom."

Rosie got up, took her clothes from Benny, and, realizing she was quite drunk, slinked carefully off to the bathroom, while Tony called Benny an *ass-wipe* and Rosie a *tease*. She closed the bathroom door and sat down on the toilet. She'd had to pee for some time but didn't want to leave the table half-naked. She had just wiped and stood up to pull up her undies, when the door burst open, and Tony came barreling in. "You prickteaser! You owe me a look at your knockers." He lunged toward her and yanked at her bra, pulling one of the straps down and revealing a breast. It all happened so fast. Rosie screamed and a few seconds later Benny burst through the door with Carl in tow. Benny jumped on Tony and they both fell to the floor, leaving Rosie standing there with her panties at her ankles and her right breast exposed. Poor Carl covered his eyes with his hand.

Benny walked her home. He kept saying, "Sorry. Sorry. I'm so sorry." Just like on the first night they'd met.

"It's not your fault. I'm the one who agreed to play."

"Yeah, but who knew he would go ballistic? I've never seen him act like that before."

"It's me, I bring it out in men."

"What?"

"Nothing."

"Rosie, I'm so sorry. Are you going to be okay? What can I do?"

"I'm fine. He didn't hurt me."

"Maybe not physically…"

"Let's forget about it, okay?" But when Benny tried to grab her hand, she pulled it away. She just didn't want anyone touching her. And when they arrived home, instead of making out for a while on the back porch like they usually did, she gave him a peck on the cheek and ran up the steps, saying, "Goodnight. Tell Carl thanks for dinner."

The next day she was supposed to be at the Dome at seven. She called in sick. She had never called in sick before in her life. Her boss wasn't happy, but she had not only never missed a day of work, she was never late, and often filled in for others when her boss was in a jam, so what could he say but "feel better." So, she slept in. Her roommate Lindy came in three times to tell her she had phone calls—two from Benny and one from Alisha. "Tell him I'm still sleeping." "Tell him I have the flu." "Tell her I'm in the shower."

She called in sick the next day too. She wasn't herself. She stayed holed up in her little closet bedroom and tried to study but she found herself reading the same sentence over and over…"*Monarchy, aristocracy, and democracy will become tyranny, oligarchy, and anarchy, respectively*." She closed her book. So much for Machiavelli. She fell asleep and dreamed about Stella Maris. Her mother pointed a finger at her. "You my dear, are an ignorant girl who puts herself in compromising situations like skinny-dipping and playing strip-poker and then wonders why she keeps getting accosted by young men. You brought this on yourself, Missy. You have only yourself to blame."

Rosie woke up to find Alisha sitting on the edge of her bed.

"Tell me," Alisha whispered, wiping a tear from Rosie's cheek with her finger.

Monday morning, Rosie was back at the Dome, pouring coffee and listening in on her customers' conversations. It was good to be working. She could forget about Xavier and Tony and just think about who gets their eggs over easy and who gets them scrambled.

Still, the incident, *incidences*, invaded her thoughts. What was it about her that brought this on? Her looks, her personality, her demeanor? She was bossy; that she would own. But she'd become bossy to stick up for herself and Camille. *Bossy* was her defense mechanism. Alisha said men were probably threatened by her strength and intelligence. (What a best friend would say.)

Alisha said Rosie should report Tony for attacking her. "Go to the university. They will expel him." But Rosie just wanted to put it behind her. "Benny better kick him out," Alisha said.

Her shift ended at three and at about two minutes to three Benny showed up, hands in his pockets, waiting near the front door. Rosie gave a little wave. She punched out and said goodbye to her boss and grabbed her jacket and purse. She didn't say anything to Benny as she walked past him, but she motioned for the door, and he opened it for her. They walked out into the sunlight of a perfect autumn day. The trees were dressed to the nines; the sky seemed to be wearing velvet. It was a day just begging a person to be joyful. They walked. "You're mad at me," Benny said.

"I'm not mad at you."

"You are."

"It's complicated."

"It's just stupid. Really. Tony's a jerk. We drank too much. I should never have let the game get started."

"It's my fault. I have a problem with men. We seem to clash."

"Nonsense. You don't clash with me."

Rosie let Benny take her hand.

"Carl and I kicked him out."

Alisha's brother Jeremy was right: for all intents and purposes, the bombing of the Army Math building was the death of the peace movement at U.W. The impact of the death of the graduate student brought a sudden end to the violence to which both the protestors and the police had resorted. No one had an appetite for it. Adding to the climate was the fact that the bombers were still at large. The FBI had put the four suspects on the most-wanted list, but they so far had eluded law enforcement. The police believed they may have interacted with the bombers on two occasions: one, on the night of the bombing, when a sheriff's officer stopped four men in a white Corvair en route to Devil's Lake State Park, about an hour northwest of Madison. They questioned the men but released them after an hour. The second interaction occurred about a week after the bombing, when one of the bombers was stopped for a traffic check in Little Falls, New York. The officer didn't recognize the name or face of the bomber and released him. It always gave Rosie the heebie-jeebies knowing they were still out there. Just as it did knowing that Xavier was still out there. And Tony.

It was weird, but hardly anyone even talked about the war anymore. It seemed like a lifetime ago that all Rosie and her friends had cared about was ending the Vietnam War. Protesting had become a part of their everyday lives. And not just theirs. Young people across the country had been voicing their anti-war sentiments. There was the march in Washington, D.C., the *Dow Day* protest in Madison, the Kent State shootings, the Weatherman bomb in the D.C. Capitol Building, the Sterling Hall bombing, as well as thousands of protests and demonstrations around the world. But now here it was almost twenty years in, and there was fatigue. Rosie wondered if Woodstock and all the protests had even made a difference.

Rosie's life got quieter. She got assiduous with her studies. UW students were traumatized after the bombing—assaulted with guilt in the part they played, frightened by the police investigations (Paul and many others had been hauled in for questioning), and somber about the seriousness the bombing itself represented. It seemed kids retreated into themselves—they stayed in, smoked dope, played music, made love. The UW campus was so quiet that fall semester of 1970, it was dubbed "The Year of Grave Calm." Professors reported that student attendance went back to normal after the bombing and that kids' grades improved markedly. Rosie spent more time at the library studying and more time hanging out with Benny and Carl. Carl was even more shy around her now that he had seen her semi-naked, but they enjoyed their dinners and Scrabble games. They felt older. They quietly questioned everything. If there wasn't anything to fight against was there anything to fight for?

A couple of weeks before Christmas, Rosie sat with Paul Soglin at the bar at the Library Lounge. Diane had backed out last minute with a headache and Benny was running late, so it was just the two of them talking and sharing a pitcher of beer. He seemed a little melancholy. "Rosie, it's gut-check time," Paul said. "I'm thinking about running for mayor."

"Wow! Really?" He was serving his second term on the city council, but Rosie never imagined he'd actually run for mayor.

"Here's the thing. There's not going to be a revolution. And we can't have any more violence. Obviously, we still want political change but we have to adjust our strategy. Beatings and bombings don't make a revolution. We have got to change things from within. And we don't have much time. The primary's in March. You'll help right?"

Rosie smiled and tapped her beer glass to Paul's. "Of course!"

Some said Paul used his notoriety as a radical activist to launch his political career. The fact that Nixon had signed an extension of the Voting

Rights Act of 1965 lowering the voting age to eighteen helped Paul. In the end, the student vote wasn't enough; Paul didn't get past the primary. He learned a lot though and promised to run again in two years.

One day, Paul called Rosie with big news: One of the bombers was caught! Karleton Armstrong, a former UW student. "They're saying he was disillusioned by Vietnam and by the violence between police and protestors," Paul said. A year and a half after the Sterling Hall bombing, he'd been found hiding in Toronto. Even though the other three bombers were still at large, the capture of Armstrong brought a sense of relief to Rosie. When word came out that the four bombers had in fact met at the Nitty Gritty to plan out the bombing, Rosie got spooked, thinking about how she had been just a barstool away from murderers.

When Paul announced in November of 1972 that he would run for mayor again, he put a team together and asked Rosie to be his Campaign Scheduler. She would be responsible for accepting and declining invitations, seeking out political events, and briefing him on all the details—directions, contact information, personal backgrounds of the people with whom he was meeting. Benny offered his writing skills and Carl promised to keep the team well-fed. Rosie knew it would be a challenge to juggle her studies and the job, but she was determined to get her degree *and* get Paul Soglin elected as mayor.

The campaign office was conveniently located not far from the capitol in a building on West Gilman Street. Rosie walked through the door on the first day to find the place already filled with people and cigarette smoke. She found a wobbly folding chair and sat pen in hand and notebook on lap, listening to Paul introduce his team. Paul's good friend, Jim Rowen, a fellow student who was dating Senator George McGovern's daughter, had agreed to be Paul's campaign manager. Jim slightly built, but with big Afro style hair, worked for the Cardinal student newspaper. Paul introduced Jim who was both communications director and pollster. He then introduced the field director, the volunteer coordinator, the office manager, and finally, Rosie.

Paul's eyes gleamed as he spoke. "We've got our work cut out for us, people. Let's face it—I'm an oddity. I'm twenty-seven years old. All people know about me is probably what they've read in the papers. I'm the troublemaker, the hippie kid, the protester, the cab driver. I'm going to be viewed as a radical. And radical I am, but that will be for later. We're going to be professional and nice. We are not going to be inflammatory. We'll save that for later, too." Everyone laughed.

Rosie took scrupulous notes. Paul was running against incumbent Bill Drake, who had been elected in 1969 mainly by promising to get control of the increasingly violent campus protests. He was criticized for being deliberately polarizing, welcoming what the Soglin campaign would call "heavy-handed" police tactics. Paul's campaign promised to make regaining control over the police force a priority.

Rosie wrote down and then circled the words "public transportation" because Jim Rowen said that was going to be a key issue in the campaign. "We're going to stay on message," Paul said. "We want to talk about public transportation, housing, urban planning, the elderly, and downtown development. We won't mention Vietnam in any of our campaign materials."

Rosie looked up from her notepad, surprised.

"We learned a lot after losing the last primary. This time we have to show we can run the city, or we've lost before we started," Paul said, seeming to read Rosie's mind. "What that means for our supporters...well, they have to be patient."

The primary was only three months away. Rosie was never as busy and happy in her life. Up at five every morning and working all day, sometimes having to skip night class to get work done. The former straight-A student was now getting B's and C's, and she was fine with it. She was grateful when the fall semester ended, and she could fully devote her time from December 11th through January 21st to the campaign. Benny asked her to go home to Winnetka with him for Christmas (she'd gone for Thanksgiving) but she told him that Paul needed her. She ended up celebrating Christmas with Paul and his wife and a few other campaign members at the Soglin home.

Benny's birthday was on December 31st and they had spent the last two New Year's Eves at the Nitty Gritty. This year, they spent it at the campaign office, affixing stamps to campaign flyers. Benny's disappointment with how he was celebrating his twenty-second birthday was softened when some members of his favorite local band stopped by and joined the group in singing Happy Birthday.

Alisha's birthday was on January 27th and she got the best birthday present of all: Nixon announced, and Kissinger signed, the Paris Peace Accord, which called for a ceasefire and a withdrawal of U.S. troops, with the intent to finally end the Vietnam War. It was what they'd all been fighting for! Rosie cried when she watched Nixon make the announcement on TV that night. "I don't trust Tricky Dicky," Alisha said. They both looked at their POW bracelets and hoped and prayed that "their" servicemen would be returned home safe and healthy.

With just two months to go until election night, everybody operated in overdrive. Benny was interning at the Capital Times Newspaper and arranged for several interviews with Paul that led to a surprisingly positive article about the "smart and capable hippie alderman." The article lent credibility to Paul's campaign and gave Benny a much-needed boost in the boyfriend department. Rosie knew she had not been a very good girlfriend, but she was caught up in the frenzy of the campaign. The energy level was incredible. She ran on adrenaline fueled by a diet of coffee, Morning Buns (a heavenly, pillowy pastry made by a Madison bakery called the Ovens of Brittany), and corn curls. She talked faster than she used to, she moved faster than she used to, everything was faster. It was insane, but there was a good chance Paul could win this time.

"You think *I'm* busy," Rosie said to Benny who complained about her absenteeism, "think about Paul. In one year, he got his law degree, was elected to the City Council for his third term, and then announced he would run for mayor in the spring election. The guy's a machine." Did Rosie pick up on the clues that she was losing Benny? Of course, she did, but nothing felt more important than Paul's election.

As campaigns go, Paul's was not the most organized, nor could it be described as a brain trust. Truly, they were running by the seat of their pants. There was a lot of bickering and infighting and "you-don't-know-what-you're-talking-abouts." Rosie tried to stay out of most of the hullabaloo, but over time, she found she had good political instincts, and she wasn't afraid to speak her mind. Once, the field director told her to keep in her own lane, but Paul intervened on her behalf and said all ideas were welcome. She mostly stayed focused on getting Paul in front of as many people as she could, setting up meetings with key influential city and university men and women, with students, and booking as many neighborhood coffees as she could. An insufferable amount of coffees. The team decided to concentrate on the Crestwood area, the 19th district. They needed intelligence on what the level of acceptance or hostility would be with these residents. Madison knew who Paul was—the anti-war, hippie student who got himself beat up and arrested—but they also needed to know he was smart and hardworking and understood city government. Of course, he had the support of the students, but that alone wouldn't get him elected.

On a rare night off, Rosie had dinner at Benny and Carl's. She hadn't been there in months. Even though the boys had kicked Tony out, somehow, he lingered in the air. Carl placed two huge slices of homemade pizza on her plate and afterward they made banana splits. After they'd cleaned the kitchen, Carl said he was off to a meeting but Rosie said, "No! Stay! Let's play Scrabble like old times!" Carl's face brightened as Benny's dimmed and Rosie realized she'd just sabotaged Benny's romantic plans. They hadn't had much romance lately. Carl fetched the game and the mood softened, and it did seem like old times, until Rosie spelled the word *mayoral* and got a triple word score.

Benny was incredulous when, a few nights before spring semester began, Rosie announced she was quitting school. They were in bed in Rosie's claustrophobic bedroom closet. Paul had dropped them off at Rosie's after they had attended the zillionth neighborhood coffee. Benny was already in a mood because he thought they were going to have the night to themselves, get something to eat, see a movie, do something non-political, but at the last minute Rosie told him she needed to go to this particular coffee (she went to *all* the coffees) because it was at a home in the Crestwood area and she felt she was sending Paul into a lion's den. Benny reluctantly tagged along and yawned through heated discussions about downtown development and transportation. (He did wake up though when one old guy said, "Promise me you won't smoke any of that 'marry-ja-wanna' and I'll vote for you.")

"I *have* to quit," Rosie said, as she rolled over in bed. "I can't do both and the most important thing right now is to get Paul elected."

"The most important thing right now is to graduate."

"Ok, *Dad*."

Benny rubbed his eyes, his signature move when he was exasperated with Rosie.

Rosie said, "So I'll graduate in December instead of May."

"This is a mistake you will regret," Benny said. "You have one semester left." He held up a finger.

"Paul needs me."

"To set up coffees."

"It's more than coffees! I set up meetings, speeches, lunches, and dinners. This is important! What's this really about, Benny?"

"I think you need Paul more than Paul needs you."

"What's that supposed to mean?" she asked, knowing exactly what it meant.

On March 6th, the night of the primary, the team and dozens of supporters crowded in the campaign office. Benny and Carl joined Rosie, Carl toting a tray of his famous chocolate-pecan cookies. All eyes were on the television as the votes came in. Eight candidates were running in the primary; everyone expected incumbent Bill Drake to make it through, but it was anybody's guess who the second candidate would be. The way Wisconsin primaries worked, the top two candidates with the most votes in the runoff would face each other in the general election. Rosie was nervous. She overheard some woman say, "Do you really think a young hippie that many of the townspeople consider to be the Anti-Christ can actually make it?"

A little after nine o'clock the results were announced. He'd made it! Paul had made it! Rosie jumped up and down and hugged everybody—even people she didn't know. The final votes came in at 16,243 for Bill Drake, 11,485 for Paul, with the next two candidates getting 10,350 and 6,150 respectively. A fine showing!

Paul stood with his wife and thanked each campaign member by name. "I could not have done this without this great team. Now that we've come this far, I know we can make it over the finish line."

The next twenty-eight days happened in fast motion. The team knew the student base of 10,000 to 12,000 had propelled Paul through the primary, but he would need to change some minds of independent and undecided voters. The only way to do that was with more coffees. And with solid issues that people cared about.

Now that Paul was the official candidate, interest in him grew. Instead of a handful of people coming to a coffee, now it was more like fifteen to twenty people—once Rosie counted twenty-eight!—jamming into someone's living room to find out for themselves what this guy was all about. It was working. A recent quote in the newspaper from a man who had attended a coffee: "I was expecting a dirty, scruffy scoundrel. What I met was smart young man, with five years of City Council under his belt, who knew what the hell the Planning Department does and what the Board of Estimates is."

When the Capital Times endorsed Paul over incumbent Bill Drake, the team was beside themselves. Hope turned into expectation. "We are going to win!" the campaign manager said over and over, sometimes to himself. Whenever anyone approached him with news or a question, Jim greeted them with: "We are going to win!"

Even Benny seemed to get more excited, now that the possibility of Paul winning was within reach. He enthusiastically canvassed door to door, stuffed envelopes, wrote copy, made phone calls, whatever Rosie asked him to do. Word on the street was that the long-haired, hippie, anti-war protester alderman was making inroads. In cafes and bars across the city, the talk was all politics, all the time. As election day neared, it seemed that Bill Drake's supporters teeter-tottered between arrogance and actual fear. Drake's campaign did their best to paint Paul as the boogeyman. They had distributed a pamphlet entitled "Lest We Forget," describing Paul's radical anti-war rhetoric. The pamphlet also criticized him for his stubborn dislike of haircuts.

There was intense personal reaction to each of the candidates, but Paul kept reiterating to the team, that the polls showed there was only one real issue: the transportation issue. "And that's what we're going to talk about ad nauseam now until election day." Madison was growing and public transit was a problem. It was a simple, straightforward issue that people could understand, and a campaign promise Paul knew he could keep.

Rosie and Benny clicked their beer glasses as they sat at the bar at the Nitty Gritty. Benny had just found out his internship at the Capital Times had earned him a job offer upon graduation. "So, it looks like you're stuck with me." They got a little drunk and walked back to Rosie's. She went to sleep contented... until she woke up at two-something in the morning worried that she would fail at the biggest task Paul had asked her to undertake: get Bill Drake to debate him.

Drake's people kept refusing, saying he was the incumbent, he didn't need a one-on-one debate. Madisonians knew him and what he stood for. But Paul's team knew that undecided voters were going to make the difference and there were enough of them to swing the election. Usually, the closer you get to an election, those undecideds tend to stick with the incumbent. In her heart, Rosie knew if they could just reassure those undecided voters that Paul Soglin would be a capable administrator, it could put him over the top.

A week before the election, Bill Drake caved and agreed to a debate. The big night was held at the West High auditorium. Starting time was seven-thirty, but when Rosie and Benny arrived at the school at six, people were already packing the place. Bill Drake arrived late, and his demeanor gave Rosie the impression that the event was beneath him. Both candidates spoke on their views and ideas, they took some general questions from the audience, and then it was time for summation. Rosie was nervous; both candidates had done pretty well. There was no real standout slam-dunk or gotcha moment for either candidate. Until there was...

Bill Drake summarized first. *Blah, blah, blah. Law and order.* But then he concluded by saying, "I just hope there are enough decent people left in Madison that I'm reelected."

"Woa!" Benny whispered, "he just insulted the voters!"

Rosie squeezed his hand. "Cardinal rule for politicians: never attack the voters." She held her breath, wondering how Paul would respond. He summarized the points he had made and ended by saying, "I don't care if you're decent or indecent, I hope you'll support me on election day." It seemed to Rosie the applause and whoops and hollers were bigger and louder for Paul than for Bill Drake.

Two days later, when Rosie walked into the campaign office, it was all abuzz. The "decent people" remark had hurt Drake. "These have been popping up all over the city," Paul told her, holding up a lawn sign that said, "Another decent family for Soglin." And that was that.

They gathered at the Labor Temple on Park Street on election night, April 3rd, and celebrated Paul's victory. The vote totals were 37,548 for Paul and 34,179 for Bill Drake. Rosie got shit-faced drunk and then basically slept for the next two days in her tiny closet bedroom.

5.
rosie & alisha

GOOD THING THE election was held on April 3rd and not on April 9th, because on April 9th, 1973, the city of Madison found itself digging out from nearly thirteen inches of snow. How the spring snowstorm could have affected the election was anyone's guess, but for now it shut down the city and much of the state. (Paul's critics blasted him for the snowstorm: "This is what happens when you elect a hippie!") Rosie was half sad, half not sad that she had to miss her brother's wedding. Benny was disappointed because he was anxious to meet the notorious Stella Maris. "You dodged a bullet," Rosie told him.

After the election, Paul asked Rosie to stay on and work for him. This was both a surprise and a dream come true. She was honored, but she knew she had earned the position by proving herself worthy during the campaign. On April 18th, she stepped into the mayor's office in Madison City Hall on Monona Avenue in a brand-new navy business suit. She even wore lipstick and a necklace! Her title was *Executive Assistant to the Mayor*, which meant she pretty much did anything and everything Paul needed. She coordinated his events, developed correspondence, worked with the media, served as the lead person for the clerical and administrative staff, and sometimes made coffee. She hated when she had to make coffee. But Paul treated her with great respect, calling her his "right hand woman." She got a bump in pay and bought her first car, and was able to move out of the apartment with the closet bedroom and move into the upper of a house on the corner of Basset and Washington with Alisha. Benny was elated. He bought her a housewarming gift: a full-size bed. But the gift came with one condition: that she would go back to night school and finish her degree.

She had been waffling. Just a few weeks into Paul's first term she got a glimpse of what his schedule was going to be like. He put in at least eighty hours in a six-day week, which meant she put in at least eighty hours in a six-day week. There were days when they got to the office at five a.m. and didn't leave until midnight. How could she juggle the job, classes, and Benny? Wonder Woman she was not.

In the end, she registered for night classes, but not because of Benny, but because of Paul. He insisted. She missed more classes than she attended, but hung on by the skin of her teeth.

One night after her night class, Alisha asked Rosie to meet her at the Nitty Gritty. Alisha took one sip of her beer and started crying. Ugly-face crying where she couldn't catch her breath. The bartender offered a glass of water, but she couldn't even stop to take a sip. People were staring. Alisha caught her breath and said, "Let's go home."

Rosie sat at the kitchen table. Alisha got out a half gallon of Neapolitan ice cream from the freezer and a spoon and handed them to Rosie.

"Uh-oh." Rosie said. "Buttering me up with ice cream. This could be bad."

"You're going to hate me," Alisha said.

"How many years have you been saying that? Since we were in kindergarten, and I've yet to hate you!"

"This time you are really going to hate me."

"Come on, Leesh, spit it out."

Alisha sat down across from Rosie. She sighed and said, "I've been seeing Tony."

"Tony?"

"Yes."

"Tony, as in the Tony who assaulted me?"

Alisha nodded.

Rosie felt her face flush with shock and anger. She sprang from the chair. "What the hell!" she screamed. "What the hell!" Alisha started crying again, which made Rosie angrier. "Shut up!" she shouted, as she paced around the kitchen, trying to absorb what she had just heard.

"Let me explain," Alisha pleaded.

"What's there to explain? First Becki and now you. Maybe it's genetic. Maybe it runs in your family. Maybe the women in your family are attracted to abusers. Is that it?"

"Rosie!"

A million questions ran through Rosie's head. *When? How long? Why?* And even though she wanted answers to her questions she wanted to be able to breathe more. Because she couldn't breathe. She could not take in a breath of air. She bolted and ran down the back stairs. On the landing, she bent over to catch her breath and momentarily wondered why people did that, what were the physics behind it? It helped. She caught her breath. Alisha was right behind her, so she ran. She ran faster than she knew she could run. It felt so good. If only she weren't barefoot, she probably could have run a marathon.

Benny made her a cup of tea and Carl put some chocolate-pecan cookies on a plate before retreating to his bedroom.

"Alisha," Rosie said to Benny, "is no longer my friend." She lay her head down on the table.

"You don't mean that."

"But I do," she said, popping her head up. "You are not going to believe this." She proceeded to tell him what Alisha had told her.

Curiously, Benny didn't look surprised, or shocked, or even appalled. He looked...nervous. Then it dawned on Rosie why. She shook her head. "Benny! You knew?" It wasn't really a question.

"It wasn't my place to tell you," he said, reaching across the table to take her hand. Rosie yanked her hand back. "She's your best friend, Ro. She asked me not to tell you. That she would tell you in her own time."

A punch in the stomach. A double betrayal. She looked at Benny, squirming in his chair. "Wait. Wait a minute! Are you ... are you still *friends* with him?" She had assumed that when Benny kicked Tony out, he'd also ended the friendship.

"Rosie, I've known Tony since we were in diapers. You can't just throw someone away because they made one mistake."

Mistake? Sexually assaulting someone? A mistake? She looked at Benny and said, "You wanna bet!" She turned on her heel and left.

Where to go? She couldn't go home. She had a key to the mayor's office, but the building itself would be locked up for the night. In her car? But the car was locked and the keys were in her purse which was in her bedroom. Okay, she would go home, but she wouldn't say a word to Alisha and then tomorrow she would decide what to do. The house was quiet and Alisha's bedroom door was closed. Rosie tiptoed to her room and went to bed without washing her face or brushing her teeth. And wonder of wonders, she slept.

She left the house at six the next morning, without showering, just a quick change of clothes, and a brush through her hair. She jammed her toothbrush, toothpaste, and deodorant into her purse to use at work. She wanted to escape before Alisha awoke. She drove over to Johnson and State and hung out at the Baker's Room above the Ovens of Brittany and comforted herself with one of their famous Morning Buns (the perfect intersection between a croissant and a cinnamon roll). At six-thirty she went to the office, thinking she might beat Paul, but, no, there he was in his office, where he could be found at almost any time day or night, on the phone, with his head in a bunch of papers, chain-smoking cigarettes, pen a scribbling, usually in his stocking feet.

"Oh, good, Rosie!" he greeted her. "Get a look at this!" he told her, coming out of his office.

She dropped her purse on her desk but brought along the bag with the two Morning Buns she'd bought for him and walked over.

"Ta-da!" he said, closing his office door so she could see the golden plaque on the door. "HIZZONER Da MARE" it read.

Rosie smiled. "Nice!"

"A gift from Mel. A little irreverent, huh?"

"A little," Rosie said. It certainly was a reminder of who he was. As was the old campaign poster on the wall inside his office that had warned: "If you don't vote, this student will be your next alderman." The poster, from years back, compliments of a Madison alderman, pictured Paul as a scruffy, radical young man, with long hair and bushy mustache, a sure troublemaker.

"You okay?" Paul asked. "You look a little tired. Are we working you too hard?"

"Not at all. Up early because I had a hankering for one of these." She dangled the tell-tale bakery bag.

"Now I know why I love you, Rosie. Is there coffee?"

The day was a blur, an endless sea of people vying for Paul's time. This is how it had been since the inauguration. Capitol Hill reporters, aldermen, UW students, the chancellor, the school superintendent, the police chief, and everyday citizens. So many people! Rosie swore, at one point, Clara, Paul's secretary, was going to scream: "Take a number!" It was amazing how people thought they could just walk into the mayor's office without an appointment.

A couple months in and the team was still in the orientation stage. Even with Paul's years of experience on City Council, he had much to learn. Rosie set up meetings with all the department heads including finance, public works, public safety, transportation, etc. to aid Paul in understanding how all the pieces fit together. He wanted to do a thorough review of everything from the current operating and capital budgets, meeting minutes from the last year, human resources and other administrative policies, organizational charts, staff roster, annual financial reports, to mission statements and goals. He kept Rosie and the team on their toes.

And tours! Paul set up tours of all the physical facilities of the city and points of interest. He also rode a city bus, walked to the public library, and checked out the public works garages, snow plows, and garbage trucks, just to get a feel how the city and its services worked. He saw many things he wanted to change or improve, but believed it was best not to jam his own agenda through too soon, but to learn all he could, prove that he could run the city smoothly, gain the confidence of citizens, and then introduce and implement some progressive programs.

Rosie sat in on the last meeting of the day. Afterward, when it was just the two of them in Paul's office, he said, "Rosie, can you believe this? That

I am sitting here in this office? That I'm the damn mayor of Madison, Wisconsin."

"You are *Hizzoner da-Mare*," Rosie said.

"You know, on my first day, I came in here, shut the door, said out loud, 'My God! What am I going to do now?' This is scary! I don't want to be one of those incompetents who ruin cities."

"You won't. You'll improve this city. I know you will."

"I feel kind of old, Rosie," he said, rising from his desk.

"Says the twenty-seven-year-old."

"Twenty-eight, remember?" When he smiled, his thick mustache which curled rakishly downward, turned up a little. He'd just celebrated his birthday a few weeks after the election. The youngest mayor in Madison's history.

When Rosie got home from work, Alisha was waiting for her with wine. And cheese and crackers. And olives, the Greek kind that Rosie loved. "Please listen," Alisha pleaded with puppy-dog eyes. Rosie remembered what Benny said: "I've known Tony since we were in diapers. You can't just throw someone away because they made one mistake." She sighed. Okay, she would hear her out.

Alisha handed her a glass of wine, and said, "You know I had a crush on him for two years. When he dropped me without so much as an explanation I was crushed. You knew that."

Rosie nodded, helping herself to an olive.

"So, I hadn't seen him in like a year. I thought maybe he dropped out. But then he shows up at this party. Remember that girl I hate, Stevie Donalds? Her party. You were in Winnetka with Benny that weekend. So, at first, I don't recognize him. He looks completely different. Cut his hair short. No scruffy beard. The way he stood was even different. So, he tries to talk to me, and I tell him he has got nerve even making eye contact after what he did to you."

Rosie made a double-decker sandwich: cracker, cheese, cracker, cheese, cracker, topped it with an olive, jammed it into her mouth, and washed it down with some wine.

"So, he says, 'Hear me out. That was the old me. I've been through rehab. That's where I was last semester. I'm clean now—no drugs, no booze, no acting stupid with women. It's been four months and nine days.'"

"Oh, and you believed him?" Rosie said.

"He had proof! He showed me a card in his wallet from Alcoholics Anonymous. It had a prayer on it."

"So, he's found Jesus, now."

"Rosie."

"Leesh."

"But he *has* changed. We've been together for two months."

"Wow," Rosie said. "Then let me ask you this. My uncle went through AA and I remember one of the steps is to apologize to everyone you've hurt. I've received no such apology."

"But Rosie! He didn't really hurt you…"

"What did you just say?"

"You told me that he just pulled down your bra strap. He barely touched you…"

Rosie looked at her friend. They had known each other, not since they were in diapers, but from kindergarten. Who was this person? "If that's what you believe, if that's what you really believe, then we can no longer be friends."

"Rosie! That's not fair!"

"Fair?" Rosie stood up. She felt her face flush. She started crying—something Rosie was programmed not to do after years of Stella-Maris-style abuse. She yelled: "He came into the bathroom, saw me naked from the waist down, tried to rip off my bra, and exposed my breast. If you don't think that hurt me, as I said, we can't be friends." Rosie turned to go to her room.

"Why didn't you lock the door?" Alisha called after her.

Rosie stopped in her tracks and turned around. "*What?*"

"Tony wondered why you didn't lock the bathroom door."

Rosie was speechless. She turned around again, walked into her bedroom, and slammed the door, wishing *it* had a lock. She fell onto her bed and sobbed. It all came rushing back at her: Xavier with his dirty hands, the animal feel of his bite on her neck; Tony clawing at her breasts. She remembered why she didn't lock the bathroom door—the lock was broken, something Benny had told her about the first night she was there for dinner. Something Tony would have known.

"Rosie!" Alisha was outside her door. "Rosie, you have to understand ... I'm in love. He was drunk that night. He's different now."

Rosie kept quiet.

"One thing is for sure," Alisha said, "you were stupid to play strip poker."

Ah, there it was. No matter what, the woman was always to blame. Rosie got up and opened the door to face Alisha. "You are not my friend, and I will be moving out tomorrow."

"You can't move out," Alisha said. "I can't afford the rent by myself."

"Well guess what? I can, so maybe *you* should move out."

"Fine. That's what Tony predicted anyway. He said I could move in with him."

"Good luck with that," Rosie said and slammed the door.

Rosie cried herself to sleep, knowing that she still had to deal with Benny.

She was so busy at work the next day, the only time she thought about Alisha and Benny was when she went to the bathroom, otherwise her mind was occupied, and her body was moving. Clara, the secretary, had a family emergency so Rosie juggled six things at once.

At the end of the day, she wasn't surprised to see Benny waiting for her outside the entrance of city hall. As she walked toward him, she rehearsed in her mind what she had planned on saying. *We've been drifting apart anyway. You've always been unreasonably jealous of Paul. You need a more attentive girlfriend. You deserve to be happy.* But she wasn't prepared to see Benny's tears. She had never seen him cry. They walked to the parking garage and they sat in her hell-hot car with the windows rolled down. She had tissues in her glove compartment and gave him a few. He proceeded to blow his nose.

"What are we going to do?" he asked.

Poor Benny. He was kind of like Camille. He was easy going and let the world unfold around him as it pleased. Rosie had never told him about Xavier. Only Alisha and Becki knew about that. She tried to bury that awful attack deep, deep down. Maybe she owed it to Benny to tell him about it so he could understand where she was coming from.

"Remember when I told you I went to Woodstock?" Rosie asked, using a tissue to wipe her brow.

"No, I don't remember how you told me a million times that you went skinny-dipping at Woodstock. You wear it like a badge."

"Really? You think this is the time for sarcasm?"

"Sorry."

But the moment was over. Rosie didn't feel like telling him about it now. What did it matter? The incident with Tony stood on its own and was serious enough without bringing Xavier into it. "You know what, Benny, never mind. *We've been drifting apart anyway. You've always been unreasonably jealous of Paul. You need a more attentive girlfriend. You deserve to be happy.*"

"Come on, Ro. We can get through this."

Rosie didn't want to break up. She sighed. Looking straight ahead through the windshield at the concrete block wall, she posed a "what-if." (She had no intention of going through with it, but it would validate her decision.)

"What if…" She paused for affect. "What if I reported Tony for sexual assault?"

"But Rosie, he would be arrested. You would ruin his life."

"Okay, Benny. That's all I needed to know. Now get out of my car. But one last thing. When, not if, Tony hurts Alisha—and I mean both emotionally and physically—some of that blame will be on you."

"I'm sorry, Rosie, I really am."

"But are you really?"

How adaptable humans are! Alisha had been in Rosie's life for fifteen years and Benny for more than three, but somehow their absence went largely unmissed. (Lie!) Workaholic Rosie sometimes worked eighteen-hour days. There were breakfast meetings and lunches and dinners and speeches and fundraisers and enough work to fill 24 hours if that were humanly possible.

Paul grew concerned. "You're working too much. Where's Benny been? I haven't seen him lately."

"Alas, we are no more," Rosie said. And nothing more. People in the office learned the hard way that Rosie was fiercely private about her personal life. When a new staff member casually asked if she had a boyfriend, Rosie rudely replied, "Next I guess you'll want my height and weight." The girl said, "Sorry I asked."

Rosie was not even aware of the wall she was putting up. Eight months into the job, she realized that at times city government could be tedious. What happened to her dream of changing the world? Even some of Paul's supporters expressed disappointment that Paul seemed to have mellowed too much. Where was the leftist firebrand they had been so passionate about? Where was the guy who was going to blow up the status quo? Just the other day she had overheard some guy in Paul's office raising his voice and saying, "Come on, man! Where is the shit-starter I used to know?"

Rosie herself was a bit disillusioned. She had always been a forward-looking person; these days she found herself more reflective. She questioned her journey. She'd had big dreams of making the world a better place—and now it seemed the only way she contributed was helping to get a stop sign strategically placed. The sixties seemed kind of silly now—a romantic vision of the world, a daydream with nightmarish edges of assassinations, war, civil unrest. Hope had been at the heart of the sixties. Hope for a better world, a society that would wake up from oppression—oppression of sexual hang-ups, race and gender inequality, mass consumerism, and political conflicts. Nixon had resigned. Shouldn't the world be a better place? But then Ford pardoned him, and the world seemed to be just as dirty and corrupt as ever.

Rosie concentrated on the job and the job was hard. People were mean. Hateful even. You could barely please half of the people half of the time. People could lose it over a streetlight or a stop sign. Barking dogs were worse than devils. Some whacko had come in and demanded the city ban homeowners from painting their houses white...white houses reflected the sunlight and bothered his eyes when he looked out the window at his neighbor's house.

But Rosie's devotion and loyalty to Paul never faltered. She admired him. He really tried to listen to Madisonians and solve their problems. He had an open-door policy which made her job challenging, but it allowed access to all citizens. Sometimes, Paul would set up a card table in the town square and would take complaints from citizens, jotting them down on a yellow legal pad. Who did that? He seemed to gain popularity with the moderate voters and lose some with the radical voters who thought he sold out. What did they think, Rosie wanted to ask them, that he would come in and legalize marijuana, arm the student body with machine guns, defund the police? Paul Soglin did not sell out; he just put on a suit and his big-boy shoes and did his fighting inside rather than outside on the streets. He did keep his promise to get better control of the police and pleased the lefties and ticked off the conservatives by hiring a new police chief who wore a ponytail.

All in all, Rosie's job was to help Paul get through his "piles": the important pile, the urgent pile, and the pile than couldn't wait.

Rosie left work with a throbbing headache. As she turned her key in her door, she could hear the phone ringing. She decided not to answer it. First, she would take some aspirin and close her eyes with a cool rag on her forehead. But the phone kept right on ringing and the only way to make it stop was to answer it. She was glad she did when she heard her little sister's excited voice on the other end. Camille was a senior in high school now, a pretty little thing. But Rosie worried about her—she was what their mother cruelly called a *featherbrain*. The girl was sweet and innocent and did not have an ambitious bone in her body. She was bright, a "B" student, but she wasn't passionate about anything. She liked children, so she babysat a lot. She liked movies and books. She played the piano well. But she wasn't interested in the important (in Rosie's opinion) issues of the day: equal rights, civil rights, or politics. "That stuff is for you Rosie, not for me."

Rosie was pleased to hear that Camille and her best friend were coming up to Madison to take a tour of the university, but her bubble popped when Camille said, "Rhonda's looking at UW, not me." Stella Maris was pressuring Camille to go to nursing school in Rockford, but like Rosie, Camille wasn't interested in a nursing career. Rosie kept telling her little sister to make her own decisions about her future, and that whatever those decisions were, they should include getting away from Stella Maris ASAP.

While Camille's friend toured the campus, Rosie took Camille to a new Italian restaurant that had opened up on Hamilton Street near the Capitol Square. Rosie asked Paul if she could take a couple hours for lunch so she could spend some quality time with her sister when she visited. He waved his hand and said, "Take all the time you need."

Over pasta, Camille said, "Mom's gotten worse."

"Could that even be possible?" Rosie asked.

"She washes the kitchen floor every night now, on her hands and knees. And did you ever know this? When she cleans the bathroom, she ladles out as much of the toilet water as she can into a bucket so she can scour the bowl better?"

"I knew. It's nuts."

"Now she's been going through my room and purging a lot of my favorite things, like that pillow Grandma crocheted for me."

"That's terrible!" Rosie said. "She has no right!"

"And it's not like she's even donating the stuff to charity. She just throws it in the trash! She's driving me crazy. She's in all my business. I caught her paging through my history notebook just to see if I'd written anything personal in there. And she thinks I'm fat."

"You are not fat."

"Last Sunday, she made her stupid cherry cobbler, set one in front of Dad, and then said to me, "You don't need dessert, Chubby.""

"No!" Rosie said. "Cammy, you have to get out of there as soon as you graduate. Come to school up here!"

"Rosie, my grades aren't good enough for UW."

"Then apply in-state. You have to get away."

"I know," Camille said, tearing up.

It was bound to happen sooner or later. Rosie bumped into—literally bumped into—Alisha. Coming out of The Mifflin Street Community Co-Op where Rosie bought her groceries. Rosie, with her hands full, backed out of the door, bumping shoulders with someone. When she went to apologize, she saw it was Alisha. They hadn't seen each other in months.

Alisha looked gorgeous as usual, with her big loose hair. "Rosie!" she said. "How are—" Rosie walked on. Just the sight of Alisha raised her blood pressure. Really, what was there to say?

When Rosie picked up the phone later that night, she was expecting Camille. Senior prom was coming up and Camille wasn't going. She had started to see some Scottish guy she met at a bar. Rosie was concerned because he was eleven years older. She couldn't help but think of a lion and a lamb. She rehearsed what she would say to Camille without sounding like Stella Maris, but when she answered the phone, it was Alisha on the other end. "Rosie, don't hang up." Rosie sighed heavily. It took all her strength not to bang down the receiver.

"I wondered when we would run into each other," Alisha said. "You probably don't know, but we live just two blocks west of you."

"I should be thankful I haven't seen you more often then."

"That's mean. Listen to me. I miss you so much! There is so much I've wanted to tell you. I'm working for Flad Architects. We're designing a new biochemistry building at the University."

What did she want Rosie to say? That she was happy for her?

"Rosie, aren't you happy for me?"

"Are you still with Tony?"

"Yes."

"Then I cannot be happy for you. Oh, but he's changed, I know."

"Actually Rosie, he's had some relapses and being with Tony has its challenges. See, I'm being honest with you, but I love him and I'm going to stick by him."

"And what do you want from me, my blessing? You want me to invite you over for dinner? I can't be associated with him in any way—for my own physical and mental health. So, as long as you are associated with him, I can't be associated with you. Nothing has changed, Alisha."

"You hate me."

"I could never hate you."

"At least that's something, I guess."

Rosie hung up but was surprised when the phone rang again almost as soon as she put it down. It was Camille. "She's making me go to prom with Owen Ford."

"She can't *make* you, Cammy."

"She already told Owen's mom I would go, and the poor kid already rented the tux, made dinner reservations, and ordered the corsage. So, I'm going. Mackinney is fine with it. He doesn't want me missing out on senior prom. He knows Owen and I are just friends."

Good old Camille. She wouldn't, couldn't, hurt a flea.

"Mom did let me get a pretty dress. It's periwinkle blue."

"Have you decided on NIU or Illinois State?" Rosie asked. Camille had been accepted at both, but now that she was seeing this older Mackinney dude, she was wishy-washy about committing. "Cammy, school is your way out. And I know I'll sound like Mom for saying this, but I am concerned about the age difference with this guy."

"But Rosie! Jackie Kennedy was twelve years younger than JFK. That never bother you..."

"But she was *ten* years older than you when she met him."

Camille changed the subject. "You're coming to my graduation party, right? You promised. Peggy's parents are members of Rockford Country Club so they let Mom rent it for the party. She's acting like it's a damn wedding."

"I'll be there. I wouldn't miss it for the world."

"Good! Because I have some big surprises for you! I gotta go."

6.
rosie & paul & alisha

PAUL'S ELECTION CAUSED a buzz across the country. The press loved his story as the young rebel mayor made for some great copy. Journalists from all over converged on his office to interview him. It wasn't every day that a radical, twice-arrested, anti-war protester was elected to run the same city whose police had tear-gassed, beaten, and arrested him. Paul would sit in his paneled, carpeted office and answer questions, sometimes while he ate his lunch or dinner. Rosie often found it hard to tear herself away from the office to attend classes because she worried she might miss out on meeting someone interesting or famous. Paul's heart still had enough rebel in it that anytime a noteworthy musician came to town, he would name the day for the person, whip up a proclamation, and present a blue ribbon. And if an opportunity came up to present a key to the city, Paul did that too.

In December of 1973, Rosie found herself backstage at the Dane County Coliseum, shaking hands with rockstar Alice Cooper, who was in town for his *School's Out* tour. Although not a fan, she was a bit starstruck. Paul awarded Cooper the key to the city in the form of a giant beer bottle opener. The best part of the whole affair was when the musician asked Paul if he was the mayor's son. Paul got a real kick out of that. He said, "No, I'm the mayor." Alice Cooper in turn got a big kick out of that. He smiled and said, "Alright!"

Working for Paul was a little like working for a rockstar. There was never a dull moment; there was never even a *free* moment. Due to Rosie's falling out with Alisha and her break-up with Benny, Rosie was relatively friendless. Who had time to make friends with work and classes and homework?

But lonely she was. She found herself talking to Camille on the phone more often. In some odd and pathological way, she sort of missed Stella Maris. How sick was that? And how sad that the only people who came to her graduation ceremony were Paul and Diane, because her father, as a high school teacher/coach, was required to be present at his own school's graduation ceremony, which happened to fall on the same day. Camille told Rosie that she begged John-O to take her to Madison, but John-O was a mama's boy and did not want to risk his mother's wrath. He knew where his bread was buttered. Even knowing this, Rosie couldn't help herself and scanned the audience to see if maybe, just maybe, someone in her family found a way to show up.

"Congratulations!" Paul said, hugging Rosie after the ceremony. Diane handed her an envelope and a bouquet of pink and yellow roses. Rosie started crying. "I'm very proud of you," Paul said.

Rosie quickly wiped the tears away and smiled her best smile. She fibbed to Paul and Diane, telling them that her dad and Camille were taking her out for dinner later. Instead Rosie went home, put her flowers in a vase, and ate two bowls of Raisin Bran while watching the old movie "His Girl Friday" with Cary Grant and Rosalind Russell. She opened the card from Paul and Diane and was touched by the gift of money and the handwritten note: "Family is just the name for the people you belong to." They were pretty words; problem was Rosie didn't feel she belonged to anyone. A few months ago, the sentiment would have rung true: Benny was her family, Alisha was her family, Carl was her family. But that was then... Never mind, she thought, waving away the self-pity. Focus on the good! She had a fantastic job and had earned her degree. It was all good. Then why did she start crying when she bumped into the end table and sent the vase of roses shattering to the floor?

Back then, Madison mayoral terms were for just two years. It seemed Paul and the team had just gotten their feet wet when it became time to start planning for reelection. Rosie was glad—she realized that campaigning was far more fun than the everyday ins and outs of city government. And even though in just a year and a half Paul had become a fairly popular mayor, there were always those critics who were against him. Still, the team felt confident about his reelection.

Rosie, Paul, and some of the staff were hanging out at a new bar that had just opened up in the Cardinal Hotel. Paul had befriended the owner, a gay Cuban refugee. The place was the perfect hiding place—none of the politicians and city leaders would be caught dead there as it was a comfortable haven for gay and bisexual Madisonians. Rosie wasn't really surprised when from across the bar she saw Carl sitting at a table with a good-looking guy—she'd always suspected Carl was gay. He saw her and waved. She excused herself and went over to say hello.

"Rosie! You're a sight for sore eyes!" Carl said, greeting her with a hug. "This is Oliver."

Rosie shook Oliver's hand. Then, because she couldn't help herself, she asked about Benny. She had heard he moved from the Capital Times Newspaper to the Wisconsin State Journal, which was great for him, but meant that sooner or later he'd be stopping by the mayor's office to cover Paul's reelection. It was inevitable. She hadn't seen him since they broke up. No, she did see him once riding his bike down Broom Street and—to her dismay—her heart skipped one little beat.

"He's good," Carl said. "Never see him, though. He's so busy. He's not dating anybody if you were wondering.

"I wasn't wondering," Rosie said, though of course she was.

"Rosie," Paul said one day when she returned to the office after an external meeting, "there is someone I want you to meet. This is Kathyrn Clarenbach. Kathryn, this is my assistant Rose Quinlayne."

"Please, call me Kay," the woman said, extending her hand.

Rosie had no idea who she was, only that she looked like a force to be reckoned with. She had to be almost six feet tall, because she towered over Paul, whom Rosie estimated to be about five-ten. She wasn't unattractive, but her facial bone structure gave her a more "handsome" look. She had brown hair and an aura of quiet elegance and intelligence, all straight lines and librarian-like until she smiled. Rosie was immediately drawn to her. In a weird way, the woman reminded her—just in physicality—of her mother. They were probably near the same age, early to mid-fifties.

"Paul tells me that you and I need to have lunch and get to know each other," Kay said.

"I'd like that," Rosie said, not knowing at all if she'd like that. Was she getting fired? Was Paul dumping her onto someone else?

"Kay," Paul said, "Tell Rosie what your husband said when you told him I won the election."

The tall stately woman standing in front of Rosie smiled and said, "That mustachioed hooligan?"

Rosie laughed as Paul said goodbye to Kay.

"Rosie, join me in my office, will you?" Paul said.

Oh no! She was getting fired! She sat down across from Paul and twirled the mood ring on her finger.

"So," Paul said. "Now that you have graduated and you seem to have no social life to speak of because you work way too hard for me, I had an idea. It just came to me when Kay came in for our meeting…"

"You want me to go work for her?"

"Rosie, as long as I'm mayor, you have a job here with me."

"Well, who is she then and why do you want me to have lunch with her?"

"Kay Clarenbach is a political science professor at UW and a former student herself. She put together a program at UW-Extension for women returning to work. But she also happens to be a founding member and first chair of N.O.W. You know about N.O.W., right?"

"Of course. The National Organization for Women. I thought Betty Friedan started it."

"She did as well and was the first president."

"Wow. You'd never take Kay for a feminist. She's got the prim and proper look of a school marm."

"She never considered herself a radical feminist. Prefers to stay behind the scenes. Her big issues are education, health, and family. She's a real champion of women. We met today about efforts to get more women working in city government. Anyway, she said something today that really struck me. We were talking about the old days. While I was consumed with the anti-war efforts, Kay was fighting for women's rights. And she asked me: 'Was it all worth it?' Of course, I got all high and mighty and said that we the passionate youth who marched and occupied buildings and argued and protested about the war and got our heads cracked with billy sticks did so with a powerful conviction that we were on the right side of history. And then she said, 'Funny how such noble idealistic impulses turned so quickly to violence.' Rosie, it was like my mother was lecturing me! The woman is fierce in a most disarming way. If she told me to jump in a lake, I just might."

Rosie nodded, but said, "Paul, I'm just not following…"

"The long and short of it is this: we did win the war, the *culture* war. Kay said the product of the sixties was actually feminism, and now that I think about it, I have to agree with her. Rosie, if you are anything, you are a feminist at heart."

"Not me!" Rosie said. She had been with militant feminists at demonstrations. They were laughed at. Even *women* patronized them, calling them "frigid" and "emotionally-disturbed man-haters."

"Yes, you are."

"I've never burned a bra, thank you very much."

"What if I told you that you earn less money than the last executive assistant?"

"Do I?"

"You do and don't get mad at me. I don't have anything to do with employment compensation. But when I asked about it, I was told that it was because you were a woman and the last assistant was a man."

"Well, that's not fair!"

Paul didn't say anything. He just held his hands out to imply *there you go.*

And there she went. The following Wednesday Rosie met Kay Clarenbach for lunch on campus at the Rathskeller in Memorial Union. The woman was impressive. Why hadn't Rosie heard of her before? In addition to co-founding N.O.W., she had served as the Chair of the Governor's Commission on the Status of Women from 1964 to 1969 and started serving again in 1971. She was the first president of the National Association of Commissions for Women, and the founding organizer of the National Women's Political Caucus. Here it was almost 1975, Rosie lived in Madison, and had never heard of Kay. She knew of other big names in the women's movement: Betty Friedan, Gloria Steinem, Margaret Mead, Dorothy Day, and Shirley Chisholm.

"I shy away from the limelight," was Kay's explanation.

As Rosie broke bread with this unsung heroine she knew she'd found a mentor. But she couldn't figure out what Kay wanted from her.

Kay shared her background. Rosie was surprised to learn that she was married to the same man, Henry, for twenty-eight years, and had three children.

"My oldest Sara is probably near your age. She's twenty-five."

"I'm twenty-three," Rosie said.

Kay was born and grew up in Sparta, Wisconsin, got her undergraduate and graduate degrees from UW Madison and then went on to get her PhD. (Kay was too modest to speak of such things, but later Paul told her that Kay was so brilliant she started school at age two and a half, completed first and second grades at the same time, and was valedictorian of her high school class at the age of sixteen.)

"It's in my blood," she said when Rosie asked how she managed it all. "My mother was active in the community and as a matter of fact, she was the first woman on the Sparta school board."

Kay looked around the room. "I guess you could say the fire was ignited right here in the Rath. When I came here in 1937, women were not allowed to even sit in the Rathskeller."

"Are you kidding?"

"I'm not kidding. And it irked me. Only men were allowed. I would buy my morning coffee—three cents back then!—and walk as slowly as these long legs would take me through the Rath to the claustrophobic Paul Bunyan Room, that they set up in 1934 when female students complained. That was my first quiet act of protest."

"Paul says I'm paid less than the last assistant because I'm a woman."

Kay smiled and put down her sandwich. "Yes, women have been addressing the gender pay gap since the late nineteenth century. We've made progress but I hate to tell you, Rosie, it's likely you earn 58.8 cents to the last assistant's dollar."

Rosie gestured with her hands. "That really stinks!"

"Yes, it does."

"But wasn't there an amendment?"

"The Equal Pay Act of 1963, part of President Kennedy's New Frontier Program."

"So ..."

"So ... we keep working at it."

Kay told Rosie the Wisconsin commission uncovered almost 300 provisions in state statutes that treated women differently than men. "That discovery not only changed my life, it has *become* my life."

Rosie was shocked to learn that even in 1975 there were some states that required a husband's signature before a wife could get a driver's license. Women's advocates had to lobby the telephone company to list both husband and wife's names in the phonebook without charging extra for the wife's name. They had to convince the Equal Employment Opportunity Commission to stop segregating the "help wanted" ads in the newspaper by "male" and "female" jobs. They fought discrimination for airline stewardesses who were forced to retire at age thirty-two or when they got married because the carriers thought they weren't "sexy" enough.

"Just this year," Kay told Rosie, "the U.S. Supreme Court threw out distinctions in the age at which girls and boys are entitled to child support. The case was Stanton v Stanton. A divorced father in Utah stopped paying child support for his daughter when she turned eighteen but would continue to pay for his son's support until twenty-one. You see, Utah defined adulthood differently—for females, it was eighteen, and for males, twenty-one. The Utah Supreme Court said there was a 'reasonable basis' for the differential: that women matured earlier and married younger; and men had a greater need for education. In 1975 for goodness' sake!"

"That's crazy, but it actually hits home. My parents were happy to send my brother to college, but it was nursing school or nothing for my sister and me," Rosie told her. "I put myself through college."

"Paul told me how hard you've worked and what a bright—he might have said brilliant—and extraordinary young woman you are."

Rosie could feel her cheeks blush.

"We could use your help, Rosie. I'm not offering you a job—we have no money!—but I am inviting you to join us in our efforts. Come to our meetings. Help spread the word. Paul's agreed to put together a team and he wants you to head it up. You are perfect since you work for the city and you're young and vivacious. Convince Paul to allocate a budget so you can travel to our meetings. I promise, you will meet some of the most extraordinary people and will get so much fulfillment knowing you are helping women to see their value and potential."

Rosie sat up straight and jumped in the proverbial lake, headfirst.

Now she was really swimming. There was the reelection in April, which Paul (described this time as the "*twenty-nine*-year-old-radical,") handily won over his opponent, former mayor Henry Reynolds, aged sixty-nine. It had proved easier to campaign for the second term because Paul had established a good record. People, even the critics who didn't agree with all his policies, had to acknowledge his successes: he regained control over the police force, appointing a chief who was viewed as more humane, and opening up the department to female, gay, and minority applicants; he provided public daycare; funded the tenants' union; opened up the city budget to greater public scrutiny; municipalized the bus system; and completed the first components of a popular city bicycle route system.

After the election, where Paul won 61% of the vote, Rosie sat in his office and they simply basked in the moment. Paul, with his stockinged feet propped up on the desk, said, "A part of me wonders why I am so happy when I know damn well how hard this job is. Oh! I almost forgot. Look what I got!" He handed Rosie a manilla envelope. She opened it and found an autographed color photograph of President Ford. She laughed. "Shall I put him in with the Nixon?" Paul had found the perfect place for the autographed photo of Nixon he'd received upon his first election: the wall above the toilet in the mayor's bathroom.

"Yes, please. They can keep each other company. Hey, Rosie, do you have a passport?"

"No, should I?"

"Yes, you should. I've got a couple of things planned. First, how would you like to join Kay Clarenbach next month for the World Conference of the International Women's Year in Mexico City?"

"In Mexico?" She cringed as she heard the words popping out of her mouth. Where else would Mexico City be?

Paul smiled. "Yes, but you don't need a passport for Mexico. But you do for Cuba."

"Cuba?"

"Strangest thing. Castro has invited a delegation from Madison for a visit in July."

"Wow! Why?"

"It's being called a 'goodwill' visit. They want us to take a tour of the agricultural center and some dairy farms. The state department approved the trip in hopes of speeding along a U.S.-Cuban anti-hijacking treaty."

"Paul, this is so cool! I have never been anywhere! I've never even been on a plane! It's so exciting! Wait, did you say *hi-jacking*?"

"Don't worry!" He chuckled. "They don't hi-jack a plane that's already going to Cuba. Why don't you go to the post office over lunch and apply for your passport? We'll cover all your expenses."

Rosie called Kay Clarenbach and told her how excited she was to join her for the conference. But when Kay gave her the dates for the trip, Rosie's heart plummeted. She would miss Camille's graduation party. She couldn't miss Camille's graduation party, could she?

"I understand, Rosie," Camille said on the phone that night.

Rosie could hear the disappointment in her voice. "How about this," she said, trying to sound chipper, "I'll come and pick you up in a couple of weeks and you spend a few days here with me. We'll go to Ella's Deli and wherever else you want to go. Now that your eighteen, Mom can't stop you."

"That sounds nice, Rosie, but I might not be around."

"Why? Are you guys going on vacation?"

"Well… Rosie I gotta go. Barnaby just peed on the rug and Mom is going to kill me because I was supposed to take him out."

Rosie bought three new outfits for her trip, and a new pair of shoes that she wore around the house to break in. She splurged and bought a crayon yellow American Tourister suitcase, wishing she could show it off to Stella Maris. She wanted badly to buy a Polaroid Instamatic Camera, but decided to wait a bit to see how her finances looked. She even broke out her Spanish dictionary to brush up.

Two nights before her Mexico trip—bags packed, plane ticket in the zippered pocket of her purse—loud banging on her front door brought her out of the bathroom where she'd been brushing her teeth before bed. She looked at the clock. Almost ten-thirty. The banging increased as she approached the door and she heard a female voice calling her name. "Who's there?" Rosie said.

"It's me. Alisha."

Rosie opened the door and Alisha nearly fell inside. She stumbled, regained her balance, and slammed the door shut. "How does this lock? How does this lock?" she cried, fumbling with the handle.

Rosie reached around to secure both the lock and the dead bolt.

Alisha leaned her face on the door and sobbed. Bewildered, Rosie asked what the hell was going on.

Alisha turned around to reveal a black, swollen eye, a bloody nose, and a laceration on her cheek. Rosie gasped. "Tony?"

Alisha nodded and fell into Rosie's arms. "I didn't know where else to go!"

"That's okay," Rosie said, patting Alisha on the back. "I'm glad you came to me."

Alisha pulled back and said, "You are? Really?"

As Alisha pulled away, Rosie noticed black and blue finger marks on her neck. "Cripes, Leesh, did he choke you?"

Alisha nodded and crumbled to the floor.

She wouldn't go to the hospital. She wouldn't go to the police. She tried to convince Rosie to go to a hotel with her because although she didn't think Tony knew where Rosie lived, she was afraid he could find out. Rosie said, "I doubt if he ever even knew my last name," but she felt a shiver of fear run down her spine as she thought about Tony coming at her in Benny's bathroom.

Rosie got out her first aid kit and cleaned up Alisha's face as best she could. There was another injury—her wrist. "It could be broken!" Rosie told her, trying to persuade her to go to the hospital.

"No, I can't!"

"If you don't get in the car right now," Rosie told her, "you can just leave and handle this on your own."

"You'd do that to me?"

"Yes. You are seriously injured. You need stitches on your cheek. And your nose and wrist are probably broken."

"How about a whiskey?"

"How about I'm getting my keys."

On the ride to the hospital, Alisha opened up. "Things were good. Well, things were never good, if I'm being honest. But things were normal for us. We fight a lot. He's jealous all the time. Anyway, he got fired from his job and wasn't in a hurry to get another one. He bummed around the house in sweats all day and greeted me at the door when I came home from work with: *What's for dinner, woman.*"

Rosie scowled. "He called you *woman*?"

"Rosie, that was just teasing. That wasn't the problem."

"What was the problem?"

"He started dealing. All of a sudden people were in and out of the apartment at all hours. I was scared the cops were going to raid us. I couldn't live like that. I lost like twelve pounds. Plus, he was always wasted out of his mind. *Quaaludes.* 'Party drugs,' he calls them. Oh my god, Rosie those things are awful. They can relax you and help you to sleep, but it's so weird, they also make it so you can't resist sex. And what it does to him! He's a maniac in bed. An animal. He drew blood once he scratched me so hard.

"Anyway, tonight, this guy comes over and I think he's a buyer and I let him in. But he's not a buyer; he's a seller, and he has a gun. Turns out Tony owes him a ton of money. I calm the guy down and give him a hundred dollars of my money and tell him we'll go to the bank tomorrow, to come back."

"This is like a movie," Rosie said, turning into the emergency entrance at Methodist Hospital.

"So, the guy leaves and I'm screaming at Tony that he is going to get us killed. He just laughs at me and says he has everything under control. 'My cousin's a cop in Madison PD, remember?' I told him I was done. I was leaving. I was going to stay at a hotel and then move out as soon as I could. And that's when he went after me. I thought he was going to strangle me to death. Good thing he tripped."

Rosie pulled into a parking place and put the car in park. "I am so sorry, Leesh."

They got out of the car and began walking to the hospital entrance, when Alisha stopped in her tracks, and said, "Oh, God! It's him!" She pulled Rosie by the arm and they ran back to the car. Rosie started it up while Alisha ducked down in the passenger's seat. Alisha was screaming and Rosie had to tell her to shut up three times before she went quiet. Rosie slowly backed out of the parking space and scanned the area. Sure enough, Tony Apello, creep and beater-of-women, sat in Alisha's VW Beetle, his eyes steeled on the entrance. Rosie held her breath as she drove past him. She exited the hospital parking lot and turned onto West Washington. She was headed back home when Alisha popped up and said, "Rosie, please get me out of town. He's going to find me and kill me."

"You really think he would?"

"Yes. I threatened to turn him in to the police."

Rosie took a left instead of a right. What should she do? What else could she do? She drove north and then got on Highway 94 and drove and drove, not knowing where to go. Finally, after a little over an hour, they found a Motel 6. Alisha waited in the car while Rosie paid the thirty-dollar room fee to the front desk clerk who checked her in. "Business or pleasure?" the lady asked in a chipper voice.

"Neither," Rosie said, with no other explanation. What could she say? Escaping a madman? On the run from a killer?

It was nearly two in the morning when the girls climbed into bed. The room darkening drapery smothered out any light. The bedspread was thin but the mattress itself was comfortable enough. Rosie could hear Alisha's soft breathing. She had always been able to fall asleep quickly. Rosie lay awake for hours, her mind ping-ponging from thought to worry to panic.

She'd set the clock radio for six-thirty because she wanted to call Paul as soon as he got into the office to tell him she wouldn't be coming in. Crap, they had a big meeting about a conference on alternative state and local public policies that Paul was hosting in Madison. With Alisha still asleep, she carried the phone into the bathroom, pulling the cord as far as it would go, and dialed up the mayor's office. "Paul, it's Rosie. Something terrible has happened…"

Vintage Paul—calm, wise, practical. He had always liked Alisha and felt bad when Rosie had told him of their falling out. "First," he said, "you've got to get her to a doctor."

"I tried that. Tony was there in the parking lot at Methodist, waiting for her. It scared her to death."

"Then she's got to go to the police. The guy is dangerous. Tell her I can help. What about her parents? Can she go home?"

"I can't go home!" Alisha said when she woke up and Rosie urged her. "I won't let anyone see me like this. My dad will make me go to the police. I won't go through that. You know what always happens to abused women—everyone turns on them."

Rosie couldn't argue with that.

After Alisha phoned her boss and told her she'd fallen down the steps and wouldn't be in for a few days, she agreed to go to the hospital, so they drove back to Madison and again pulled into the emergency entrance at Methodist. "This time," Rosie said, "I'm dropping you off and then I'll go park."

Because Rosie wasn't immediate family, the ER attendant asked her to take a seat in the waiting room. Poor Alisha! Poor, stupid Alisha. Rosie wondered…could I forgive her? And then she realized that she already had. Rosie was so exhausted she fell asleep in the chair.

Alisha nudged her awake. "Let's go, Rosie."

She had a broken nose and a sprained wrist, both which would heal on their own with ice and rest. The laceration on her cheek should have had stitches, but she'd waited too long. "If a wound isn't stitched up within twenty-four hours, the stitches won't take, and the wound risks infection. At least that's what the high and mighty nurse said," Alisha told Rosie as they walked to the car. "I guess I'll have a scar, but I really don't care how I look. I'm done with men."

"Aww, don't say that," Rosie said, as she got into the car. "There are some good ones out there."

"Like who? And don't say our dads or our brothers."

"Well, like Paul and—."

"Rosie! You're still in love with him!"

"I am not. But he is one of the good ones." Rosie thought of her conversation with Paul that morning. *"Take care of your friend, Rosie. She needs you."*

Alisha asked if they could swing by a drug store. "They gave me a prescription for the pain. Oh, Rosie, this is so perfect. Guess what they prescribed?"

"What?"

Alisha read from the prescription: "Methaqualone. The generic name for Quaalude."

"You have got to be kidding me."

"Ironic, huh?"

"Well, if they help with the pain…"

"Oh, they will help with the pain. Believe me."

"Listen Leesh. Tomorrow morning, I leave for Mexico for a week for work."

"Mexico! With Paul?"

"No, with this cool feminist lady named Kay Clarenbach. It's for a women's conference. So, the way I see it, we have two options: I take you home to Rockford or you stay at my apartment."

"I'm not going home."

"Then you stay at my place. My neighbor downstairs is a bouncer. So, what do you think? You'll be okay?"

Alisha turned her head to look out the window. "Sure, Rosie. Thank you."

When they got home, Alisha took a bath. Rosie told her to help herself to clean clothes. Alisha came out of the bedroom wearing the tie-dyed T-shirt Rosie had bought at Woodstock. "I remember this," Alisha said, smiling. Rosie made lunch and they ate their peanut butter and jelly sandwiches on the back porch and talked as if nothing had happened. They reminisced about high school and Woodstock and their early days at UW, the protests and demonstrations. "I've never felt as alive as I did then," Alisha said. "We had a purpose. To end that fucking war. I wonder if we had any effect at all, or if it simply ran its course."

Rosie said, "I guess history will tell. But I agree with you. We knew it was wrong in every cell in our bodies. Paul says LBJ bailed on a second term because he knew the war couldn't be won and he would rather be remembered for advancing civil rights and not a stupid war."

"Oh, Paul says that, does he," Alisha teased.

Alisha took a nap on the sofa while Rosie called the office to see how the meeting on the conference went. Later in the afternoon, she ran out to the Co-Op to get a few groceries since she'd purposely run through her perishables knowing she would be gone for a week.

Together they made dinner. "Hamburger Helper Cheeseburger Macaroni! My favorite!" Alisha said. "You remembered." A cook Rosie wasn't. They ate at the kitchen table and threw back a couple of beers. Kay Clarenbach called to confirm she would pick up Rosie at six-fifteen in the morning.

They played a few games of Backgammon and watched *Happy Days*. At ten o'clock, they went to bed in Rosie's room. (Alisha's old bedroom had become a junk room, a catch-all place for cross country skis, tennis rackets, laundry baskets, and such.) As they wound down, the girls giggled about sleepovers they'd had since kindergarten. "I love you, Rosie. Thanks for not hating me," Alisha said.

"Leeshy, honey, I could never hate you," Rosie replied.

Rosie couldn't sleep—her head danced with thoughts and worry. She realized she had forgotten to call Camille back and tried to remember if she put the Travelers Cheques in her wallet or the zippered part of her purse. She wondered what would happen to Alisha. What if that monster did come here? Should she even go to Mexico? How could she not? The trip was paid for.

She finally slept and woke up the next morning vibrating with both anticipation and guilt. She got up to use the bathroom, and when she returned, she saw that Alisha was not in the bed but sprawled out on the floor. Rosie gasped, and as she approached, she saw the pill bottle beside her. Rosie fell to the floor and starting screaming and shaking her friend. But she couldn't rouse her. Flynn, the bouncer from downstairs, must have heard her and banged on the back door. Rosie ran to let him in and led him to the bedroom. He told Rosie to call an ambulance and he started CPR.

When the EMS workers arrived, they pushed Rosie and Flynn out of the way and attended to Alisha. Rosie cried on Flynn's shoulder, certain her friend was dead. Flynn drove Rosie to the hospital and dropped her off at the ER entrance. Rosie told the lady at the front desk that she was the sister of the girl the ambulance had just brought in. A guy in scrubs brought Rosie back into a room and grilled her for information. Rosie decided the truth was best (except for the sister part) and shared as much information as she could. The EMS workers had the medicine bottle, so they knew what Alisha had taken. Rosie sat in the waiting room, not knowing if Alisha was dead or alive. Torture. She used the payphone to call both Kay and Paul to tell them what was going on. They both understood that Rosie needed to stay with her friend.

Finally, a doctor emerged from the swinging doors and approached Rosie. "She's a lucky young woman," he said.

Rosie was so relieved to hear those words she sank down in her chair and cried. The doctor sat down next to her. "We've pumped her stomach and administered medications. She's conscious but weak. We're going to admit her. Do you think she's addicted to Quaaludes?"

Rosie said she honestly didn't know. "But I think this was a one-time thing. Can I see her?"

"Not just yet."

Rosie called Paul to let him know that Alisha was all right. She sat in the waiting area and reflected on the last couple of days. What the heck had just happened? Reunited with her best friend only to almost lose her! She wished she was on the plane to Mexico City. She could picture herself shaking hands with important women, ordering room service in Spanish, and swimming in the hotel pool while a handsome Mexican flirted with her. Life is weird. She wondered if she had blown it now with Kay Clarenbach. The woman had a husband, three kids, and a full-time job and she was able to manage the trip. And what about Paul? Had she dropped a notch in his estimation? Probably not, but somehow, she'd dropped a notch in her own estimation.

A few weeks later, Rosie found herself seated between Paul and Diane on a plane to Cuba. When they landed in Havana, Rosie felt like Dorothy in the Wizard of Oz: she wasn't in Kansas anymore. Cuba was such a colorful place, the houses painted in pastel shades of blue, yellow, and pink. The people were friendly; all the children seemed to smile and wave. There was also extreme poverty, the likes of which Rosie had never encountered. Crumbling architecture, closed-up buildings. But the thing that made the biggest impression? The cars. Classic American cars from the forties and fifties filled the streets. Paul explained that back in the early 1900s Cuba was the top Latin American importer of U.S. cars. "Cubans love cars and cigars," Paul said. He had done his homework, hoping in all unlikeliness, that he would get a chance to meet the notorious Fidel Castro himself. Their escorts told them if they were to meet Castro, it would happen on the last night of the trip. Rosie heard her mother's voice in her head: *"Why would anyone in their right mind want to meet that awful communist dictator?"*

The trip was a whirlwind of meetings and tours. Being shuffled from here to there by Cuban officials. There was a sense of tight security and

Rosie found herself in a state of high alert throughout the trip. That's not to say she didn't enjoy herself, she did. Paul's entourage, in addition to his wife and Rosie, included a WISC-TV reporter/photographer named Ron Backman and he was loads of fun. Being around Ron, a chain-smoker and snappy dresser, was like being with a stand-up comic—he had quick comebacks, corny puns, and was never at a loss for words.

Rosie brought along a notebook for travel journaling and was documenting as much as she could about the trip so she could share the experience with her dad, Camille, and Alisha. She felt guilty about leaving Alisha. The poor girl was not herself. The ER doctor had referred her to a psychiatrist, but Alisha wouldn't go. "I'm fine, Rosie. It was just one moment of stupidity."

Alisha stayed and they turned the junk room back into her room. She never did go back to work though. She told Rosie she had it under control, that she had a plan. Rosie didn't want to press her. She knew Alisha needed time to heal physically and emotionally. Alisha showed her appreciation by cleaning the apartment and cooking a nice dinner every night. Rosie felt like she had a damn wife. *"Honey, I'm home!"* All teasing aside, having Alisha around felt good; it felt normal, like they were still in school. They had been so happy back then. Rosie hadn't realized how achingly lonely she was until Alisha came back into her life. She hoped she was doing okay. She'd left her with a full refrigerator and Flynn's phone number. "I'll be back in five days," she'd told her.

On the last night of the trip, they were in the middle a wonderful dinner at a restaurant, with Ron keeping them all in stitches about his escapades as a TV anchor, when their Cuban escorts interrupted and hurried them back to the hotel. It was only seven-thirty, but they were told they needed rest for their long trip back home. Rosie found this odd. Once they were back at the hotel, two Cuban officials came to their room and told them that Castro was on his way to meet them. Paul was beside himself and suggested someone go get some ice so they could offer a drink like good hosts. But they were told the elevators were out of order and guessed that might have been part of the security detail.

Paul brought a giant map of Wisconsin to show Castro and he had just laid it out on the bed when the door opened and Castro walked in, bigger than life, signature cigar hanging from his mouth. He walked right past Paul and greeted the two Cuban officials, asking in Spanish, "Where is the mayor?" One of the officials explained that he had walked right past him. Castro looked at Paul and laughed. "I thought he was one of your assistants," he said, smiling. "He looks like a Cuban!"

He shook Paul's hand and they sat in two club chairs and talked for at least two hours, with the help of a translator, while Ron filmed them. Rosie sat with Diane off in the corner while the men spoke. Castro was charismatic, as people said, but Rosie had to pause and remind herself he was also a brutal dictator. She noticed that he had delicate hands for such a big man and a quiet speaking voice, which surprised her after seeing him on TV belting out speeches at the top of his lungs. He and Paul talked about farming, cross-breeding cattle, nuclear energy, baseball. It was clear Castro knew American politics inside and out. Paul told him about how he found his way into politics through his anti-war activism. They found some commonality there and in the fact that they were both lawyers. Castro gave his views on America's free press, something he did not believe in for Cuba. (Little did Paul know that this diplomatic trip and his fraternizing with Castro—giving him a key to the city and a baseball signed by Hank Aaron—would later lead to his critics calling him "The Red Mayor.")

Rosie stayed up late that night to write in her journal while the experience with Castro was fresh in her mind. She was so hyped up she had trouble falling asleep and then when she finally drifted off, she woke with a start from a terrible nightmare where she arrived home only to find Alisha on the floor at the side of the bed, unconscious again, with a bottle in her hand. She couldn't get back to sleep after that, so she packed up her suitcase and waited for the Cuban officials to escort the group to the airport. She couldn't wait to get home.

At O'Hare, Rosie called Alisha, but there was no answer. She tried not to worry, but her antennas were up. By the time Paul and Diane dropped her off at home, Rosie was sick with worry. Paul brought her suitcase up for her, and she almost asked him to stay until she knew for certain Alisha was all right. They said goodbye and she turned her key in the lock. "Honey, I'm home," she called out. Nothing. "Leesh?" Nothing. Rosie's heart went into overdrive. "Alisha?" Rosie went into the kitchen, looked in the bathroom, and held her breath as she checked both bedrooms, but Alisha was not home. The place was spotless and a vase of white roses sat on the kitchen counter. Rosie walked downstairs and knocked on Flynn's door. He said he hadn't seen Alisha in a few days. Rosie climbed back up the stairs and then plopped down on the couch. There on the coffee table was a note. Scribbled on a sheet of notebook paper: "Now, you really are going to hate me. But I love him."

7.
stella maris

IF BLAME MUST be laid, then place it at the oversized feet of Stella Maris Quinlayne. She will not accept it, mind you, but it belongs to her just the same. If you reverse engineer things, you will discover the reason Camille ran off in the first place was to get as far away from her controlling, neurotic mother as possible, just as her sister before her had. Same reason; different route.

Just a couple of months after her eighteenth birthday, two weeks after her high school graduation, and the day before her graduation party at Rockford Country Club, Camille Quinlayne hopped on the back of her boyfriend's Harley with no more than an overnight bag, and beat it out of town. Stella Maris was not at home at the time of her daughter's escape/betrayal; she was busy hanging green and white crepe paper (Camille's school colors) around the dining room at the country club, setting place cards on the tables, and rejoicing that her daughter-in-law's parents, longtime club members, had arranged the rental. For a few glorious hours, Stella Maris pretended she herself was a member, part of the country club set. (Upper crust she wasn't. Stella Maris came from Wisconsin farm people with thick hands, strong lungs, ruddy complexions, and big feet. All the Quinlaynes had big feet, men and women alike, even petite Camille.)

Stella Maris had just finished hanging the "Class of 1975" banner when she looked at her watch and clucked. Late as usual. She shook her head. "Tcch! My daughter the graduate was supposed to be here to help decorate," she told the assistant club manager. "I swear that girl will be late for her own wedding."

Of course, the mother could not possibly know that the daughter would not be late for her own wedding. She was very much on time. At the precise moment of Stella Maris' clucking, Camille and her boyfriend—more of a *man*-friend at eleven years her senior—were tying the knot at the Winnebago County Courthouse. After the groom slipped a pawnshop ring onto Camille's finger, they kissed, signed some papers, hopped back on the bike, and drove to Beloit, Wisconsin, a half hour north of Rockford, Illinois, where the groom worked at a bar called *Lenny's*. (He'd told Camille he *owned* the bar which was a bold-faced lie.) They would live with "Uncle" Bob in the apartment above the bar until they could get on their feet.

Stella Maris found her husband in his recliner when she got home from the country club. "Where's your daughter?" she asked.

"Not home yet," Barry said, not looking up from the TV.

"She was supposed to meet me at the club."

"What club?"

"Barry! What *club*? The country club? Where I have been all day, preparing for the party tomorrow. Where else would I be?"

"Oh, *that* club. How about dinner?"

For the last four years, Barry's bald head had been getting on Stella Maris's nerves. She especially did not care for the sheen. "Barry! I just walked in the door. There's beef Stroganoff in the crockpot. Can I at least catch my breath? Sheesh!"

In the kitchen, she lifted the lid on the new avocado green crock pot, her daughter-in-law Peggy had gifted her. The Stroganoff looked good. Then she saw it: a coffee cup in the sink. *Her* coffee cup, no less, the porcelain one with dainty pink roses on it. Stella Maris could not tolerate a dirty dish in her clean sink. Everyone in the family knew that.

"Bare, did you have coffee?" she called into the family room.

"No, I did not."

"There is a dirty cup here in the sink and it wasn't there this morning when I left for the club." (Notice how Stella Maris is now on familiar terms with Rockford Country Club?)

"I didn't have any coffee, but I would like to have dinner…sometime in this century."

"As soon as Camille gets home."

But Camille did not get home. At six-fifteen Barry demanded nourishment, saying even prisoners got three squares a day. Stella Maris served him up and then stood at the kitchen wall phone and called each of Camille's three best friends. There was no answer at Rhonda's or Marilyn's, and Mrs. Nelson said Martha was babysitting. Stella Maris murmured the St. Anthony prayer for finding lost people, because Camille never went anywhere without telling her mother where she was, whom she was with, and what she was up to. The wheels in Stella Maris's head started to turn, but never in her wildest dreams could she have imagined what had really transpired. Camille was not Rosie.

"She just graduated, for crumb sake," Barry said, picking out the mushrooms in his beef Stroganoff. "She's off gallivanting."

Stella Maris sat down at the table across from him.

"Let her be, Stell. She's a good girl."

"I don't appreciate your tone. I'm just worried about my daughter." She sat up straighter in her chair.

"It's not like she wanted a fancy party anyway."

That much was true. Camille had said, "I don't need a big fuss."

When the front door slammed, Stella Maris expected Camille to come sauntering into the kitchen with some lame excuse about forgetting her promise to help decorate. But it was John-O, their eldest, and only son, and he was starving. John-O had a new wife and home of his own, but one or two nights a week he somehow found his way to Stella Maris's dinner table. Usually, this made Stella Maris happy (and Peggy not so happy), but tonight, Camille's absence agitated her to no end. She set a plate in front of her son and sat down to watch him eat.

When the phone rang, John-O jumped up to get it and then handed it to his dad. "Camille," he said.

Barry wiped his mouth on his napkin and said, "Hello, honey. I must tell you…your mother's a bit peeved at you…"

"Where is she?" Stella Maris demanded, wondering why on earth the girl would ask to speak to Barry instead of her.

Barry waved his hand at his wife. "What was that, honey? What did you do? Oh, no! Cammy, you didn't. Please tell me you didn't!"

Stella Maris stood up. "What did she do? John-O, do you know?"

John-O shook his head and continued to shovel Stroganoff into his mouth.

"Barry!" Stella Maris barked and snatched the phone out of her husband's hand. But when she put the phone to her ear all she heard was the dial tone. "Barry?!"

Barry's bald head went from rosy to red. His eyes welled up. "She's run off, Stell. Run off and got herself married."

"She did no such thing!"

"Who the hell did she marry? That Scottish dude?" John-O asked. "I'll kill him!"

"You'll do no such thing," Barry said.

Stella Maris slammed the phone back on the hook and then stood over her husband with her hands on her hips. "Tell me exactly what she said. Word for word."

"She said she got married at the courthouse and they're going to live with his Uncle Bob in Beloit."

"That's it? That's all she said?" Stella Maris grabbed hold of the chair to steady herself.

"And that she'd talk to you once the dust settled."

Stella Maris put the back of her hand to her forehead. "Remember what I told you, Bare? I didn't like that boy from the start. I said that boy has bedroom eyes." She began to pace around the kitchen. "What about the party, Barry? She's coming to the party, right? I have sixty people coming! I've got the cheese balls and the Watergate salad, the pineapple chicken, and the three different kinds of quiches. I baked three carrot cakes and skewered fruit chunks until my fingers pruned, and I hung green and white crepe paper for goodness' sake. Peggy's bringing the helium balloons. And what about

Rosie? Rosie's coming in from D.C. She wouldn't stand up Rosie. She's still coming to the party, right?"

"She didn't say anything about the party. For crumb sake our little girl has been abducted! Who cares about the party?" Barry said.

Stella Maris sunk into her chair. "*I* care. All my planning. All my hard work! The time and the money. Stop chewing!" she snapped at John-O. John-O set down his fork and swallowed.

"I don't know how to react to this," Stella Maris said, holding her head in her hands. "Nothing has prepared me for this moment."

Barry started to cry. "My little girl. She couldn't have gone on her own volition. He brainwashed her. She just turned eighteen. It's almost illegal." He blew his nose with his napkin.

"I'll kill him," John-O said again.

"I'll kill her!" Stella Maris said. "How could she do this to me? She knew this party was important to me. And I bought that lovely lavender dress with the shoes to match! I can't cancel the party, Bare. How am I going to call all those people? I'm mortified! What will my friends think?"

Barry stood up, his chair screeching on the kitchen floor. "Is that all you care about? Your dad-gum party at your dad-gum country club?"

"How dare you! Certainly, that's not all I care about."

"My little girl. My sweet baby. That loser is eleven years older than she is. We've met him three times. We know nothing about him!"

"You spoiled her. This is your doing," Stella Maris said."

"Oh, no. This is on you. You drove her out, just like Rosie."

"What did I ever do to make my daughters hate me?"

John-O said, "Maybe she's PG."

"Bite your tongue!" Stella Maris said.

"I'll kill him!" Barry said.

No one said, "You'll do no such thing." For a full minute no one said a word. John-O took the lull in the brouhaha as permission to resume eating. "Here's an idea," he said. "Why don't you just play dumb? Pretend you don't know about Camille and what's-his-name."

"His name is Mackinney. Mackinney Lennox. I guess our daughter is now Camille Lennox," Stella Maris said.

John-O continued. "Anyway, just play dumb. Have the party and tell everyone she's on her way. When she doesn't show up say she died in a car acci—"

"John-O, shut your trap," Barry said. "That's not helpful."

Stella Maris massaged her chin. "Actually, John-O, darling, it's brilliant!"

"Stella Maris, you wouldn't."

"Oh, I most certainly would. Except for the dying part. John-O, how could you even say such a thing! But anyway, the party is on! I'm going to steam my dress."

The next day, Stella Maris stood in front of the full-length mirror in her bedroom and twirled like a debutant in her lavender dress and matching shoes. The dress, with its accordion pleat skirt and attached sheer cape, was too formal for the occasion, but she fell in love with it the moment she saw it on the mannequin in the department store and knew it would make her feel like a queen. And the shoes! Her first ever pair of platform shoes, the heels so high it made her size ten feet pass for size eight.

"You're sure you want to go through with this?" Barry asked her as he tied his tie.

"The party goes on," Stella Maris said, with one last twirl.

In the car on the ride over to the country club, Stella Maris went over their story. "Remember, Bare, we know nothing. We will act just as surprised as everyone else."

"I can't believe I let you rope me into this. It won't end well."

Stella Maris touched up her lipstick. "You think calling the party off, losing all that money, much less our reputations…you think that would be a better ending?"

"But what about the gifts? How can we accept gifts?"

"They are *graduation* gifts after all. Our daughter did in fact graduate, did she not?"

"What if I just drop you off and fake a stroke or something?"

"You will do no such thing. When the timing is right, John-O will lean in and give us the bad news."

"What bad news?"

"That Camille and her boyfriend were on their way over to the party and they got in a little bitty accident. Nothing too serious, but they thought they'd better go to the ER just to be sure. Don't wait for them."

"This is not going to end well."

"You know what this is, Barry? This is making lemonade out of lemons."

"I never much liked lemonade."

Stella Maris had expected guests to be more formally dressed for the party. It surprised her how casual some of them looked. Pantsuits, leisure suits, and track suits were all the rage, but some guests promenaded in wearing those awful bell bottom hip-hugging jeans, T-shirts, and ratty sandals. When she spotted one of her nephews wearing a *Cheech and Chong* T-shirt, she wished she had included a dress code on the invitation. This was a country club after all, not a commune. Even her own daughter-in-law arrived looking like a hippie-dippie in her one-piece denim pantsuit and those dreadful Dr. Scholl's wooden clogs.

"What time is Rosie supposed to get here?" Barry asked Stella Maris, interrupting her as she spoke to a group of ladies.

"How am I supposed to know?" Stella Maris barked and returned to telling her friends where she found her lovely lavender dress and shoes. Stella Maris had been dreading seeing Rosie. She'd never forgiven the girl for running off with the hippies. At least Rosie would see her in her glory—at the country club, all decked out, surrounded by friends. Life went on without Rosie and would go on without Camille.

"I just can't imagine where those girls are," Stella Maris told her mother-in-law when she approached.

Barry gave his wife a look.

At one o'clock, Stella Maris feigned exasperation at the inexcusable unpunctuality of her daughter. "Please, please, make your way to the buffet table, everyone," she announced to the guests. "We will have to start without the little imp."

With her plated food, Stella Maris joined Barry, John-O, Peggy, and her mother- and father-in-law at an eight-top. Two chairs sat empty—reserved for Camille and Rosie. They ate the three different kinds of quiches, the pineapple chicken, the Watergate salad, and the fruit skewers.

"Wonder where Rosie is?" Barry said.

"Bare, this isn't about Rosie," Stella Maris said. "Today is about Camille."

"I wonder where Camille is," said Mother Quinlayne.

And *poof!* she appeared. The graduate herself floated in on the arm of Mackinney Lennox. Stella Maris had to admit the couple made quite the entrance: petite Camille, a brown-eyed, blond beauty, dressed in an off-the shoulder cream linen dress with a handkerchief hem and clunky platform sandals, and Mackinney, dark and bearded, eleven years her senior and probably as many inches taller, in skin-tight, burgundy-colored bell bottoms with a thick white belt, a multi-colored polyester shirt—unbuttoned nearly to his navel, revealing a healthy plot of chest hair—and pair of suede moccasins. That darn Mackinney Lennox was a looker...but those bedroom eyes. A sight to behold, the couple glided around the room, greeting the guests and apologizing for their tardiness. What an entrance!

"Well, I never," Stella Maris said to her husband, blotting her mouth with her napkin. She faked a smile, as her eyes followed Camille and her— oh, dear lord—her husband, and she joined in on the applause that had erupted. But she wasn't happy. Camille's absence had provided an unexpected benefit—Stella Maris herself had been treated as the guest of honor, the main attraction, the VIP. How many compliments had she received on her lovely lavender dress and shoes? Dozens upon dozens. Even snooty Greta Kennedy told her she looked fantastic.

When Camille finally made it over to the table, she greeted her mother with a kiss on the cheek. Stella Maris stood up and dramatically embraced her, all the while whispering in her ear: "I am *not* a happy camper." To the guests she said, "Finally!" in a booming, put-out voice. "The princess has arrived!"

Camille smiled obligatorily and then sat down at the table with Mackinney. Stella Maris noticed that he didn't bother to pull out her chair. "I'm starving," were the first words out of his mouth. Stella Maris hated that she found his Scottish accent so appealing…the way he rolled the 'R' in *starving*.

Barry said, "Camille, I'm a bit worried that Rosie isn't here yet."

"Oh, Daddy, I forgot to tell you. Rosie's in Mexico!"

"Mexico?" Stella Maris repeated. "Whatever could be more important than your own sister's graduation party?"

"Mom, it's for work. She couldn't get out of it." (Camille didn't know that Rosie had never actually made it to Mexico.)

"I counted her in the attendees," Stella Maris said. "She should have RSVP'd."

Mother Quinlayne's face puckered in disapproval. "Cammy, darling," she said, "aren't you going to introduce us to your friend?"

"Try *husband*," Mackinney said, as he attempted to tuck a dinner napkin into his shirt. (He'd apparently forgotten that it was unbuttoned nearly to his navel.) He set the napkin on his lap and scanned the table to assess the effect of his verbal grenade.

"How amusing," Grandmother Quinlayne said.

Camille looked around the table, beaming. "Actually, Grammy, this is a doubly special day!" She took Mackinney's hand in hers and announced: "One, I graduated, and two, I got married!"

To feign shock, Stella Maris dropped her iced tea glass. As it hit the edge of her dinner plate, it shattered to pieces. So did her nerves.

"Oh my," said Grandmother Quinlayne.

Back at home, Stella Maris lay on the sofa. Barry brought her a couple aspirin and a glass of water for her headache. She didn't bother to thank him. Barry collapsed into his recliner. They both stared off into space, trying to figure out what the hell had just happened.

Stella Maris blamed everyone but herself: Barry had babied and coddled the girls; the girls themselves were spoiled and ungrateful; and those damn hippies and their rock music. She'd done her job, hadn't she? She had clothed and fed them. She made sure they had good medical care, braces, nice clothes, piano lessons, the best education. They'd been exposed to culture—museums and art galleries, concerts and plays. They'd had more privileges and opportunities in their childhood years than she'd had in her lifetime. They were so self-absorbed! Their whole generation was. Hippies and protesters. Anti-everything. No respect for authority or their elders. Going braless, wearing tube tops, and halter tops, and hip-hugger jeans, and hot pants, for god's sake. Rebelling against the entire universe.

No one appreciated how hard she tried. She had to *earn* her children's respect, whereas when she was a child, respect for your elders was a given. She often felt threatened by her own children. She'd had to pretend for example when she and her family visited the Art Institute or the Museum of Science and Industry in Chicago that it wasn't her first time. Stella Maris's life had been a lot about pretending. Her greatest fear was that people would view her as a country bumpkin. And even though Barry was not the most handsome, charming, and clever man she could marry, he did come from a good, upstanding, middle-class family. She did appreciate the bump in social standing the marriage had provided, but it was never enough. In her eyes, Barry could have and should have been more successful. For Stella Maris, the epitome of success would have been that coveted country club membership. She often day-dreamed about lying in a chaise near the pool sipping on some cool drink while displaying her tanned and slender figure. But her practical, unassuming husband was never interested and renewed their YMCA membership every year.

Stella Maris hadn't even changed out of her lovely lavender dress. She cared not if it wrinkled. "Barry?" she said.

Barry had fallen asleep in the recliner with the dog on his lap.

"Bare?"

"Hmmmm? What?"

"Would you have married me if I hadn't been pregnant?"

Barry popped open his eyes. Not in thirty-one years of marriage had this question ever come up. Not that he hadn't thought about it himself. He did. Often. Sometimes daily. Today, almost hourly.

"Who knows?"

"What kind of answer is that?" Stella Maris snapped, sitting up.

"An honest one, Stell. You know I was crazy in love with you. But we were pretty damn young. Who knows what would have happened? We'd only known each other for a couple of months."

"Do you regret marrying me?" She asked, lying back down.

"Of course not. But I do have regrets. What happened with our girls? Why did they giddy-up outta here the first chance they got?"

"Well, I guarantee you that Camille is pregnant. I know she is."

"She says she's not."

"A mother knows these things."

"Your mother didn't know."

"Thank God for that."

"I guess time will tell."

"That's your answer?"

"Stella Maris, after thirty-one years of marriage, you of all people should know—I have never had the answers."

Dinner was leftovers from the graduation party. The kitchen light seemed dimmer than usual. Stella Maris ate but didn't taste. "What now?" she asked.

Barry put down his fork. "We go to church tomorrow. I go to work Monday. We wait for things to settle down. I predict in a month or two she'll call and beg us to come and get her."

"Oh, no you don't, mister. That girl made her bed. There's no turning back. She will never step foot in this house again!"

"But Stell, she's eighteen. She's our little girl."

"Ha! Little girl, my foot. Good lord, my nerves..."

"I'm going to watch the ball game," Barry said, getting up from the table. He rinsed his plate and set it on the counter.

Stella Maris cleared the table and did the dishes. She washed the table three times—once with a dishrag to get up any crumbs, the second time with a sponge soaked in *Mr. Clean*, and the third time with a paper towel and a spray bottle filled with her own concoction of two parts water, one-part vinegar, and one-part *Windex*. The floor was a four-step process. First remove the two rugs and shake them out at the back door. Then a good sweeping with the broom, third, down on hands and knees to clean up any trouble spots on the linoleum, and fourth, a thorough mopping. The countertops took the most time. Everything—the canisters, the toaster, the mug tree, the blender, the knife holder—was moved to the kitchen table so that the complete surface could be cleaned and sanitized. Then everything was returned to the exact same spot. Please do not move an item in Stella Maris's kitchen or her nerves will jump out of her body. Everything had its place after all.

"Oh no!" she screamed as she returned the toaster to its spot next to the blender. "Barry! Bare!" When Barry appeared in the kitchen, she said, "An ant! I just saw an ant!"

"For crumb sake, Stell, I was right in the middle of a foul ball."

"You know how I feel about ants."

"I'll get a trap from the basement."

"How do you think he got in here?"

"Who?"

"The ant. Who do you think?"

"Stella!"

"My house is the cleanest house on this block. I guarantee it! There is not a loose crumb to be had."

"Stell, it has nothing to do with cleanliness. Ants are everywhere. Sometimes they get in."

"Maybe I need a better disinfectant. Maybe we need that pest control man to come back. Maybe I'm missing something." She started crying. Stella Maris who never cried. "Barry, I can't believe we have ants! We're being invaded! I can't sleep here tonight. Let's get a hotel. Or maybe John-O will let us spend the night."

"Honey, settle down. You're upsetting yourself."

"No, *ants* are upsetting me. The whole house is contaminated. We can't eat in here, now."

"Honey, sit down. I'm going to get you one of those pills Dr. Loden prescribed for you."

"No, they knock me out."

"You *need* knocking out."

Luckily, the anxiety pills worked quickly, and Stella Maris fell asleep within a half hour. But she slept fitfully, dreaming that Camille had planted the ant on her mother's counter and placed the dirty cup in her sink before she ran off to get married. That stupid, ungrateful child.

8.
camille

AT FIRST GLANCE Camille's story might seem like a love story. But it wasn't a love story. It wasn't even a *lovely* story. But it was an old story—countless naïve teenage girls used the institution of marriage as a means of escaping their overbearing, overcritical monster mothers. Scores of girls took that route, and when Camille realized it was her only way out, she jumped at the chance. And no, she wasn't pregnant.

Her sister Rosie had led the way with her own great escape. But Rosie didn't leave for a man. Her passions ran deeper than for one mere man—she was out to save the whole damn human race. Rosie had made a quick, clean getaway. Camille was determined to do the same. But she wasn't out to save the world. Camille was just in love.

It all started when Rhonda, Camille's best friend, wanted to do something special for her eighteenth birthday. Since grade school, Camille and her three best friends—Rhonda, Martha, and Marilyn—were inseparable. They were good girls who attended Boylan Central Catholic High School. Rhonda was in Poms, Martha was senior class treasurer, and Marilyn played guitar at all the school masses. Camille took part in the "Natural Helpers" program, an organization composed of students and staff gifted in their listening and counseling skills.

Rhonda was the leader of the pack. Friendly, bubbly Rhonda infused fun into the group of otherwise serious girls. "I have a great idea for my birthday tomorrow," she told Camille, as they gathered at their lockers. She leaned in and whispered into Camille's ear, "Road trip."

"Where to?" Camille asked.

Rhonda hand-signed (her brother was deaf) B-E-L-O-I-T.

Camille's eyes widened. They had never been—only heard stories from the popular kids about going up to Beloit bars. Twenty-five minutes north, the drinking age in Wisconsin was eighteen; in Illinois, it was twenty-one.

The girls were giddy on the way. A girl Rhonda knew on Poms suggested they stay away from the big bars and visit a small place where this gorgeous guy worked, a place called *Lenny's*. Camille, sitting shotgun, and playing navigator with a map and a flashlight, barked out directions. "Turn left, no right, now left, left again." It was a minor miracle they found the place. As Rhonda pulled into a parking space they squealed with anticipation. Camille's three friends liberally applied strawberry-flavored lip gloss and sprayed their Farrah Fawcett hairdos with hairspray until the fog was so thick, they started choking and were forced to exit the car. Camille wore her blond hair long, loose, and parted down the middle. Her lips were full and heart shaped. Her friends often chided her about her natural beauty and not needing any makeup.

Lenny's looked like someone's house on the outside and like a ski lodge on the inside, with its dark paneling, dim lighting, and deer heads on the walls. It smelled like stale beer, and the air was warm with the alcohol-infused exhalation of about a couple dozen patrons. Some scruffy old men sat at the bar, but young people occupied the tables. To Camille, it seemed like a place that had once been a neighborhood watering hole but was now being overtaken by kids. A band was setting up on a makeshift stage. Three stools sat empty at the bar, and a nice old guy moved down a seat so the girls could sit together.

They almost gasped when the bartender came out from the back room. He was large-boned and handsome, with dark brown curly hair, and sleepy-looking green eyes. He had full lips and when he smiled, it was darn right flashy.

"Hello, loves," he greeted them, in a Scottish accent.

Rhonda was the only one who could find her voice and return the greeting, but she flubbed it saying, "Huh-yo. I mean hello."

"Loves, I hate to tell ya, but ere's a little problem 'ere."

The four girls stopped breathing.

"You got the wrong night—next Saturday is *movie star* night."

They exhaled in unison.

Rhonda said, "Oh, you!"

The bartender said, "Oh, you!" but he wasn't looking at Rhonda. He was looking directly at Camille.

"Me?" Camille asked, putting her hand to her heart.

"Ya, you. I know you. You're Michelle, aye?" (He pronounced it Mē-shell.)

Camille shook her head and looked at Rhonda.

The bartender said, "You mean you're not *Michelle ma belle*?"

She shook her head, smiling.

"Oh, wait. I know. You're *Lovely Rita Meter Maid*."

Camille loved how he pronounced meter "me-tah" just like Paul McCartney did in the Beatles song.

"*Lucy in the sky? Lady Madonna? Long Tall Sally?*"

Camille looked at her friends. She could tell they were a little jealous of the attention she was getting. Rhonda said sardonically, "She's Mother Mary."

The bartender held out his arms and sang, "*Mother Mary, come to me!*" He didn't even card them, just filled four glasses of beer from the tap. He went to take care of another customer but not before turning back to flash Camille with a big smile.

"He's the yummiest thing I've ever seen," Marilyn whispered.

"You lucky thing," Martha said.

"He's old," was all Camille said, but tingles ran down her spine.

Later, when the band started and the girls got up to dance, the bartender put his hand on Camille's and said, "Stay." She stayed. He told her his name was Mackinney Lennox. "Mac to friends." He was quote-unquote twenty-something, his parents were from Scotland, he had two brothers, but one died. He owned the bar and was saving up to open another one in—"Wait, where do you live? Rockford? Yes, a second bar in Rockford."

He cleared away her warm beer and brought her a glass of ice water. "Yer not a big drinker, are ya, love."

"Not really. What time do you work until?" she asked, just to make conversation.

"Why, love, do ya want to get together after?"

Camille felt her cheeks flush. "No, I—"

"Just giving ya a hard time, love. I can tell yer a good girl."

"You can? How?" She was genuinely curious. "Because I don't wear makeup?"

"No, it's not that. Ya have an aura about ya, love. Pure. Almost holy."

"Good grief, I'm not a nun."

"Prove it!"

"Excuse me?"

"Prove it."

"How?"

"Let me take ya for a ride on me motorcycle."

"Now?"

"Not now. How about tomorrow?"

"It's the middle of March!"

"Hold on." He turned to address an old man at the other end of the bar. "Eugene, weather report for tomorrow?"

"Unseasonably warm for March. Sunny with a high of sixty."

"Perfect bike riding day," he said, and slipped a bar napkin and a pen in front of her. "I'll give ya a call after ya get back from church."

"How do you know I go to church?"

Mac just smiled and made an air circle above his head.

Camille said, "Because I'm cuckoo?"

"Love, I was pantomiming a halo."

"Oh." Until he said that, she wasn't going to give him her number. But it was almost a dare. She wondered if he meant it as a dare. She found herself writing her number on the napkin.

Rhonda was too drunk to drive home. Camille took the wheel. Marilyn and Martha slept on the way back, but Camille insisted Rhonda stay awake to keep her company. She had never driven on the highway at night before. When Camille confided that she had given Mackinney her phone number, Rhonda went nuts. "You lucky brat, you! I am so jealous. Don't you think he looks like Cat Stevens? You're so lucky. Maybe this is it?"

"What?"

"Your first."

"My first what?"

"Your first screw, you idiot!"

"Rhonda, please! I'm almost a nun. I've only kissed three guys in my whole life and never French kissed one. These boobs have never been touched by a human, except for my doctor, and she is a she."

"Gag me with a spoon."

"I know."

Camille couldn't sleep that night. Mackinney monopolized her thoughts. What was it about him? He had some kind of animal magnetism. Maybe he was a magician or hypnotist—she felt mesmerized. And foolish. Who was she kidding? He wasn't going to call her. He was just flirting.

But he did call. The following day, just as she walked in the door from church—as if he were psychic or something. She picked up the phone in the kitchen and hoped her mother wouldn't pick up the extension in her bedroom. Camille told Mackinney she'd meet him at The Waffle House on North Main Street in one hour. Just as she said goodbye, she heard the click of the phone upstairs. "Hang up mother," she said. The phone clicked again.

One thing Camille was not: a good liar. The life she'd led up till now had not required any level of deception. Here was an average American girl in the mid-seventies who was content with a simple life. She enjoyed school, her friends and babysitting. She loved to read and play the piano. She was no trouble at all—not like Rosie who rebelled at everything. Still, Stella Maris didn't trust her.

While Camille was changing into jeans and her favorite powder blue cowl-necked sweater, Stella Maris knocked on her bedroom door and entered. "Who was on the phone?"

"A boy I met. I'm meeting him for lunch at The Waffle House."

"How nice? Do I know him? Or his family?"

"I don't think so."

"Where did you meet him?"

Stella Maris asked this just as Camille was slipping her sweater over her head and that one split second of camouflage gave her the time she needed to come up with a lie. "He's a friend of one of Rhonda's friends from Poms." She popped her head out to look at her mother with a straight face.

"Yes, but where did you meet him?"

"Mom, I'm eighteen, I don't have to tell you every detail of my life, do I?"

"As long as you live under this roof, you do!"

"I'll be going off to college soon and then you won't be privy to my every move."

"What do you mean—going off to college? We agreed you would go to nursing school and live at home. Daddy and I aren't made of money, Missy." She folded her arms for effect.

"That's all your idea. I'm not even sure I want to be a nurse. I think I'd like to be a teacher. You know I was accepted at Illinois State and NIU."

"And who is going to pay for room and board?"

"But John-O went to college. You and Daddy paid for University of Illinois for four years!"

"John-O is a man. It's different for a man."

"You're so old-fashioned."

Stella Maris flinched. Camille knew that would get her, for her mother tried to be trendy and relevant. "I am not. Tell me about this young man or you are *not* meeting him for lunch. And why isn't he picking you up, anyway?"

"Like I said, you're so old-fashioned. Kids *meet* nowadays, Mom. And they go—as you would say—'Dutch.'"

"His name?"

"Mackinney Lennox."

"Where does he live?"

"I don't know."

"Where does he go to school?"

"He graduated."

"How old is he?"

"I don't know, Mom. Are we done with twenty questions? May I please take your car for an hour?"

"You may not."

"Then I'll just ask Daddy."

Barry Quinlayne was a pushover when it came to his daughters. Camille found him sitting in his recliner with the basketball game on. She kissed him on the cheek and asked if she could use the car to meet a new friend for a bite to eat. "Sure, honey. Have fun."

Camille kissed him again, and thanked the good Lord for her dad. He was such a sweetheart, so easy-going and easy to please. After a hard day's work as a high school math teacher and basketball coach, all he wanted was dinner, his slippers, and his recliner. Camille knew her dad spoiled her, attempting to compensate for Stella Maris's toughness. It was Barry who encouraged and complimented his children. When Stella Maris delivered compliments, they were brisk statements of fact: "Very nice." "Clever." "Adorable."

As Camille backed out of the garage, she could feel her mom's angry eyes watching from the kitchen window. Stella Maris was a pretty woman when she smiled; when she scowled, she was darn right scary.

Camille pulled into the parking lot and fast-walked into the diner. She spotted Mackinney sitting in a booth by the window. She waved (and immediately wished she hadn't—it seemed so juvenile!). She self-consciously walked across the room—what if she looked different than he remembered?

"You showed!" Mac said, giving her hand a little squeeze.

"I showed," Camille said, feeling shivers from his touch. Mackinney looked just as fabulous in the daytime as he did at night, but he did look a bit older. She peeled off her coat and slid in across from him in the booth.

She noticed that he was drinking a cup of coffee. That made him seem even older. None of her friends drank coffee. It was Sprite or nothing, thank you very much.

"Coffee, hun?" the waitress said, as she warmed up Mackinney's cup.

"Sprite, please?"

"For breakfast?" Mackinney said.

"Coffee is for old people," she teased.

"Right, I know I'm old. Now, tell me—and ya must be quite honest—how old are ya, love? I canna be robbin' no cradles."

"I really am eighteen, Mackinney."

"Good to know. These young vamps come in and lie about their age. A guy could get into a heap a trouble with an under-aged lassie."

"Okay, I told you, now you tell me. What's the 'something' in 'twenty-something'?"

"Nine. I'm twenty-nine." He scrunched up his face. "Too old, love?"

"Not for me, but my parents would have a shit fit."

"And rightly so. But I couldn't help myself. The moment I laid eyes on ya…well, believe me, this isn't like me, but little darlin', ya have knocked me off me feet!"

Suddenly the room grew unbearably hot and Camille's eyes began to water. What was happening to her? When the waitress returned with her Sprite and to take their orders, she blurted out the first thing she could think of: waffles. Mackinney ordered toast and eggs. *Waffles*? She could have kicked herself. What an absolutely childish order!

He smiled. "So, tell me about yourself. What do ya do for fun?"

"I'm a pretty boring person, really."

"I'm quite sure that's not true."

"Oh, but it is. Honest. I go to school. I babysit. I do homework. I play the piano. I go to church on Sundays and then to my grandma's for dinner, but luckily, she was sick today. Well, not luckily, but—"

"I know what ya mean, love. So, yer still in school then. How about after graduation? What are yer plans then?"

"My mom wants me to be a nurse, but I think I'd rather be a teacher. Actually," she said, surprising herself, "I don't care what I do; I just need to get away from my mother."

"Ah, yes, mothers. I'd gamble mine is worse than yours."

"Impossible!"

"Sometime we'll share mommy horror stories, but here comes our food. Let's talk of something lovely. Do you like the Beatles, Camille? Cuz, if you don't, I will have to fall out of love with ya quite immediately!"

A week later, on April Fool's Day, Camille found herself on the back of Mackinney's motorcycle. A first for her. He picked her up from the downtown library (where she was supposed to be researching a paper). Notwithstanding the deception, Stella Maris would have a conniption if she knew her daughter was riding, helmet-less, on the back of a motorcycle. Camille had pulled her hair back in a ponytail but the wind whipped it loose and wild, obscuring most of her vision. The air was cold, and she wished she would have worn a warmer jacket and a hat, but she held on tight to Mackinney and enjoyed the ride. The sun was out, and the trees were just thinking about budding. They drove up Route 2, through Rockton and South Beloit, about a twenty-five-minute ride. Their destination: Mackinney's bar.

It was Sunday so the bar was closed. Camille thought Mackinney would take her upstairs to the apartment he shared with his Uncle Bob, but once inside, he had her take a seat at the bar and told her he had a surprise for her. He went around to the other side of the bar and started mixing up a drink, pouring in a little of this, shaking, pouring in a little of that. He garnished the drink with a cherry and a paper parasol, and then presented it to her. "Taste," he said.

Camille had never tasted hard liquor in her life. She braced herself and took a small sip. It was delicious.

"I call it *The Camille*."

"You named a drink after me?"

"I *created* a drink for ya. Ya really like it, aye?"

"I really like it." (How could Camille know that Mackinney had created the same drink for Jean and Scarlett and Theresa and Robin and Lynn and

Donna and dozens of other girls.) He made one for himself, sans the umbrella, and came around and sat on a stool next to Camille. They sipped their drinks and talked about a stupid movie Camille had seen the night before with Rhonda and Marilyn.

"How late can you stay, love? Don't wanna cause any trouble."

"I need to be back to the library at quarter to five. They're picking me up at five."

"Well, if you are supposed to be *at* the library, love, don't ya think you should be learning something?" He leaned in to kiss her. "I'm quite a good teacher."

Mackinney took her hand and led her to a small backroom that held an old sofa and a desk with a stereo system on it. And yes, Mackinney Lennox was a good teacher. Like all young girls, Camille had dreamed and wondered and fantasized about her "first time." But she could never have imagined something that combined bursting fireworks with gentle fingertips. Parts of it hurt, but most of it was spectacular! She kept thinking, "Oh my god, I'm having sex!"

Safely deposited back at the library, Camille prayed that her father would pick her up, not her mother. Her mother would know. Her mother would be able to *smell* it. When she saw her father's car pull up, she exhaled deeply.

"Hey kiddo," Barry greeted her when she got in the car. "Make progress on your paper?"

"A little," she said. She wasn't proud of the lying. She didn't like it at all. But love made you do things you never thought you'd do.

Her dad sniffed the air. "New perfume, honey? You smell a little minty."

"Ummm, yeah. Do you like it, Daddy?"

"Yes, but for some reason it makes me want a Margarita."

Rookie mistake. She wouldn't make it again. She pulled a stick of gum from her purse and chewed it before she came face to face with her mother.

John-O and his wife Peggy joined them for dinner. Grandma Quinlayne was still not feeling well, thus dinner at her house was cancelled again. Camille chastised herself for not having even thought to call her grandma to see how she was doing, something she would have normally done, before her mind was flooded with love chemicals.

Over roast chicken and potatoes, Peggy said to Camille, "Honey, what's different? There's something different about you? Your hair?"

Camille touched her hair. "No, nothing's different."

"Well, you look gorgeous as usual. I don't know, you look older or something. I can't believe you're graduating soon!"

"I can hardly believe it myself."

Stella Maris said, "I'm just glad she's keeping up with her studies. She spent hours at the library today. What's your paper on?"

"The Holocaust."

"Oh Camille, don't bring something horrific like that up at the dinner table. We're trying to eat."

"Sor-reeey, but you asked."

Stella Maris stared at Camille. "Peggy, I think you're right, our little girl does look different, doesn't she?"

After that remark, Camille noticed that her mother's eyes barely left her. That damn sixth sense that Rosie always talked about. Camille chewed a mouthful of food slowly. Her mother knew. Somehow, she knew. Or maybe it was all in Camille's head. Her guilty conscience playing tricks on her. The thing was, Camille was a nice girl and she wasn't a liar and she didn't like sneaking around. It was exhausting! So, after she had been with Mackinney for four weeks—actually just four Sundays, since their school and work schedules made it impossible to meet on weekdays—she told him that she would like to invite him over to meet her parents.

"Oh, love, I dun know if that's such a hot idea, aye? I donna do well with parents."

"What does that even mean?"

"Parents don't like me. Me own parents don't even like me!"

"You're being silly. Come over at one on Sunday and you can meet my mom and dad."

"But, but, but …your mother's a monster. So ya've been telling me. What if she tries to put a stop to us?"

"Let her try!" Camille said, shocking herself by her newly found courage.

Stella Maris had decided before she even met Mackinney that she didn't like him. Camille had provided her mother with spotty information since being grilled on that first Sunday, but once Camille realized that she was head-over-heels in love, she decided the truth would be the best thing. *He's twenty-nine, Mother; he owns his own business; he's a good driver; he has good manners; no, I haven't met his family; he treats me very respectfully.* In all fairness, Camille knew her mother had every right to disapprove—what mother would want her innocent eighteen-year-old Catholic school girl to date a man eleven years her senior? It wasn't right. What good could come of it?

"He wants one thing, Missy, mark my words. And when he gets it, he'll move on and break your heart."

When Mackinney arrived at the front door, Stella Maris pushed Camille out of the way to open it herself. Camille watched her mother's face when she got her first glimpse of Mackinney Lennox. Camille thought she heard her mother gasp, but she knew in her heart Mackinney's good looks and charm couldn't win her mother over in the end. "Hello Mackinney, I'm Mrs. Quinlayne. You wouldn't mind removing your shoes, would you?"

Camille had set ground rules (who the heck did she think she was?!) before Mac arrived. She didn't want a fancy Sunday dinner, just pizza. "You may not interrogate him, Mom. If you do, we'll just leave and go out for pizza by ourselves." Little did Camille know, it was her father she should have been worried about.

In the basement rec room, over a game of pool, Barry went after Mackinney with abandon. Barry, dressed for company, had removed his sport jacket and tie, but in his cuffed trousers and white dress shirt, he looked a little intimidating…bald head and all. Stella Maris was like a straight line—tall and thin in her tailored black slacks and silk cobalt blue blouse. She'd been to the beauty shop that morning—her auburn hair teased up high, her lips a flashy red. And those dark, Joan Crawford-Mommy-Dearest eyebrows.

"Well, young man," Barry said, as he handed Mackinney a cue stick. "Maybe I shouldn't call you *young* man, now, should I? Twenty-nine, is it?"

"Yes, sir."

"Camille tells us that you're an entrepreneur. What line of business?"

"A bar, sir. A nice little neighborhood tavern. Lots of regulars. Never any trouble, aye." Mackinney nervously chalked his cue stick. Camille thought his anxiety made him seem younger. He wore a forest green turtleneck sweater with a pair of jeans that seemed so new and stiff they could stand up on their own.

"Pretty impressive for someone so young," Barry said.

"He's not that young," Stella Maris said, while attempting a shot. (Stella Maris loathed billiards but had always agreed that it was a good game to play with her children's friends. Something to do while you interrogated them.)

"And you're an immigrant. Scotland, was it?" Barry continued.

"Me parents came over in nineteen-thirty-eight. I'm the baby of the family. I was born here."

"He's a United States citizen," Camille said, unnecessarily.

"You have siblings then?" Stella Maris asked.

"Two brothers, but one died in a car accident."

"Speaking of accidents, Mackinney," Stella Maris said, "I do not want my daughter riding on the back of a motorcycle. I had a cousin who was killed in a motorcycle accident. He was so mangled up my aunt had to have a closed casket. Don't you have a car?"

"No, Ma'am, but I was planning on trading in my bike for a car quite soon."

"Hmmmph," Stella Maris said, accidentally poking the back of her stick into Camille's stomach.

Barry said, "I've got to be straight with you, Mackinney, I'm concerned about the age difference."

"I'm a gentleman, Sir. I've treated all me ladies with respect."

"*All* your ladies," Stella Maris said. "How many have you had? You've never been married? Barry was twenty years old when we were married. You're kind of old *not* to be married."

"*Mom!*" Camille said. She pocketed the eight ball on purpose and the game was over. Thank goodness.

"Let's have some pizza, why don't we," Stella Maris said and led the way upstairs.

In the kitchen, Mac sat across the table from Camille. She gave him her "I'm so sorry" look. The table looked as if it were set for a holiday, with a lace tablecloth, cloth napkins, and candles. "Good grief," Camille said, "paper plates would have been fine."

"Yes, Mrs. Quinlayne, you went to too much trouble."

"Nonsense. I treat *all* my guests the same."

"Yes, she does," Camille said. "She interrogates all her guests while sitting at a beautifully-set table."

"Just wait until you're a mother, Camille. You'll see. You have to worry about everything. This crazy world has turned upside down. The sexual revolution has made parenting so much more difficult!"

Stella Maris served the pizza, setting two slices on each plate. She sat down in her chair and said grace. When Mackinney picked up his pizza with his hands, Stella Maris looked at him as if he had just drunk soup from a bowl. "We Quinlaynes usually eat our pizza with utensils," she said, cutting into her slice with her knife and fork.

"That's nice," Mackinney said. "We Lennoxes usually eat pizza with our hands. Quite boorish, aye?"

"You said it, not I," Stella Maris said, dramatically putting her fork to her mouth.

"Ok, Stell, ease up on the boy," Barry said.

"He's not a boy!" Stella Maris said, a bit too loudly.

Camille was mortified. "Come on Mac, let's take our pizza downstairs."

"Camille, love, let's not be rude. I understand your parents' concern. I am older and I talk funny. I don't come from upper crust, but I do have good manners. And good manners require that we finish this lovely dinner. If the tables were turned, and you were my daughter, I'm sure I'd have quite the same concerns."

"There now," Stella Maris said, wiping her mouth with her napkin, "the boy does have some sense."

"He's not a boy," Barry said.

When Rhonda asked Camille what it was like to be with Mackinney, the best way she could describe it was that it felt like a sunny day, like in the Beatles' song *Good Day Sunshine*. It was just easy to be with Mac. Simple, no stress. They spent most of their dates outdoors—either on Mac's bike, in parks, or on the bike path. They both liked long walks, just holding hands and taking in nature. Mac played the guitar and often brought it on their jaunts. Camille loved to lie on a blanket while Mac serenaded her.

One day, after she and Mackinney had been together a little over two months, he said, "I think I love you, little darling. Marry me and I'll take ya away from your mommy monster." Camille, without hesitation, said *yes*.

9.
camille & mackinney

CAMILLE DIDN'T KNOW it, but her husband hailed from a long line of handsome, lovable losers. Not the Charlie-Brown-deep-thinking-existentialist kind of lovable loser and not the socially-awkward-late-blooming kind who sucked at dancing but got the girl in the end. The Lennox men could charm snakes with nothing more than their good looks and lilting accents, but in the end, they always came up short. Mackinney's grandfather had been a popular British film star; his uncle, a famous stage actor. Mackinney's own father was a real looker who played the field and probably would have continued playing if he hadn't met Elspeth at a friend's wedding. The Lennox men all started with a bang but ended with a whimper. Elspeth called it the Lennox curse.

At first, Camille was happier than she had ever been. Riding on the back of Mac's Harley, she hadn't a care in the world. With her long blond hair blowing in the wind, she felt free, loved, and beautiful. It was hard to believe that just a short while ago she was wearing a Catholic school uniform, taking exams, and eating French fries in the cafeteria. Now she was married to this hunk of a man who told her everyday how lovely she was and how crazy he was about her. And she was crazy about him. He was such a beautiful creature! But arguably, the most fascinating and frankly irresistible thing about Mackinney Lennox was his Scottish accent. The way he bent words, slightly rolled his R's and ended everything with "aye?" Yes, Mackinney was the man of her dreams. He made her feel like a woman and not a little girl. He was so romantic! In lieu of a honeymoon (*someday, sometime, someplace wonderful, I promise!*) he had served her breakfast in bed, gifted her with her very own bike helmet, and then took her for a ride through some rolling Wisconsin countryside.

When Camille first called Rosie in Madison to tell her she was in love, Rosie, being Rosie, wanted to know his political leanings, his philosophy on life, what he did for a living, his dreams, his passions, whether he liked children and treated waitstaff with kindness. Short on answers, Camille said, "I don't know, he just makes my knees go weak."

Rosie said, "Camille, please take it slow. You're so young. Keep your eyes focused on your future. Education is crucial for women! Don't get sidetracked."

"I won't get sidetracked."

She didn't get sidetracked; she got run off the track.

Everyone thought she was pregnant. Why else would she run away and marry this guy? For what? Stella Maris had cornered her in the snazzy bathroom at the country club the day of her graduation party. "You're PG, aren't you, Missy. I can see it on your face."

"I am not, Mom. Look at my face." Camille pointed to the pimple on her chin. "I have my period right now as we speak. I always get this zit on my chin."

"Pregnancy can cause acne, too."

"I am not pregnant."

"Then why? Why on earth?"

"I'm in love. We're in love."

"You're a baby! You're throwing away your life! What about nursing school?"

"That was your idea."

"What do you want then? How do you see your future?"

"Maybe I just want to be a wife and mother and an Avon lady, like you." (She knew that last dig was mean.)

"Then why the hell did your father and I spend all that money on private school?"

"It's always about money, isn't it?"

"Don't be ridiculous. And go ahead and make fun, Missy, but I've been a top earner at Avon for three months in a row now!"

"Think positive, Mom! Spend my nursing school money on a trip or on jewelry, or, I know, a membership to this country club! That would make you happy!"

"I'll never be happy again! I don't understand. I think you're lying to me. You must be pregnant. Tell me why are you doing this?"

Then Camille did something she hadn't done in ages. She leaned in and drew in her mother for a hug. She lay her head on her shoulder and just stayed there for a moment. Stella Maris was stiff; she didn't return the hug. "Okay, Mom, here's the real reason: I love you, and Daddy too, but I have to get the hell out of your house, or I will die."

Stella Maris pulled away. "You're just like your sister. You are a stupid, stupid girl. Go! Go to that man. See if I care. And don't call me when your little brat comes along!"

Two weeks in, Camille phoned her dad at school to let him know she was doing fine. "I love you, Daddy. I'm sorry if I hurt you."

Barry said, "If he hurts you, baby girl, I'll kill him."

Camille would never admit the first month spent with Uncle Bob was a little awkward. She had understood "Uncle" Bob to be literally Mackinney's *relative*, and an older man at that, but it turned out he was just a guy in his early thirties—skinny and balding—who worked for Mac at the bar. Bob's apartment, upstairs of the bar, made his and Mac's commute to and from work a breeze, but it also meant that Bob was always around. He didn't say much, just whistled a lot, chain-smoked, and coughed incessantly through the night. And he stared at Camille. When she complained about this to Mac, he just laughed and told her Bob had one bad eye. "It only seems as though he is staring, aye?"

They needed a place of their own and soon. Without school, without a job, without friends or family, Camille found herself bored and restless, in an indeterminate state of being. She had applied for a few jobs—at the drug store, the dry cleaner, and a pet store—but grew discouraged when she was rejected for having no experience. Other than babysitting, Camille had never held a job.

Since Mac worked all night and slept all day, she found herself falling into his schedule—sleeping most of the day, too, and then watching TV all night. Wouldn't Stella Maris have a hissy fit if she knew her daughter was polluting her mind with inane boob tube shows like *Welcome Back Kotter*, *Wonder Woman*, and *One Day at a Time*. Camille had never watched so much TV. She had to turn up the volume to drown out the ambient noise from the bar crowd below.

Mac forbade her from coming downstairs to the bar. She'd only been there when it was closed. "Cammy, love, I don't want ya in the bar," he told her once they were married. "Please don't just come down or drop by when yer out and about, aye? (She loved how he pronounced it "*oot* and *aboot*.") I don't want my drunken customers ogling my lovely wife, aye? It's not a place for ya."

She wished her dad could hear him—how protective he was of her. She missed her dad terribly. Mac asked her one night as they lie in bed, "Do ya miss the family, love?"

She teared up. "My sister and my dad. But not my mom." What was there to miss? More than once, Stella Maris had told Camille, "Good heavens, I should have stopped after Rosie!"

Rosie had explained once to Camille that their mother was a neurotic. She'd been reading about women who suffered from anxiety disorders that caused them to try to control everything around them. Stella Maris's variety of obsessive-compulsive disorder included some interesting behaviors and rituals. She hated toilets and even in her own home she covered the seat with toilet paper before sitting on it. She overcooked food to kill pathogens. She disinfected and polished every doorknob and every drawer pull, every day. She scrubbed the walls and ceilings of all the rooms once a week and color-coordinated the clothes in the closets. She wiped their dog's feet with a soapy washcloth every time he came in after being outdoors. Shoes, friends, and neighbor kids were not allowed in the house.

For the first time in her life, Camille could be a slob. Mackinney *was* a slob. They both threw their dirty laundry in the corner of the bedroom until they could get to the laundromat. And Bob couldn't care less if dishes piled up in the sink. This was something new and liberating. In Stella Maris's home everything had its place. Here at Bob's, everything had its place, too—wherever it fell.

Camille felt emancipated. But she never anticipated being alone so much. Mac worked crazy hours. "That's how it goes when ya own the place, love." There was always work to do…equipment would break down, employees wouldn't show up, bands would cancel, inspectors would surprise him, suppliers would change. Before long, loneliness set in. Camille missed her friends desperately. Bob wouldn't let her make long-distance phone calls on his phone, so she had to use a pay phone at a nearby drugstore to call her dad, Rosie, and her friends. Once a chatty-Cathy, she drew inward and quiet. She mentioned to Mac that she hadn't realized he was a man of few words. He responded with two words: "I'm not." When Mac finally climbed up the backstairs from a "hellish day" at the bar, he was spent. Not in the mood for chitter-chatter. (He was always in the mood for something else though.)

She needed something to do! Mac told her she shouldn't worry about getting a job, he could support his wife just fine. "It's not about money, Mac. I just need something to do! Maybe I can take in a couple of kids to babysit."

"Or, I know, maybe you can learn to cook!"

"When we get our own place, I will learn to cook. But I could do both—cook and babysit."

"Awww, come on, love, I don't want any brats running around the house when I'm tired."

"I could give piano lessons if I had a piano."

Mac motioned around the room. "'Fraid we're fresh out of pianos, aye?"

There may have been moments along the way when a little inner voice gave her a dressing-down. *"Oh, girl, you may have screwed up big time."* How could it be that she was married to a man she'd only known for a few short months! What did she really know about him? He had a snarky side that had never surfaced before they were married. Was she in over her head?

She did her best to shake off negative thoughts. She could just hear Stella Maris's voice: "You made your bed…" Camille shushed that voice, hopeful that once she and Mac had their own place things would be better.

One day, after lunch, Mac sat in the living room practicing a song on his guitar. The folk singer who was booked for Wednesday's Happy Hour had cancelled, so Mac was going to be the entertainment. During a pause in the strumming, Camille asked him when they could look at apartments. He looked at her as if she had interrupted the symphony orchestra. "I don't have time, love. Ya married a man who works twelve hours a day and needs a good solid ten hours of sleep every night. The bar is hard work, aye?"

So, Camille took the apartment-hunting mission upon herself. Once Mac and Bob went to work, she walked the nearby neighborhoods to get a feel for the area. Beloit was a nice little town, population around thirty-five thousand. As a high-school girl she'd only thought of the town as a place for underage Illinois teenagers to come to party, but the townspeople were proud of their city. After a month of apartment hunting, she grew discouraged. They couldn't afford much since Mac told her that all his money was tied up in the bar. He had a certificate of deposit but early withdrawal would mean a penalty. "Be patient, love, aye?" All she knew was she had to get out of Bob's apartment or she would go insane.

This morning she'd found an ad that looked promising. She'd left Mac and Bob sleeping and walked eight blocks to meet up with the landlord who'd advertised a cheap upper apartment.

Good thing for her graduation money! And good thing for her father, because if not for him there would be no money. At the conclusion of her graduation party, Stella Maris marched right over to the gift table, swooped in, and snatched the card holder box.

"You don't *deserve* this money!" she'd told Camille, hugging the box, which she had so carefully decorated with Camille's school colors, to her chest. "I'm keeping this money to cover the expense of this party and all the pain and heartache you caused me."

"But Mom, I need that money!"

Her dad, not one to get involved, threw his hands up in the air, but later, he put a check for five-hundred dollars in the mail to her. She kept the check hidden in her wallet. Something told her not to cash it right away. She also had a secret stash of babysitting money she'd saved. One-hundred dollars in fives and ones lay hidden in the zippered pocket of her overnight bag. (She'd experienced a twang of guilt for not disclosing the money to Mac, but it was hard-earned, representing two hundred hours of babysitting.)

The landlord turned out to be a land*lady*, a friendly, bubbly, sixtyish woman with a double chin and dimples. She stood on the front porch of a red brick house, her dyed hair the same color as the brick, waving as Camille approached. "Hello! Hello! You must be Camille!"

"I am."

"I'm Sadie. Nice to meet you! Isn't it a glorious day?"

Sadie weaved her arm through Camille's and led her through the front door. "Let's give you a look at the place. My husband Wally and I live on the lower level. We would love to have newlyweds as renters. Our last renter was an old geezer with a bent toward hoarding, but that's another story altogether. Utilities are included, cupcake. It's a cozy space plus it comes furnished! Though very *humbly* furnished."

She wasn't kidding there. After they'd climbed the steep staircase and Sadie caught her breath, she opened the door to reveal a small but sunny space: a perfectly square living room, a postage-stamp-sized kitchenette, a small bedroom with a surprisingly large walk-in closet, and a tiny bath (shower but no tub). *Humbly furnished* turned out to be one saggy beige sofa, a scratched coffee table, a floor lamp that listed to the right, a card table and three mis-matched chairs in the kitchen, and a chest of drawers in the bedroom.

"You'll need your own bed naturally. And I'll need a deposit and the first month's rent. What do you say, cupcake? I might be able to drum up a couple of throw pillows and a tablecloth for you. Girly it up a little." Sadie shimmied when she said "girly it up a little."

Camille looked around, trying to picture herself and Mac here. The place was small but immaculate. It was close to a grocery store, the bus stop, and not too far from Mac's bar. It fit the bill and she wasn't really excited about looking at other places, so she decided to surprise Mac. She signed the lease and signed over her father's check to Sadie right then and there. She couldn't believe it! Here she was, eighteen years old, married, and signing important documents. She'd never even held a job—other than babysitting—or owned a bank account.

"You can move in today if you'd like, cupcake. If you need help hauling your stuff, the mister can come around with the pickup." Sadie winked and Camille fell totally in love with her.

"You what?" Mac barked when she told him. His tone surprised her— he'd never raised his voice before. She chalked it up to him just waking from a sound sleep. He rubbed his eyes. "Sorry, love, but we don't have the money yet."

It wasn't fair that Mac looked beautiful at all times of day...shaven, stubbly, unshaven, dressed, half-dressed, undressed. He definitely had that something-something.

"I had the money...from my graduation."

"I thought yer mum confiscated your loot, aye?"

"She did, but my dad sent me a check—I used it for the deposit and first month's rent. We can move in today."

"Damn it, Camille, I wish ya would have discussed it with me."

"What's to discuss? We can't live with Bob forever." She lowered her voice, twirled her long blond hair around her fingers. "He creeps me out."

"Oh, Bob's okay."

"Mackie, I thought you'd be pleased! Wouldn't you rather be alone with me? Don't you want to start our life together?"

He pulled her into bed and started kissing her all over. When they came up for air, he said, "Does that answer your question, little darlin'? Did ya know ya have perfect, heart-shaped lips?"

Camille fixed Mac and Bob baloney sandwiches. After they went downstairs to the bar, she packed her small bag. The original plan had been to return home after her graduation party and pack her clothes and things into Rhonda's car, but her mother's wrath put a kibosh on those plans. Mac said they would come back in a few days when things settled down, but her father told her things hadn't settled down. "So be it," Camille said to Mac as she hugged his neck. "I have all I need right here with you." Since she wasn't working, she didn't have much use for the clothes she'd left behind. At least not for now.

Camille hummed while she gathered up Mac's clothes and loaded them into garbage bags. So many clothes and shoes and toiletries—shampoos, crème rinses, shaving items, and colognes. After stopping to eat a sandwich herself (Camille was one of those girls who often forgot to eat) she called Sadie the landlady and told her if the offer still stood, she'd take her up on her husband's help.

"I'll send him by after lunch, cupcake," Sadie said.

One trip with Wally did the trick. They didn't have much. Mac said he had sold the furniture he'd had in his last apartment to buy his Harley. She and Wally packed up the bags of clothes, a box fan, a television set, a stereo and console, a "table" made of macramé that you could hang from the ceiling, two guitars, three milk crates of albums—mostly Beatles' albums, and three boxes of Beatles' memorabilia. Wally was a gem. On the way to the apartment, he ran through McDonald's drive-thru and treated Camille to a strawberry shake.

When Sadie greeted them at the door with the throw pillows and tablecloth she promised, Camille almost cried. "I was a newlywed once myself," Sadie said. "We didn't have a pot to pee in, did we Wall? But that's what makes it fun. We've got a Salvation Army and a Goodwill nearby and of course the garage sale season is in full force. You'll make it homey, cupcake. It won't take much."

Wally told her it would take a couple of days to get the phone hooked up. Camille asked Sadie if she could use her phone to call Mac. She could barely hear him above the din. "Make it quick, love, the bar is hopping!" he barked.

She couldn't contain her excitement. "I'm here! At the apartment. We're all moved in! Here's the address. Now write it down. Okay?" It was so noisy in the bar, she was worried he wouldn't get it right, but Mac said, "Okay, got it," so she said, "See you tonight—or this morning, I guess. About three? Oh, Mac, you're going to love it! Our first place."

"Gotta go, love."

"Mac, wait! Could Bob bring our bed over in his truck?"

"Gotta go, aye!"

Before she hung up, she heard him ask a customer, "What can I get you, love?" Call her silly, but she thought Mac only called her "love."

After hanging up Mac's clothes in the bedroom closet and storing all his toiletries in the medicine cabinet in the bathroom, Camille realized they had no dishes or cookware to speak of. Sadie had left a newspaper with nearby garage sales circled in red. Camille had never been to a garage sale—Stella Maris would never stoop so low—but they proved to be a gold mine. She bought a set of dishes, in a cheery blue tulip pattern. The whole set for a dollar! She bought some silverware, a toaster, a clock radio, and a teakettle. She also picked up an iron and ironing board. A broom with a dustpan that cleverly affixed to the handle completed her purchases for the day.

Her bounty required two trips back and forth to the apartment, but it was worth it. She stopped at the grocery store to buy a few items and then set up her little kitchen, while sipping a cup of Earl Gray and listening to music on her new clock radio—Frankie Valli's *My Eyes Adored You*. Dinner was a toasted cheese sandwich and a second cup of tea, steeped in the same tea bag as the first, for economic reasons, of course. She sat at the card table which was covered in Sadie's whimsical rooster-adorned tablecloth and wondered if she would become a coupon clipper like her mother or a frugal woman like her Grandma Quinlayne, who, having lived through the Depression, still used socks for oven mitts, and wrapped gifts in the cartoon "funny papers."

After tidying up the kitchen she retreated to the sofa in the living room. The house was quiet, which Mac would love, but which she found unnerving. She'd grown accustomed to the background noise of the bar crowd. She looked at her watch—it was only seven o'clock. Sick of TV, she curled up on the sofa, and read a few pages of *Jane Eyre*, her favorite novel. But the day had proved to be exhausting and after reading just a few pages she fell asleep with the book open on her chest.

She awoke to a darkened room. Disoriented, she sat up, regaining her bearings. Oh, right, the apartment. She rubbed her eyes and flicked on the floor lamp to look at the time. Almost midnight. At least three more hours until Mac would arrive. She read a few more pages, but sleep overtook her again, and the next thing she knew it was morning. She sat up. Bright sunshine and the tweets of raucous birds outside the window greeted her. Her husband, on the other hand, was nowhere to be found.

At first, she couldn't breathe. Her hand went to her chest as she tried to calm herself. Questions—rational and otherwise—whirred through her mind: Did Mac decide to dump her already? Or did he just lose the address? Did he come home but then leave to get breakfast? Or did he get killed in an accident on his bike? How awful to be without a phone! Should she run downstairs and ask to use Sadie's, or should she just head over to Bob's? Too embarrassed to reach out to Sadie, she washed her face, brushed her hair and teeth, and locked the door. As she walked the eight blocks to the bar, she realized for the first time that her shorts were a bit tight. She guessed her diet of baloney and cheese sandwiches and corn curls was taking a toll. She blamed her tears on that—that she was putting on weight and not that her husband was AWOL. When she was a little girl and she lost something, she used to pray to St. Anthony, the patron saint of lost people and things: "Good St. Anthony, look around, someone's lost and must be found."

At Bob's she had to knock a full minute before he came to the door in his boxers and grayish undershirt. He blinked and took a step back to let her in, wordlessly closing and locking the door behind her.

Mac: asleep in his bed. Never did a man look more beautiful when he slept, especially with the window open and a light breeze fluttering the curtain. The man slumbered in the nude, with abandon, spreading out to all corners of the bed, tangled in sheets and pillows. His tanned skin and dark hair stood out against the white sheets and Camille suddenly pictured him on a movie set doing a love scene—he'd be right at home, so comfortable with his body, so sure of its power. She sat down at the end of the bed and studied him. Even his hands were beautiful. Camille swallowed hard realizing, yes, she was in over her head. Maybe he didn't really love her. Maybe he realized he had jumped in too fast. Maybe—"

"Sweet cheeks!" He woke, smiled, and grabbed her arm, pulling her in for a kiss. "Yer a sight for sore eyes!" He rolled over on top of her, but she squirmed out.

"Mac, wait. Mac! What the heck happened? I was waiting for you!"

"Oh, love, don't get all bent out of shape. Bob and I had a late night. A belligerent drunk started a fight, and we had the cops in right before closing time, and then it was like three-thirty. The napkin I wrote the address on got wet and the numbers were smudged so there was no way to reach ya, darlin', was there now? Plus, I was dead tired, aye. I was sleepwalking by the time Bob and I walked up the back steps." He tried to kiss her, but she wasn't having it.

"Weren't you worried about me? Didn't you think I'd be worried about you?"

"Yes and yes, but there was nothing for me to do. I couldn't go house to house throughout the entire city looking for ya, could I now?"

"No, but…"

"No, but nothing. You're here now and if you make Bob some eggs, I think he'll let me borrow his truck to haul the bed. Then we'll be on our way to our little love nest. And I know just how we'll celebrate!"

She hated to admit it, but he had her at "sweet cheeks." She knew she was looking at a man who could charm the skin off a snake.

Camille stood in the phone booth in front of the drugstore, pocketful of dimes. Mac had postponed the phone hook-up saying they couldn't afford the extra expense. "I'm sure ya can use the landlady's phone if ya need to." What she needed was to talk to Rosie, but Rosie didn't pick up. Neither did Rhonda. Neither did her second-best friend Martha. She re-deposited her coins, intending to try her third best friend, Marilyn, but before she realized she had misdialed, her mother's voice materialized on the other end of the line.

"Hello," Stella Maris said in what Rosie called her "synthetic" voice, the one she used on the telephone and with salespeople and waitresses, the one that told the world who was boss.

Camille was shocked into silence. Should she speak or hang up?

"I said *hell-ooooo*. Hello."

Camille froze, put her hand to her heart, angry that her mother's voice still put the fear of God in her.

"Who's there?" Stella Maris asked in a voice that seemed to soften around the edges a bit. "Is it you?" she said in a near whisper.

How did she know? Camille wondered. Rosie often said Stella Maris had psychic power, extrasensory perception, clairvoyance. The woman could scope out cigarettes in your purse with her X-ray vision, she could smell beer on your breath despite efforts of camouflage with minty chewing gum, and she could smell McDonald's grease on your clothing when you were supposed to be at the library.

"*Camille.*" It wasn't a question.

"Yes."

"I knew it was you."

"It's me," Camille said, closing the accordion door on the phone booth a little tighter.

"Well."

"Well ..."

"Well, why are you calling? What do you want?" The synthetic returned to Stella Maris' voice, sharpening her articulation.

"Nothing. I don't want anything."

"You need money, don't you? I told your father after he sent you that check that you'd come begging for more. The answer is no."

"I don't need money, Mom."

"State your business then."

"If you must know, I misdialed. I meant to call Marilyn."

"Marilyn's mother doesn't want you talking to her daughter. Said you were a bad influence."

"Okay." Camille wanted to hang up, but she couldn't bring herself to do it.

"Don't *okay* me, young lady. And who is Sadie, anyway?"

Camille almost gasped. (Rosie was right—she was clairvoyant.) How did her mother know about Sadie?

"I already know who Sadie is. She's your landlord because you signed Daddy's check over to her."

"Yes, Mom, Sadie Phillips is my landlady."

"And I have a question for you. Did you leave a dirty coffee cup in the sink the day you ran away?"

"What?"

"I got home from the club that day and my favorite cup was in the sink. Did you or that man of yours put that cup in my sink?"

"Are you serious, Mom? This is what you're worried about?"

"You disrespected me."

Camille shook her head in disbelief. She had run away and married an older man, given up nursing school, shamed Stella Maris in front of all her friends at the graduation party, dashed her dreams of having a nurse as a daughter to care for her in her old age…and she was disrespected by a dirty coffee cup left in a clean sink?

The line went quiet. "Mom?"

"I'm here." Camille detected a catch in her voice. "How could you do this to me? You hate me so much?"

"Mom, I don't *hate* you. And I didn't do this *to* you. I fell in love."

"Oh, spare me. I know you're PG. I could see it on your face."

"Thing is, Mom, I'm not. Why won't you believe me?"

"You can't expect me to be happy about all this. The only way I can survive this is to pretend it never happened and to do that I have to pretend *you* never happened. YOU and ROSIE never happened. I have one child, a son, and his name is John Oliver." And with that, she hung up.

Camille walked back to the apartment. She refused to cry. How many tears had she shed after a run-in with her mother? Marilyn's mother was difficult, but both Rhonda and Martha had wonderful mothers, kind and gentle, on their side no matter what. Rhonda's mom never belittled her because of her weight. Martha's mom worked Saturdays at a medical clinic for two years to pay for her daughter's braces, happy to do it. When Camille got her braces, Stella Maris said, "There goes my European vacation."

When Camille returned, Mac was still sleeping. In the few weeks since they had been at the apartment nothing had changed. In her innocence and naïveté, she believed that once they were settled in it would be like playing house. She would learn to cook more than just canned soup, scrambled eggs, and macaroni and cheese, and Mac would keep more regular hours. When she'd asked him if he could possibly hire an additional bartender so that he could work a little less—he was the owner after all—he said, "It doesn't work that way, love." Which made her wonder how it did work? She had fantasized about making friends with other couples, maybe even having guests over for a cookout sometime. They could cruise the garage sales together and purchase things they would need for the apartment. Plus, she didn't want to be a nag, but Mac had promised to introduce her to his family, but whenever she brought it up, he scrunched his nose and said, "In good time, love."

She tiptoed around the bedroom and changed out of her shorts and halter top into a more presentable sundress to wear to a doctor's appointment she had later that morning. Mac had asked, now that they were married, if she would please get on the pill so he could stop using those damn condoms. He said he would come with her, but now, when she tried to rouse him, he rolled over and groaned. "Come on, Mac, you promised. And I need a ride."

He covered his face with his arm. "You know, love, I didn't sleep well at all and it's going to be a bitch of a night. We got baseball teams coming in and I'll be up to my arse in beer and shots. Can't you ask Sadie to take ya? I hate all that lady shit."

"Lady shit? Really, Mac?"

"Aww, you know what I mean, love. Don't be getting all bent out of shape, aye."

But she was bent out of shape. In a few short months, this man who couldn't keep his hands off her, who worshipped the ground she walked on, had somehow…cooled. Camille didn't want to admit it to Mac, but she had never been to a doctor by herself much less an OB-GYN. She walked ten blocks to the clinic, all the while arguing with her inner voice: *Is this normal? Are you happy? Is this what you thought it would be?* She arrived at the clinic agitated and anxious.

The nurse did not put her at ease. When she looked over Camille's intake form, she pointed out the missing phone number.

"Oh, um, we don't have a phone yet."

"You don't have a phone?"

"No, we do not have a phone."

"How are we supposed to get a hold of you? For test results and such?"

"I guess by mail?" Camille offered.

"By mail." The nurse frowned and made a notation on the form.

The doctor, a middle-aged, bespectacled, bow-tied snob was not happy with Camille at all. Judgmental was what he was. When he asked what brought her in today and she told him that she wanted to get on the pill, he said, "How old are you and do your parents know you're here?"

Camille said, "I'm eighteen. I've been married for a few months and my husband and I don't want to have children right away." Camille bit her tongue. She and Mac had never even discussed children. She assumed he wanted children. Wasn't that the natural course of events?

Camille had never had a pelvic exam. It hurt. She even cried. The whole process was humiliating—peeing in a cup, spreading your legs while your feet were in stirrups, probing hands and fingers. Simply mortifying.

At home, she found Sadie sweeping the front porch. "There she is! I thought maybe you'd moved out. You two are quiet as mice!"

"Well, Mac works a lot and…"

"Oh, I'm not complaining, cupcake. You are a landlord's dream. How's things? How's married life treating you?"

"Well…" Camille couldn't help herself. She teared up, covering her eyes with her hand.

"Oh dear, someone needs a nice cold glass of lemonade." Sadie leaned the broom against the wall and grabbed Camille by the hand. She led her to the kitchen and sat her in a chair. The dog, Henry the Eighth, a straggly-haired mutt who looked nothing like his aristocratic name, sniffed her legs. He was a sweet old thing and took a liking to Camille, who missed her own dog more than she ever imagined she would.

"Believe it or not, I was seventeen when Wall and I got married," Sadie said.

"You were?"

Sadie set a glass of lemonade on the table along with the pitcher. "I was. How about an oatmeal cookie? Store bought. Too hot to bake."

Camille honestly couldn't remember the last time she'd had a cookie. She happily accepted one when Sadie held out the plate.

"I never even finished high school. I thought, what was the point? I was going to be a wife, a mother, and a housewife, so what did it matter if I finished school? I was never a very good student anyway. Wally was nineteen. He'd graduated and got a job at Hormel Foods. We rented the upstairs apartment that you're in and eventually bought the house when our second son was born."

"Was it hard at first?" Camille asked.

"Oh, cupcake. It was so hard. I was a baby! For a fact, I was the baby…in my family. I had four older sisters and two older brothers, and they all doted on me. I was like the family puppy. Adored and petted. We had a small farm in Stoughton and I basically wandered my childhood away. I had a horse, Cooper, and I spent most of my time with him. Anyway, I came into the marriage utterly ignorant and naïve. But Wally was kind and patient. He even taught me how to cook!"

"Wally is the sweetest!"

"So, what's the trouble, cupcake? You can tell ol' Sadie."

"It's nothing…well, it's everything. It's confusing is what it is."

"I just think you need something to do with yourself."

"That's what I told Mac! I applied for a few jobs, but I have no experience. All I can do is babysit and maybe give piano lessons, but obviously I have no piano."

"I have a piano," Sadie said, as if it were the most wonderful coincidence ever. "It's sitting in the living room unused since the boys are gone. You can use it."

Camille perked up. "Oh Sadie, you're an angel from heaven."

That night, Camille lay awake in bed, while Mac slept soundlessly beside her. She thought about Sadie and what an amazing woman she was. So different from her own mother! She couldn't think of a time she sat at the kitchen table—or anywhere—and had an honest heart-to-heart with her mother. There was no communicating with Stella Maris, no back and forth. You listened. You did what you were told. Sadie Phillips was Stella Maris's opposite, her contrary, her antonym. Sadie was the mother Camille always wished she'd had.

That's why Sadie was the first person Camille sought out after a letter came from her doctor's office a week after her appointment. Camille was already in tears when Sadie answered the door. "I'm going to make a pot of tea," Sadie said, as if lemonade were not a serious enough drink this time around.

"I'm pregnant!" Camille blurted out, plopping down in a kitchen chair.

Sadie set down the teapot and squeezed her hand. Camille loved how she didn't say anything right away. She probably didn't know if this was wonderful news and Camille was just overwhelmed with emotion or if this was terrible news and she was overcome with dread. Camille didn't even know herself.

"And..." Sadie said.

"And...oh my god. I am pregnant!"

"So, it's a surprise?"

"Oh, Sadie, it's a bombshell."

"Tell me."

"Well, one, I've only been married for three months! Two, Mac and I never even discussed having kids. Three, even if he does want kids, it's way too soon. That's why I went to the doctor in the first place—to get on the pill. And four, my mother will think she was right and I *had* to get married." Camille lay her head down on the kitchen table, almost turning over her teacup. Sadie caught it just in time. She stroked Camille's hair and let her cry it out.

"You poor little thing! Okay, cupcake, let's take things one at a time. Number one, you've only been married three months. To that I say—at least you're married. No scandal there! Two, I bet Mac wants kids. And if he doesn't, too late buddy, time to grow up. What do the kids say nowadays? *Time to grow a pair?*"

This made Camille pop her head up and smile. Sadie handed her a napkin and Camille wiped her eyes.

"As for your mother—well, time is on your side. When the baby comes your mom will count backwards and see that you were telling the truth. I say Congratulations! Being a mother to my two hooligans has been the biggest blessing in my life."

"Oh, Sadie, why couldn't you have been my mother?"

"Oh, cupcake, we can pretend, can't we?"

How to tell Mackinney. It seemed there were two options—at least from what she'd seen in the movies: the "sexy" approach (greet him at the door completely nude with a can of whipping cream) or the gastronomic route (his favorite dinner and dessert). Two problems: she could never bring herself to play the sex kitten and she didn't know how to cook. In the end, her tears gave her away. That night after lovemaking, Mac joked that his sexual prowess had never moved a woman to tears before.

"You idiot," Camille said. "I'm pregnant."

Mac sat up. "Aww, Cammy, I told you to get on the pill!"

"And I went to the doctor for that very purpose, didn't I? I had to be informed by letter since we don't even have a phone. I knew you'd be mad!" She cried harder.

"There now, little darlin', I'm not mad, I'm just surprised, aye? It's just so soon."

"I know."

"I just wish we were more settled."

"I know."

"How far along are ya, aye?"

"I have no idea. I didn't even know I missed a period. I don't keep track! I never had to keep track. I just got it when I got it. Come to think of it, my last period was unusually light."

"Cut it out, I hate that lady shit. Wait, maybe it's a mistake. Maybe the doctor's office made a mistake."

"Maybe? Or you hope?"

"Jesus Christ, Camille, I *hope*. Is that so bad? We're not ready. At least *I'm* not ready."

Neither said anything for a while.

"A baby, huh?"

"Yes, Mac, a baby." She almost asked if he thought it might be a puppy, but she caught herself.

He drew her closer to him. "I think it's actually quite wonderful, love." He kissed her forehead.

"You do?"

"Aren't you happy? I thought all women wanted babies."

"I am happy. I've always wanted to be a mom. But I'm scared. But now that I know you're happy, I'm happy."

"I'll have to work harder at the bar. Longer hours."

"Mac, I've been thinking, maybe you shouldn't open a second bar in Rockford."

"What?"

"The second bar. You said you were going to open a second bar in Rockford. The night we met. You said that."

"Camille! I was just kidding. I was flirting with you, aye?'

"You were?"

"Yes." Mackinney laughed and laughed.

Camille felt like a two-year-old. She got up to use the bathroom. When she came back to bed Mac was asleep. She was glad.

The next day, Sadie let Camille use her phone to call Rosie and Rhonda. Neither one was very excited about the news. "It's so soon," Rosie said. She had just moved last month to Washington, D.C. This big-shot feminist she knew found her a job with U.S. Congresswoman Bella Abzug, and although her boss, the mayor of Madison, Wisconsin, was sorry to lose her, he supported the move. Rosie said, "I just wish you two had more time to get to know each other." She had to go. She was meeting with a senator in half an hour. "Keep me posted. I'm sure once the shock wears off, I will be happy. I will love being an aunt. Go to the library and get the Dr. Spock baby book. Quit eating baloney—ugghh, all the preservatives. And make sure you take the prenatal vitamins they prescribe. No alcohol. No cigarettes. And no pot!"

When Camille called Rhonda with the news, she was more focused on the physical ramifications: "You're going to get so fat."

"You brat!" Camille said.

"I'm teasing you. Think how gorgeous your kid is going to be!"

Camille decided to be happy. She started thinking about how much she adored children and how having one of her very own would be pure bliss.

She had no doubt that she would be a good mother. Her road map would be simple—do the opposite of what Stella Maris had done. Be like Sadie.

Sadie helped Camille to make some fliers advertising piano lessons and shortly after she'd hung them at the library, the grocery store, and the drug store, Camille received five responses and booked two students. She was elated! Sadie had saved all her children's sheet music so Camille could start her business without a penny's investment. Sadie suggested a fee of five dollars per lesson.

"Sadie! I'll be making ten dollars a week. Forty dollars a month! That's better than babysitting!"

Camille blossomed. Everything about her softened and rounded. She looked and felt wonderful. No morning sickness. No mood swings. None of the scary stuff she'd read in the books she borrowed from the library. She read as much as she could about pregnancy and childbirth, forbidding Mac from smoking in the apartment once she learned about the dangers of secondhand smoke.

She changed her diet completely, adding cottage cheese and whole milk. She replaced baloney with lean turkey. She ate her vegetables like a good girl. Mac complained about the cost of all this healthy food, but she ignored him.

"You're blooming, aye?" Mac said one night when she was getting ready for bed. He gently touched her belly. "I like it," he said. "I think I'm going to like ya barefoot and pregnant."

Camille slapped his shoulder. "Don't be a male chauvinist pig."

"Aw, don't get all bent out of shape, love, I just mean I will love ya when ya are fat and walking around like a walrus."

"Sometimes, Mackinney!" Tears welled in her eyes. It had never occurred to her that Mac might not be attracted to her when she was pregnant. Now she couldn't get it out of her head.

10.
camille and sadie

ON AN AFTERNOON in late September, Sadie drove Camille to some neighborhood garage sales. She parked Wally's truck in front of a huge old Victorian home and the two walked to the back of the house to the detached garage.

"I hope it's still here," Camille said to Sadie.

"I have a good feeling, cupcake."

They had come for a crib, the final thing on Camille's list. Over the last few weeks, she and Sadie had foraged and found a highchair, a walker, a changing table, a car seat, a stroller, a few toys, and some books at local sales. Sadie had surprised Camille with a beautiful blanket she'd quilted and some sleeping gowns she'd sewn for the baby. Rosie insisted on paying for a diaper service, a lifesaving luxury that made Camille cry in the phone booth when her sister told her about it. And her dad had sent a check for a hundred dollars with a note that read "Don't tell Mom." As if she would.

The crib was still there, and it was in good condition. The homeowner and his son hoisted the crib and mattress into Wally's truck. The man's wife was kind; she threw in two sets of sheets for free.

"I think it's a boy," Sadie said on the way home.

"I kind of want a girl," Camille confessed.

"You'll take what you get!" Sadie teased.

Later, when Mac left for the bar, Wally and a next-door neighbor brought the crib upstairs and set it up in the nursery, which was really just the oversized walk-in closet off their bedroom. Only the crib and the changing table fit into the space, and Mac was ticked off that his clothes had been moved to the front hall closet and a secondhand wardrobe that Sadie had lent them, but Camille was pleased. She couldn't wait to show everything to Mac.

But Mac came home in a mood. Camille had been reading in bed. "Another belligerent drunk?" she asked, watching him undress.

"More like a belligerent ex-girlfriend."

Camille sat up, eyes wide. Naturally she knew Mac had girlfriends before her—he was gorgeous and twenty-nine years old after all, but he had never talked about them before. Then she noticed some puffy scratches on his right cheek. "Good grief! What happened?"

Mac tossed his jeans, T-shirt, and underwear in the corner of the room— something that irked Camille to no end now that she was "nesting"—and plopped his naked body onto the bed. "I'm fine." He touched his cheek. "She wouldn't take 'no' for an answer." He smirked as he rubbed his cheek. "It better not scar, aye?"

"What are you talking about...*she wouldn't take no for an answer?*"

"Aww, don't go getting bent out of shape, aye? She wanted to get back together. Wanted me to go back to her hotel with her."

"Mac!"

"Well, I didn't, love, did I now? Nothing to worry about. She's only in town for her class reunion, *our* class reunion."

"Why did she scratch you?"

"We were dancing and—"

"Dancing?!"

"Don't get all bent out of shape. I often dance with customers. It's part of the job. Hey, will ya get me a cold wash rag for my cheek? Please, love?"

For a full six seconds, Camille didn't move. She knew moving would be giving in. She knew getting up and fetching Mac a washcloth for his stupid scratched cheek meant that she wasn't getting all bent out of shape. But was she bent out of shape? Yes, she was. She so badly wanted to say, "Get your own damn washcloth." Why didn't she? What made her get up and grab one from the linen closet and run it under cold water in the bathroom? What made her fold it in half and then in half again and place it gently on Mac's cheek? Weakness? Inferiority? Living in a world of male domination where talk of feminism and liberation was just beginning to trickle down to the average American woman? Was it because he was gorgeous? Was it his charming Scottish accent—the way he rolled the R in *wash rag*? Maybe it was because of the crib and the nursery and the fact that she had just felt the baby flicker inside her that very evening after dinner. A fleeting, but certain, tickle. Maybe she just wanted to be a family.

Mac held the washrag to his cheek and stared up at the ceiling. "I can anticipate your next questions, love, so I'll just answer them. Her name is Scarlett and we dated for about a year and it ended about a year ago. That's it."

Camille hated herself for asking: "Is she pretty?"

"Oh, yeah. She's a knock-out. But an utterly terrible person. A trickster and a double-dealer. A she-devil." He turned to look at her. "You're not mad, love, are ya? Dunna be silly now."

"Why'd you go and dance with her, Mac?"

"Is that what's bothering you, little darlin'? We can fix that." He jumped up from the bed, tossed the washrag to the floor, and pulled Camille up by the arm.

She moaned. "What are you doing?"

"It's called *dancing*," he said, taking her hand and wrapping his arm around her waist.

"There's no music, you idiot," she said, already falling into an imaginary rhythm.

"We'll make our own music."

Mac hummed a Scottish folk song. Damn it, even his humming had a charming lilt to it. Camille's body danced, but her mind was in a big, fat pout. About Scarlett, yes, and the fact that Mac hadn't even noticed the crib and the makeshift nursery.

She couldn't sleep. How could she sleep? She tiptoed out into the living room and curled up on the sofa, staring at the wall. She lay frozen for several minutes then retrieved her journal that she'd hidden under the sofa cushion. She began doodling—random thoughts, word balloons, worries, prayers. Baby names. Hearts and cubes. She wrote the name *Scarlett* and it looked like a dirty word. She wrote out what she remembered the Justice of the Peace saying at the civil ceremony: "By joining hands, you are consenting to be bound together as husband and wife. You are promising to honor, love, and support each other for the rest of your lives." She rubbed her stomach. "I will make this work," she said out loud. She tiptoed back to bed, but sleep did not come.

Camille wondered if she should be riding on the back of Mac's motorcycle when she was five months pregnant. Hadn't he been telling her that she shouldn't? Hadn't he been using it as an excuse *not* to accompany her on her doctor's appointments? Oh, but she was going stir-crazy, cooped up inside. It was a crisp October day—the trees dripped golds and ochres and the sky looked like Van Gogh himself had painted it. The sun was bright and warm on her face. Sunday was the one day they had together, and she lived for Sundays. Sunday was the only day the bar was closed and the only day she had Mac's full attention. This was the Mac she had fallen in love with. The 'Sunday Mac.' The Mac who laser-pointed his green eyes on her and seemed to drink her in. The Mac who sang love songs to her. She had packed a picnic lunch and hoped they could spend the whole day outdoors.

At Riverside Park, she was a little self-conscious of her appearance. Mac talked her out of wasting money on buying maternity clothes ("Ack! They're so ugly!") and talked her into wearing some of his soft flannel shirts—he had many in a variety of plaid patterns. "Get yourself a pair of maternity jeans from the Goodwill and then wear me shirts. Who cares how you look now anyway?" *She* cared, for one. All her life, she'd been the pretty one. Now she didn't feel pretty at all.

On a blanket in the grass they munched on cheese and crackers and apple slices, while people-watching.

"Come closer," Mac said. "Let me feel me baby."

Camille scooted closer and Mac placed his hand gently on her belly. The baby responded to the touch and something akin to a flutter danced across her stomach.

"Well, what do ya know?" Mac said, smiling. "He's really in there, isn't he?"

"How do you know it's a 'he'?"

"I'm hoping. I always wanted a son. I sometimes wonder if perhaps I have one or two out there somewhere that I dunna even know about, aye."

Camille pulled back a little. "What do you mean?"

"Now, love, don't get all bent out of shape. All I mean is that I've been around the block a few times, aye, and so who knows where me seed may have sprouted."

"That's disturbing."

"Just a fact of life, darlin'. Not fair to ya, I know, that I got to marry a sweet, unplucked virgin, and ya get this used-up, traded-in model. I've been running since 1961. Popped my first cherry in the backseat of me dad's '55 Chevy. I was fourteen. She was eighteen."

Camille shook her head. "You know, I would really prefer *not* to hear about your sexual escapades. It makes me uncomfortable."

"Why, love? Ya know I had a life before ya and I know ya had a life before me. What matters is now. Here we are now."

Camille, lay back on the blanket and shushed that inner voice that said, *Who is this guy? What are you doing here?* She stared at Mac while he strummed his guitar. He had such beautiful hands. Wait just a minute…where was his wedding band? "Mac, where's your ring?"

He stopped strumming, looking annoyed. "In me pocket, love. Don't go getting all bent out of shape, aye. It messes up me guitar playing." She didn't see how, as he strummed with his right hand, but she didn't say anything. He sang, "Good Day Sunshine," her favorite Beatles' song and that lightened her spirits.

More than anything else—more than making love, being pregnant, or signing rental agreements—giving piano lessons made Camille feel like a real adult. She took her job seriously. Julia Martinson, age seven going on seventeen, was a quick learner, but easily distracted. Jack Anderson, six and front-toothless, stole her heart. "You're pretty but fat," he told her on day one. Camille looked forward to Monday and Wednesday afternoons when the kids came for lessons. She wished she could find a few more students. She almost had a third, but when the mother came to interview her and saw that she was young and pregnant, she told Camille she didn't think she was the "right fit." Disappointing. Still, the extra ten dollars a week that she socked away for the baby made Camille feel proud.

She also felt frightened. Every night for an hour or so she read the *Dr. Spock's Baby and Childcare* book she had picked up from the library. At first, the main message of the book gave her a sense of comfort—caring for your baby won't be hard if you trust your instincts. But then Dr. Spock asserted that we all end up "at least somewhat like our parents" in the way we deal with our children. If you had an easy-going parent, you will likely be an easy-going parent yourself; if you had a strict parent, chances are you will be a strict parent. One thing Camille knew for sure: she did not want to be like Stella Maris.

Sadie answered a lot of questions Camille had about pregnancy and babies. She'd been having Camille downstairs to eat dinner with her and Wally. "We get a little lonely down here, just the two of us." Sadie filled Camille's plate with a thick slice of meatloaf, a baked potato, and green beans. Then she filled a glass of milk and placed it in front of her. "Pass the rolls over to her, would ya Wall?"

Camille chose a warm roll and buttered it. What would she ever have done without these two kind people? It felt so good to sit at a real table and enjoy a real meal. It was funny, Mac was interested in her, but not in anything *about* her—not in her friends, her family, her past. "I live in the NOW, love. There's nothing but today."

So, when Wally asked about Camille's siblings, she jumped at the chance to talk about Rosie. "Rosie's my older sister. Six years older. She's working in D.C. now. She's wanted to save the world ever since she was a senior in high school. Remember how crazy things were with Vietnam and the anti-war demonstrations and everything? Nixon was just elected and, man, how my sister despised that man."

"Those were crazy times," Wally said. "We thought the world was coming to an end. Lord Almighty, the sixties were nuts."

"Before Rosie moved to D.C.," Camille said, "she lived in Madison and worked in the mayor's office."

"That teenage mayor?" Wally asked.

"Yes!"

Wally said, "I remember the bombing in Madison on the UW campus a few years back. Terrible!"

"Rosie was there. She actually overheard the bombers planning the event at a bar!"

"Oh, my!" Sadie said.

"I love her so much! I wish I was as strong and brave as she is."

"Do you see each other?" Sadie asked.

"Not often enough. I haven't seen her in about eight months. She's busy fighting to get the E.R.A. ratified."

"That's the Equal Rights Amendment, Wall," Sadie said.

"I know what the E.R.A. is, woman!" he shouted. Then he grinned and said to Camille's shocked face: "That was a joke, honey."

"Don't mind him," Sadie said. "Did Mackinney ever meet her?"

"No, but he will when the baby comes. She's staying for a whole week!"

Mackinney loved the "care package" Sadie sent for him and gobbled up the meatloaf, potatoes, and green beans even though it was two in the morning and he'd already eaten dinner.

Camille was folding laundry. "Look at this!" she said, holding up a pink sleeper she found at Goodwill.

"Uh huh," Mac said, barely looking up.

"Mac, we really should talk about names. If it's a girl, what do you think of Charlotte or Caroline? I like old-fashioned names. I even considered Sadie. Do you like the name Sadie?"

"Sadie, like our landlady?"

"Sadie, like my dear friend."

"Sadie Lennox. It's alright."

"For a boy, I like—"

"Damn it, Camille, cut it out with the names, will ya?"

"Excuse me, Mr. Crabby Pants."

"I'm sorry, love. I'm just beat. Let's go to bed."

But once they were in bed, Mac didn't seem to be beat. He reached out to her. She had started to hope her blooming stomach would tamp down his desire, but Mac was always hungry for her body. "God, you're so gorgeous, love," Mac said afterward. "Even as fat as you are." Then he turned over and fell asleep.

"Do you have any Thanksgiving plans, cupcake?" Sadie asked. Camille had been spending most of her days downstairs now with Sadie and Wally. If she wasn't practicing the piano or giving lessons, she was lying on the sofa with the dog.

"I asked Mac if we might get an invite from his family, but he said, 'They're Scots, Camille. Scots don't celebrate Thanksgiving.'"

Sadie frowned. She sat in her rocking chair, crocheting scarves for Christmas presents. "But they're Americans now. When in Rome?"

"That's what I said. Sadie, be honest. Don't you think it's a little odd that I haven't met anyone in Mac's family? Whenever I bring up his family, he changes the subject. Don't you think that's weird?"

"Maybe they're on the outs, too, like your family. No worries. You'll join us on Thursday. Our sons and their families are coming. We would love to have you and Mackinney."

"We'd love to come, Sadie. What can I bring?"

"Bring your appetite, cupcake."

Mac whined when she told him. "Aww, why'd ya go and promise we'd come?"

"Why? Do we have other plans?"

"No, but…"

"But you like Sadie and Wally."

"I like staying home and watching TV in me underwear better."

"Then be my guest. I'll be downstairs stuffing my face with turkey and dressing. And I won't even bring you a slice of pie."

"Aww, love, don't get all bent out of shape. I just thought we could have some alone time together."

"Mac, all we have is alone time together! No family or friends!"

"I meant alone time before the wee bairn comes."

"Oh." She'd read that men could get jealous of a newborn baby.

She gave in. On Thanksgiving Day, they slept in and then ate turkey TV dinners in bed. It was torture to hear all the hustle and bustle of Sadie's family downstairs. To make matters worse, Mac got ticked off that Camille forgot to buy a pumpkin pie. Then they got in a fight about money. Camille had depleted her secret stash and she wanted to buy herself a nice nightgown and slippers for the hospital. Her due date was looming, and she had no decent bed clothes to wear.

"That's not in the budget, aye," Mac said.

"We have a budget?"

"Yeah, I make the money and I decide how to spend it."

"But Mac, I've asked you for nothing all these months! We live like we're paupers and here you own your own business."

Mac sat up in bed. "You know nothing about it, love. I work twelve-hour days. Ya've never worked a day in your life. Babysitting and a few piano lessons don't count. Who pays the rent? Who pays the utilities? Who pays for me bike?"

"Which is impractical now. We need an actual car."

"Who pays for your food and your doctor's appointments? Who pays for all this garage sale shit ya brought home?"

Camille got out of bed and walked to the door. "I did, you idiot! I paid for all this garage sale shit." She slammed the door. Curled up on the sofa, she waited for Mac to emerge from their bedroom and apologize. But he didn't. Her inner voice was getting quite loud. *Girl, you are in deep.* She fell asleep. When she woke up, Mac was up and out. The sun streamed in through the slats of the shade. He couldn't have gone to the bar yet. She'd thought the bar would be closed today but Mac said that the day after Thanksgiving was one of their busiest days—people needed strong drink after suffering through time with relatives.

Sleeping on the sofa was a bad idea—her back was killing her. She made a trip to the bathroom and then in the kitchen poured herself a bowl of cornflakes. She sliced up half of a banana into the bowl and then realized they were out of milk. She ate the cereal/banana dry. This is what it had come to.

Having no energy for anything other than worry and apprehension, she trudged off to bed. When she woke up Mac was lying next to her with a shopping bag between them.

"What's going on?" she asked, sitting up.

"I'm sorry, love. I was an ass, aye?"

"A big fat ass."

"This is new for me, love. I'm an old bachelor."

"You're not old."

"I feel old. And to be honest, the closer we get to the baby coming, the more nervous I get."

"You? What about me? I'm the one who has to go through labor and delivery. I'm so scared, Mac."

"I know, love." He tucked a loose strand of her hair behind her ear. "We'll get through it, won't we now. Open your present, aye?"

He handed her the shopping bag and she reached in and pulled out a pink flannel nightgown. "I don't know much about lady shit. It's not maternity so I just got ya an extra-large. There're slippers, too."

She pulled out the slippers and knew by looking at them that they would be too small for her large Quinlayne feet, but she said, "Thank you, Mac. It was so nice of you." She hugged him.

"So, I need to head to the bar. Ice machine is on the blink."

After he left, Camille tried on her nightgown and slippers. The nightgown was roomy enough for a hippopotamus and the heels of her feet hung over the back of the slippers by a good inch. Looking in the mirror she realized she was at the fifty-fifty mark: she could laugh or cry. She decided to laugh and join the millions of wives whose silly husbands—bless their hearts—tried but failed in the gift department.

She made herself a cup of tea and sat quietly at the card table. How she wished for a phone! She wondered what Mac would do if she went behind his back and had it hooked up herself. She'd had a cool phone at home—a pink *Princess Trimline* with push buttons that lit up, perfect for sneaking late-night calls to Rhonda. She missed that silly phone. She sat and sipped her tea. The house was quiet as a cup.

At midnight…a knock on her door. Heart beating, she walked barefoot to answer it, finding Wally in his bathrobe, holding the dog, saying, "Don't worry, nothing serious. Mac just phoned though. A pipe burst at the bar. He'll sleep at Bob's tonight. Didn't want you to worry."

"Wally, he woke you up! I'm demanding we get a phone!"

"I was up. Henry and I were watching a John Wayne movie."

Camille patted the dog's head. "Take Wally to bed, Henry!"

When Camille was seven months along, she asked Sadie if she thought she should call her mother. Sadie, always honest, told her that if she were her mother, she would surely want to know. "What if it's the turning point in your relationship? You never know, cupcake. Either way, you can use our phone. I don't care if it's long distance."

"I will pay you for the call."

"Nonsense." Sadie went off to the kitchen to give her privacy.

Camille dialed and held her breath. When her mother answered, Camille thought she sounded old. It made her sad. "Hi, Mom."

"Hello. Who is this please?"

"Camille."

"Oh."

"How are you, Mom?"

"I'm fabulous. Your father and I are off to Greece soon."

"Greece? That's wonderful. Daddy didn't mention it."

"Daddy doesn't know. It's a surprise for his fiftieth birthday. Don't you dare say a word. Why are you calling? For money, I'm sure."

"Nope, don't need money, Mom."

"You're leaving him. Or, he's leaving you."

"No, Mom, we're fine. Still married."

"State your business please."

"Well, I'm preg—"

"I knew it! I knew you had to get married. I knew it."

"Wrong again, Mom. I was not pregnant when we got married. I'm only seven months along. I've been married for nine months."

"Uh huh."

"I just wanted you to know. Wanted you to hear it from me."

"Ok. I heard it from you. Thanks for calling."

Camille hung up the phone and sat at Sadie's piano. She banged out a poor version of "Fur Elise," her go-to song (she could play it in her sleep). One should not play "Fur Elise" when one is angry.

Camille's water broke on Sunday night, a week before Easter, just before the ten o'clock news. At first she thought she peed her pants—what an odd sensation! But then she remembered what the doctor had explained, and she calmly got a towel from the bathroom and mopped up the floor. She changed her underwear and put on the nightgown Mac had bought her.

There was a plan. When she was ready to go to the hospital, and if Mac was at work, she was to knock on the floor of her bedroom three times with the broom handle. Her bedroom was situated right above Sadie and Wally's. They would hear the signal and Sadie would come upstairs while Wally would call Mac at the bar, then pick him up in the truck (there was still snow on the ground despite it officially being spring and Sadie didn't want Mac riding his bike to the hospital). Sadie would drive Camille to the hospital in the Buick and stay with her until Mac arrived. It had seemed like the perfect plan, but now that everything was coming to a head, Camille started to panic. Where was the broom? How many taps was it again? What if Sadie and Wally slept through her taps? Would they hear a knock at their door? Would she have to put on coat and boots and trudge to the pay phone at the drugstore to tell her husband the baby was coming? Oh, why hadn't she insisted on a telephone? Normal people had telephones!

But the worrying was for nothing. Sadie and Wally heard her signal and came up to her apartment in a jiff. They helped her into her coat and boots, carried her bag, and held her arm as she descended the stairs. In the garage, Sadie said, "Wall, you forgot to call Mac!"

"Should I go back and call him or just go to the bar?"

"Oh, please just go!" Camille said, suddenly stabbed by a pain that couldn't possibly exist in the universe. "Ohhhhhhhhhhh!" she said and steadied herself on the car.

"There, there, cupcake," Sadie said, opening the door to the Buick. "Breathe, cupcake. Breathe!"

"Ohhhhhhhhhhhhhhhhh!" Camille said again. The pain was so overwhelming and frightening that right then and there Camille made a promise to God that if she lived through this ordeal she would go back to church, she would have her baby baptized, and she would send him or her to a Catholic school. She just knew she was going to die!

11.
camille and leo and mackinney

LEO MACKINNEY LENNOX was born on April 11, 1976, at 3:06 a.m. No hippie names for her son; no Marley or Ziggy or Orion. She and Mac had never agreed on any names, but when the nurse placed the eight-pound-two-ounce bundle in her arms, Camille looked at him and said, "Hello, Leo." The name just came to her out of nowhere. She'd never even considered Leo. She didn't think she had ever known a Leo. But Leo he was. Not Leonardo, not Leonard, not Leon, just Leo.

Mac sat in the chair next to her bed and held his son who was all wrapped up like a tamale. Leo made his little noises, squeaking and squawking like a baby bird. Mac got up and paced around the room, bouncing the baby lightly.

"You look like a pro," Camille said. She could barely keep her eyes open. She was bewildered by what she had just gone through—the labor, the delivery, the episiotomy, trying to nurse the baby. The nurse said Leo was having difficulty "latching on" and they'd called in a lactation specialist.

"He's amazing!" Mac said. "Not crazy about the name, though."

"Too bad. I did all the hard work."

"True enough, little darlin', true enough. Was it so terrible?"

"Yes, it was so terrible. But I'm so in love with him, Mac!"

"He's something, isn't he? I think he looks like me. The nurse said so too." He came back and sat down in the chair. Leo protested with a weak squeal. "How does he know I'm sitting?" He rose and began walking again.

Camille said, "I called my dad. He was happy we are all healthy. Mac, I want him baptized."

"Your dad?"

"Mac!"

"Where's this coming from?" Mac said, placing the baby in the bassinet. It was true, Camille hadn't stepped into a church once since they'd been married.

"It's different now. I want him baptized and I'm going back to church."

"Have at it then," he said, retrieving a pack of cigs from his shirt pocket. He tapped one out.

"Mac, you're not smoking in here." He defiantly placed a cigarette between his lips but didn't light it.

"Mac, can I ask you a question?"

"Aye."

"Does your family even know about me?"

"Ridiculous question!" he said, without answering the question.

After Mac went home, Camille had a bout of what the nurse called the postpartum weepies. "Perfectly normal," she said. "Your body has been through a lot and now your hormones need to level out. Plus, you're a young thing. You should have your mama with you."

That only made her cry harder.

Camille wasn't sleeping. Who could sleep with machines beeping and nurses coming in to check you every five minutes? She'd finally dozed off and then at four in the morning, a nurse brought Leo in from the nursery. She thrust him into Camille's arms and barked: "Feed this baby. His wailing is disturbing all the other babies." Camille blinked back tears and tried to nurse Leo, moving him from one breast to the other, trying to remember all the tips the lactation specialist had given, but Leo didn't latch on. "I'm no lactation specialist," the nurse said, "but I think you have inverted nipples."

When Rosie arrived at nine o'clock the next morning, the scene was a rerun of the night before: blubbering mother and hungry baby.

"Rosie!" Camille said. It was as if an angel had appeared, only this angel was pint-sized and brown-eyed like Camille, but chunkier, with darker, curlier hair. What a sight for sore eyes!

Rosie set down her bag and suitcase and leaned in for a hug, embracing both mother and baby. "Let me see him, Cammy! Oh, look at this little guy! He's gorgeous! Look at that head of hair!"

"Rosie, he won't eat. I have weird boobs."

Rose Marie Quinlayne could calm a tornado. Wise beyond her twenty-five years, and always the big sister, she shushed Camille and gently scooped up the baby, who was beet-faced and quite put out. "So, if your boobs don't work, we get the little fella a bottle. No biggie. Where's the nurse?"

And with that, Camille stopped her crying. Rosie was here. Rosie the pocket-sized ball-buster (her father's term of endearment). Rosie pushed the call button for the nurse. When the poor girl arrived, she didn't know what hit her. "Hello, I'm Rose Quinlayne, sister of the patient. This baby needs a bottle of formula. NOW!"

The nurse said, "The chart says she wants to nurse."

"Yeah, well, maybe that's what your chart says, but her boobs aren't cooperating. I'd like to speak to whomever is in charge. Where's the doctor? Who is the head nurse?"

In a matter of minutes, the floor supervisor, the nurse, and the lactation specialist gathered in Camille's room. Rosie held a screeching Leo in her arms, bouncing him, as she excoriated the hospital personnel. "Why isn't this baby being properly cared for?"

"Excuse me? Who are you?" The supervisor asked.

"I'm Rose, Camille's sister and this little peanut's aunt. This baby hasn't eaten properly since he was born. Can't you see he's starving!"

The nurse looked at her supervisor. "She's been trying to nurse."

The lactation specialist said, "She has inverted nipples."

"Please stop talking about my nipples!" Camille blurted out.

The lactation specialist said, "I was going to try a breast pump."

Rosie cut her off. "Listen, I am not a mother, so I don't know anything about this stuff. But if the point of breastfeeding is to nourish your baby and he is not getting nourishment, isn't it time for plan B?"

"Is this what you want, Camille?" the lactation specialist asked, with obvious disappointment in her voice.

"Yes."

"Please bring us a bottle. STAT!" Rosie commanded. How a five-foot-three, one-hundred-fifty pound, twenty-four-year-old woman could make people who out-aged and out-ranked her jump into action was something Camille never understood, but she had witnessed it many times in her life.

By the time Sadie and Wally arrived with a shopping bag full of gifts, Camille was half-asleep and Leo was fed and sleeping peacefully in the arms of his besotted aunt. "I just know you're Rosie!" Sadie whispered upon entering.

"And I just know you're Sadie!" Rosie answered.

"I am! And this is Wally. Oh, look at him, Wall, he's precious! Look at all that hair!"

Camille woke up. She looked around the room and smiled.

"How's our cupcake?" Sadie asked.

"Better now that Rosie's here. I had a hard time nursing, Sadie, so I have to bottle feed him."

"So, what's so wrong with that? I bottle-fed my two boys and they turned out just fine. Believe it or not, we fed them condensed milk and corn syrup!"

"But the books say nursing is better."

"Not if he can't do it," Rosie said. "He'll be fine, won't he Sadie?"

"He'll be more than fine; he will be amazing."

Rosie got up and offered her seat to Sadie and then placed Leo in her arms. "Oh, look at you! Look at you!" Sadie cooed. "He's a little peanut butter cup!"

Camille started to cry and when Rosie asked her what was wrong, she said she wished their mother and father were here too. "And John-O and Peggy, too. It doesn't seem right that the whole family isn't here. And Grandma and Grandpa Quinlayne. Oh, I don't know what's wrong with me. I guess it's the hormones."

The person who wasn't there was Mackinney. Camille looked at the time—it was nearly one o'clock in the afternoon. Last night when he left, he'd kissed her on the head and said, "See you in the morning." She was just about to pick up the phone to call the bar when he appeared. Camille did a double take—he looked disheveled and hung over.

"The man of the hour!" Sadie said as Mac entered.

"Morning," Mac said.

"It's afternoon," Rosie said.

"The famous Rosie! You're here."

"I'm here."

Mac nodded to Sadie and Wally. "How's my son doing?" He peeked at his little face, snuggled up against Sadie's ample bosom and sang a line from the Beatles' song about golden slumbers. Mac looked around the room. Camille could tell he was looking for a place to land—Sadie and Rosie occupied the two chairs and Wally held up the wall—so she patted the bed and told him to come sit. The closer Mac got, the stronger his aroma. Alcohol seeped from his pores.

"Were we celebrating last night?" Camille asked him.

"Everyone at the bar kept buying me drinks and toasting me. Until *I* was toast. Sorry, love, my head feels stuffed with rocks."

"Mackinney," Sadie said, rising. "Come sit and hold your son. Rosie, how about grabbing a cup of coffee with Wall and me?"

When they were alone, Camille told Mac about having to bottle feed the baby, that something was wrong with her breasts.

"Your breasts are quite perfect, thank you very much."

"Don't tease. I feel like a failure."

"Failure? Little darlin', you just performed a miracle!"

At that moment, she never loved Mackinney Lennox more.

Mac pulled an envelope from his shirt pocket. "From Bob," he said. "A bonus."

Camille opened the envelope and found a hundred-dollar bill. "How nice! But why is he giving you a bonus? You're the boss. Don't you hand out the bonuses?"

"I meant baby gift. It's a baby gift."

"How nice! Tell Bob thanks."

Mac kissed Leo softly on his head. "He has my nose, aye?"

"He has my long fingers."

"And your heart-shaped lips. I hope he won't have the Quinlayne feet."

"You're so mean!"

"I love to rile ya up." He rose and passed the baby to her. "But hey, I gotta get going, love."

"But you just got here!"

"Got three mouths to feed now! Trying a new idea at the bar to bring people in. A wet T-shirt contest! We're bringing Spring Break to Southern Wisconsin. The kids are all home from college right now, so we're hoping for a big crowd, aye."

"Mac, that's disgusting!"

"But necessary. Especially now that your udders don't work, and we have to buy formula. I bet that's not cheap."

"Mac, you just compared me to a cow!"

"Now you're being *udderly* ridiculous, love."

"Mac!"

"Don't get all bent out of shape. I was just teasing, aye?"

"My hormones are raging, and I just pushed something the size of a canned ham out of me. I am in no mood for teasing."

Mac laughed. "Okay, okay. I'm outta here. Can I get you anything, love?"

"Yes, a phone. We need a phone."

"Well, if the wet T-shirt contest is a success, I'm sure it will pay for installation of a phone. If that'll make you happy."

"That will make me happy."

Leo—for the most part—took to the bottle, but he was hard to burp and cried after his feedings. The nurse told her, "You got yourself a little fuss budget."

Rosie said, "How dare you!" and the nurse just shrugged.

At last, it was time to go home. Rosie packed up Camille's overnight bag and the nurse demonstrated one last time her no-fail technique of swaddling the baby in the receiving blanket, and then she wheeled mother and baby down to the hospital entrance where Wally was waiting in the warmed-up Buick. Sadie was back at home preparing a welcome home dinner. Mac was at the bar.

Sadie insisted that Rosie cancel her hotel reservation and stay in their guest bedroom for the last three days of her visit. Camille was a bit jealous— the bedroom was beautifully appointed with antique furniture and carpet and draperies. Her bedroom upstairs held a double bed, a pine wardrobe, and pull-down shades. This new desire for nice things was surprising, but Leo had changed everything. Where last week, she was an unmaterialistic free spirit, this week she was a mother who wanted nice things for her baby. This must be latent *nesting* she thought as she helped Rosie unpack her suitcase.

Rosie was uncharacteristically quiet. Camille knew this to mean she was gathering her thoughts; she braced herself for a lecture. She definitely did not need a lecture. It was as if the two sisters read each other's thoughts, for Rosie's pensive facial expression changed, and she said cheerfully, "Why don't I see if Wally will take me to the store after lunch and I will buy you a couple of cases of formula."

"Only if I pay. Bob gave Mac a bonus, I mean a baby gift."

"Camille…"

"Rosie, please don't say anything. I am going to make this work. I *have* to make this work."

Rosie paused at the closet. She closed her eyes and took a breath. "Okay, but I'm a phone call and a plane ride away if you need me."

"He loves me, Rosie. He does. He just has to work so much. That's how it is when you own a business."

"Time for dinner!" Sadie called.

Three days later Wisconsin Telephone Company hooked up the phone in their apartment and Rosie left for D.C. The two events made Camille feel simultaneously connected to the world and abandoned from it. She accompanied Rosie to the airport with Wally, while Sadie stayed back with the baby, or as she was calling him, "my sweet sugar lump" (she'd taken to calling him three-word nicknames, which Camille found herself doing as well). Camille sat in the back and listened as Rosie told Wally about her job and why passing the E.R.A. was so critically important. She talked about how she shared a house with five other women who were all passionate about women's rights and how they dreamed about equal jobs, equal pay, equal opportunities, and equal education. "We need thirty-eight states to ratify the amendment before the deadline of March 22, 1979. Wally, did you know that a married woman can get fired from her job if she gets pregnant? And that most women can't get a credit card unless their husbands co-sign for them? In some states, women can't serve on juries. Women still earn forty-five cents less an hour than a man for the same exact job.

"Discrimination happened in our own home, didn't it, Cammy? Remember how Mom used to make you and me drink powdered milk, but John-O got real milk because he was 'a growing boy'? Remember?"

"Yes, I do."

The last thing Camille heard Rosie say before falling asleep was, "You know, Wally, you can judge a society by how well they treat their women."

At the airport, Rosie hugged Camille goodbye. Between her tears she said, "Thank God you have Sadie and Wally. I don't think I could leave you if you didn't have Sadie and Wally."

But then she didn't have Sadie and Wally. A week after Rosie left, Sadie got word that her sister died. "We'll be gone for a week, cupcake. We have to drive to St. Louis. Wally doesn't fly. It's a long story. But here's what I'm wondering. If you'd be willing to dog sit for Henry the Eighth. You, Mac, and the baby can stay down here in our apartment while we're gone. There's more room and we have the rocking chair and the queen-size bed. Could that work, cupcake?"

"Of course!" Camille said.

But Mac said, "Nothing doing. I want to sleep in my own damn bed, aye?" So, he did. And Camille slept in Sadie's guest room with the baby, who grew fussier and fussier as time went on. "I hate to use the 'C' word, cupcake," Sadie told her before she left for St. Louis, "but I think our little pumpkin-poo-pie has colic. My Peter was colicky and Leo's tummy gets hard as rock, just like Peter's did. And I couldn't get a good burp out of my Petey either."

The week passed like this: Mac slept in as usual and then came downstairs before he went to work. He usually couldn't last even an hour because the baby's crying got on his nerves. More often than not, when he left for work, he left a crying baby and a crying mama. He often returned at three in the morning to a crying baby and a crying mama.

"What's wrong with him?" Mac asked, as he bounced the baby in his arms, pacing around Sadie's living room and dining room.

"Sadie thinks he has colic."

"Take him to the doctor then. The kid is miserable and so are we."

"What a terrible thing to say! I'm not miserable!"

"All ya do is cry."

"That's just the hormones."

"Call the doctor. Maybe there's medicine or something."

"And how will we get there, Mac? On the back of your bike?"

"Wally left me the keys to his truck."

"He did?"

Mac pulled the keys out of his pocket and tossed them to her. She missed and had to lean down and pick them up.

"Let me know what the doctor says," he called as he left, singing that Beatles song about Dr. Robert.

Ironic that the pediatrician Camille had chosen—on Sadie's advice— was named Dr. Robert. "Everything is fine," he said after examining Leo. He had to speak over Leo's screaming. "Looks like a little colic to me. See how his belly is hard and how he arches his back? His tummy hurts. Some doctors treat with phenobarbital or paregoric, but I don't believe in drugging babies, do you?"

"Of course not."

"Let's try a different formula. They make a soy version now. It's expensive so I'll have my nurse give you some samples to try. He'll grow out of it, but in the meantime, it's hard on you. Be sure to sleep when he does. And don't be afraid to have your husband take a shift when this little guy wakes up at night." Dr. Robert handed Leo back to Camille. "At least he's cute or you might be tempted to trade him in."

Camille smiled, but because there was a smidgen of truth to his words, it wasn't really funny. She trudged out of the clinic, carrying a wailing Leo in his infant seat, her diaper bag, and a bag containing four cans of formula. She tripped on her own feet and nearly fell. She righted herself, took a deep breath, and walked carefully the rest of the way to Wally's truck. She seat-belted Leo's carrier in the passenger's seat, facing backward as Sadie had shown her, and because she was feeling sorry for herself, she stopped at McDonald's on the way home and had herself a cheeseburger, fries, and a strawberry shake. Leo screamed the whole time. "I'm sorry your tummy hurts my doodly-doo-bug."

At home, she fed Leo a bottle of the new formula. He drank it up and even burped. Maybe this would help, she thought, crossing her fingers. Finally, Leo fell asleep and the silence was better than a million dollars. Camille took a bath—a luxury since their apartment only had a shower—leaving the door open to listen for Leo. She lay back in the tub and wondered what Stella Maris would do if Camille called and asked for her help. Could she bring herself to do it? She shooed the thought away. If she could just get through the week, things would be better when Sadie and Wally returned.

When the phone rang, she jumped, realizing she had fallen asleep in the tub. Perfect, she thought. She could see the newspaper headline: *Mother of Newborn Drowns in Tub*. She couldn't make it to the phone in time but assumed it was Mac calling to find out what the doctor said. She dried off and put on her humongous pink flannel nightgown, then sat on the sofa and called the bar.

"*Lenny's*," Bob answered.

"Hi Bob, it's Camille. Hey, thank you for the baby gift."

"What baby gift?"

"The hundred dollars."

"Oh, er, you're welcome."

"Can I speak to Mac, please?"

"Uh, er, he's indisposed. I'll have him call you back."

Henry the Eighth jumped up onto her lap and Camille realized she'd forgotten to feed the poor dog! Another headline passed before her eyes: *Sleep-deprived New Mother Starves Landlord's Dog*. As she scooped Henry's food into his bowl, she remembered that she'd forgotten to eat as well. She wasn't really hungry due to her McDonald's lunch, but she knew she should eat something. Sadie had stocked the refrigerator and said she would be angry if she came home and still found it full. Camille warmed up some beef stew and ate it while Henry the Eighth stared at her. She petted him and then added a couple of nice cubes of beef from her stew to his bowl.

When Mac called back, he was steaming mad—someone had slashed the tires on his bike.

"Good grief! Who would do such a thing?"

"I have an idea…"

"Mac! That's very concerning."

"Listen. Ya have two choices: come get me at three o'clock with Wally's truck or I sleep at Bob's."

"Can't Bob drop you off? I don't want to take the baby out that time of night."

"Ya can leave him home for ten minutes."

"Mac, I cannot! And it scares me that you think I would."

"So, I'll just stay here then."

"Fine. Don't you even want to know what the doctor said?"

"Oh, yeah. Uh…That's why I called."

"He's fine but probably has colic."

"Is there medicine?"

"Only opiates. It's controversial. I don't want to drug our baby."

"Well, if it's the only thing that will shut him up…"

"I can't believe you would say such a thing!" Camille hung up without saying anything else. She hated him for saying that. But when Leo woke up and cried for two hours straight, she considered calling the doctor and saying, yes, she did want to drug her baby.

The next day, Bob dropped Mac off about noon. "He's picking me back up at one to take me to get new tires. The good news is I think my insurance covers vandalism one hundred percent with no deductible. Can you fix me a sandwich?" He was cheerful, singing a line from the Beatles song *Here Comes the Sun*. It was as if their awkward conversation the night before had never taken place. He sat waiting for his sandwich, drumming a beat on Sadie's card table.

"Hello baby," he said to Leo, who was sitting quietly in his infant seat. "Hey, did I tell you how well the wet T-shirt contests are going? We're packing 'em in on Friday nights, now. Bob is so pleased!"

"How nice," she said, the sarcasm lost on Mac. "Oh, we're almost out of formula. I wondered if you would run out today or tomorrow before work and get some. Please?"

"Sure, love. Oh wait, no wheels."

"Wally's truck?"

"Oh, right. Give me an empty can so I know what to buy."

Camille hadn't expected that to be so easy. Maybe she was too hard on Mac. Sometimes he surprised her. Like on Sunday, they spent the entire day together. Mac fed Leo, he played guitar and sang for Leo, he bounced him when he had a screaming fit, and he splurged for delivery pizza for dinner. They ate the pizza with cold bottles of beer while the baby slept and Henry the Eighth kept watch for crumbs.

Out of the blue, Mac said, "I thought maybe next weekend I'd take ya and the wee bairn out to meet the folks, aye?"

"Oh, Mac, really?" She loved when he called Leo the *wee bairn*.

"Sure. I'll ask Wally if we can borrow the truck."

"I'd like that."

"Don't be so sure about that. They're not very sociable people."

"But they're your family, so I will love them no matter what."

Mac laughed. "I don't even love them no matter what."

Maybe they were falling into a groove. For the first time in a long time, they slept together in Sadie's guest room.

The next day, Mac woke up with a fever. "Damn, I never get sick," he said. "Better get me a bowl, love, I might lose my cookies." He never did throw up, but the fever held and he ached all over. "Why don't I take meself and me germs upstairs, away from ya and the wee bairn." He took the back stairs, carrying the stainless-steel bowl she had given him. She had to smile; he looked so helpless. She spent the day going up and down checking on him. Mostly he slept, but then he started coughing. A deep, chesty cough.

When she went to feed Leo, she remembered they needed formula. She ran upstairs to tell Mac that she was running to the store for formula and did he need anything. "Seven-up? Maybe some saltines. And cough syrup." He kicked off the blanket. "I go from the chills to the sweats."

"Poor thing. I'll be quick."

Leo wasn't happy about getting strapped into his infant seat. "But I have no other choice, my little root beer float," Camille told him. "I can't leave you home with your sick Daddy and you need food." But Leo didn't listen; he just kept crying.

In the store, Leo continued his yelping and Camille noticed people were staring. She hurried to get what she needed, finding the soda, saltines, and baby formula right away. But when she stopped in the cough and cold aisle, she was confused by the different formulations, so she decided to consult the pharmacist.

"What do you recommend for a bad cough?" Camille asked the young man behind the counter, whose white coat was so big in the shoulders and long in the arms he looked as if he were playing dress-up for career day.

"Adult or child?"

"Adult. My husband."

"Is it a chesty cough or a dry, hacking cough?" he asked.

"I think it's more chesty."

"Is it productive or nonproductive?"

"I don't—"

"Is he spitting up any mucus?"

"I don't know."

"Fever?"

"Yes."

"Any allergies that you know of."

"Sorry, I don't know."

"Is he a customer of ours?"

"I don't know."

"What's his name? I can look him up in our system."

"Mackinney Lennox."

"Mackinney Lennox? Mackie?"

"You know him?"

"*Know* him, he's my drinking bud— Wait, did you say *husband?*"

"Yes." Camille suddenly felt as if illuminated by a spotlight. She looked around to see if there were customers behind her.

The pharmacist looked her up and down and then glared at Leo, who was working his way up to another frenzy. "Mackinney Lennox? The *bartender*, Mackinney Lennox."

"Yes, he owns Lenny's."

The pharmacist laughed. "Sure, he does, Sis. Why don't you just get old Mackie a bottle of Vick's Formula 44 and some Smith Brothers Cough drops. That should do the trick. God forbid if we give him anything with alcohol in it, right?" He snickered. "Aisle twelve, Sis."

Camille felt like she was in grade school and had told the teacher the dog ate her homework: *Sure, he did, Sis.* Her heart started to beat faster as she found aisle twelve and grabbed a bottle of Vick's Formula 44. To heck with cough drops. She quickly walked to the front counter to pay. She couldn't get out of the store fast enough.

After buckling Leo in, she started up the engine and sat motionless behind the wheel to gather her thoughts. She took in a deep breath and closed her eyes. She replayed the conversation. This supposed drinking buddy had no idea that Mac was married. Had no idea that Mac had a baby. He seemed surprised to learn that Mac *owned* Lenny's and his comment about alcohol in the cough medicine implied a drinking problem. Her inner voice said, *"Damn, this could be bad."*

When she got home, Mac was asleep. She set the bottle of cough medicine and a glass of water on the windowsill near the bed and let him be. Downstairs, Henry the Eighth guarded Leo, still asleep in his car seat. He slept so peacefully she almost didn't want to take him out of the seat, but one whiff and she knew he needed changing. Sure enough, he woke up and started his screeching. He settled down after his bottle, and mom and baby had some quality time in Sadie's rocking chair. Sadie and Wally would be home tomorrow afternoon. Sadie would know what to do. A tiny part of her, just a tip of her heart missed her mother. But most of all, she missed Rosie. Rosie was the one she turned to in times of distress.

She looked at Leo's sweet face as he slept in her arms. He was so beautiful, just like his father. She found herself hoping that was where the resemblance ended and then realized it was a terrible thing to hope for. But the information the pharmacist told her earlier lay heavy on her heart. Could it be true? Why would he lie?

The next morning, Camille got up early and cleaned the apartment from top to bottom while the baby slept. She wanted the place to sparkle when Sadie and Wally returned home later that afternoon.

At noon, after putting baby-muffin-cake down for a nap, she climbed the stairs to check on Mac. He was still asleep, but the cap was off the bottle of cough syrup and the water glass was empty so at least he'd taken the medicine. She let him sleep.

Hearing Sadie's voice later that day—"Yoo-hoo! We're back!"—was music to Camille's ears. With Leo in her arms she greeted Sadie and Wally at the door, hugging them both. Sadie took the baby and covered him with kisses. "Look how he's grown in just a week! Oh, my little biscuit 'n' gravy. I missed you!"

"Was the funeral okay?"

"It was fine. Full of family drama though. My sister didn't have much, but her daughters-in-law were vultures. They'll never forgive me—she left me our grandmother's engagement ring. Look." She held out her right hand to show the vintage diamond ring in all its glory.

"It's humongous!" Camille said, leaning in for a closer look.

Wally said, "I told her to let them have it. I didn't want any trouble."

"But I told him my sister wanted me to have it."

"Ahh," Wally said, waving his hand. "Much ado about nothing."

Sadie asked how Mac was.

"He's upstairs. Been sick with the flu for a couple of days."

"Oh dear, I hope you've been keeping the baby away from him."

"Oh yes. We've been down here the whole week. Thank you for letting us. Leo slept well in the cradle."

"Wally will take it upstairs for you later. With Mac sick, you two should stay down here another night or two."

"Thank you, Sadie. Let's see how he feels." Secretly, she wanted to stay downstairs forever. She didn't want to face Mac and find out the answers to her questions. Even though her heart already knew the answers.

12.
mackinney

SOME MEN ARE masters of their own misfortune. Mac's fourth wife once said that he had a master's degree in "useless," but his first, second, and third wives—for a good while anyway—believed him to be a workaholic entrepreneur.

The truth was Mackinney Lennox peaked in high school. Attribute it to his striking good looks, endearing Scottish accent, and his fetching physique. He sailed through with passing grades and unfettered popularity. He was the guy everyone aspired to be or longed to date. Go ahead and call him a "dumb jock," what did he care, because he'd turn around and surprise everyone by landing the lead in the school musical, confounding everyone who tried to label and typecast him.

Mackinney was not dumb—but he didn't apply himself, nor was he encouraged to excel in academics by his immigrant parents. Mac's father, Donald Lennox, was a butcher; his mother, a cashier at the Piggly Wiggly. Mac's two older brothers got in with the wrong crowd early on and dabbled in gambling, dealing pot, and check kiting. Both moved out of the house when Mac was still in high school, their whereabouts unknown until they resurfaced needing money for one thing or the other.

The downward spiral for the Lennox family began with the death of their eldest son Ewan. Ewan was best friends with Bob Paulson, who owned Lenny's. On the night before the two boys were to report to duty for Vietnam, a sleep-deprived truck driver crashed head-on into the car that Bob Paulson was driving. Ewan, in the passenger seat, died instantly. Bob sustained serious injuries including losing the sight in his right eye. Bob was not at fault (thankfully they were *on their way* to getting stinking drunk rather than *returning from* getting stinking drunk or else Bob's ass would be in jail); still, the survivor guilt ate him up. It was guilt that compelled Bob to hire Mackinney when he came looking for a job a few years after the accident. That and the fact that Mac's mother had completely fallen apart after her favorite son's death. She couldn't get out of bed for months and then only to drink her breakfast, lunch, and dinner. In his own grief, Donald Lennox inadvertently cut off his thumb and index finger with a meat cleaver which brought an end to his butchering career. Soon Donald and Elspeth were both diabetic alcoholics living on government disability benefits. It was the least Bob could do, to give his friend's younger brother a job. Mac had no bar experience so Bob wasn't expecting much. But Mac surprised him. He was a quick learner and the customers adored him.

"*Lenny's*" Mac said, answering the phone on a busy Saturday afternoon. Three customers had just bellied-up to the bar and he was about to take their orders.

"Is that guy here yet? The plasterer?" his boss, Bob, calling from the upstairs apartment, asked.

"Not yet."

"I'll be down in five."

Bob Paulson, lucky stiff, had inherited *Lenny's* from his uncle, Leonard (Lenny) Paulson, in 1971, when Leonard suffered a massive heart attack, and, having no children of his own, left the building and the bar to his one and only nephew. Uncle Lenny felt sorry for the kid, what with the accident and all and being blind in one eye. Bob was a skinny, homely, diffident, unmarried guy whose mild manner was a facade—inside he was a bundle of nerves.

Nobody in his family thought Bob had a chance of keeping the bar afloat. His own father chided that he should rename the bar "One-Eye Tap," but Bob kept the name *Lenny's* out of respect to his uncle. And it turned out he had a good head for business. In 1972, when the state of Wisconsin lowered the age of majority from twenty-one to eighteen, Bob saw the opportunity to transform *Lenny's* from a neighborhood tavern filled with old-man Packer fans and political pundits to a hip watering hole for thirsty eighteen-, nineteen-, and twenty-year-olds. But he didn't have the charm and charisma needed to transform the bar into a cool hangout. That's where he hoped Mackinney Lennox could help. And help he did.

Mac had watched now for three years as customers patted Bob on the back and congratulated him for the great success of the bar, but the acclaim was misplaced. He knew the truth—and so did Bob—that the bar was successful because of *him*. Without his creative and money-making promotional ideas, without his good looks and charm, without his musical talents, they wouldn't be packing them in Monday through Saturday. It was Mac who had come up with a theme for each night of the week: Monday was *Monday Night Football Night*; Tuesday was *Quarter Beer Night*; Wednesday was *Ladies' Night*; Thursday was *Crazy Contest Night*; Friday was *Date Night*; and Saturday was *Harvey Wallbanger Night*. It was Mac who came up with the fun contests for Thursday nights: the *"Fishbowl" Beer Contest*, the *Wet T-Shirt Contest*, the *Drinks for Card Tricks Game*, *Name that Tune*, *Arm-Wrestling Match*. It was Mac's idea to sell punch cards—ten punches got you a free beer. And it was Mac who boosted the bar menu from cheap, salty fare like peanuts, pretzels, and popcorn (provided to increase thirst) to beer sausage, cheese curds, Slim Jims, pickled eggs, and hot spicy weenies (provided to increase thirst *and* soak up alcohol). Mac knew everyone's name and favorite drink. Mac made the homely girls feel beautiful and the wimpy guys feel worth their weight. He brought in live music on weekends and he would play his guitar and sing sometimes on Friday Night Date Nights.

By the time Bob came down the plasterer had arrived and the two went off to the kitchen to haggle about repairing the ceiling that had been damaged by a burst pipe. Mac was in his element, on a roll—filling chilled mugs with draft beer, pouring some girls their favorite Carlo Rossi Rhine wine on the rocks, and mixing a *Fuzzy Navel* for a little blond cutie he knew for a fact was underage.

At nine o'clock, the place was mobbed, and Mac realized he hadn't eaten anything all day. Camille offered to fix him eggs for lunch, but he had passed—her eggs were always slimy and unseasoned. His stomach was still a bit "iffy" after a bout of the flu. He grabbed a Slim Jim, unwrapped it, and placed it between his lips like a cigar, biting off bits as he worked. A dumb choice for an empty stomach, but portable.

He was both starving and dead on his feet. Turns out, his baby was a screamer. Something he never expected, although somewhere in the back of his mind, he remembered his mother complaining about him being colicky when he was a wee bairn. He didn't share that information with Camille though—he didn't want her blaming Leo's gastrointestinal issues on his genes. (Surely if the day came when she actually *met* his parents, she would have great concerns about his genes.) To make matters worse, he'd woken up with a huge zit on his forehead, right smack dab in the middle. He'd tried to squeeze it and ended up making it worse. Now it was red and swollen. He feared he looked like Cyclops.

When the plasterer left, Bob joined him behind the bar. He was in a foul mood, complaining about the cost of the ceiling repair. He helped Mac behind the bar, mixing up the night's drink special, *Harvey Wallbangers*. Mac could mix them in his sleep: three parts vodka, six parts orange juice, one-part Galliano, garnish with lemon. In the 70's, drinking was just an accompaniment to the night out, not the main attraction. These kids didn't care about how their drinks tasted—cheap beer, watered down whiskey, it was all the same going down.

Lenny's was like any other dive bar in Wisconsin—walls and ceilings paneled with dark wood, a big oak wrap-around bar edged with hunter green-colored vinyl bumpers, hardwood floors that had gone wavy over the years from heavy shoe trafficking. The floor was always sticky despite getting a good mop every night. The lighting was terrible, which made the women appear hotter. You had your pool table and your dartboard, pictures of past patrons (nobody famous) thumbtacked to the wall, tchotchkes on the shelves above the bar, and the dance floor.

Above the bar, five deer heads looked down on customers—Uncle Lenny had been a hunter. Now some jerk customer sitting at the bar was trying to "ring" one of the heads with his still-looped necktie. He kept missing. Each time, Mac picked up the tie and tossed it back to him. The guy tried a couple more times until Bob blurted, "Cut it out!" See? That's where they were different. Mac would have let the guy have his fun. What was the harm? Sometimes—often—Bob cramped his style. And his tips.

Three parts vodka, six parts orange juice, one-part Galliano, garnish with lemon. Repeat.

Two hot young blondes took seats at the bar. Mac had never seen them before. They looked like many of the girls that frequented the bar: low cut tops, Farrah Fawcett hairdos, blue eyeshadow. It made him think how gorgeous Camille was—she needed no makeup to enhance her appearance. But she just wasn't *stylish*, like these young ladies were. She wasn't…well sexy. She used to be sexy, but ever since the baby, she seemed matronly and older. It was no secret: Mackinney Lenox liked his women young.

And these two sitting in front of him were definitely young. Since Bob was around, he would have to card them, but he knew they weren't yet eighteen. After a while, you could just tell.

"Need to see some IDs, lassies," Mac said.

"Oh, my gawd," said one of the girls, "I love your accent!"

Mac smiled. "IDs please, loves."

The girls retrieved their terribly fake IDs from their purses and flashed them in front of Mac. He told them it was Harvey Wallbanger night. They ordered two, drank them, and then took to the dance floor. Mac got busy with other customers and forgot about the girls until it was closing time. One of the girls had left with some guy and Bob found the other with her head down on a table. "Mac, take care of her, will ya?" Bob said. "I'm heading up,"

"Thanks a lot," Mac said.

Bob saluted him and headed for the back steps.

"Miss, Miss," Mac said, gently shaking the girl's shoulder. "Come on, love, wake up."

The girl lifted her head. She'd been crying and her mascara had smudged. "She ditched me again!" she told Mac. "She's supposed to be my best friend and yet she does this all the time."

"Can I call someone for ya, love? You didn't drive here, did ya?"

"No, I came with Renee."

"Let me call someone for ya. A friend? A cab? Your parents?"

"Very funny," she said, dropping her head onto the table again.

"Listen, love, it's after three. We're closed and ya have to go. Either ya tell me who to call or I call the police. How about a cab?"

She started to cry. "Please don't call the police. I'm not eight— Listen, can't I stay at your place? Or here, can't I just stay here for the night? Renee told me you have a room with a bed behind the bar."

"Oh, she did, did she? Where do you live, love?"

"On Broad Street, but I can't go home. I'm supposed to be sleeping at Renee's and I can't go to Renee's because she's supposed to be sleeping at my house."

"Hate to tell ya, love, but I'm dropping ya home. Make up a story to tell the folks on the way."

After Mac dropped her off and made sure she got in okay, he headed for home. He knew the night could have ended differently, *had* ended differently many times. How easy it would have been just to lead the young, beautiful but dumb girl to the room behind the bar, just as he had led Camille and dozens upon dozens of others before her. He hated to admit it, but not spending the night with the girl had more to do with being too damn exhausted than it did being faithful to Camille. In fact, he had *not* been faithful to Camille. No one in his world knew that he was married except Bob. Mac always took off his wedding ring before he went to work, telling Camille that it got in his way when he was grabbing bar glasses and mixing drinks, in addition to messing up his guitar-playing. Why? Why did Mac hide his marriage and his son from the world? He had no good answer for that. He loved Camille, and he loved the *idea* of his son, but the little screamer was a little hard to love. When the colic ended maybe it would be a different story, but the howling shredded his nerves. He couldn't describe it. Anyway, he was pleased with himself. Pleased that he hadn't taken an underage drunk girl to bed. Maybe he was growing up. Maybe he was finally taking responsibility for his life. Maybe, but maybe not.

When he got home, he found Camille pacing the apartment with the little screamer and immediately wished he had spent the night at the bar, with or without the girl.

"It's a different cry," Camille said. "I think he has a fever. Feel his forehead."

Mac lay his hand on Leo's forehead. "He's quite cool, Camille. Listen, I've got to get some sleep, or I am going to fall over, aye?" She couldn't expect him to walk the baby, could she? He just worked twelve straight hours. She could nap when the baby napped. She could get Sadie to help her. Even when he wore earplugs to bed, he could hear the crying. He wondered how Sadie and Wally put up with it.

"But Mac, I need to talk to you. It's important."

"If it's so important, love, it better wait till tomorrow. I have nothing left to give. Plus, I feel like puking." (He made that part up.)

The next morning, Mac woke up earlier than usual. A terrible thing had happened: the pimple on his forehead had doubled in size while he slept. It felt hot to the touch, sensitive, and painful. When he looked at himself in the bathroom mirror, he recoiled. "Camille!"

Camille joined him in the bathroom. "What's wrong?"

He gestured with his hand toward his forehead.

"Oooo. Owww."

"What the hell, aye?"

"Did you squeeze it?"

"I didn't touch it."

Camille stood on her tiptoes to get a better look. "Maybe it's a boil. Or skin cancer."

"That was mean!"

Camille shrugged. "I'm feeling a bit mean this morning."

"Well, I can't go to work like this."

"What do you mean?"

"I can't be seen like this, aye?"

"It's not a big deal. Who are you trying to impress anyway?"

"My customers, aye?"

"Good grief. You're vainer than a woman. Come on, I'll make you some eggs and toast. I really need to talk to you."

Mac ate some slimy eggs, and then listened while Camille talked about one of her piano students whose father was selling a nice, used car for cheap. Hint. Hint. He ignored her and picked at his eggs. When he could tune her out no more, he pushed away his plate and said he needed to get to the bar early today. He stood and kissed his son on the head. He could tell by the look on Camille's face that she was hoping he'd stick around, hold the baby, and be all Norman Rockwell.

"Before you go," Camille said, "I need to ask you something."

"What is it, love?"

"When I went to the drugstore when you were sick…the pharmacist knew you."

"Who? What's his name?"

"I don't know. But he was extremely surprised to hear you were married and had a kid. Said you were his drinking buddy. Insinuated that you didn't own the bar? And alluded to a drinking problem…"

"Camille, I dunna know any pharmacists and I dunna *drink* with any pharmacists. Why were you discussing me in the first place?"

"He was trying to figure out if you had any allergies."

Mac ran his hand through his hair. *Kevin Orrie*, the asshole. "Oh, wait. I know who ya are talking about. Really tall? Blonde hair? Pockmarked face."

"He was tall—"

"I haven't seen that guy in years. I drank with him a couple of times. That was before I bought the bar from Bob. He's a *bawbag*."

"I didn't know you bought the bar from Bob."

Mac shrugged. "Yeah, he was running it to the ground. Is that it? Are we good?"

Camille said, "I guess, I just—"

"Okay, good." And off he went.

Once outside, Mac wondered if Camille believed him about the bar and about Kevin Orrie. What did it matter? If she found out he didn't own the bar, what would she do, leave him? Where would she go? Mac started up his Harley. He thought about Leo. The baby was really getting on his nerves—not the baby, who was really quite lovely—but his crying. Sadie said colic usually resolved by three months, but a guy could go berserk in the meantime. There was affection there, but if he was honest, it wasn't as strong as he thought it would be. Leo was…a wrench in the plan. He never realized how expensive a baby could be, what with the medical bills and special formula.

He kept the fact from Camille, but they were strapped. He'd insinuated that there was money in the bank—CDs he'd told her. There was no money; there was just the opposite, there was debt. He owed people. He was paying off a gambling debt that he'd racked up when he played poker with some old dudes at the bar. And he was still paying off his bike. Yeah, he told Camille he owned the bar because, well, he was trying to impress her, and he got carried away. Hell, he *should* own the bar. But Bob denied him even the title of assistant manager and paid Mac just a smidgen above minimum wage. (Justification for Mac appropriating a few bucks from the cash register every now and then.) Dashed were his hopes of saving enough money to buy his own bar. Hell, he was three months late with rent money. He avoided Wally like the plague, but he knew Wally and Sadie would never evict them; they loved Camille and Leo too much.

The warm air felt good against his skin as he cruised through town. Blue skies above him, it felt so good to be moving and free and out of doors. So good, in fact, that when he should have made a right on Broad Street, he just kept going and somehow ended up on some back roads. The roar of his engine, the velocity, the piercing wind—it was just what he needed to clear his head. Figure out how he'd ended up here, with a wife and a kid and hunted by creditors.

What was he thinking all those months ago? He'd never fallen so hard for a girl, and Camille was just that, a girl. She was lovely, yes, and sweet, and her body…well her body used to be darn right irresistible. She was like an unwrapped present. But the baby changed everything. Not true, actually.

Things had changed before that. What had made him think he could be monogamous? There'd been no history of monogamy. But he was twenty-nine when he met Camille, not getting any younger, and the thought of settling down with a good woman was appealing. Maybe he just wanted a family. Guess he'd forgotten: families were complicated.

He kept driving north until he ended up in his hometown, Janesville, Wisconsin, and zigzagged through neighborhoods that had seen better days. Houses with faded siding and roofs missing shingles, rusted-out cars in the driveways. Without intending to—at least consciously—he found himself on his parents' street. He hadn't been home in three years, not for a holiday, not for a visit. As far as he knew, his parents didn't know if he were dead or alive. Come to think of it, he didn't know if his parents were dead or alive. He pulled up in front of the drab green bungalow. The paint was chipped in so many places the house looked like camouflage. The front porch sagged; the wrought iron railing angled to the left. Home sweet home. Mac cut the engine and swung his leg around. He paused. Did he really want to do this?

After a wee while, his father answered the door. He looked a million years old. His hair was yellow-gray, his face prickled with patchy whiskers, his belly protruded audaciously under a dingy T-shirt. "Good god almighty," Donald Lennox said. "Am I seeing a ghost?"

"I'm no ghost, Da."

"If you're looking for money, ya come to the wrong place, eh?"

"I'm not looking for money…I just thought… is Mom here?"

"She's here. Where the hell else would she be?" Donald stood at the door and waited for Mac to ask if he could come in.

"May I?"

"If ya must."

"Who is it, Don?" Mac's mother called from the living room. Mac would bet a trillion dollars he would find his mother just as he had left her three years ago—lying on the couch. After his brother died, she suffered from extreme vertigo. Of course, the alcohol didn't help the condition one bit.

"Yer long-lost son."

"Which one?"

"The pretty one. 'Cept I wouldn't call him pretty at the moment. What the hell is wrong with yer forehead, eh?"

"Mackie? Is it really Mackie?"

And there she was on the couch. The scene frozen in time. His mother, dressed in what she called a *duster*, a casual, boxy, serviceable dress that snapped up the front. It was her signature "at-home" article of clothing that had embarrassed Mackinney to no end when he was young. Her hair was grayer, and she was thin and patchy. She sat up slowly and began to cry. "My baby!" She held her arms out.

Mac leaned in to hug her. She smelled sour. A rush of memories overcame him. There had been good times in the early days. His Dad had a good job with benefits. The three boys played baseball and were boy scouts. They went to church on Sundays and had neighbors over for cookouts. Once, they looked like a normal family. But they were never a normal family. They had secrets. Mac wondered for the millionth time if there would ever be a day of reckoning.

His mom patted the cushion on the couch. "Sit down. Let me look at you. You look wonderful!"

"Looks like Cyclops," Donald said, plopping down in his recliner. Mac noticed three beer cans on his TV tray. It wasn't even noon.

"Don, get him a soda. Would ya like a crème soda, honey?"

"No, no. I'm fine. Don't fuss, aye? I just came to see how ya were doing."

"Seems strange that ya'd start caring now," Donald said. "Ya must be after something."

"Da, I am not after anything. I just thought ya should know that, well, I'm married, and I have a wee bairn."

Elspeth clapped her hands. "Glory be! Married! And a wee one! A boy or a girl?"

"A boy. His name is Leo."

"Leo?" Donald said. "What kind of name is that?"

"His mother named him."

"Oh Mackie, tell me about your wife."

"Her name is Camille."

"And…?"

"And she's good, Ma. She's nice."

Elspeth looked confused. "Do you have any pictures?"

He shook his head. "No, no pictures."

"Might you bring them round for us to meet sometime? Or, are you too ashamed of us, Mackie?"

He looked around the room. The house wasn't dirty, but it was shabby. The drawn tattered window shades blocked the light, leaving the room the color of dusk, and the air was warm and thick. Now the walls were closing in and Mac felt as if he were breathing underwater. He shouldn't have come. He stood up and said he had to get to the bar.

"You're still at Lenny's then?" his dad asked.

"Yes."

"Hard to believe."

What was hard to believe was that he'd been so stupid. Why in God's name had he stopped? He closed the door behind him, knowing it would be the last time he would come back. To hell with them. They weren't fit to be parents. Pretending as if nothing had ever happened. Sweeping it all under the rug. "Oh, Mackie, I'm sure you're mistaken. It's all in your imagination," his mother had said when he came to her. She refused to believe that her precious brother, the star child in the family, the first to come to America, would do that to her son. Mackinney was only seven at the time. Surely, he didn't understand things like that. But it didn't just happen once, and it didn't just happen to him. When he approached his older brothers, asking if Uncle Stewart ever…er, touched them…the blood had drained from Ewan's face and Brody had run off in tears. Mac had nightmares about Uncle Stewart. He even dreamed about killing him. He would wake from the dreams with his heart racing, his body drenched in sweat. He found ways to bury the shame—sports helped, and music, a guitar for Christmas one year, and then the musicals at school. Keep busy. Keep moving. Then later there was pot— that quieted the voices. But truth be told, the best way to combat the shame of being molested by your uncle as a child was to have sex, lots of sex, with women, as many women as possible.

His bike had a mind of its own today. He drove past his grade school and his high school. Old girlfriends' homes. His Uncle Stewart's house. Stewart didn't live there anymore—he'd died years ago. But this didn't stop Mac from getting off his bike and picking up a rock and throwing it at the abandoned house. He aimed for the picture window, but the rock bounced off the faded aluminum siding. The clunking sound it made was satisfying, but only for a couple of seconds.

Now Mac was more revved up than his bike. He recognized this feeling, this state of being. This is where he intentionally screwed things up when they were getting too heavy, too serious. This wasn't what he wanted in life, to be weighed down by a wife and kid. He wanted his own bar, to run his own way. He wanted to sing in a band. But what he wanted most was a different woman every night to wipe away the damage of Uncle Stewart.

Hell, right now what he wanted most was Gerianne Parks.

Mackinney looked at his watch. *Boaby!* It was after three in the afternoon! Bob would be having a conniption. Good thing he'd never given Bob his phone number or surely he'd have called Camille looking for him. He'd never been late to work before. He leaned over to kiss Gerianne. She lay naked on top of the sheets. No, her body wasn't what it used to be—she was the same age as he was, but she was still good. With some women, and Camille was one of them, you did all the work. But with other women, and Gerianne was one of them, it was an interactive thing. She blew him away. Just what he needed.

"Stay," Gerianne said, stroking his cheek.

"I'm late for work. Gotta go."

"One more time?"

How could he resist?

When Mac walked into the bar two hours late, Bob said, "Well?" There were two customers at the bar—regulars who drank their dinner Mondays through Saturdays. They usually hightailed it out of there before the young kids descended on the place.

"My bike wouldn't start. Spark plugs."

"Get a phone, would you? So, you can call your boss."

"Sorry, Bob. Really. Come on, I've never been late once in all these years."

"Don't let it happen again."

"Or what?"

"Or I'll fire your ass."

"Fire me? I've MADE this place, and ya know it, aye? You might as well change the sign to "Mackie's." Most people come for me Scottish charm, me music, me marketing ideas. Ya were close to running it into the ground. I saved ya, so shut the hell up, why don't ya."

Bob stared at Mackinney. "What the hell happened to your face and neck?"

Mac put his hand to his forehead. "I know, the worst zit I ever had. Like a third eye, aye?"

"Does your wife know about the hickies?"

"Hickies?" Mackinney hurried off to the men's room to have a look in the mirror. Sure enough, three dark-colored marks lined the right side of his neck. "Damn Gerianne!" he said out loud.

Mackinney called out to Bob. "I'll be back in a minute." He jogged a block up to the drugstore and bought a tube of what the clerk at the makeup counter called "concealer." She smiled a knowing smile.

Back in the men's room at the bar, Mackinney applied the concealer to the marks on his neck, and what the heck, he gobbed some on the zit too. He stared at himself in the mirror. He had never looked worse. He had bedhead and bags under his eyes, and even though the hickies were concealed, the zit now looked like a zit with makeup on it. He looked ridiculous. What a day!

As he trudged off to his place behind the bar, under Bob's evil eye, he thought about how things were only going to get worse. The rent was due in a week and Mac had blown the rent money on hotel rooms (in addition to Gerianne, there was Lisa and Kate and Carol and Sheila and Lynn and Celeste and Pauline and Heather and DeeDee; mostly there was DeeDee) and lottery tickets (he just knew he would hit it big one of these days) and new tires for the bike since Lisa or Kate or Carol or Sheila or Lynn or Celeste or Pauline or Heather or DeeDee slashed them, and drugs (speed—how else could one endure twelve-hour work days?). If Bob knew that the bar had become a choice hub for drug deals, he'd strangle Mac with his bare hands. Death by strangulation might be the best option at this point. He certainly deserved it.

Speak of the devil, a little after eleven o'clock that night, DeeDee Cambridge came in and took a seat on a stool at the corner of the bar. DeeDee was one of Mac's girls. That's how he thought about the women he slept with—they were his girls. DeeDee was twenty-one and worked as a hairdresser at a shop up the street. She wasn't really his type in that she wasn't an absolute knockout, but she was a natural redhead, cute and willing, and somewhat of a hero-worshipper. She once told Mac that he was absolutely the most handsome man she had ever seen in her life, bar none. She lit up a cigarette. He finished pouring some wine for a customer and came across the bar.

"Hello, little darlin'. You look ravishing tonight."

"I look like shit, Mac. I have to talk to you. It's important."

On closer inspection, Mac could see that she had been crying.

"Can we go in the backroom?"

"I can't leave my post, love. I've already ticked Bob off, aye."

She motioned for him to come closer, then whispered, "I'm pregnant."

He pulled back. "No way. No possible way."

"Yes way. And there's only been you."

Mac ran his hand through his hair. "*Boaby*, love, I thought you were on the pill," he whispered.

"I am!"

"Maybe it's a false alarm."

"I did a test."

"But love, I'm…I'm married; I have a baby."

DeeDee's whisper modulated to a screech: "YOU'RE MARRIED AND YOU HAVE A BABY?!"

Everyone in the bar turned to look at them. The crowd mumbled and the news spread. *He's married? No! He doesn't act married. I've never seen a wife. I've never even seen a ring. And a baby? Mackinney Lennox cannot have a baby—he IS a baby.*

Bob came over and shook his head. "Take this into the backroom, will ya please?"

DeeDee sat on the couch in the backroom and wiped her eyes with a tissue. Mac paced. "I'll take care of this," he told her.

"What does that even mean?"

"I dunno. I need time to think. Go home. I'll call ya tomorrow."

"I'm keeping this baby, Mac."

"Course ya are, love."

At two a.m., Mac phoned Camille and told her he had a splitting headache and that he didn't trust himself to drive. He was just going to sleep on the couch at the bar. He heard Leo screaming bloody murder in the background. A normal husband would feel guilty. Mackinney wasn't a normal husband.

He lay on the couch in the backroom saturated in his own self-loathing. This is how things went with him. There was a definite pattern. He would vow to live a better, cleaner, more decent life, making promises and resolutions, and he would make some progress. But he would always find a way to sabotage anything good. It was his thing. With Camille, this was the closest he'd come to a normal life. But now everything had turned to shit: his job, his finances, and now DeeDee. If he were a praying man he'd pray for a miracle. He knew what he'd have to do—he'd have to beat it out of town. What other choice did he have? He couldn't provide for one child, let alone two. Camille and the baby would be better off without him. She had family…well, she had her sister. She would be fine. He'd have to wait until Friday when he got his paycheck and then he would get on his bike and just drive.

He woke up at ten in the morning with a backache, his forehead throbbing. He went to the bathroom to pee and then looked at himself in the mirror. Ugly reflected back. He couldn't help himself—he took his thumbs and squeezed the zit. Pus splattered the mirror. He wet some toilet paper and cleaned the mirror, then moistened another few squares and held them to his forehead. How could it hurt so much? Maybe it was infected. Maybe it wasn't a zit, but it was some kind of cyst. Maybe the abscess would spread to his brain and he could mercifully die. He found a box of bandages in the cabinet and applied two in a crisscross fashion. Maybe he could say he had a mole removed.

He went back and lay on the couch with every intention of sleeping until two, but—maybe he was partly human after all?—he experienced a brief pang of guilt. Poor Camille. She was a nice kid. He never meant to hurt her. He decided to go home for a while. Spend some time with her and the baby. In two days, he'd be out of their lives forever. He'd always wanted to live in a warmer climate, and he'd heard that places like Nashville and Austin were booming. Surely a bartender with a charming accent would be a novelty in the south? A plan was developing…he would need to sell his Beatles albums and memorabilia. He knew the value hadn't increased that much since the band broke up in 1970—the plan was to hold on to them for years in hopes their value would increase enough to buy a bar—but he'd have to get what he could. He'd ask Wally if he could borrow the truck tomorrow and haul the boxes over to the pawn shop. He'd tell Wally he needed to sell the stuff to pay him the rent money. He ripped the band aids from his forehead and headed home.

Mac was surprised and relieved to find a calm and quiet mother and baby sitting on the couch. Camille looked bright-eyed and cheerful—she was dressed and looked lovely in her jeans and pretty blue top. And Leo smiled at him when he approached. "Come to Papa, wee one?" Mac said, taking the baby from Camille.

"Mac, your forehead is worse! You squeezed it, didn't you?"

"I had to! The pressure was unbearable! Hence, the headache." He sat down and faced Leo to him and bounced him a bit. "His hair is getting curlier."

"He's been so good this morning." Camille smiled. "Keeping my fingers crossed. You hungry?"

"I could eat, aye."

Sitting at the card table in the kitchen, Mac felt another pang of guilt. A card table. Imagine. He couldn't even provide his wife with a proper kitchen table and yet she didn't complain. For a fact, Camille never complained. She was a stout-hearted girl. She served him some slightly burnt French Toast. Mac handed her the baby so he could eat.

Camille sat down and said, "Sadie said when Leo starts on solids his tummy may settle down. I hope so."

Mackinney nodded and smiled. He looked around at the domestic scene, Norman Rockwell, Father Knows Best. He was the one wrong thing in the picture. But…what if he was being too rash in his decision to bolt? What if things could get better? If the baby stopped wailing and Camille was sexy again and if he could get his finances back in order—maybe he could trade in his bike for that used car—maybe he could stay? But what about DeeDee? Could Camille forgive him for DeeDee? If there was ever a woman with a heart big enough to do it, it would be Camille. There had to be a way to figure this out.

Leo needed to be changed so Camille took him, cleaned him up, and put him down for his nap. Mackinney rinsed his plate in the sink. Camille came up from behind and wrapped her arms around his waist. It was a rare moment. She took his hand and led him to their bedroom. It had been a while. Long enough that all of Mac's original desire for Camille welled back up. This was the Camille he remembered—her perfect breasts, her long pretty fingers, the curve of her neck, her lips.

Afterward, he lay spent. He spooned his wife and felt like crying. What would Camille think if she knew all his secrets?

Camille turned to face him. "Mac, I know it's been hard since the baby, but I promise, things are going to get better. I know I've been a wreck. Crying all the time. I woke up feeling so good today. Maybe my hormones have leveled off. I've got a doctor's appointment tomorrow. I'll— Hey, what's on your neck? Zits? No—"

"What?" Mac slapped his hand to his neck. So consumed with vanity about his face, he'd forgotten all about the hickies.

"Mac! Are those love bites?"

"I gotta pee, love. Be right back."

In the bathroom, Mac searched in the medicine cabinet for makeup, but Camille didn't wear makeup so of course he found nothing to hide his sins. Camille walked in.

"How could you? You didn't sleep at the bar last night, did you?"

"No, I did. Honestly!"

Camille scowled and folded her arms. "Explain yourself."

"I didn't want to alarm ya, love, but Bob and I got in a fight. He was late for work again and I just can't have that, aye? I threatened to fire him, and he came at me. I thought he was going to strangle me!" He looked into Camille's eyes. Would she buy it?

"What? That's awful!" she said. "Good grief! I didn't know Bob had such a temper."

"If you only knew what I've been through."

"Did you fire him?"

"Hell yes, I fired him. The bad news, love, is I'll be working night and day until I can hire a replacement. You'll have to be patient."

"Mac. Please. You've been gone night and day as it is. I can manage. But I do need you to watch Leo Thursday at nine o'clock. I have my doctor's appointment and Sadie and Wally are spending a few days at their son's house, so they won't be around. They took the bus, so they left the car and the truck for us. Wasn't that sweet?"

"Yes. Okay. No problem, love. Just remind me, okay? I'm going to get going."

"Okay. Good luck!"

"What for?"

"For finding a new bartender!"

"Oh, right."

13.
camille & rosie & leo

THE BEST PART of the day—she would admit this to no one—was when her little salt-water taffy napped. Camille knew this was a terrible thing for a new mother to say. But when Leo napped, she napped. Leo was getting better, but he was still a fussbudget.

There were hints of a happy, contented baby. For about an hour in the afternoon, after his nap and feeding, he was happy—smiling and cooing, wiggling and waggling, finding his hands. He started to gain weight and his chubby arms and thighs were irresistible. Camille loved him so much. She couldn't wait for her dad to meet him. He was planning to sneak up to Beloit next month when Stella Maris was set to attend an Avon convention.

Her dad had surprised her with a gift shortly after Leo was born—a camera and twelve rolls of film so she could capture each month of his first precious years. "Have double prints developed, honey, a set for me," the card said. Cash was included for developing fees. She waited for Leo's happy moments to snap his picture. She wanted to capture only the wonderful pictures of his babyhood. Once when Leo was in an especially good mood, she asked Mac to snap a picture of the two of them—mommy and baby.

After finishing up the afternoon's piano lesson, Camille put Leo in the stroller and walked over to the drugstore to pick up her latest set of photographs. It was mid-August hot, and she arrived with beads of sweat on her forehead. The air-conditioned store felt glorious and she roamed the aisles just to cool down. Who should she run into in the oral-hygiene section but good old Bob-recently-fired-Paulson.

"Bob?"

He turned at the sound of his name. "Oh, hi, Camille." He put a bottle back on the shelf. "How are you?"

"How am I? I'm shocked is what I am. How could you?"

"How could I what?"

"Bob!"

Bob waved his hands in the air. "Camille, I honestly don't know what you're talking about."

"Mac told me about the fight and about having to let you go."

Bob squinted with his good eye. The bad eye didn't move. He shook his head. "Camille, wake up and smell the coffee."

"What? What are you saying?"

"I'm saying your husband is a loser." He turned and walked away.

"That just sounds like sour grapes to me, how about to you, Leo? Sour grapes, I say."

But then again, she wasn't so sure. She'd had her doubts all along. Earlier, she had called Rhonda and asked her what love bites looked like. "Oh my god, Camille, no one calls them that. They're hickies and they look like little bruises."

Even after looking at the adorable photos of Leo, she couldn't divert her attention away from her encounter with Bob. "Are you up for a longer walk, my little chocolate-chip-cookie?" she asked Leo. She turned the stroller around and headed in the direction of the bar.

Bad idea. It was so hot and humid, she arrived sweaty and irritable, and Leo arrived with a wet diaper and hungry for his bottle. Again, the air-conditioning felt wonderful when she entered, pushing backwards through the door at Lenny's while maneuvering the stroller. Mac was behind the bar, washing glasses. Two old men sat at the bar, hunched over their beer bottles.

"Hey! What are ya doing here?" Mac said when she entered. "Is everything okay?"

Leo had begun to wail. "I need to change him," Camille said, heading for the ladies' room. Once she changed him, she ran his bottle under hot water in the sink. She took a deep breath and decided to be direct and just ask Mac point blank: do you own this bar or not?

"Do you own this bar or not?" she called out as she exited the bathroom, hoping to throw him off guard.

"Little darlin', what are ya talking about? Of course, I own the bar. Don't be ridiculous. The name on the sign is Lenny's, isn't it? Short for Lennox."

"That's not proof, Mac."

"Proof? What do you want to see, a deed? My mortgage?"

"Yes."

"That's all in a safe deposit box at the bank. Guys," he said to the two old drunks sitting at the bar, "who owns this bar?"

"Why, you do, Mackie!" one man said.

"Been yours long as I can remember," the other man said.

"See, love? Where is this coming from?"

"I just ran into Bob at the drugstore. He told me to wake up and smell the coffee. That you were a loser."

"Something a guy who has just been fired would say."

"Mac, I don't know…"

"Love, come sit down while ya feed the baby. Come on, hop up on a stool. How about a nice cold soda? It's hotter than hades out there, aye? Or I can whip up a *Camille* for ya! Eugene, Elden, this is my wife, Camille, and that little guy is my son, Leo."

The men nodded, obviously uninterested.

Camille wanted to believe Mac. She carefully climbed onto a stool and sat while Leo sucked on his bottle. She'd only been married a little over a year, but one thing she'd learned: life was easier if you believed Mackinney Lennox.

On Wednesday evening, Camille reminded Mac that she needed him to watch Leo the next morning while she went to her doctor's appointment.

"Why can't Sadie watch him again?"

"I told you, Mac, she and Wally are at their son's house for a couple of days. Remember, they left the car and the truck for us. Or we all three can go. Like a little family."

"You know I hate that lady shit," Mac said.

"Whatever. But I need to leave at eight forty-five, okay? I'll have a bottle ready, but Leo will probably sleep until I get back. You'll be okay, right?" She'd never left the baby with Mac before.

Thursday morning, she woke Mac up right before she left for the appointment. If she hadn't made him get up and come into the kitchen for a cup of tea, he probably would have just rolled over and gone back to sleep. "Go," Mac said, as he sipped his tea. "We'll be fine."

At the doctor's office, Camille sat in the waiting room until her name was called. Her legs were nervous-jittery. She'd only shared this little piece of information with Sadie, but she was worried that she was pregnant again. After Leo was born, her periods never went back to a regular cycle. She prayed that she wasn't, then felt guilty about praying, since she hadn't kept her first promise to God that if she survived childbirth she would go back to church. She shook her head. How dare she make bargains with God!

She wasn't pregnant and the doctor put her on the pill to regulate her cycle. To celebrate, she thought she would splurge and bring home fast food for lunch. She phoned Mac to see what he would like. He didn't pick up. He was probably changing Leo's diapers and had his hands full. She wondered: had he ever changed Leo's diaper? Did he even know how? She hadn't thought of that.

She was hungry for tacos, so she went through the drive-up and purchased four soft-shells. Just as she pulled into the driveway at home, Mac was getting out of Wally's truck. Her first thought was she hoped he knew to face Leo's car seat backwards for safety.

She got out of the car. "Hi," she called out. "Where'd you guys go?"

Mac didn't say anything. He just stood there with his hands in his pockets.

Camille was confused. The back of the pickup was filled with his cartons of Beatles albums and memorabilia. She opened the passenger seat door to retrieve Leo, but instead of Leo, she found a young redhead.

"Where's the baby?" Camille shrieked.

The redhead said, "Baby? I'm just a couple of months along."

"Where's MY baby?" Camille cried. She moved towards Mac and started hitting him with the bag of tacos.

"He's fine. He's upstairs, sound asleep."

"You left him alone?" she said as she threw the bag of tacos at him and ran up the porch. She could hear Leo crying. What the hell was happening? Poor Leo! She found him in his crib, blubbering his head off, his little face red as a cranberry. She picked him up and held him close, rocking him. She realized she was dizzy and hyperventilating; there was a chance she might faint. She made it over to the bed and sat. Once she composed herself, she looked out the window. Mac and the redhead were standing by a car parked on the street. She hadn't noticed it when she got home. The girl was gesticulating wildly while Mac stood there with his head down, hands in his pockets. Not until that moment did Camille realize that the redhead, whoever she was, was pregnant. Suddenly (finally), Camille smelled it. She smelled the goddamn coffee.

She heard Mac going in and out of the house and realized he was bringing his boxes back in the apartment. He seemed to care more about that stuff than he did about his own wife and son. So be it. She could wait him out. She lay back on the bed and sat Leo on her stomach. He was happy and smiling. "We'll be just fine," she promised.

Then the house grew quiet and she heard Mac's bike start up. She jumped up and reached the window just in time to watch him speed off down the street. She opened the window and shouted, "Coward" as loud as she could, but she was sure he hadn't heard her over the rumble of the engine. All it did was scare Leo. It all fit together now: why he banned her from ever coming to the bar, why there was never enough money, the hickies, the scratches on his cheek, the slashed tires, the dozens of nights he slept at the bar. A pregnant woman. Probably many women. She had been a fool, an absolute fool.

How she wished Sadie were home! She fed Leo and then put him in his baby swing. "Give your mom just ten minutes, will you chicken-pot-pie?" It took fifteen minutes, the last five of which Leo screamed bloody murder, but the job was done. Every one of Mac's boxes of Beatles' albums and memorabilia was packed safely away in the trunk and backseat of Sadie's car. She wondered if Mac was on his way to sell them or was returning from having tried to sell them. Camille assumed they probably were not worth what he had hoped. Good grief, the Beatles had only been broken up for six years. These things take time to become valuable collectables. It wasn't stealing. For all she knew, Mac was never coming back. It was her insurance policy.

As far as exits go, Camille's was not noteworthy. Not like Thelma and Louise gleefully driving their car over a cliff, or like Eugene Cernan, the last astronaut on the moon who left his daughter's initials—T D C—behind, etched in the dust, for all eternity. Not like Elvis when he left the building. Camille's departure was calm and quiet. She packed up the baby's things and the few things she had, and when Sadie and Wally returned home from their son's house later in the day, Camille cried on Sadie's shoulder, and then they went to work packing the Buick and the truck. One call to Rosie and everything was set in motion. Sadie and Wally would drive Camille and Leo to a safe house an hour north in Madison. Rosie's friend, Eleanor, helped women who were fleeing bad or dangerous situations. Rosie would fly out that night from D.C. and meet them in the morning. Just like that, it would all be over.

Camille and Leo rode with Sadie; they followed Wally's truck—Henry the Eighth peeking out the back window—until they reached the house. Camille was in a daze the entire car ride. Leo and Sadie cried the whole way, but Sadie didn't badmouth Mac and she didn't lecture. Wally pulled up to a big white Victorian house and Sadie parked behind him. Three women, hippie types dressed in long, flower-patterned dresses, met them and whisked them along inside, at a pace that made Camille feel as if she were doing something illicit. The women then went back and forth unpacking the car and the truck, and moving Camille's belongings to a small bedroom on the second floor.

Eleanor was thirtyish, with short brown hair and big hoop earrings. She wore jeans and a black T-shirt adorned with a gold peace sign and no shoes. She sat everyone down in the living room. Sadie rocked Leo in her arms and

Wally held Henry the Eighth. A young woman brought in a tray with glasses of iced tea. Camille almost had a heart attack—it was Alisha, Rosie's estranged friend. Camille knew all about what had happened to poor Alisha, and when she put two and two together, Camille was happy to see her here.

"Camille!" Alisha said when she saw her. "What are you doing here?"

"Alisha!" scolded Eleanor. "You know the rules."

"I'm so sorry, Eleanor." Alisha said.

Camille jumped in. "It's okay, Eleanor, Alisha is a friend from way back." They hugged and Alisha said, "We'll talk later." Alisha backed out of the room, smiling when she saw Leo.

"Camille, we're pleased you're here," Eleanor said. "Rosie is like a sister to me."

Leo started to fuss, so Sadie stood up and walked him around the room. Eleanor handed a card imprinted with a phone number to Wally. "We don't list any identifying information for the safety of our girls, but if you need to get ahold of Camille, call this number."

Wally took the card. "This is all my fault," he blurted out.

"Wall?" Sadie said.

"I should have known he was up to no good. He hasn't paid the rent in three months."

"Wally!" Camille said. "Why didn't you tell me?"

"I didn't want to worry you, honey."

"I will pay you back when I get on my feet."

"No, you won't," Wally said. "That's not why I mentioned it."

"It's not your fault anyway," Camille said. "What about me? I've had my own suspicions. I just didn't want to believe them."

"Well, who would, cupcake?"

Eleanor said, "Tomorrow we'll complete paperwork. Just know that you and Leo are safe here."

Camille wasn't worried about safety. She knew Mac wouldn't come after her or the baby, but he might come after his Beatles stuff. She sat in a rocking chair feeling bewildered and disorientated. For all she knew, she could be on the moon. Sadie continued to walk the baby around the room.

Wally sat quietly. Eleanor said, "Why don't I give you all some time. Please stay as long as you like. I'll be in my office down the hall if you need me."

Wally said to Camille, "What can we do for you, honey?"

"Oh, Wally, what haven't you done for me? I couldn't have survived without you and Sadie." Camille did think of one thing. She was worried about her piano students and asked Sadie if she could apologize to them and say how proud she was of their progress.

"Of course, cupcake."

And that was it, really. Camille's only connection to the life she'd led for a little over a year: her wonderful landlords and two piano students. She couldn't think of any other loose ends she needed to tie up. She realized she had no Beloit friends—other than Sadie and Wally—no acquaintances even, who would miss her. Maybe the grocer would miss her; they'd had some nice chats. And one of the librarians, the younger one, not the old biddy who gave her the stink eye when she was pregnant. Would Mac miss her? She shook her head. How could she even answer that question when it was painfully clear that she didn't even really know who Mackinney Lennox was.

"What do you want us to tell Mac?" Wally asked.

"If he shows his face, that is," Sadie added.

Camille rocked back and forth. "I don't know. I just don't know, but something tells me he won't be coming around any time soon." She massaged her forehead. "I know," she said. "Tell him I finally woke up and smelled the coffee. Tell him that."

Camille and Leo walked Sadie and Wally out to their vehicles. "It's hard to leave you, cupcake. You're like family to Wall and me."

"This isn't goodbye, Sadie. We're only an hour away. I want you in my life. You're more mother to me than my mom ever was!"

Wally gave Camille a bear hug and caressed Leo's head. "Be good, little guy." He was crying as he and Henry got into the truck.

Sadie took longer with her goodbye. Camille basked in her hug, although she worried that they were squishing Leo. "Goodness me, I almost forgot!" Sadie said, reaching into her purse. "I have something for you and you cannot refuse it. Promise me you won't refuse it."

"Sadie!"

"Promise me!"

"Okay, I promise."

"Hold out your hand."

Camille did as she was told, and Sadie placed a ring in her hand. Camille took it and held it up to the light. "Sadie! Your sister's diamond!"

"This way, my two daughters-in-law won't fight over it."

"I couldn't take it."

"But you promised. Sell it and get yourself settled. You're a good piano teacher—I'm sure in this big town you can get a lot of students. Now put that ring on your finger so you don't lose it."

"Sadie, does Wally know about this?"

"Cupcake, it was Wall's idea!" With that Sadie got in her car and followed Wally down the street. What a sad sight!

Leo started to cry. "Oh no you don't, you apple-cinnamon-tart," Camille said. "It's my turn to cry." Out of nowhere, one of the women appeared and took the baby from Camille. She handed Camille some tissues and led her to the back porch of the big white Victorian house, where a swing awaited her. "Have yourself a good cry," she told Camille. "I'll take this little fellow inside. He'll be fine. Babies love me." She smiled.

So, Camille sat down on the porch swing and had herself a good cry. An ugly, face-contorting, snotty, throat-hurting cry. She cried for herself, she cried for Leo, and she even cried for Mackinney.

Camille could *feel* Rosie's presence. When she woke up the next morning, she knew Rosie was in the house. There was a little buzz, a vibration, a spark that seemed to follow Rosie wherever she went. Leo was still asleep. Camille tiptoed out of the room and let her nose follow her to the kitchen. There was Rosie sitting at the table with Eleanor. "I just got here five minutes ago!" Rosie said, getting up to hug Camille. "You look awful!" Rosie said when she broke from the hug.

"Thanks a lot!"

"Beautiful, but awful. Oh, you know what I mean. You look exactly like someone who has just been abandoned."

"I don't know, Rosie, technically, I may have abandoned *him*. He might have just gone off to work, came home, and found us gone."

"Camille, please."

Camille changed the subject. "You look wonderful!" she told Rosie. And she did. Rosie wore her thick brown hair back in a loose ponytail. Her large, dark-framed eyeglasses made her look older than her twenty-five years. Camille wondered if Rosie had seen Alisha yet or if she already knew she was there.

Eleanor handed Camille a mug of coffee. She sat down at the table and looked around. The kitchen was huge, with large windows, a tin ceiling, and a long oak table that could seat ten. Leo's highchair had been moved from the bedroom and placed by the window alongside another one. If these walls could talk, Camille thought. What stories she would learn about all the young women who passed through?

"Who wants pancakes?" the woman who had taken Leo from her last night asked. Her name was Dawn, and Camille would learn that she had a six-month-old daughter (hence the other highchair), an abusive boyfriend, and lung cancer. Dawn set a plate of pancakes in front of Camille. She wasn't hungry but picked at her plate to be polite.

Eleanor reviewed the necessary paperwork with Rosie and Camille. Camille signed whatever forms were put in front of her. Eleanor said, "How about a tour?"

"Sure," Camille said, "but let me check on Leo first." The baby slept soundly, so she and Rosie—holding hands—followed Eleanor around the big, old home, as she introduced residents and explained how things worked, which areas were private and which were common. Eleanor had given Camille a list of rules which was long and explicit, covering things such as no smoking in the house, no drugs, no unapproved visitors, kitchen duties, which bathrooms to use, curfew, quiet hours, etc. Rosie said, "It will be like going to college!"

"You can stay for thirty days," Eleanor said. "We usually get our girls on their feet in a month. If we need more time, we can re-apply for another thirty days."

"That won't be necessary," Rosie told Eleanor. "We're going apartment-hunting as soon as Leo wakes up and has his breakfast."

Camille sat with Rosie in the living room as Rosie gave Leo his bottle. He would stop sucking from time to time to smile and Rosie would giggle. Then Leo would giggle. It was a sight for sore eyes. Rosie was giggling when Alisha walked in the room.

"Rosie!" she said.

Rosie looked up and saw her friend.

"I was just coming to talk to Camille…and ask about you."

Rosie stood up and delivered Leo to Camille. "Let's go for a walk," she said, taking Alisha's hand.

"You're going to love Madison," Rosie said, as she zipped through neighborhoods in Eleanor's white Camaro, with Leo babbling happily in his car seat in the back. "It's so exciting with the capital and the university. It's a happening place. It's not D.C. or anything, but I loved the time I spent here. I'm glad to be back."

"How long can you stay?" Camille asked, hoping for a few more days.

"Cam, I'm here to stay!"

"What?"

"You heard me. I'm moving back! We're going to do this together."

"But Rosie, you love D.C.!"

"I love you and Leo more. Plus, I'm lonely out there. I need you."

"I need you more. I can't believe it!"

"Believe it!"

"Rosie, what happened with Alisha?"

"I about had a heart attack when I saw her!" Rosie said.

"I should have warned you. My brain is mush."

"No worries. She told me she went back to Tony and things were better for a while. He quit dealing, got a job, but when he drank, he turned into a completely different person. Mean. Last time he sprained her wrist, this time he broke it. Poor Alisha. She says she's done with him for good, but I don't know, Cam, some women keep going back."

"I always loved Alisha. We'll help her, won't we?"

"Not sure. I know that sounds heartless, but it's the opposite, my heart might not survive it."

They found the perfect place to rent—the lower apartment of a two-story brick home on the corner of Mifflin and Broom Streets. Rent was expensive in Madison due to student housing demand, but this apartment was affordable, just blocks from the capitol building, plus they could take advantage of college students who could help babysit. Rosie had lived just up the street so she knew the area well. She told Camille that "Miffland" (as the area was endearingly called) was established in 1969 as the center of anti-Vietnam War activism by the UW students who were no longer required to live in university housing. "We took over this neighborhood!" she told Camille. "I got here just a couple of weeks after the first Mifflin Block Party. Right there!" she said, pointing to a house. "At 512 Mifflin—that's where the party started. There was an anti-war dance in the street, and then a protest and then a riot and then a hundred people were arrested, including my boss. Dozens were injured. The police used gas and clubs!" Rosie spoke so wistfully, as if she missed those days. "But they couldn't stop us, Cammy. The next year, we had another block party and now it's a spring tradition, although the radical edge is toned way down. Oh, look, right there on that corner—I was this close to getting arrested. I actually squirmed under a cop's legs and got away!"

The apartment was a little dumpy, with scratched wooden floors, chipped kitchen cabinets, and a bathroom with mismatched fixtures, but the sisters loved it. Camille showed Rosie the diamond ring that Sadie had given her. "I can pay my share, Rosie. I just need to have the ring appraised. Sadie wanted me to sell it."

"Save it for a rainy day, Cam. I'm sure we'll have some of those ahead. I've got money. I'll cover the deposit and a couple of month's rent to get us started."

Camille began to cry. "You're giving up your dream for me!"

"You know what? I'm beginning to see that I can have more impact on the state level than in D.C. I've still got all my connections here. I would never ask for my job back with Paul, but I am sure I'll find a position in no time. Don't worry about anything."

Sadie called with news about Mac. He had come knocking at the door one morning asking Wally if he knew where his wife and son were.

"Wally told him he saw you leave in a taxi. That you never even said goodbye. And that we were heartbroken."

"What did he say?" Camille asked.

"Cupcake, all he said was, 'I really screwed up this time.'"

Camille touched her heart—the tiny corner that still loved him. Eleanor had warned her about her heart. "I've seen it a million times, Camille. The wife starts feeling bad for her husband, starts missing him. Wants to forgive him. Wants to change him. Don't go there. It's destructive." Camille thought about Alisha and how much better her life would have been if she had just been able to walk away.

Still, she wondered what Mac would do. Would he just take his bike and leave town? Would he move in with the redhead? Would he go home to his parents? A part of her could forgive him—for the money problems, for lying about the bar (surely it was to impress her) maybe even (probably not!) for the infidelity, but never, ever, ever for leaving her sweet baby home alone. Never.

Sadie said, "Obviously, Wally told him he wasn't welcome in the apartment anymore and that he didn't even expect the back rent. He would be happy if he just never saw him again. We'll gather the rest of your things, cupcake, your dishes and such, and bring it up to you soon."

"Throw it all away, Sadie. I couldn't eat off those dishes."

"I understand, cupcake."

True to her word, Rosie got a job with a Democratic state congressman right away. "My reputation precedes me," she teasingly boasted. Rosie and Camille settled into their new home, bringing dinner on Sundays to the safe house and sharing it with Eleanor, Alisha, Dawn, and the revolving door of young women who passed through. All their stories were so much worse than Camille's and usually involved black eyes, fat lips, lacerations, and broken bones.

Rosie and Alisha slowly spent more time together until Alisha made the decision to move out of state. She'd found a job at an architectural firm in

Denver. "It's for the best," she told Rosie and Camille when they saw her off. "My therapist says I have to put distance between us, or I run the risk of slinking back to him."

"We'll visit someday," Rosie said, tearing up.

Sadie called once a week and Camille filled her in on Leo's milestones: he rolled over on his own, he giggled whenever he heard the word "banana"—his favorite food. He loved to suck on his toes. His hair was fully curly now, his eyes were definitely green, and for better or for worse, he was the spitting image of his father.

"I miss my little bread 'n' butter pickle!" Sadie said. "Wally and I are going to drive up soon, cupcake. But we'll be staying put for a bit. Wally has to have shoulder surgery and yours truly needs a new knee."

One day, Sadie called with word of Mackinney. Camille had been in Madison for several months, but she still thought about Mac each and every day. She couldn't help but wonder where he was, what he was doing, and whether he wanted to see Leo. She wasn't sure if *she* wanted him to see Leo. He had his rights, of course, but wouldn't her life be easier if he was just out of the picture? Sadie said she received an envelope in the mail with another envelope inside addressed to Camille. "Do you want me to mail it to you, cupcake?"

"Oh, Sadie, just read it to me. The suspense would kill me."

Camille heard papers rustle. Sadie cleared her throat. "Here goes, cupcake. Oh, goodness, he has nice handwriting. I wasn't expecting that. Okay. '*Dear Camille, I sure hope that Sadie can find it in her heart to see that this letter gets to you wherever you are. I could say I'm sorry a thousand times, but I know it won't make up for what I put you through. I am a lout. I come from louts. I thought I could be someone else. I'm guilty of everything you think I am guilty of except for one thing and this I wanted you to know: I did not leave Leo alone at the house. I was packing my Beatles stuff into Wally's truck when...well, her name is DeeDee...showed up. She started ranting and raving and making a scene, so I told her to get in the truck so we could talk. I never left the driveway. I wanted you to know that. I may be many things, but I would never leave our son alone. I'm staying at Bob's again if you want to get a hold of me. Mac.'"*

Camille didn't quite know what to say. Sadie said, "Hmmmph. I don't know about you, cupcake, but I don't believe him for one minute. He's just trying to cover himself in case you bring him to court. You know I've never said a bad word about him, but he's a conniver, that one. He would lie with a straight face to the good Lord Himself. Don't you go feeling sorry for him now. I'll put this in the mail to you. You might need it later on."

Camille hung up the phone, not sure of her emotions. But her piano student was arriving shortly, and she had to find Leo's walker. A couple of days later when the letter from Sadie arrived in the mail, Camille showed it to Rosie. Her sister shook her head and said, "I'll take care of this." Camille didn't know but that evening Rosie wrote her own letter. To Mackinney. Saying to stay the hell away from her sister and her nephew or she would report him to the Department of Children and Family Services for leaving his baby home alone. "Please, Mac, if there is a speck of decency in your heart, let us be!" She sent the letter to her friend in D.C. and asked her to mail it so that Mac would see the postmark and think that Camille and Leo were living with her in D.C.

There were no more letters from Mackinney.

One Sunday night, on their way home from Eleanor's, Rosie asked Camille what she thought of Dawn's nine-month-old daughter Merricat.

"She's a sweetie-pie. Her name is a little odd though. Why do you ask?"

"Dawn is going to stop her chemo treatments. The doctor said there's nothing else they can do."

"Oh no!" Camille said. "I'm so sorry! What about Merricat?"

"That's why I am asking. What if I adopted her?"

"Rosie! Really?"

"I love Dawn. And she has no family and she asked me, and what the hell, she's a sweet baby, and we're all set up—"

"Rosie, I don't know. That's a huge step. I just pictured you going back to D.C. someday and—"

"Never! Camille, the worst people in this country are all in D.C. Selfish, greedy, power-hungry vultures. I'll never go back. Like I said, I can do a lot at the state level. I got to be honest, I vowed never to get married and never to bring a child into this screwed-up world, but I'm learning never to say never. This feels right."

And so, a few months later they became a family of four. Rosie went to court one day and came home with Merricat. The baby's real name was Mary Catherine. Apparently, Dawn took the nickname from Shirley Jackson's 1962 mystery novel *We Have Always Lived in a Castle*. (Camille later read the book and decided it was unfair of Dawn to saddle such a darling child with the name of a murderess, but her name was her name.) Merricat was a dream child—bright, curious, and willful—just the sort of child a person like Rosie should have.

The foursome made an oddball family and once when Camille was out walking Leo in a stroller, she overheard one of the college girls refer to her as one of the lesbians with the cute babies. Rosie, being Rosie, thought it was hysterical, but Camille was mortified. "We're sisters," Camille would explain. "Sure, you are. Whatever you say." Sometimes when the two were walking the babies in their strollers, Rosie would grab Camille's hand and they would walk down the street that way, just to cause a stir. At first, Camille would pull away, but as time went on, she thought it was funny too. They would laugh and laugh. It felt so good to laugh. Camille couldn't remember laughing much when she was with Mac. That time of her life was starting to fade from her memory. Funny how humans can adjust so quickly. Had she really spent a year in Beloit? Was she really still married to Mackinney Lennox? How could that be? Sometimes, when she thought about being with him, she wanted to throw up.

At times, she could hear Stella Maris' voice in her head saying, "What did I tell you, Camille? But do you ever listen to me? No, you don't." But Camille didn't regret a thing. She may have lost a husband and a year of her life but look what she got in the deal—her beautiful son, her sister back in her life, a beautiful niece, and a friendship with Sadie and Wally. Still, sometimes at night, she found herself reaching for Mackinney. She missed that safe and secure feeling of sharing your bed with someone. Everything had ended so quickly. There was never any closure. Maybe she needed some closure.

There were a few times when she had to stop herself from sneaking off in Rosie's car and driving to Lenny's. She had it all planned out. She would doll herself up and she would just waltz through the door, walk right over to the bar, slip up onto a stool, and then wait for Mac to say, "What can I get ya, love?" before he looked up and realized it was her.

"It's me, Mac!" she would say, lighting up a cigarette.

"Little darlin'," he would say. He would fix her namesake drink, on the house, of course. He would ask after Leo. "How's the wee bairn doing? I bet he's getting big, aye?"

She would tell him all the things Leo was doing—he was walking and talking, he was potty-trained, he sang songs. Mackinney would nod and smile. And she would ask how DeeDee was and whether they'd had a boy or a girl.

"We have a little girl. Cute as a button. Such a good bairn, too. You never hear a peep out of her."

"Is that so?" she would say. And even though *that* comment would make her hate him all over again, she wouldn't show it. She would keep ice cool. She would tip back her glass and finish the last of her drink, snub out her cigarette in the ashtray, and then walk on out. No goodbye, no toot-a-loo, and definitely no tip.

Other times she pictured him alone in a park, heartbroken, and singing "Yesterday"—asking himself why she had to go…

She'd asked Rosie, "What about a divorce? Shouldn't I file for a divorce or do you think he will?"

Rosie, being Rosie, was way ahead of her. "Just wait a bit. My lawyer friends are trying to decide what would be better for you: a fault ground divorce for abandonment, desertion, and infidelity, or a no-fault divorce. The state of Wisconsin is looking to adopt a no-fault divorce law. We've been working on this for a while. I'm pretty sure it's going to pass. Be patient. I'll take care of everything for you."

"I want sole custody."

"Oh, you'll get sole custody."

Rosie, so worldly in so many ways, was pretty naïve when it came to babies. She wasn't prepared for how much work a baby would be. "You made it look so easy," she said to Camille. They agreed that while Rosie went to work, Camille would stay back with the kids. She tried to keep up with giving piano lessons but now that she had two little ones running around, it proved impossible. Leo had started walking and Merricat had taken to running.

Rosie knew Camille was disappointed about giving up her piano lessons, but she never complained. Although when Rosie got home from work, she was often met at the door and two kids were wordlessly dumped into her arms. Rosie suggested Camille go to college.

"College! What would I do? Where would I go? *When* would I go?"

"Just give it some thought."

Camille did think about it and surprising even herself she decided she would like to be a nurse after all. (Good grief, was Stella Maris right all along?) Camille's experience of childbirth had left her thinking about the nursing profession. She knew she could do a better job than the nurses who had taken care of her during her stay, dishing out insensitive comments like "you have inverted nipples" and "I think you have a fuss budget on your hands." She attended night classes, doing her homework while the kids napped and she finished up a two-year program in four and a half years, timing things perfectly so that she started her job when the kids started kindergarten.

Rosie threw Camille a graduation party. Sadie and Wally came up from Beloit and of course Barry came. He'd been visiting once a month or so since Rosie rescued Camille. Barry adored his two grandchildren. He could never get Stella Maris to come. "Not over my dead body," she'd say.

"How could a woman be so stubborn and hateful?" Camille asked Rosie.

"Because, Cam, she's mentally ill."

Camille and Rosie sat with their father in the living room after her graduation party and sipped brandy. "I have one more gift for you," Rosie said. "I've been saving it." She handed Camille a clipboard with a form

THE WONDER OF IT ALL

attached, and said, "Sign this." Camille signed it. Rosie said, "There! You are now officially divorced." She took a bow.

"And to think, it only took five years!" Camille said, clapping. "I'm glad it's done. Thank you. She's a good sister, isn't she Dad?"

"She is at that. Maybe she can get me one of those."

Camille stared at her dad.

"Girls, I'm leaving your mother. I'm telling her tomorrow."

"Good for you, Daddy!" Rosie said.

"What happened?" Camille asked.

"Nothing really, no bombshell, no other woman. But I've been seeing a counselor and I've discovered how miserable I am. It's been thirty-five years and I just can't take it anymore. My blood pressure is up; I'm agitated all the time. I'm sixty years old and I just can't live with her anymore. I love her, I do, but she won't get help and her neuroticism is getting worse. I can never forgive her for how she's treated you two. And not wanting to even meet her grandchildren..."

Rosie said, "You deserve happiness, Dad."

"Poor miserable Mom," Camille said. "Where will you go? We can make room for you up here."

"No, no, honey, I have a few more years before I can retire. I already rented a place. Remember those nice brick four-families on Melrose where John-O and Peggy lived when they first got married? I put a deposit and the first month's rent down."

"It's a big step," Camille said. It made her sad. Two marriages were ending—one that was a farce, lasting but a year and one that had always seemed like the real thing and lasted thirty-five years. What was the point, she wondered. She was doubtful she would ever try it again. Here's to being single!" Camille held up her brandy glass. She wondered if Mackinney was somewhere celebrating as well, singing the perfect Beatles song...was there one that fit divorce? She remembered Mac telling her that Paul had written "Hey Jude" to comfort John's son Julian when his parents broke up.

As for Camille, she was going to take her own sad song and make it better. Much, much better.

14.
rosie & camille & leo & merricat

LEO AND MERRICAT rode their new bikes—which had been in storage since Christmas—up and down Mifflin Street. It was March, vestiges of old snow remained in patches on the ground, but the sidewalks were clear, and the kids couldn't hold out another minute. Camille reluctantly brought the bikes up from the basement. "It's still so cold out!" She made them wear hats and mittens, which they quickly peeled off once they were outside. They rode up and down the block all that cold Sunday morning while their moms prepared for their weekly women's group potluck lunch. Their version of *church*.

It was 1987 and life was good. Camille worked as a labor and delivery nurse at St. Mary's Hospital. Rosie was a registered lobbyist for the Wisconsin Women's Network, still fighting for equal rights and equal pay and loving every minute of it. Ten years later they still lived in the house on Mifflin. They bought the place after having rented it for three years. Now they were landlords, renting the upstairs apartment to various college students.

Mifflin Street was inhabited (overrun) by college students, many of whom Leo and Merricat had befriended. It was Merricat who did most of the befriending—Leo was shy and unadventurous. Both children were eleven years old now, but Merricat was inches taller and more mature than her cousin. She was an early bloomer, getting her period and breasts at age ten. Leo was the opposite, a late bloomer; he could pass for a third grader when he was actually a fifth grader.

Leo pedaled as fast as he could, trying to keep up with Merricat. Story of his life. She was bigger and stronger and faster than he was—better at just about everything. But he adored her. He pretended he was riding a motorcycle—something he'd always wished he could do. Some of the college kids had mopeds. He had asked for one for Christmas. That got a good laugh.

Merricat hit the brakes at the three-story, gray-sided house at the end of their block, the one nicknamed the "Flag House" due to the various flags— American, Wisconsin Badgers, Green Bay Packers, and Chicago Cubs—that hung year-round from the porch railings. Leo and Merricat weren't banned from fraternizing with the students who lived on their block, they were just admonished by Rosie to be "smart about it." Camille was warier: "They're wild! A bad influence." Rosie said, "Yeah, but some are guys, and our kids need to be exposed to guys."

Rosie was right about that. Being raised by your mother and your aunt and living with your cousin set one up for some major razzing. *"What, Leo, are your parents lesbians or something?" "Is Merricat your sister, your cousin, or your woman?"*

Camille worried that Leo would grow up thinking all women hated men. Not that Rosie *hated* men… Well, she hated some. Xavier, Tony, and Mackinney were high on her list. An ex-boss in D.C. who had groped her, Benny for not fighting for her, and the guy who rear-ended her car and then left the scene of the accident. Also the employers who still paid females less than males—she *really* hated them. Whenever Rosie would go on one of her male-bashing rants—"MEN ARE MALE CHAUVINIST PIGS"—she would make sure to qualify the statement: "But not you, Leo, you're not a pig! And you won't ever become one, right? Promise me."

"I promise."

The sisters found that the only arguments they ever had about parenting were about the level of honesty they used with the children. Rosie was all for disarming honesty: "Yes, Merricat, you were adopted. Yes, your mother died because she smoked cigarettes—never smoke cigarettes. Yes, your mother named you after a character in a book. No, I never met your father. No, I don't think you're part Chinese; we don't know your ethnic background." Camille was softer with Leo; she divvied out the truth in dribbles. "Yes, of course you met your dad. You knew him for several months. I know Merricat never met hers. Yes, he loved you. No, I don't think I'll ever get married again. Of course I don't hate men! Yes, you have grandparents on both sides. No, I never met your father's family. Yes, Grandpa Barry has a wife—she's my mother. No, Mommy and Aunt Rosie aren't queers! Who told you that?"

Merricat had a crush on Drake, one of the guys that lived in the flag house. Leo stopped his bike behind Merricat and frowned when he saw Drake and his buddies up on the third-floor balcony drinking beers, doing what they always called "Sunday-ing it up."

"My lieges," Drake called down, "I dig your new human-powered, pedal-driven, single-track velocipedes."

"Come down and get a better look," Merricat shouted upward, blatantly flirtatious. At eleven!

Leo didn't think Drake would come down, and he got a little nervous when Drake's roommate, Alex, grabbed Drake and pretended he was going to throw him off the balcony. But moments later, Drake and Alex and a couple of the other guys came down to check out the bikes. "You didn't steal them, did you?" Drake teased.

"Drake!" Merricat said.

"Honest, we didn't," Leo said.

"That-a-boy," Alex said.

Drake told them their bikes were nice. Leo could tell he was just pretending to check them out.

Alex said, "My favorite thing about riding bikes when I was your age was riding out to the creek and smoking cigarettes with my older brother and his friends."

Merricat and Leo didn't say anything. Cigarettes were the devil to Merricat since her mother had died of lung cancer.

"Here," Alex said, retrieving a pack of cigarettes from his coat pocket and shaking a couple out. He held them out to Merricat. "Go, have yourself a little smoke."

Merricat looked at Leo and shrugged. Leo couldn't believe she would even touch the cigarettes! But she opened her hand and he dropped them in. Then he handed her a book of matches and said, "Don't light anything on fire, now. Promise?"

"I promise," Merricat said.

Drake said, "You guys don't have to if you don't want to."

But Merricat wanted to. The fact that Drake smoked overrode the fact about her mother. She rode off with Leo trailing her, passing the apartment building and stopping in the back parking lot, where they were sure to be out of their mothers' sight.

Leo didn't think smoking cigarettes was a good idea. He asked his cousin, "You're not really going to smoke, are you?"

"I'm thinking about it. I kinda want to know what it's like."

"But what if you like it and you end up like your mom? I'd rather you didn't."

"Just a puff. I'll do it if you do it."

"But I don't want to do it. It's gross."

"But who knows if we'll ever get the chance again? It seems like an opportunity has been presented to us. Maybe we are supposed to try it now, not like it, and never become smokers."

"Like destiny?"

"You're such a serious kid, Leo."

Merricat made sure the coast was clear and then she got off her bike and clicked the kickstand. Leo did the same. She handed him one of the cigarettes and placed the other one between her lips.

"Can I light the match, please?" Leo asked.

"Sure." She handed him the matches.

They'd seen enough smokers on TV to know that you had to puff. Merricat puffed and choked. Then Leo puffed and choked. They took a couple more puffs and choked a couple more times. Leo dropped his cigarette to the ground and squashed it with the toe of his shoe. Merricat did too. "You were right; it's gross."

"At least now we know," Leo said.

"Yes, now we know," Merricat said and got back on her bike. "We can check that off our list."

"We have a list?"

Feeling guilty, wondering if his mother or aunt would smell it on him, Leo rode up and down the block, to "air himself out." Over the years, he'd heard Rosie and his mom talking about their mother—his grandmother, Stella Maris, whom he'd never met—and how she could smell anything on them. It was quite possible that his mother and aunt had inherited their mother's olfactory skills. Merricat suggested they go in—she was getting cold. But Leo, being Leo, just had to go back to the parking lot to make one-hundred-percent sure they had snubbed out the cigarettes completely. "We promised we wouldn't start a fire."

Leo worried about the smoking—should he just confess to his mother and promise never to do it again or just shoulder his guilt as he had done so often so as not to implicate Merricat? It wasn't that Merricat was bad or mischievous, she was just uber curious. Anyway, he was so preoccupied with worry that he barely noticed the man leaving their house and getting into a rusted silver sports car. People were always coming and going on Mifflin Street. Men and women in business suits—lobbyists and lawyers, politicians and newspaper reporters—often stopped at the house to meet with Rosie. And the girls who rented the upstairs apartment always seemed to have visitors. Camille worried they were prostitutes or something. *Those* girls were definitely off limits to Leo and Merricat. Camille wanted to evict them, but Rosie said they paid their rent on time and took pretty good care of the place.

Suddenly, Merricat braked so quickly she left a skid. Leo just about rear-ended her. "Merricat! What the heck!"

"Sorry, Leo, but...did you see that guy?" She pointed to a silver car. The engine started and the car began heading down the street.

"Yeah. So?"

"I think that was your father."

Leo followed the car with his eyes until it turned left on Bedford Street. "You do? Why?"

"He looked *exactly* like you."

At least Leo was sure of a couple of things: he knew he *had* a father and his mother knew who he was. Not so for Merricat. According to Rosie, Merricat's mother had been a "free spirit," "she was comfortable with her sexuality," "she was uninhibited."

"You mean she slept around," Camille had said.

Rosie explained to Camille how Merricat's mother had ended up at the home. Dawn's boyfriend found out that the baby wasn't his and he beat the crap out of her. "Dawn didn't know who the father was—she had narrowed it down to three guys."

Camille always felt bad that Merricat would never know her father. Her sympathy was misplaced though. It was her own son who was more affected by not knowing his father. "How come me and Merricat don't have fathers?" Leo asked one night before bed.

"Merricat and *I*. You do have a father. He's just not in our lives."

"How come?"

"It's complicated. I'll explain when you're older."

"Will I ever meet him?"

"I honestly don't know."

"Was he bad, Mommy?"

"No, honey, he just…wasn't good. Now go to sleep."

Camille changed her story from time to time depending on which psychology book she'd been reading: "Leo, Daddy's not a bad person, he just made bad choices and hurt us when he left, but it wasn't your fault. I can love you for the both of us." The next time the message could be: "Daddy left us because he was selfish. He never should have gotten married and had a child in the first place." And then, maybe more realistically: "You know what, Leo, I really don't know why he did the things he did, but I am here for you, and I will never leave you."

Rosie, being Rosie, tried too, in her Rosie way. "Kid, the truth is we barely knew your dad. Your mom was only with him a little over a year. He was good-looking, I'll say that. We can't control these things. We take what life gives us. I have a super dad and a crappy mom. You have a fantabulous mom and a cruddy dad. But the four of us are a family and we live in a house of love. Come on now, chin up!'"

Sometimes when they were on family excursions—for Rosie and Camille made a point of exposing the kids to something new every Saturday: museums, the arboretum, plays and musicals, concerts, parades, rallies, camping, tobogganing, ice-skating—Leo would look at the kids with fathers and his heart would ache. "We do everything with you kids that fathers would do with their kids and then some," Rosie told him when Leo played victim. They'd gone to hockey games and boxing tournaments. They'd golfed and played paintball. They hunted deer and even ice-fished once when a friend of Rosie's invited them to his cabin on a lake in northern Wisconsin. They'd been on archeological digs, got to witness a baby being born at St. Mary's Hospital when a friend of Camille's invited them to be in the delivery room. They got to meet a real-life astronaut and a presidential candidate. Camille and Rosie thought by keeping the kids busy and giving them wonderful opportunities, they would not miss having fathers.

When Leo and Merricat brought their bikes to the back door, Camille met them and carried them back down the basement.

"Who was that man?" Merricat asked on Leo's behalf.

"What man?"

"We saw a man just leave in a silver car."

"Oh, him. Nobody important. Go wash your hands. The Femmys will be here soon."

The *Femmys* were Rosie's feminist friends. The same group of ten ladies had been arriving at noon on Sundays carrying their pots and dishes and trays for as long as Leo could remember. He and Merricat looked forward to the lunches for the delicious food the ladies brought—"hippie food" Rosie called it. Rosie was a vegetarian and had converted Camille early on, hence, Leo and Merricat by default. Another way for Leo to feel different—at lunchtime, his lunchbox contained tofu, whole grain bread, and sliced carrots and celery, while his classmates' lunches consisted of baloney sandwiches on white bread, chips, and Hostess Twinkies and Suzie-Qs.

Today, the Femmys brought red beans and brown rice, tabouli salad, tofu and bean sprouts, falafel, dolmades, tahini, chickpeas. They brought vegetable curries, olives, and cheeses. And wine! Rosie allowed Leo and Merricat a half-filled shot glass of wine every Sunday. "So they'll have a healthy respect for it," was how Rosie explained it to Camille, when Camille protested. Rosie always got her way which led Leo to sometimes wonder if Camille were an "assistant mother" of sorts.

After hippie lunch, Leo and Merricat were excused so the Femmys could have their meeting. The kids were instructed to retreat to their shared bedroom and read books—comics or classics, it mattered not—for a full hour. Merricat loved "reading time" but Leo often got restless, and after a while would sneak out into the hallway and lie on the floor and listen in on what the Femmys had to say. Good thing, too, or today he may have missed some juicy discussion about his long-lost father, who *had* visited today.

"He just showed up out of nowhere!" Camille said. "No idea how he found us."

"Could have hired a private detective," one of the ladies said.

"I read an article," someone else said. (She was a low-talker and Leo couldn't make out all of what she was saying.) "...and that the quality of relationships in a child's life helps determine his well-being."

"I say let him meet him," someone else said. "The statistics about boys raised without fathers are horrifying. They're more likely to drop out of school, be incarcerated, take drugs, and drink alcohol."

"I don't know, Camille." (This voice Leo knew. It was Eleanor.) "Leo's doing great! Do you really want to expose him to Mackinney and everything he brings to the table?"

"It might confuse him," Rosie interjected.

"Yes, but it also might help him," his mom said.

"She's right." (The low talker again.) "My son's psychiatrist said that there's some evidence that fatherlessness can permanently alter the brain, causing higher levels of anger and even aggression in boys."

Rosie's voice: "A bunch of hogwash! Our kids are two of the sweetest, healthiest, happiest, most grounded kids in the world!"

Camille said, "Leo is the *least* angry child I know!"

"Have you ever asked him, Camille?" someone said.

"Asked him what?"

"Asked him if he would like to meet his dad."

"No," Camille said, quietly. "No, I haven't."

"Yes," Leo whispered, "I would very much like to meet my dad." A thrill reverberated through him when he realized that his dad wanted to meet him!

"Just a minute," he heard his mother say. Quickly, he "swam" to his room across the hardwood floor and made it back before he was discovered. (He'd been discovered before.) He ran to his bed and grabbed his book just as the bedroom door opened. Camille peeked her head in. "You guys okay?"

"Yep, just reading," Leo said, his heart ba-bumping in his chest. He quickly righted his book which he realized was upside down.

Camille gave him a knowing look and closed the door, returning to the group. Leo wanted to jump up and immediately tell Merricat about what he'd just heard, but something made him pause to think it through. Leo, always sensitive about Merricat, thought maybe this news would be hard for her to hear: that he might be able to meet his dad, but she never would. But he had to tell her! They told each other everything!

"Told you that was your dad!" Merricat said.

"You really think I look like him?"

"Exactly like him."

"Did he seem…nice?"

"Leo, I only saw him for a split second. But if he was so nice, don't you think your mom would still be married to him?"

Leo knew that was true, but maybe he had *turned* nice. Maybe he had repented and changed his ways. Maybe he'd found religion. Leo had to wonder, why now? Why had his father waited eleven years? Or had it just taken that much time to find him?

"What if he's a jerk?" Leo asked.

"Leo, of course he's a jerk. He left you and your mom when you were a baby and he never paid one cent of child support."

"What's that?"

"It's when dads pay moms money every month to help take care of the kid."

"And mine never did?"

"Not a penny."

"How do you know?"

"You're not the only one who spies on the Femmys."

Suddenly Leo wasn't in such a hurry to meet his father. What if he was stupid or pathetic? And if he treated his mother so badly, did he really want to get to know him? His excitement quickly downgraded to confusion and then degraded to apprehension.

These thoughts weighed heavy on him; he hid his disquiet from Camille, but Rosie sensed his uneasiness and invited him to go on a walk with her one night after dinner. "Only if you don't try to hold my hand!" Leo said. He was eleven years old for pete's sake! It was humiliating! Rosie promised.

Mifflin Street was quiet. The last patches of snow had melted and the days were getting longer. "Your mom and I were thinking of going to California for vacation this year, Rosie said. "See the redwood trees and Yosemite. Then stop in Denver to see my old friend Alisha."

Only Rosie would travel across the country to see some darn trees. "Could we go to Disneyland, too?"

"That god-forsaken, overpriced, overcrowded, fairyland that masquerades as a park but is just hot and expensive and full of strollers? I'm disappointed you'd even ask. Oh, it's lush and fanciful all right, but it's designed to trick your brain. It's a fake, a big fake. For example, you can ride on a submarine, but it's a *fake* submarine in a *fake* ocean, and the fish are fake too. Let's go find ourselves a *real* submarine. See where I'm going with this? There are no real surprises at Disneyland. Everything is manufactured."

"Have you ever been there?"

"Of course not."

He wanted to ask how she knew then, but knew better.

"You wouldn't like it, I'm telling you."

"Maybe my dad will take me."

This stopped Rosie in her tracks. He hadn't meant to say it out loud.

"So, you *were* spying."

"Yes."

"We've talked about this…"

"I know, but Merricat saw him coming out of the house and she said I think that's your dad because he looks exactly like you and then we asked Mom about him and she said he was nobody important but that's not true, he is somebody important because he's my dad and I want to meet him even if you and Mom don't think I should because he's my dad and it's my life."

Rosie tried to take his hand, but he snapped it back. "Come on," she said, "let's keep walking." She was quiet for a while and then she said, "You're right, kid. Let me see what I can do." Leo took her hand then and they walked the rest of the way like that, and he didn't even care who saw.

After Leo and Merricat went to bed, Camille tiptoed in and woke Leo up. She put her finger to her lips and then motioned for him to follow her. In the living room, Rosie was sitting in an armchair, wearing her serious look. Camille sat on the couch with Leo and slung her arm around his neck. "So, I understand you really want to meet your dad."

"Yeah."

"That's okay, honey. I'm not upset."

"You're not?"

"Of course not. It's perfectly normal and natural. I just want to do what's best for you. That's why when he showed up here, I needed some time to think about it."

Leo rubbed his eyes with his fists. Maybe he was dreaming. "Then I can meet him?"

Rosie said, "He left his phone number. Why don't you start with a phone call? Talk to him. See if you still want to meet him after that."

"I know I will!" he said, incredulous she would think otherwise. "Thanks, Mom. I love you." Leo went to bed happy.

Merricat asked if she could listen in on the extension when he called his dad.

Leo considered it. "Maybe on the second call."

He was given complete privacy and allowed to use the phone in Rosie's bedroom. His mother had written the phone number on a piece of paper in big, neat digits. After dinner, he was excused from the table to make the call. He sat on Rosie's bed and punched in the numbers, realizing that if he didn't need an area code, his father must not live that far from him. He counted the rings…six, seven, eight…and then his dad's voice. But on the answering machine. "*You've reached Mackinney Lennox. I can't come to the phone right now. Please leave your message at the beep and I will return your call directly.*"

The disappointment of not reaching him was mitigated somewhat by the sound of his father's voice. That accent! Leo knew his father was Scottish, but he didn't know he was *that* Scottish! The accent was so cool! The word "you've" sounded like "Ya've" and the R's in the words "reached" and "right" and "return" all had that rolling sound and the word "directly" was pronounced "*di*-rectly" not "*dir*-ectly." He hung up the phone and took a breath. Maybe it was better this way, to meet his dad in increments: a figure coming out of his house, a silver car driving down the street, and now a voice. Next time, a live conversation and then a face-to-face meeting.

"Well?" his mother said when Leo returned to the kitchen. He could tell they had been on pins and needles, waiting for him, his mother doing the dishes while Merricat and Rosie sat at the table with homework and paperwork spread out before them.

"What did he say?" Merricat asked.

"I got his machine," Leo explained.

"Did you leave a message and ask him to call you back?" she asked.

"No, I didn't think of it. I was so surprised by his voice…"

"Why don't you try again tomorrow," Camille said.

The next day, he got the answering machine again. When he announced this to his mother and aunt and cousin, who were again gathered at the kitchen table, his mother gave Rosie a worried look.

"Maybe he's out of town," Leo said. "Or maybe he works nights. Do you know where he works, Mom? Maybe I can call him at work."

Camille looked at Rosie, who nodded. "He does work nights, honey, at a bar."

"My dad works at a bar? Which bar?"

"A bar called Lenny's. It's in Beloit."

What? His father was only an hour away? All this time?

Rosie said, "But he wouldn't be able to talk at work. Why don't you call again and leave a message so he can call you back."

Leo went back to Rosie's room, called his dad, and left a message: "Hello? This is Leo Lennox? Your son? Can you please call me at your earliest convenience?"

His father didn't call. A week went by and Camille and Rosie exchanged worried looks. Camille's look said: *This is why I didn't want to go there.* Rosie's said: *Yes, but now he knows his father is a loser.*

Merricat told Leo as they lay in their side-by-side twin beds, "Who needs him anyway? We're doing fine without him. Maybe we can use this to our advantage. Act really bummed and I bet we can get a trip to Disneyland thrown into our vacation."

Leo didn't have to *act* bummed.

Merricat was right about Disneyland as a consolation prize. After Leo moped around for a couple of weeks, Merricat told her aunt and mother she knew just the thing that would cheer him up. Disneyland. So, they made Anaheim the first stop on their trip out west. But no sooner had they parked their car in the lot than it began to rain and then storm—with lightning and thunder—on and off again all day long. The crowds were horrendous, the lines were long, some rides were closed down completely due to the weather, and someone ran over Merricat's foot with a double stroller. Leo ended up throwing up after a ride on Space Mountain. And seeing all the happy families—real families with actual mothers and *fathers*—well, for Leo, it was like rubbing salt in the wound. He sulked for the rest of the trip. Later, when he stood under the great redwoods, he felt small and insignificant. By the time they got to Alisha's in Denver, the last leg of their trip, all four of them were exhausted and irritable. And Rosie got more irritable when she met Alisha's new boyfriend.

The first thing Leo did when he got home was check the answering machine. It blinked compellingly. He held his breath and hit the playback button. And there was that voice, that accent! "Hello. This is Mackinney. I'm calling to speak to my son. I have to leave for work in a few minutes so I will try back tomorrow, aye? Have a good day!"

Leo sighed. "He called! I knew he would!"

The next day was Sunday and Leo wanted to sit by the phone all day, but his mother shooed him outside to ride bikes with Merricat while she and Rosie prepared for the Femmys' lunch. "If he calls, I'll come find you," Camille promised.

But he didn't call. When Camille rounded up Leo and Merricat for hippie lunch, Leo looked expectantly at her. She smiled and shook her head. Leo picked at his food, and when it was reading time and he was supposed to be in his room, he again slipped out to eavesdrop. Sure enough, he was the main topic of conversation again.

"It's been like a rollercoaster for him," he heard his mother say. "Mac's playing with his emotions. Just as I feared."

"He's so selfish," Rosie said. "He always was."

"Poor Leo," Eleanor said. "I still think it's best to keep his father out of the picture."

The low talker said something but the only thing he could make out was "see a counselor."

"Just a minute," he heard his mother say. Footsteps... This time, Leo didn't even bother making a run for it. He stayed right where he was. "Leo Mackinney Lennox, you are in big trouble, young man. Go to your room and we will discuss this later."

Leo was grounded the next day, relegated to his room after dinner, punishment for "his undercover espionage." "Don't you budge from this room," Camille told him, "I'm walking up the street with Rosie and Merricat for ice cream. Real ice cream, not frozen yogurt."

Leo took his punishment like a man. Getting a scoop of ice cream would have been nice but getting the scoop about his dad was way more important. He lay on his bed thinking about next steps and was just drifting off to sleep when his mother knocked on his door and said, "The phone is for you."

Leo popped up in a flash and said, "I didn't hear it ring." (He didn't know that Camille had initiated the call.)

Camille pointed to Rosie's room and nodded. The phone lay on the nightstand. He sat on the bed and put the receiver to his ear. "Hello?" Camille closed the door.

"Leo?"

"Yes, sir."

"Well, hello there, me wee *bairn*. I'm your father!"

"Hello," Leo said tentatively, not sure what his father had just called him…a *barn*?

"I can't believe it's you, son. We had a hellava time connecting, aye?"

"Yes, sir."

"You're a polite one, I see."

"Yes, sir."

There was a pause. Leo heard ice cubes clink and then the sound of gulping. "So, how do you like school?"

At first, Leo thought his father was asking him how he liked "skull." He pronounced school *skull*.

"I like school all right. We're on summer vacation right now."

"Do ya play any sports then?"

"I play basketball but I'm not that great."

"What else do ya play, aye?"

"I play piano."

"Do ya now, like yer bonnie Ma."

"Yes sir."

"You can call me Da, if ya want to."

"Excuse me, sir?"

"Da or Dad or even Papa."

"Okay."

"Do ya fancy the Beatles, son?"

"The Beatles?"

"Don't tell me ya dunno know who the Beatles are?"

"Oh, the band. Mom and Aunt Rose love them."

"Hmmmm, they have lots of Beatles' albums then, aye? And boxes of promotional stuff? Does she still have that stuff?"

"I don't know," Leo said, confused.

"Should I ring you up tomorrow then, same time?"

"Yes, please." Leo liked how his dad said r-r-r-ing.

The next day, Leo sat by the phone after dinner, pretending to do homework. When the phone rang at 6:30 he jumped to answer it. But it was Eleanor calling for Rosie.

Summer passed with no more calls. Leo sulked and turned inward. He was already shy and introverted and his father's rejection only exacerbated things. At first Rosie said to let him be, but when he started showing signs of anger and aggression, once pushing Merricat off her bike and another time throwing his soup spoon across the room, she and Camille grew concerned. Rosie remembered the low talker warning about anger and aggression in fatherless children. One day after school, Camille informed Leo that she was taking him to "see someone." His name was Jim Lockwood and he was a counselor.

Leo liked Jim well enough. He was funny. When he first introduced himself to Leo, he said his name was James Lockwood, but his nickname was "Jimmy the Lock." "Do you get the joke, Leo?" he asked. "*Jimmy* can mean to open. And I try to get people to open up about their locked-up feelings."

Over the weeks, Jimmy explained to Leo that he'd got a bad rap. "Sometimes people draw the short end of the stick when it comes to fathers." Jimmy explained that it wasn't Leo's fault. To internalize it and let it eat away at his insides was the worst thing he could do. And though it was painful, talking helped. Jimmy said he would discuss some of the things they talked about with Camille, but if Leo asked him to keep something just between them, as long as it wasn't dangerous, he had his word to do just that.

"The most important thing is honesty. If we can't be honest with each other, then this is a waste of time."

Leo asked Jimmy to keep something just between them.

Jimmy pantomimed zipping his lips. "Give it to me kid."

"Maybe he never called back because after talking to me on the phone once, he, he, he didn't like me so much." Leo blinked several times to hold back the tears. He hoped that Jimmy wouldn't say something stupid like, "What's not to like?" Or "Who wouldn't like a great kid like you?"

Jimmy said: "Hmmmm. I can see why that might cross your mind. Tell me what gave you that impression."

Leo thought about it for a moment. "I don't think he liked that I was so polite. He said I was sure a 'polite one.' It made me feel like I was a sissy or something."

"What else."

"He asked what I played, and I told him I played basketball and the piano. Then he told me I could call him Da, or Dad or Papa because I was calling him sir. And then he said he had to go to work and that he would call me tomorrow. He said he would 'ring me up.' That's what he said. And then he never called." Leo couldn't hold back the tears any longer.

Jimmy leaned back in his chair and gave Leo some time. There was a box of tissues on the side table. Leo had spotted the box on his first visit and vowed he would never use it. He wiped his nose on his sleeve, knowing it was childish. "I think I messed up," he said.

"Oh, no you don't. You are not blaming yourself for your dad's actions. You're a kid. He's an adult."

Leo sat quietly.

"So, Leo, listen, with me, you can be sure of one thing, I will always give it to you straight. And here it is: these things are tricky. From what your mom told me about your dad, he seems to be a complicated person."

Leo squirmed in his seat. "But he's my dad!"

"Right. And he sought you out, right? He found you."

"Right. But he was also the one who left me and my mom."

"Yes, he was."

"And he was the one who said he would call and then never did."

"Yep. So, here's where we are. You're not coming here so I can make you feel better. I can't do that. You're coming here so I can help you see the truth, and help you choose options that are healthy for your well-being. Only you can help yourself feel better. Are you following me? You know I'm not a bullshit artist."

This made Leo look up and smile. "I know."

"Leo, your dad might be an asshole or he might be a good guy. I don't know. You don't know. Even your mom doesn't know. Years change people. What you have to decide is—what do you want? Do you want to pursue a relationship, knowing that this person is unreliable and will probably continue to hurt you? Or do you want to put up a wall and say nope, can't do it. There's no right or wrong answer. Either way it hurts. Either way, I will help you."

Leo said, "I don't know."

"It's not set in stone. You might make a decision now and then in a year or five years change your mind and that's fine. But I have found when people make a decision and then move forward, it helps."

"I think I need to put up a wall and say nope—at least for now."

"Okay, then we make a plan for that. Okay? Now, tell me about Merricat."

"What about her?"

"What's she like?"

"She's my best friend."

"Is she more of a friend, a sister, or a cousin, would you say?"

Leo was confused. What did it matter? "I don't know. She's just Merricat."

"Is there anything about her that makes you uncomfortable?"

"Just that she's so much taller and stronger than me. I feel like a wimp sometimes."

"Awww, don't worry. You'll grow. Girls go through puberty earlier than boys. Has, uh, er, has Merricat gone through puberty yet?"

Leo was mortified to be discussing such things. He felt his face turn red and flushed. "I don't know," he said. Of course, he knew. Merricat had shown him her sanitary napkin pads (gross) and her bras were strewn around their room. And she shaved her legs, and armpits, too, which really irked him. He had no hair anywhere on his body yet!

"The only reason I mention it is that you are almost twelve. You need your own room, your own privacy. I talked to your mom about it. Since your house only has three bedrooms, your mom and aunt are going to give you and Merricat your own rooms. They'll take the room you and Merricat are in now."

"What? Mom and Aunt Rose in twin beds?"

"It's amazing the sacrifices parents make for their kids, Leo."

Leo thought about it and decided he didn't like the idea. And not only because he would miss sharing a room with Merricat, but also, and probably more so, because he thought that now people would really think his mom and Aunt Rose were lesbians!

15.
leo

THE "PLAN" THAT Jimmy the Lock and Leo came up with—putting up a wall and moving ahead—had an unintended side effect. It wasn't Jimmy's fault really; it was more about genetics and wiring and introverted personality types, but Leo put up that wall and often it was so strong it was impenetrable. By the time he was a teenager he developed a closed-off-you-can't-hurt-me attitude that seeped into other aspects of his life until it became his M.O., his way to self-protect. Walls were good. They kept feelings in and people out. As time went on, Leo put on a good face for his mom and Rosie—everything was fine! He found that busyness helped. Throw yourself into stuff—basketball, piano and guitar lessons, and now a new interest, making money. He met a man who owned student housing on Mifflin and started working for the guy, mowing lawns, shoveling, and painting. By the time Leo graduated from high school he had a nice sum in his bank account.

When you asked him about his future, what he wanted to do, Leo would say, "I want to be an entrepreneur." He didn't know what kind of business he wanted to start, just that he wanted to be his own boss and he never wanted to wear a suit and tie every day.

On the outside, Leo emanated cool and collected, but inside he buzzed with anxiety. Even when things were going well, he could never fully let go and enjoy it. Even his good looks didn't boost his self-esteem. He was well-liked by his teachers and classmates, especially the girls, but his shyness kept him from asking girls out. He did attend Sadie Hawkins dances, but more often than not he and Merricat would show up at school functions together. (Classmates were often confused by their relationship—they seemed like brother and sister, but they were really cousins, but they weren't really related at all since Merricat was adopted. Were they secretly boyfriend and girlfriend?)

Leo never changed his mind about not wanting to meet his dad. He pretended he had moved on. Camille wasn't so sure…Rosie always tried to convince Camille it didn't matter. She'd recently read an article reporting that up to thirty-six percent of U.S. students lived without their fathers. It was actually very common. She'd even found a study that showed there was even a bright side from not growing up with a father—it might increase a person's creative outputs, especially rebellious, novel ideas. "Leo, I read that seventeen percent of all Nobel Peace prize winners for creative writing lost a father during their early years," Rosie told him once.

A curious thing happened as Leo matured. Suddenly, in his senior year of high school, he had sort of morphed into his father—at least in appearance. He was always the spitting image, but now he was *the* image. It was darn right spooky. Leo noticed his mother staring at him sometimes with a funny look on her face. Leo was oblivious—he'd never even seen a photograph of his father. To complete the metamorphosis, Leo had embraced his Scottish ethnicity and had added little nuances subtly into his vernacular. Suddenly when he was telling a story about some kid at a party who was drunk, he said the guy was *blootered*. And when Merricat was extra chatty and he'd had enough he would say, "Stop your *havering*." And then, before long, it was, "*Stap yer haverin.*'" And suddenly people were asking themselves did Leo always have a bit of an accent? Did I miss it before? Did he always say things like "That's pure deed brilliant!" or "This band's well good"?

He continued his guitar lessons and then he started singing, too. He had a beautiful voice! He wasn't brave enough to try out for school musicals, but he did join the glee club. Upon his high school graduation, Camille gifted him with cash and his father's Beatles albums and memorabilia. She made him promise that he wouldn't sell the stuff. "Leave it alone and it will continue to increase in value. And, please, please, honey, don't you ever lose this stuff!"

Just a blink and off they went. Leo and Merricat to the University of Illinois at Chicago (yes, Leo followed Merricat there), leaving Camille and Rosie behind to miss them desperately. By the time Camille and Rosie visited on Parents Weekend in October, Leo's transformation was complete. Leo was Mackinney. And now he spoke with more of an accent and with more colloquialisms than Mac ever did.

"Who is this guy?" Camille asked Rosie back at their hotel.

"Maybe it's how he's dealing with his father now as an adult. Embracing the heritage but not the man."

"It's weird. I hope it's not pathological," Camille said.

Camille worried for nothing. By sophomore year, Leo seemed to have rounded out a bit. He lowered the wall, made some friends, and toned the accent way down. He cut his hair short, grew a beard, and sported John-Lennon-like glasses, lessening the resemblance to his father. He got a job at a coffee shop and ended up playing guitar and singing there on weekends.

"He's finding himself," Camille said.

"I think he's in love," said Rosie.

The girl who rocked Leo's world was a pretty Chinese-American architecture student from Chicago. Her name was Poppy Li Chang and she— "please don't mention it," Leo had asked—was only four-foot-eleven. Her passions ran high for architecture, politics, Mexican food, and baseball (the White Sox, not the Cubs). She talked a mile a minute and she never stopped moving. She had a nervous habit of flipping her long, silky black hair with a flick of her fingers. She dished out opinions liberally, followed by a "don't you agree?"

"Ain't she sweet?" Leo sang to his mom.

At first Camille liked her. "She's a mini version of you," she told Rosie as they walked to the Student Center for the Parents Weekend kickoff.

"Pa-lease," Rosie said. "A hundred bucks that girl ditches architecture and becomes some kind of CEO or event planner. Bossing people around is in her blood."

The truth was Leo liked having a woman in the driver's seat. Always had. He liked to be taken care of. He liked not having to make decisions about where to go, what to do, how to dress, what to eat.

"He's turned into such a wuss," Merricat groused as she walked up Taylor Street with Camille and Rosie to the coffee shop where Leo worked.

Poppy Li pounced on Camille, Rosie, and Merricat as they entered the coffee shop. She jumped up and down. "I made Leo's boss tell him he has to sing for us, or he'll fire him! Isn't that great?"

Camille looked at Rosie, who looked at Merricat, who said, "Poppy Li, you're a big fat bully!"

Poppy Li just continued bobbing up and down. Over coffee she told Camille why she was so short. "I imagine you are wondering why I am so short?"

Camille didn't know what to say. She sipped her coffee. "No, Poppy Li, it never crossed my—"

"I had this disorder as a child: Central Precocious Puberty. It's where you go through puberty too soon. I started at age five!"

"Good grief!"

"There was medication, but my stupid mother chose acupuncture instead, and now I am a 'little person.'"

"You're a big, fat bully," Merricat told her again. "Look at poor Leo!"

Leo did fine, great even. He sang two Beatles' songs, *When I'm Sixty-Four* and *Hey Jude*. During the "Nah Nah Nah Nana Nah Naaaaah" part, Merricat whispered to Camille, "He thinks she's the one, but she's not."

Funny, Leo expressed similar concerns about the boy Merricat was crazy about. At breakfast the next morning in the Student Rec Facility, Camille and Rosie got to meet Merricat's fellow. His name was Brice Davinsky and he wanted to be a doctor more than anything.

"I want to be a doctor more than anything," he said as he buttered his toast, making sure to cover every square inch.

Leo rolled his eyes. Camille gave Leo the eye.

"My mother is a nurse practitioner and my father, a biomedical engineer," Brice told them, grinning. "Medicine's in my blood."

"Right, *anti-psychotics*," Leo whispered to his mother.

Camille gave him the eye again.

Merricat called him her gorgeous "gingerbread man" on account of his bushy red hair. She was a little bit taller than him, not to mention a little bossier. The synonymity of the two relationships could not be ignored. Two bossy girls fell in love with two passive guys.

Later, as they walked to a restaurant, Camille overheard Merricat tell Rosie she thought Poppy Li was a "flat out bitch" and that she couldn't understand what Leo saw in her. When Leo asked Camille what she thought of Brice, she shrugged and said he seemed like a confident young man, a match to Merricat's healthy self-esteem.

"But, Mom," Leo said, "he's a Republican!"

Camille stopped in her tracks. "Oh, dear lord, Rosie will die!"

"I'm just joshing you, Mom. Merricat wouldn't date a Republican. But I don't care for the guy. He's persnickety and he insists on calling Merricat 'Mary Catherine.'"

Camille was glad that Leo and Merricat were so protective of one another, but she hoped they would give each other some slack. She knew it was time for these two to make their own way. At least Brice and Poppy Li seemed like decent, if not eccentric, kids.

She said as much later that evening to Rosie. Rosie, being Rosie, said, "Truth be told, Cam, I'm not a fan of either one of them. But our babies are growing up and we have to love who they love."

Camille never really warmed up to Poppy Li. Oh, how she tried. One weekend, when both kids came home for a visit, they brought Brice and Poppy Li with them. When they were all deciding on lunch and a movie, Poppy Li overrode the majority vote and got her way on both accounts:

Mexican food and The Titanic (even though she had already seen it twice before).

"She pushes my buttons," Camille told Rosie in private.

"Mine, too," Rosie said. Rosie started to call Poppy Li (oh, this is so mean) *Poopy* Li and soon Camille was calling her *Poopy* Li too. They prayed they wouldn't slip and say it to her face.

One weekend, after Leo and Poppy Li had been together for a little over two years, and Camille had resigned herself to the fact that she wasn't going away, the two kids came up to spend the weekend in Madison. The Sox were playing the Brewers in a special inter-league game and the four of them were heading to Milwaukee for the event. There was some commotion. Leo had lost the tickets, and then Poppy Li found them, but just as they were getting ready to leave, Camille complained that she was short of breath and clammy. "Maybe I'm coming down with something," she said. Rosie said she would stay back with Camille. Leo wanted to skip the game all together, but Poppy Li put up a fuss. "Your mom will be fine, right Camille? Your mom wants us to go, right Camille?"

"Of course," Camille said. "Of course, you two go. Can you sell the other tickets when you get there?"

"That's called *scalping* Camille," Poppy Li said, "and it's banned in Wisconsin."

In the end, Leo and Poppy Li went to the game and decided to drive straight back to Chicago afterward.

"What does he see in her?" Rosie said, reading Camille's thoughts.

So, they were both relieved when three months later Leo phoned to say he'd broken it off. "It was always her way or no way," was how Leo explained it. Camille had him on speaker phone and Rosie mouthed, "Ya think?"

Leo explained: "She started talking about marriage and babies!"

Camille was smart enough to know that saying anything negative about Poppy Li could come back to bite her in the butt if the kids got back together, so all she said was, "I'm so sorry to hear it, honey." After she hung up, Rosie and Camille broke out a bottle of sparkling wine and clinked their glasses. "To Poopy Li!" Rosie said.

"To Poopy Li!" Camille said.

Rosie took a long swig of her bubbly. "There's only one thing that would make this moment better…" Camille raised her eyebrows in question. "If we could get rid of Brice, too!"

Merricat was elated that Poppy Li was out of the picture, but she did report back that Leo, even though he'd been the instigator, was taking it pretty hard. "Not even Paul McCartney getting knighted could lift his spirits. And just so you know, Aunt Camille, he says he's not coming home for summer vacation."

"You're not coming home for summer vacation?" Camille asked Leo when she immediately called after hanging up with Merricat.

"Merricat has a big mouth."

"Why aren't you coming home?"

"I've lined up a summer job—painting the residence halls. It's good money, aye? I'm thinking about taking your advice and studying abroad next year. Maybe I'll go to the British Isles. I'll need the money."

"I see," Camille said, trying to hide her disappointment. "How's Merricat?" she asked to change the subject.

"She and Brice are going strong. It's obnoxious," Leo said.

"She loves him, Leo. You'd better get used to it."

Leo could not get used to it. After the breakup, he was hoping to hang out more with Merricat. But she was obsessed with Brice. She acted differently. She even looked different. She'd slimmed down and had become partial to wearing tank tops, with simple black skirts, and flats that made her feet look big. He didn't see her for most of the summer since she'd gone home to do an internship with Catholic Charities, but she did call him every few days to provide updates on Rosie and Camille, and yes, Brice. At these times, when it was just Leo and Merricat on the phone in the quiet of the evening, Merricat seemed more like herself. She'd regale him with Mifflin Street stories—the flag house had to be evacuated for a month due to bedbugs; there was a fire caused by a towel resting on a nightlight in one of the dorms; that man who always fed the ducks on Lake Mendota was beaten up; Rosie and Camille were starting to look older and this was making Merricat sad.

Rosie *was* looking a little ragged. She'd been putting in long hours working on a proposed bill that would require insurance companies to cover breast reconstruction following mastectomy. And Camille had increased her hours at the hospital. She would come home spent like a dishrag. Rosie tried to convince her to cut back. "And what's with the hiccups?" Rosie asked.

It seemed these days Camille had chronic hiccups. "I'm just trying to drink more water," Camille said. "Maybe I'm gulping." Since she'd also been experiencing some difficulty swallowing and a burning in her throat, she consulted her medical books, but she couldn't come up with a definitive diagnosis—those symptoms could be related to any number of things or to nothing at all. She felt fine, really. A little more tired than usual. She was only forty-one, but she felt so much older.

She couldn't put her finger on it, but she was melancholy. Leo didn't need her anymore. Boys were different that way. Merricat called Rosie from school each evening whereas Camille was lucky to get her Sunday evening call from Leo. She found herself thinking about Mackinney and Sadie and Wally and about that one year of her life in Beloit. She'd grown up that year. In a snap she went from child to adult. Sometimes she found herself wondering if she should have handled things differently. What if after watching Mac drive off on his motorcycle that fateful day, after calling him a coward, what if she had stayed back, waited for him to come home? If he hadn't come home, would she have called him at the bar? What if he was telling the truth when he said he didn't leave Leo alone that day? Would she still have left? And even though she left, should she have contacted Mac to let him know where she was? Should she have let him see Leo? These questions never left her. Oh, they had faded over the years, they weren't top of mind, but they bubbled up at odd times. Especially when she contemplated her own mortality.

That summer, Leo painted dorm rooms at UIC and dated six different girls. He'd met them all at bars in Wrigleyville following Cubs games. He was glad to get back to Wrigley Field after a couple of years of Poppy Li dragging him kicking and screaming to Comiskey Park. He'd looked into studying abroad and decided he just didn't have the energy for it. Truth be told, he didn't really have the energy for much these days. He painted the dorms; watched baseball; drank beer; picked up girls, some of whom he had his way with; and he slept. His favorite thing really was sleeping. Poppy Li had stolen something from him. As he sat belly up to the bar at Rizzo's he figured out what it was she had taken. It was his "give-a-damn." Poppy Li had stolen his "give-a-damn."

That was why when he got back to his apartment at two a.m. after a night of drinking and behaving badly with some stupid girls, and saw his answering machine blinking, he didn't check it. He didn't really give a damn who it was or why they were calling. He crawled on top of his bed. He woke to the sound of Merricat's voice on the machine: "Leo! Damn it! Pick up! It's important." He looked at the clock. It was two-thirty-five. Leo was sure she was calling to say she was engaged because Brice was taking her to her favorite fancy restaurant in Madison this weekend and she was sure he was going to pop the question, so he didn't pick up. He'd kind of had it up to there with Merricat and Brice. But when she called again a few minutes later and said, "Come on, Leo. It's about your mom," he slid across the floor in his stocking feet as if skating on ice and picked up the phone.

"What's going on?"

"I'm sorry to be so blunt, but—"

"I just walked in the door. What is it?"

"Your mom, Leo, she's sick!" Merricat was crying.

"Sick with the flu?" he said.

"The four of us were out to dinner and she started choking. She's been having trouble swallowing. They did tests. It's cancer, Leo. Esophageal."

Leo's legs gave out and he actually collapsed to the floor.

If he hadn't been so damn blootered he would have driven home that night. But he told Merricat he'd have to wait until he sobered up. He made coffee and drank enough to convince himself he was good to drive, but in fact, he wasn't truly sober until he reached Janesville. By the time he pulled up to their house, it was just before nine o'clock in the morning. Now he was clear-headed, sober as a judge.

He was glad to find out that Merricat and Brice had already left.

"To announce their engagement to his folks," Rosie said.

"You should see the ring, Leo," Camille said, "it's vintage."

They were skirting the issue.

Rosie said she had just made some homemade granola and was going to fix him a dish of yogurt and granola. "I can tell you haven't eaten anything."

"So," Camille said, leaning back on the sofa.

Leo sat across from her in the rattan Papasan chair. "Tell me," he said. He moved the chair closer and held her hand.

"Well, I didn't think it was anything," Camille said. "A little heartburn, indigestion, sore throat. But then we were at dinner and I was just eating my salad when I started choking on a radish. It was as if I forgot how to swallow—the strangest thing—I just couldn't *make* myself swallow. It was so embarrassing. This man at another table rushed over and did the Heimlich on me. Then Rosie insisted we go to the ER and they did tests…cancer. I still can't believe it, honey."

"Does it hurt? Are you in pain?"

"No, I'm fine."

"So, what does it mean?"

"Treatments. Chemo. Radiation. We'll see what the plan is. I'm going to see an oncologist Thursday. At least I know all the good doctors!" She smiled and patted Leo's hand.

"I'll drop out."

"Over my dead body. Oh, sorry, not a good choice of words."

Rosie came in with the yogurt and handed it to Leo. "Nobody is going to talk about death or dying. Nobody is going to ask about what stage it is or about life expectancy. Not allowed. We're just going to move full speed ahead." Thank God for Rosie. She sat next to Camille on the sofa. "And nobody is dropping out of school or delaying an engagement or a wedding. We keep going, that's what Quinlaynes do."

"I'm part Lennox, though," Leo said, trying to be funny. "They seem to be quitters."

"Very funny," Rosie said, throwing a pillow at him. She gave him one of her signature Rosie looks that said the topic was closed.

When Leo visited his mom on weekends during the first semester of senior year, there seemed to be less of her. She was thinner, paler, and weaker. They lost her bit by bit. First, she had to go part time at work, then two days a week and finally she had to quit altogether. Rosie, being Rosie, subjected Camille to some alternative treatments: an acupuncturist, a homeopath, a naturopath, a holistic medicine practitioner, a chiropractor who practiced something called Zen Physical Medicine. Rosie mixed organic concoctions—green shakes made with algae and seaweed—until Camille said one day, "Good grief, let's go out and get a good steak, why don't we?" A testament to how much Rosie, the die-hard vegetarian, loved her sister: she not only treated Camille to a steak, she had one herself.

One Saturday afternoon when Leo was visiting, Camille suggested they take a ride and "leaf peep"—what the Femmys called looking at the autumn foliage. The trees were especially colorful after a wet spring and a late summer full of sunny days and cool nights.

Leo got in the car. "Where to?" he asked.

"I think it's about time we took a trip to Beloit."

"Beloit?" Leo said, unsure if it meant what he thought it meant.

"Not sure if he's even still around..."

Leo got on Highway 14 and then took the winding back roads to Beloit, through Oregon, Evansville, and Magnolia. The trees were gorgeous against a sky so blue it made Leo's heart ache. In Orfordville, Camille said, "Stay on this street all the way to Beloit."

Camille told him to turn left, then right, then cross the Rock River. "There's the park where your father and I had picnics in the grass. Now go up three blocks and then pull up there. Right there," she said, pointing. He stopped in front of a red brick two-story, generic-looking home. The house itself was in good shape, but the white wood trim could use a coat of paint.

"That's it!" Camille said. "That's where you were born! Well, not born. You were born at Beloit Memorial Hospital, but that's where we lived. Upstairs. Wally and Sadie lived downstairs. You remember Wally and Sadie. Oh, lord, I really should call Sadie, shouldn't I?" She was rambling. "Course this place wasn't so run down twenty years ago."

Leo didn't really know what to say. He had no emotions either way. The house was a house. It didn't provide any answers for him.

"It wasn't all bad, Leo. But we were—I was so young. Eighteen! Can you imagine?"

"I can't."

She stared at the house. "To a captive bird, it looked like freedom. But it was just another cage."

"Are we getting out?"

"Good grief, no. I just wanted you to see it. Wally and Sadie have lived in Appleton for years. Now, drive up a ways. There. That's St. Thomas Church where I wanted to go but you were so colicky, I couldn't take you anywhere."

Again, Leo didn't know what to say…sorry that he was so colicky? It was dawning on him that this trip was more for his mother than it was for him. Camille took him past the grocery store and the pharmacy. She was sad to see the phone booth outside of the pharmacy had been removed. "I made many a call from that phone booth."

"You didn't have a phone?"

"Not at first, but I insisted on it once you were born."

She pointed out the clinic she went to, the library, even the Salvation Army, "where I bought most of your baby clothes and things."

That was eye-opening. Leo never realized they were dirt poor! It was pathetic that these were the landmarks of his beginnings.

"That's where I bought your crib! At a garage sale." She pointed to an old Victorian house. "The lady threw in the crib sheets for free."

Damn, they were a charity case! Leo was thinking that maybe this wasn't turning out to be the best idea, when his mother said in a Rosie-ish voice, "And now for the pièce de résistance."

"Go straight for five blocks, turn left, go up three blocks. Park in the lot."

Leo's heart started racing.

"Honey, we should have done this years ago. For both of us."

It seemed to Leo as though she was trying to convince herself. He pulled into the lot and parked the car beside the only two other cars. "The place looks hopping," he quipped.

"Good grief," Camille said. "This place has seen better days."

Looked to Leo like Lenny's had once been someone's home. The only thing that made it look like a bar was the sign that said *Lenny's* in faded lettering. The font they had used for the sign was so amateurish it almost seemed to say: *Sorry, this is the best we could do.*

"Now listen," Camille said, again sounding more like Take-Charge Rosie than Go-Along Camille, "who knows if he even still works here. We'll just go in and have ourselves a beer."

"You hate beer."

"I know, but I *want* a beer. Unless Mac is working. Then I'll ask for a *Camille.*"

"What's a Camille?"

"Some drink he created for me."

It wasn't fair that she had these memories, these little nuggets of nostalgia, and he had nothing. Suddenly, he was a little miffed at his mother. Was this all because she was dying? Was she giving up? Was she keeping something from him?

"Now or never," Camille said and opened the car door. Leo felt about five years old as he walked across the parking lot. His dad's voice came back to him, "You can call me Da, if ya want to."

They entered a cavern-like room, dark and nearly empty. Typical Wisconsin bar, Leo thought as he looked around, taking in the wood paneling, the large wrap-around bar, the vinyl-covered bar stools, and all the deer heads. Strands of colored Christmas lights hung willy-nilly from the ceiling, as if someone had taken them and thrown them up haphazardly to see if they would suspend themselves from the exposed pipes and ductwork. Three old geezers sat at the bar watching a wrestling match. The guy behind the bar—a skinny, round-shouldered, balding fellow—said "Hey."

"Hey yourself," Camille said as she settled onto a bar stool. She smiled at the man and paused. "You don't remember me, do you?"

Leo watched the man squint as he looked Camille up and down. It wasn't until he glanced at Leo did he place Camille. A smile spread across his face. "Well, I'll be damned. It's you!" he said.

"It's me!" Camille said, seeming suddenly very young. "This is my son, Leo. Leo, Bob Paulsen, proprietor." Leo extended his hand across the bar for a shake.

"It's scary how much he looks like him," Bob said to Camille. Turning to Leo, he said, "How old are you, buddy?"

"Turned twenty-two in April."

"Criminy, I knew your dad when he was your age. You're like a ghost. Kid you not."

"Is he here?" Camille asked, looking around.

Bob shook his head. "Nah. Hasn't worked here in three years."

"Ahhhh," Camille said. "We just took a chance, seeing that Leo has never met him and all."

Leo thought Bob was staring at him but then realized he had a bum eye. Bob said, "Can I get you something, Camille? On the house."

"Sure, thanks, I'll take a beer. Just whatever you have on tap."

Bob nodded to Leo. "Coors?" Leo asked.

"Ha!" Bob snorted.

"Make it a Bud, then."

Camille took a sip of beer and made a face. Leo shook his head.

"So, Bob, you still live upstairs?"

"Sad to say I do. My life hasn't changed much since I last saw you, twenty-whatever years ago. Pretty pathetic when I say it out loud."

"You look exactly the same!" Camille said. She took another generous gulp of beer.

Bob blushed again. "Nah, you do."

Camille said, "No, really, you do."

Leo was getting antsy. He took a long swig from his bottle and said, "Bob, tell me something I don't know about my dad."

Bob shrugged. "How can I tell you what you don't know if I don't know what you know?"

"I know *nothing*," Leo said.

Bob looked to Camille for help. "It's true," she said. "He knows nothing. I just never knew what was best—to tell Leo his father was a loser, a narcissist, or just a lost soul. I never really knew myself..."

"That's easy," Bob said. He looked Leo straight in the eye. "Your dad is a loser. No question about it. You're better off not knowing him. I only put up with him for economic reasons—he brought business to this place."

"The ladies loved him," Camille said, batting her eyes.

Could someone get tipsy in five minutes? From three sips of—oh, she'd finished her beer. Bob was filling a fresh glass. He'd never seen his mother drunk. She usually had one glass of wine on Sundays with the Femmys or when they went out to dinner, and that was it.

"Here's the thing, Bob," Camille said, leaning in over the bar. "I knew Mac for about a minute and you knew him for, what, thirty plus years. Just give Leo an objective profile of Mackinney Lennox."

"I don't know, Camille."

Camille batted her eyelashes again. "Please, Bob? For me?"

"Well," Bob said. "His brother was my best friend. I was an only child and I spent a lot of time at the Lennoxes. His mom and dad were good folks. Hard workers."

Camille said to Leo, "There, that's something. You hail from hard workers on your father's side."

"*Mom.*"

"Anyway, my friend Ewan and me, that's Mac's older brother. They drew our numbers and we had to go to 'Nam."

"Vietnam!" Camille said to Leo, as though he were an imbecile.

"Yeah. So, the night before we have to report, Ewan and I are going to get smashed. On the way to the bar, we get hit by a truck. Head on. Ewan is killed instantly and I...well, that's why my eye... Anyway, Mrs. Lennox went crazy and then the whole family went downhill...drinking and then Mr. L. couldn't work anymore. The other brother, Brody, was a real loser. Anyway, my uncle left me this bar and one day, Mac comes 'round looking for a job. It was the least I could do for his family. Turns out, he had a good head for business."

"He had a good head, period," Camille said. "And by that, I mean he was so stinking handsome."

Leo gave her a look.

"He's a good-looking guy," Bob said. "You can't take that away from him. But if you ask me it's his downfall. Anyway, before I know it this kid is infiltrating himself into my life. He wanted to move into the apartment with me upstairs. Save money so he could buy his Harley." Bob shrugged. "I let him."

Leo pictured a Harley. What he wouldn't have given to ride on the back of it hanging on tight to his father's waist!

"He was a real hard worker and he loved this place. I knew he used to pretend it was his. He always thought it *should* have been his."

"He lied to me, Leo," Camille said. "He told me he owned the bar. I spent the whole time thinking he owned the bar."

"Why did he lie?" Leo asked.

"Who knows? To impress me I guess."

Bob continued. "Anyway, his work ethic was never the problem. It was...er...you sure, Camille?"

She nodded and downed the rest of her second beer.

"Slow down, Mom," Leo said.

"Mind your own beeswax," she said to Leo. She banged her hand on the bar. "Give it to us straight, Bobby."

"It was the women...that was always the problem."

"Ha!" Camille said. "The women. Plural."

"I felt so bad for you, Camille."

"But in the end, you helped me, Bob! You told me to 'wake up and smell the coffee' and I did. I can take it from here, Bob. So, Leo, your dad was always working. He was always here. I was stuck in that tiny apartment with no car, no phone, no friends, none of my own stuff from back home, and my mother had disowned me. I got pregnant with you after being married just a couple of months. You came along and oh, how I loved you! But good grief, you were a little screamer. But I loved every minute of it. I loved every squeak you squawked. Anyway, one day I asked Mac to watch you and when I came home, he was getting out of Wally's truck. He had left you home alone in the house! A tiny baby! And there was this red-head in the truck that he had knocked up!"

"What?"

"Oh, yes, I'm sorry to say, honey, but you have a half-sibling out there somewhere."

"Try four," Bob said.

"Four?" Leo said.

"That I know of. Three girls and a boy. And four ex-wives."

"Good grief!" Camille said. "I think I need another drink."

"Oh, no you don't," Leo said. "I think you've had enough, and I think we've *heard* enough."

"Okay, okay, okay," Camille said. "Just one more thing, Bob. Why did he leave and where is he now?"

"I had to fire him, Camille. He was dealing cocaine. No idea where he is now and don't want to know."

Leo got up and pulled some bills out of his wallet. "Hey, Bob, uh, wondering…was he involved with any of his other kids?"

"Are you kidding? Just like with your mom, he was there for a few months until reality set in and then he scrammed."

Leo was ashamed that this gave him some satisfaction.

They sat silent in the car for a while. Camille said, "This little road trip didn't turn out quite as I imagined."

"How did you imagine it?"

"Oh, well, silly, really, but one could hope, right? I pictured your dad behind that bar, looking handsome as ever, out of his mind with joy to meet you! I pictured a contrite, repentant Mac, full of explanations and apologies: *I have a disorder, I'm a sex addict, I was abused as a child. I'm weak. I'm sorry. I meant to call you back all those years ago. I lost my nerve. You look like such a great kid. I am so proud of you. I want to have a relationship with you.*"

"Pie in the sky, Mom."

"I know." Camille sighed. "You know what the worst part is?"

"Oh Mom, so many things could be the worst part."

"I think the worst part is that I don't get to forgive him. I mean in person. I've forgiven him in my mind or in general, or whatever. But before I die, I just wanted to unload that baggage."

"Mom."

"Honey it's in my lymph nodes."

16.
leo & christopher & veronica

STELLA MARIS SHOWED up at Camille's funeral. Rosie couldn't believe it. Her mother, now seventy-one and remarried, looked like a movie star. She'd maintained her figure and was dressed in a charcoal gray dress, belted at the waist, with a fur coat draped over her shoulders. The man on her arm wasn't necessarily handsome, but he oozed money and had a snobby name— Anders Garret. Rosie referred to him from then on as "that poor sucker." Rosie noticed a big, fat diamond on her mother's hand and was certain there was a country club membership in the deal. At least Stella Maris didn't try to stand in the receiving line or sit in the front row of the pew at church. Stella Maris didn't even shed a tear for Camille, but she did stare quite a bit at her grandson. She'd never even met Leo and here he was twenty-two years old.

Barry stood next to Rosie in the receiving line. He was remarried, too, to a nice lady who treated him like a king. Rosie was sure many of the funeral-goers assumed her dad's new wife was Camille's mother. Felicity, in her plain black dress, stood on the other side of Barry, shaking hands and accepting condolences from well-wishers.

Barry had made all the funeral arrangements, insisting on a Catholic Mass at St. Peter's Cathedral in Rockford even though Camille hadn't been to church in over twenty years. Barry explained to his pastor that his daughter had been a *believer*, just not a churchgoer. Barry asked Leo if he would like to give the eulogy, but Leo told his grandfather there was no way he could manage it. "I'm sure Aunt Rose will do it, Gramps. She knew Mom better than anybody."

The night before the funeral, Rosie, Merricat, and Leo stayed with Barry and Felicity at their home. Late into the night, Rosie came knocking on Leo's door, rushing in, all in a tizzy.

"Leo, I'm sorry!" she said.

Leo had just climbed into bed. He sat up. "What's wrong?" He hoped she wasn't chickening out of giving the eulogy. No way he could do it. Maybe Merricat would do it. Or even Eleanor.

"I've been working on the eulogy. And now I realized..."

"What?"

"I overpowered your mother."

"What are you talking about?"

"I see it now." She started to cry. Rosie, who ruled the world, who could part the seas, who could get a bill passed, who could secure a million-dollar grant, was falling to pieces before his eyes. "I'm realizing all this now. I overshadowed her. From day one! I always took control, told her what to do. I never let her make her own decisions."

"That's not true."

"Even with raising you kids, she always deferred to me. I talked her out of going back to church. Out of Catholic school. I talked her out of getting you baptized."

"Wait, what? I'm not baptized?"

Leo knew that his was an unconventional family, in every way, even in the way they had practiced their faith. Rosie, being Rosie, preferred the "female" side of God, the goddess. For as long as he could remember, Rosie had a small altar set up in her bedroom with statues of the Virgin Mary and candles. "If we are made in God's image and likeness," she'd explained to Merricat and Leo, then God is both male and female. He is not some old man with a white beard." They said their prayers at night, they said grace before meals and celebrated Christmas and Easter, but they never set a foot in a church. Leo and Merricat had attended public school and Rosie said, "Let's not," when Camille suggested they enroll the kids in catechism classes at the Catholic church. "I don't want them brainwashed!" Rosie said.

"I'm writing all about what a gentle, kind spirit your mother was and now I'm wondering…did I make her that way?" Rosie paced around the room, wringing her hands. Leo had never seen her like this.

"But you two were best friends. Where is this coming from?"

"I forced her to become a vegetarian. Maybe she liked meat! Maybe she resented me for that!"

"I don't think she—"

"Leo, do you think she was happy? Wait, let me rephrase that. Do you think she was *fulfilled*?"

"I think she was hap—"

"I mean after your dad, she dated a few guys."

"She did?"

"Yes, but I discouraged that. I used to hate men so much back then. I hated everything back then—men, the Catholic Church, politicians…did I say men?"

"My mom dated?"

"She was so naïve about men! I was so worried that someone else would come along and take advantage of her again. So, yes, I discouraged it. I wasn't interested myself—you know I've always been, I don't know…not interested anyway. We thought we had it all, our careers, our home, our friends, our beautiful kids. Who needed men?"

Leo squirmed. Where was all this coming from? "Aunt Rose, stop. Please! Everything's fine. I know you will say wonderful things about Mom, and I'll be happy. Don't fret about this. Merricat and I had a great childhood. You guys did a super job. We turned out great!"

Rosie's eyes were red and swollen. She blew her nose with a tissue. "Well, that's true."

"Come and sit down." Leo patted a spot on the bed.

Rosie plopped down. "I feel like I robbed her of a complete life!"

"You rescued her. And me." Leo slung his arm around Rosie's neck and pulled her in. She leaned on him. "I sometimes think about the crappy life I might have had if you hadn't rescued us."

Rosie blew her nose again and said, "That's true, too. You're right." She sat upright. "Okay, I feel better now."

In the end, Rosie gave Camille a lovely tribute, focusing on her warmhearted, sweet-tempered soul. "Camille didn't ask for much from the world," Rosie said as she wrapped things up. "She was a soft, gentle breeze to my tornado." (That got a laugh.) "She held a simple philosophy about taking a little goodness from life and putting a lot of goodness back. Camille was a good sister, a good friend, a good nurse, a good *daughter* (she emphasized the word for Stella Maris's benefit), and she was a fantastic mother. Oh, Camille, we are going to miss you so very much."

At the luncheon after the burial, an elderly couple sought out Leo and introduced themselves. "I'm Sadie Phillips and this is my husband Wally. Do you remember us, honey?"

Leo hadn't seen Sadie and Wally in years! He remembered visiting them when he was little, and they had attended Camille's graduation party, but once they had moved from Beloit up to Appleton, Wisconsin, where one of their sons lived, they'd lost track.

Leo said, "Of course I remember you!" He hugged Sadie and shook Wally's hand.

"We loved your mother like a daughter," Sadie said. "She was our little cupcake!"

"She insisted you were a better mother than her own," Leo said.

"Leo, you are the spitting image of your father! You even *sound* like him," Sadie said. "I was surprised but glad to see him here today."

"Here's here!?" Leo asked, his eyes darting around the room.

"Oh, honey. I thought you knew," Sadie said.

"I've never met him. That just, uh, that just never worked out. Can you point him out to me?" Leo asked, feeling ridiculous.

"Oh, honey," Sadie said, reaching out for his hand. "I saw him leave in the middle of the service."

"Oh," Leo said.

Wally patted him on the back and said, "If you ask me, it's better that way. He's a good-for-nothing."

"Now, Wall…"

"Beg your pardon. I'm outta line."

Sadie said, "Don't fret now, honey. Well, I'm sure you have people you need to visit with, but I wrote down our phone number. You call if you ever need us." Sadie handed him a scrap of paper. "We're so sorry, honey."

"Thanks so much for coming," Leo said. "It means a lot to me."

Merricat approached as Sadie and Wally walked off. "Who are they?"

"Mom's old landlords, Sadie and Wally Phillips. You remember them." Leo watched them shuffle across the room with their walkers. They had to be in their late eighties or early nineties.

"Oh yeah, I remember. How sweet of them to come, Leo!"

"Get this, Cat. They said my dad was here."

"You're kidding! Did you see him? Did you talk to him?"

"No and no. Seems like he kind of slithered in and out."

"The perfect verb: slither," Merricat said. She looked at Leo's blank stare. "What?"

"I don't know," Leo said. "I wonder if there have been other times when he's been near me, or in the vicinity, or maybe even stalking me…"

It didn't seem right to Leo that the day after he buried his mother, life continued as if this seismic event hadn't occurred. He and Merricat kissed Rosie and Barry and Felicity goodbye and drove back to UIC to finish the last few months of their senior year. Leo was glad that he had some easy classes for the last semester. He knew it was going to be hard to concentrate. Merricat called that night to check on him. "I can be there in a minute if you need me." (She lived in an apartment one block down.)

"I know," Leo said.

"I can bring tequila."

"I know," Leo said.

"We can get *blootered*!"

"Oh, I don't know," Leo said.

And the world kept turning, dishing out joy and sorrow, but not in equal measure. The joyous occasion of Merricat and Leo's UIC graduations in May, 1998—with degrees in Women's Studies and Business, respectively—was spoiled when Barry's wife Felicity fell and broke her hip. She developed an infection post-surgery, went septic, and died. Barry was devastated. Another loss. Another funeral. Then two years later, Barry was diagnosed with Parkinson's and since Merricat and Leo were living and working in Chicago by then, Rosie did the most selfless thing a person could do—she gave up her life in Madison and all its social-political excitement and all her friends and influential acquaintances and she moved to Rockford to care for her dad. (Truth was, without Camille and the kids, she was lonely.) She bought a condo, moved her dad in, and got a job working for Mayor Charles Box as Director of Community and Economic Development.

When Leo helped move Rosie to Rockford he couldn't believe all the stuff she had. "It's our whole life, Leo," Rosie said as they carried in box after box of what he called the Mifflin Street shit.

"You should have left all this, Aunt Rose, and bought new."

"Bite your tongue. I'm not materialistic, but I read somewhere that as we age our belongings embody our sense of self."

"There she goes," said Merricat.

"Listen, it's true. All these things have become receptacles for our memories. For our lives, our travels, our relationships. But if you're not sentimental about your things, I'd be happy to throw out your PEZ collection, Merricat, and the Beatles' stuff your mom left you, Leo."

"What can I do for you?" Leo asked the young, fresh-faced businessman who sat across from him at his large mahogany desk at the bank. Unlike his savvy cousin Merricat, who had done an internship her senior year with a nonprofit that advocated for victims of domestic violence and then got hired by the said nonprofit (like mother, like daughter), Leo had secured no internship and had instead partied and coasted the last semester of his senior year. Upon graduation, his job search proved difficult and he wound up having to do what he swore he would never do—take a job that required a suit and tie. After three humiliating months of searching, he got a job as a savings counselor at the Chase Manhattan Bank on Dearborne. Now he had to suit-and-tie-up every day. He hated it. Talk about boring! The best parts of the day: two fifteen-minute coffee breaks and his lunch hour.

Today, on his lunch break, Leo walked up the street a few blocks to a bike shop called *Pierre's Bikes* (named after Pierre Lallement, the Frenchman considered by most to be the inventor of the pedal bicycle). His girlfriend, Alondra, was harping on him to get a bike so they could ride together. He'd been "window-shopping" for a couple of weeks, researching his options. Leo was a careful buyer—whether it was a dress shirt or a bicycle. The owners were a middle-aged married couple who considered the bicycle to be the premier invention of the nineteenth century. "What kind of bike are you looking for?" the wife asked him.

"One with two wheels," Leo said.

She didn't think it was funny. At least she didn't laugh. "Homer!" she said, calling for her husband. "You take this one."

Homer had more of a sense of humor. Homer was also a fantastic salesman. Leo bought a fairly expensive bike. "I'll pick it up after work," Leo told the wife when he paid.

"We don't deliver," she informed him.

"No, I just said I would pick it up."

"Good, because we don't deliver."

Later, when he went back to pick up the bike, Homer offered him a job. "The wife just quit! Our daughter had twins and Mother wants to help. You're a good-looking young man with a sense of humor and I can teach you about bikes. I go by feeling. I don't need a resume or references. My stomach tells me when someone is good. I got a feeling you're good."

"I'll need to give two weeks' notice at the bank."

"Hired!" Homer said and shook Leo's hand.

Turned out, Leo wasn't the greatest salesman. He thought most of the bikes were way over-priced and so he tried to sell the economical options to customers. "Are you *trying* to run me out of business?" Homer said one day after Leo talked a customer into buying a bike that cost two-hundred dollars less than the one he came in to purchase.

"Maybe your gut was wrong about me."

"Just do better," Homer said.

Since Leo liked selling bikes better than he did opening savings accounts, and since he didn't have to wear a suit and throat-strangling tie, he stepped it up. He mimicked Homer's selling style and started breaking sales records. It wasn't hard to out-sell "Mother."

"See, I know my own gut," Homer said, slapping Leo on the back.

"But you don't want to sell bikes for the rest of your life, do you?" Merricat asked at breakfast one Sunday. The two had met for breakfast every Sunday since they graduated. (Leo didn't know that Merricat lied to Brice about where she was. Years later she would confess that she led Brice to believe she was at church.)

"Of course not," Leo said, stuffing eggs into his mouth. Although that wasn't really true. Leo just wasn't ambitious in the way Merricat and Brice were. He felt no inherent responsibility to save the world. Leo kind of coasted on air. He worked at the bike shop, he hung out at bars, he took guitar lessons, he went to concerts, he rode bikes with his girlfriend. He liked his uncomplicated life.

"You still want to own your own business, right?"

"Of course." (The answer he knew she wanted to hear.)

"Leo, you've worked for Homer for nearly three years now. You're twenty-six. You need to start thinking about your future."

"Sheesh. It can't be three years."

"Brice says—"

"Oh, no. Don't 'Brice says' me." Leo still didn't care for Brice. As far as Leo was concerned, he was a third wheel. Leo and Merricat had always been a pair. The post-graduation plan was to get an apartment together, but then Brice happened. Brice and Merricat got a place in Andersonville and so Leo moved in with three guys in a house in River West. Even though they lived only twenty minutes apart, they may as well have lived on different continents. Brice was jealous of Leo. He told Merricat he didn't understand the relationship.

Merricat pointed her fork at Leo. "You've always needed a little push. You get too comfortable."

"What's wrong with comfortable?"

"You stop growing, that's what. Listen, Brice has a friend who wants to open a bar and he's been looking for a partner. You'd be perfect. You have a good head for business, you're handy since you worked for that landlord all those years, you're charming when you want to be, and you've got your mom's inheritance to invest. The guy's name is Christopher Lynwood. He's a trust fund kid. Will you talk to him? Please Leo?"

"Hmmmm. Maybe it's destiny. My dad worked at a bar."

"Operative word—*worked*. You would *own* a bar."

"I'll talk to him."

A month after Brice and Merricat's wedding (a small affair, complete with a barefoot bride, hippie food, and all the Femmys in attendance) Leo and Christopher Lynwood opened the *Silver Darlings Pub* in an old brick-front building on Clark Street, across from the Wrigley Field parking lot.

The grand opening was a huge success. Rosie drove in with Barry for the celebration, and of course Merricat and Brice were there. They timed the opening to coincide with a Cubs home game on May 11, 2000, against the Milwaukee Brewers. Never could they have imagined that the Cubs' outfielder, Glenallen Hill, with his tree trunk sized arms, would make history at the bottom of the second, becoming the first and so far the only player to hit a pitched ball (somewhere in the neighborhood of five hundred feet) onto the roof of a five-story building across the street at the corner of Waveland and Kenmore Avenues. The crowd went berserk. Leo and Christopher heard the cheering as they were making last minute preparations for the opening. It was a great omen! They opened the door at six p.m., just minutes after the game ended, and, even though the Cubs had lost to the Brewers (14 to 8), the crowd—it seemed nearly all of the twenty thousand fans descended upon them—was upbeat and excited to try the brand-new Scottish bar with the odd name: *Silver Darlings*. Things were so out of control; the fire marshal was called in when someone reported overcrowding. They even ran out of beer.

While Leo and Christopher had both agreed they wanted to open a place in Wrigleyville to attract Cubs' fans, they disagreed on the type of bar. Christopher wanted a more upscale venue; Leo wanted a cozy tavern. In the end, they opened a sort of hybrid, calling it an "up-dive," a dimly lit, quaint gastropub with a hint of European cool. There were several Irish pubs in the area, but not one Scottish pub. Duke of Perth, a Scottish pub south of Wrigley Field, had opened up on North Clark Street and was a pleasant place complete with rock bagpipe bands and authentic British food. The other Scottish pub was Ole St. Andrews Inn, north of Wrigley Field on Broadway, a tavern with a distinctly medieval aura and an impressive collection of sabers. (Legend had it there was a drunken ghost roaming about.) Neither bar catered to loyal and thirsty Cubs fans though and that's where Silver Darlings found its niche.

Turned out, it wasn't Christopher who was a gifted businessman, it was Christopher's *father.* Somewhere along the line, Calvin Lynwood, a Chicago real estate mogul, took over the planning when it was clear that Christopher and Leo were in over their heads. "Two knuckleheads with business degrees," he lamented. "I never stepped foot in a college and look at me today." He chided the boys that they hadn't done their due diligence. "You don't just open up a bar one day." (When Calvin had asked Leo what kind of experience he had, Leo stammered and then answered, "My dad owned a pub," which was deceptive in so many ways.) Calvin had his company do due diligence—which meant he hired two guys to visit every one of the forty-some bars in the Wrigleyville area. They bought drinks, sampled food, took notes about themes and decor, and talked to the owners about their businesses. Due diligence also meant a trip to Glasgow, Scotland, to visit Calvin's favorite pub in Europe—the Bon Accord, an ale and grub pub/specialty whisky bar. The trip, written off as a business expense by Calvin, was the first time Leo had flown out of the country. Good thing his mom had made him get a passport when he started college in case he wanted to study abroad.

Leo, not wanting to appear to be a country bumpkin, pretended the international trip was a common event. When they landed in Glasgow and Calvin started asking questions about where his father was from, Leo concocted some lame explanation about how, when his father's family emigrated from Scotland, they fell in love with America and focused on assimilating quickly. His family didn't talk much about "the old country."

Leo had a lot to learn. He didn't even know the difference between whisky and whiskey. Without Calvin's help, Leo and Christopher never would have opened their doors. When they returned from Scotland, Calvin secured the tax statistics on entertainment, dining, and bar service in the area to make sure there was room for profit. He paid for demographic studies, got insurance quotes, and applied for a liquor license—you had to know people! He put a lawyer on retainer and interviewed and hired general contractors. He attended to things such as the "consent of transfer" from the current owner, blueprints of the floor-plan, and the property tax clearance from the county treasurer. Leo's head swirled with all the details—he had no idea it would be this involved. He would learn that studying business, opening a business, and conducting business were very different ventures.

Calvin had encouraged the boys to come up with a unique name. "Something catchy; something original." He'd offered the *Silver Darlings Pub* (after a 1947 British film about a Scottish herring fisherman—the herrings were the silver darlings). Christopher suggested *The Liquid Library* and Leo suggested *Ole Scotty's* or *Tip's Tavern*. Calvin had a consumer marketing company test the names and Silver Darlings tested the best.

Leo's inheritance from his mother ended up not being enough for his share. He'd had to sell Sadie's diamond ring, plus take out a loan. He was so tempted to sell the Beatles stuff, but he'd promised his mother he wouldn't. When all the paperwork was signed and everything was a "go," Leo and Christopher shook hands. "Equal partners," Christopher said. But nothing about the partnership was equal, because much too late in the process, Leo realized that their business was structured as a Limited Partnership. Calvin's lawyers set it up where Calvin was the "general partner" who would control the day-to-day operations and also take on the liability for business debt. The limited partners—Leo and Christopher—would run the bar but would have minimal control over major business decisions or operations, but neither would they be personally liable for business debts or claims. Leo, a nervous wreck after finding all of this out, called Merricat, who put Brice on the phone who explained to Leo that this was the very best set-up. It protected Leo from losing everything if the bar went under.

They got carried away with the construction. They spent too much on the bar and the dark wooden gantry behind it, but Leo insisted they needed to showcase the Scottish whiskies and the Irish whiskeys. When the shelving was lighted it was a thing of beauty. Built into the gantry were gorgeous stained-glass fronts with fish on them, custom-designed. The bar itself was a massive wrap-around with real leather high-backed bar stools for ultimate comfort. Glass lamps created by a local artist hung from the ceiling over the bar, providing a warm and cozy ambiance. The bar was edged with a thin ribbon of copper etched with humorous quotes: "*Eat, Drink, and Bring Mary!*" "*Beer does not make you fat. It makes you lean...lean on chairs, friends, walls.*" "*I'm on a whiskey diet. I've lost three days already.*" "*Beauty is in the eye of the beer holder.*" The walls were stucco and exposed brick, with wood beams on the ceiling. Christopher wanted a tin ceiling, but Leo thought new tin ceilings looked like you were trying too hard. On the walls hung gorgeous eighteenth-century prints of Scottish wild revelry and drunkenness. And in the back, two red leather couches faced each other across from the huge fireplace creating the perfect romantic spot. All in all, when you walked in the door of the Silver Darlings Pub, you got the feeling you were in a family-run candlelit neighborhood bar in Scotland.

At first, both Leo and Christopher pretty much lived at the bar. Eighteen-hour days were not unusual. Leo had glamorized it all thinking how fun it would be to spend most of the time behind the bar, mixing drinks, flirting, high-fiving customers, raking in big tips, cheering on the Cubbies. What he hadn't expected was that the work was backbreaking. It was less about charming inebriated customers as it was schlepping kegs in the basement, dealing with unscrupulous suppliers, unclogging toilets, firing inept employees, and cleaning up piss and vomit. What made it all worth it? His adoring fans. The regulars who would chant LEO! LEO! LEO! when he took his place behind the bar. Once a group of loyal regulars was established, it was as if Leo were throwing a party every night for friends. He guessed the bar business was in his blood after all.

Two years in and they were in the black. Calvin was pleased. They'd stuck to their conservative business plan, were careful with their monthly spends, and made sure cash flow was king. They'd realized early on that it wasn't the weekends that would make or break them, it was the weeknights. They treated their weeknight customers extra special.

They fell into a groove: they divvied up the duties—Christopher did the books and the payroll, Leo did all the ordering, stocking, and hiring. Christopher was good with health inspectors; Leo was good with plumbers. They both fixed what was broken and there was always something broken. When Christopher married a gorgeous girl who worked for his dad, they divided the day; Christopher managed the lunch crowd and Leo, always the night owl, took the night shift. They overlapped for an hour or two in the early evening when they conducted their "business meetings"—mostly Christopher bitching about one thing or another. But once Christopher went home for the day, Leo found his groove. He drank right along with his customers—building up a healthy tolerance to copious amounts of alcohol, and practically lived his life at the bar. Often, he ended up too drunk to walk home—he had moved out of the house in River West and rented a hole in the wall above another bar three blocks down from his own bar—and slept in a recliner in the back office. He made sure to get the hell out of there before Christopher showed up in the morning. Not once was he ever caught. Christopher lived his life like a well-timed clock; he showed up precisely at seven-fifteen and left exactly at six-fifteen.

Though he had no way of knowing it, Leo was like his father in some ways and unlike him in others. He was like him in that he was a great marketing man. It was Leo who came up with creative promotional ideas that garnered praise from Calvin Lynwood and jealous looks from Christopher. Leo came up with Scottish themed nights such as Hogmanay (New Year's Eve) and Burns Night (A birthday party for Scottish poet Robert Burns) and contests and punch cards. He sold T-shirts and baseball hats imprinted with their logo. Leo's college roommate, Caesar, an artist, designed the logo for the business' signage, website, business cards, etc. (Another move that got him praise from Calvin and snide looks from Christopher.) Caesar came up with a rendering of a gorgeous Cisco—a lake herring—with its slender, elongated body, silvery in color with faint pink and purple iridescence sides, blue green back, and white underside. Directly under the fish was the name Silver Darlings Pub in AR Christy typeface, which Caesar described as young, funky, and nerdy.

Leo was unlike his father in that he wasn't a pig with women. "Hello beautiful!" he said to Angie when he came to work on Friday night. He could say that to Angie because they were together. He'd hired her as a night cook eleven months ago when Christopher suggested expanding their menu. (Now in addition to fish and chips, shepherd's pie, Scotch eggs, and bangers and mash, they offered Scottish meatloaf, Guinness steak stew, lamb and rosemary pie, corned beef, braised short ribs and of course, the obligatory haggis.)

He'd dated a few servers who worked at the bar on and off since they'd opened four years ago. Nothing serious, but when Leo dated someone, he was loyal until the end. But now he was twenty-nine and the girls they hired were twenty-one, twenty-two. He was unlike his dad in this way also: he wasn't attracted to young girls. If anything, he liked older women.

Angie was thirty-six, a fact about which she was quite sensitive. "One of these days, you're going to dump me for a younger woman," she would say. But she in no way looked seven years his senior. Yoga and running kept her slender body in good shape and she paid good money to keep her skin smooth and tight. Her strawberry blond hair and freckles added to her youthful appearance. They'd had to keep their relationship on the down-low because Calvin had implemented a "no-dating" policy that banned dating between a supervisor and his/her subordinate. "But *everybody* is my subordinate," Leo had complained.

"Exactly," Calvin said. "Things are going great. The last thing we need is a lawsuit." (After a broker in his firm sued another for sexual misconduct, Calvin's attorneys had him implement the policy at all his businesses.)

"This is exactly why I wanted to own my own damn business," Leo told Merricat after Calvin had delivered the news. "I'm nothing but an employee."

But a year or so into the no-dating policy, Calvin (newly divorced and chasing skirts at his own firm) announced that the policy went too far and he revised it to a "notification" policy whereby employees were required to report to the managers whenever they entered into a consensual relationship.

"Got it," Leo said to Calvin. "Okay, I hereby officially announce that I am in a consensual relationship with an employee."

They were sitting in the back office having a meeting. Calvin in his three-piece suit always looked as if he had just left a courtroom.

"You have to name the person or it's not official," Christopher said. (Leo imagined Christopher got beat up a lot in school.) Christopher looked to his father, who nodded.

"Come on, you guys know I've been with Angie for months."

"But we had a no-dating policy!" Christopher said. "Dad!"

Leo said, "I have never let my relationships bleed into work."

Christopher snorted. "Well, Angie is bleeding in the kitchen as we speak."

"What's that supposed to mean?"

"She cut herself. Pretty badly."

Leo stood up, his chair screeching against the floor. "And you're just telling me now?"

He found Angie in the kitchen with her left hand wrapped in a towel. "I'm fine," she said, seeing his furrowed brow. "I told Christopher to keep his mouth shut."

"What happened?"

"Slicing leeks for the Cock-a-Leekie soup. I might have to rename it Cock-a-Leekie-Fingertip soup."

"You're exaggerating, right?"

"Just a little."

"You need to get it looked at. You may need stitches."

"I'm fine, Leo," she said, but then she started tearing up.

"You don't look fine."

"I'm fine," she repeated, mopping her eyes with the towel.

Trying to cheer her up, Leo said, "There is some good news. Calvin just updated the 'no-dating' policy to a 'notification' policy. I officially notified him that we are dating."

"We're what?"

"Dating? Together? In a relationship?"

"You call this," she used her knife to encompass the kitchen, "a relationship? We work together at the same place, but I am mostly in the kitchen and you're mostly behind the bar, and then when we close, we go to your place or my place and we don't even have energy to make love. We literally *sleep* together."

"We make love in the morning!"

"No, we sleep all morning. We make love in the afternoon. Sometimes."

"You have just described my perfect world! Aren't you happy?"

"No!"

"Oh."

"Leo, I'm thirty-six. I'm not getting any younger."

"Meaning?"

"Meaning, I want to get married and have kids before my uterus shrivels up."

"Oh, well, Angie…"

"I know, you love me, but you don't LOVE me. I get it. I love you, but I don't think I LOVE you either."

Something else Leo didn't know, but he was like his father in that he liked to match up his life experiences with the perfect Beatles song. When he was with Poppy Li, early Beatles songs—*I Want to Hold Your Hand*, and *Baby It's You* were fitting. When he and Christopher were paying the bills, *Taxman* ran through his head. Or when Christopher was acting like a bloody idiot, it was *The Fool on the Hill*. When he was in a groove behind the bar, he'd whistle *All Together Now*, and *With a Little Help From My Friends*, or *Ob-La-Di, Ob-La-Da*. After making love to Angie, it was *A Taste of Honey*, and *Till There Was You*.

So, when Angie returned to work after a couple of days off and acted as if the conversation they'd had never took place, he greeted her with, "Hello beautiful. How's the finger?" But the McCartney song, *Things We Said Today*, was running through his head.

"It's throbbing, but I had to get back to work. I couldn't stand it." She held up her hand covered in a rubber glove.

When the bar closed, Leo and Angie walked to his place. Leo could have fallen asleep standing up, but he found some strength and made love to

Angie. She had to hold her finger out of the way so as not to bump it and they ended up laughing at the awkwardness. But something had changed. They both knew it. The next morning, Leo woke before Angie. He looked at her as she lie sleeping. Suddenly she looked every bit of thirty-six; she may even have looked thirty-seven. And it wasn't about her looks; she was lovely whatever her age, but he knew she wouldn't be happy with what he could give her. Leo wasn't even sure he wanted kids. What if he wasn't cut out for it, like his father wasn't? He didn't want to put a kid through what he'd been through, because here he was, twenty-nine years old, and he still felt he had been shortchanged. He made coffee and bacon and eggs. The least he could do was make a nice breakfast for Angie.

After they broke up, Angie stayed on for another three months at the bar. This surprised Leo, but since she was a good cook, he was grateful; and since he could stay out of the kitchen, it worked. It was strange how they moved effortlessly from lovers to friends. He put out feelers for a new night cook and when Angie finally gave him her two weeks' notice ("three if you need it, Leo") he was ready with a couple of candidates. Angie left with a piece of his heart. (Later he would receive Christmas cards from her. She'd ended up traveling the country, cooking at wonderful restaurants. Last card he'd received included a family photo of her with a nice-looking—younger?—man and a baby. "Chloe Louise, seven pounds, three ounces." Leo was happy for her.)

Four years later, on New Year's Eve, or as the Scottish call it, *Hogmanay*, a man sat himself down at the bar and asked Leo in a heavy Scottish accent, "Do ya have a Glenmorangie, eh?"

Leo said they did and grabbed the bottle of one of Scotland's biggest selling single malts from the top shelf. It was one of his own favorites with its light flowery taste and strong perfume. He didn't get many requests as it was a bit pricey. "Got a nice 18-year."

"Neat, if ya don mind."

Leo poured and set the glass in front of the man, who Leo guessed to be in his late sixties, early seventies. He was big-shouldered and thick-wristed, with a full head of pure white hair, and blue-green eyes, with bushy brows.

At one time he may have been good-looking, but now he appeared haggard and used-up—you could tell drinkers and smokers by their bloated faces, broken capillaries, and reddened complexions.

The man sipped his whisky and said, "That's pure deed brilliant. G'head and keep tha' bottle close by, eh."

"Where you from, sir?" Leo asked.

"Where d'ya think?"

"Glasgow?"

"Would ya believe me if I said Wisconsin?"

Leo did a double take. Could it be? Nah. But what if it was? "Your name doesn't happen to be Lennox, does it?"

"Depends who's asking!"

Leo's eyes grew saucer big.

"That'd be a joke, eh. Name's Brody McDonaugh."

Leo released his breath. "Nice to meet you. I'm Leo Lennox. Have relatives from Scotland...that's why I was asking."

"Haven't been there in yonks. But come on, son, I can see you're talking oot your fanny flaps. Who ya really looking fer?"

"Never met my father. He's from Wisconsin. Near your age. You never know."

"True enough. Sorry fer ya, eh. But that be how life is...when you least expect it, he'll show up."

"It would be a miracle," Leo said.

"T'would indeed. Now pour me another and be generous, why don ya."

As midnight approached, Leo left the bar in the capable hands of Jules, the bar manager, so that he could hand out party favors—hats, Hawaiian leis, confetti party poppers, blowouts, fringe squawkers, and mini hand clappers. Leo's girlfriend, Veronica, was sitting with Merricat and Brice and a few other friends at a table near the windows. He brought over a bottle of champagne for the toast and uncorked it. He filled glasses with the bubbly—everyone's except for Merricat's, who was pregnant—and then counted down with the crowd to the year 2008. He kissed Veronica and Merricat and even hugged Brice, whom he still did not care for, but to whom he owed a great debt, as he was instrumental in setting him up with Christopher. The bar was profitable and Leo was in a good place. He and Veronica had been together for a little over a year. He was thirty-three, and if there was ever a woman who could make him think about settling down it was Veronica. She was a flight attendant for Delta. She enjoyed her job and like Leo didn't think she wanted children. Veronica wasn't needy like some of the other girls he'd dated. The two were...comfortable, compatible. They fit well.

When Leo returned to the bar, McDonaugh was still there, talking too loudly, slurring his words. "There's me good man. Hit me up, eh?" he said to Leo. But Jules, the bar manager, shook his head at Leo and subtly motioned a throat cut.

"Ahh, Mr. McDonaugh," Leo said. "It looks as though we're fresh out of the Glenmorangie. How about a nice glass of seltzer?" Jules sprayed seltzer into a glass with the bar gun and Leo slid it in front of McDonaugh.

"Now listen here," McDonaugh said. "Don be a dobber! Pour me a glass. A wee dram, eh?"

Leo looked to Jules, who held up four fingers. With the two Leo had served, that meant he'd consumed six glasses in an hour or so. Oftentimes, the best way to handle an inebriated customer was to recruit the help of someone in his party. A drunk usually took the news that he was cut off better from a friend. "Mr. McDonaugh, did you come with anyone else tonight?"

"It's just me. Just me. Now do I get a drink or not?"

"Sure, you do." Leo said. "Try this." Leo surreptitiously opened a bottle of Irn Bru, a caffeinated orange soda so popular in Scotland it was dubbed "Scotland's Other National Drink," and poured it over ice. He'd been successful in passing the soda off to other drunk customers as a Gin and Orange. He placed the glass in front of McDonaugh. "And how about something to eat? Some fish and chips maybe? On the house. A Happy New Year treat." That was the other tactic—to get some food into the customer to soak up some of that alcohol.

"I already had me dinner!" McDonaugh sipped from the glass and set it back down hard on the bar. Guess there was no pulling the wool over on him. "I'll just take me business elsewhere!" This was actually the best outcome—that the customer made the decision to leave on his own.

McDonaugh climbed down from his stool but was so tanked-up his legs gave out and he fell flat on his face. A couple of ladies at the bar gasped. Leo and Jules hurried around to help the man up, but he was having none of it. "Get yer hands offa me! Leave me be!" Leo moved back and gave the man some space. It took some time but he was able with some effort to right himself.

Jules said, "Sir, are you okay? Can I call you a cab?"

"No, you cannot, I'm a walkin' man," McDonaugh said, brushing off his trousers. He staggered to the door like an admonished puppy. Jules realized he'd forgotten his coat and ran it over to him. McDonaugh snatched it from his hands and pushed the door open.

"Happy New Year!" Jules called out.

Satisfied to hear the man wasn't going to get behind the wheel, Leo called, "Please come again!" Then, turning to his customers at the bar, added, "NOT!" Back behind the bar, he and Jules mixed and poured and served until it was closing time and he turned out the lights, locked up, and he and Veronica walked (holding each other up) to his apartment and fell into bed, nearly dead to the world with exhaustion.

Leo woke the next morning with a spectacular headache. He and Veronica spent the entire morning in bed. Then Veronica got up and made what she called her "Hangover Breakfast": Asian pear juice, honey on toast, two aspirin, and scrambled eggs. As an international flight attendant, Veronica had discovered these scientifically proven hangover remedies from around the world. Sprite and Pedialyte were also options. They ate breakfast in bed and watched the news on WGN. Leo nearly choked when he heard the newscaster report that a seventy-year-old man had been found New Year's Day morning beaten and bloody in an alley near the Wrigley Field parking lot (not far from Silver Darlings). The man was taken to Thorek Memorial Hospital where he was treated for lacerations and frostbite. His alcohol level was 0.299.

"Bloody hell," Leo said, "I hope that wasn't *my* drunk."

"Who? What?" Veronica asked.

"That old guy that was in last night, drunk as hell. That guy who fell off his stool? Geez, I hope it wasn't him."

It wasn't him. McDonaugh showed his face—unbeaten, but still haggard-looking—the next Friday night, pleasant as could be, not exhibiting a shred of memory of New Year's Eve. Took a place at the bar and waited patiently for Leo to get to him. Just as he was about to take his order, Leo decided to have a little fun with him. "Evening, sir. You know what, you look like a Glenmorangie connoisseur. Do you know it? Single malt?"

"Know it?" McDonaugh said. "I dream about it!" He perked up.

"I have a nice 18-year."

"Neat, if ya will. And keep tha' bottle close by," he said.

It was nine o'clock and post-holiday slow—New Year's resolutions and all. How many regulars had told Leo on New Year's Eve that he may never see them again as they were swearing off alcohol forever? (Three of them were sitting at his bar this very moment.) Leo decided to play it out with McDonaugh, more because he was bored than anything else. He winked at Jules. "Nice accent. Where you from?"

"Where d'ya think?"

"Glasgow? Or Edenborough?" Leo winked at Jules again. "Or, I don't know, maybe Wisconsin."

"Well 'at's pure brilliant! I indeed do hail from God's Country. Good guess!"

Leo decided that the guy must have already been hammered when he'd arrived on New Year's Eve—he had no recollection whatsoever of their conversation.

"You wouldn't by chance be related to the McDonaughs of Wisconsin, would you?" Leo asked.

McDonaugh raised his right eyebrow and paused, drink in the air. "*Boaby*! What are ya', a mind reader then?"

"Nah, another lucky guess."

"Come on," he said, but then he got distracted by an attractive woman. "Nice place, this is. You own it?"

"Me and two other guys."

"Ya' didn't quite pull off the Scottish bit, though."

"Oh?"

"If authentic was what ya' were looking fer, you should a consulted with a true Scot. Ya' got the delicious brew, eh, but what yer missing is the jovial backdrop with some interesting characters."

"Ah," said Leo.

"The place is too new, as well, too slick. A true Scottish pub is antiquated or at the very least, cozy, with a bit of a run-down feel."

"Ah," Leo said again.

"A place where the patrons are friendly and at any moment someone might jump up from the bar and dance a little number."

Now Leo was getting a bit annoyed.

"The floors ought to be of stone, there should be fiery open hearths and live music."

"The floors are stone and we do have a fireplace and—"

"And the gossip—Scottish pub gossip is the best. And the place should have some history to it—like it'd been the stompin' grounds for some national figger, like a poet or statesmen. Or at the very least some mysterious fellow, an old character with an accent and a look…maybe even a secret."

"Someone like you?"

"Ha!" McDonaugh said, "I ain't no national figger, I guess, but I do have me secrets."

McDonaugh finished his one and only glass of Glenmorangie, slammed down a dollar tip and left.

"Hmmm," Leo said out loud.

McDonaugh showed up again the next Friday night around the same time, near nine o'clock, sober as a stick. Chatty. With a glass of the 18-year Glenmorangie in front of him, he talked wistful-like of the old days to anyone who would listen. And folks did listen. It was that accent—it was like a magnet. Leo thought about himself in his younger days when he'd cultivated a faux-Scottish accent. He'd given up on it years ago, although vestiges of it remained when he said certain words or phrases. McDonough was full of fantastic stories that no one believed. But they were entertaining. When he wasn't drunk, the guy could be charming.

McDonaugh returned on Friday, January 25th for "Burns Night." The old guy told Leo he was impressed that a wanna-be Scottish pub like Silver

Darlings even knew what Burns Night was, much less attempt to recreate it. "Burns Night is the highlight of the Scottish social calendar," he announced to the other customers at the bar. "The day ta celebrate our most revered national poet, Robert Burns. Ya know, the brilliant baird who gave the world the poem *Auld Lang Syne*." He held up his glass and started singing, "May auld acquaintance be forgot," in a rich baritone.

Leo had worked with the Chicago Scots organization to find out how to celebrate with authentic traditions such as "Immortal Memory," the "Toasts to the Lads and Lassies" and the address to the haggis. He'd hired some students from Columbia College to recite poetry and he made sure the evening was interspersed with boozy toasts of Drambuie and Strathearn Cider brandy.

This time, while Leo was busy overseeing the Burns Night activities, McDonaugh got wasted again, despite Jules keeping an eye on him. He started arguing with a customer who sat next to him. When Leo heard the raised voices, he made his way back behind the bar. Jules held up two fingers signifying the number of drinks he had served McDonaugh. Again, Leo suspected that he'd shown up already lit.

McDonaugh pointed his finger at the man sitting next to him and, with his face inches away, shouted something about the Beatles being better than the Stones. "You dobber, you, do ya got a brain in yer head or not? I'm telling ya, there is no comparison. Hey, bartender, what say you? Best rock band a all time—Beatles or Stones?"

Leo said, "Beatles. Of course, the Beatles."

"See, see?" McDonaugh said to the guy next to him. "Good boy," he said to Leo. "Ya know what I got? I got all the Beatles' albums, every last one of 'em. Some of 'em never even removed from thair jackets. Do you have any Beatles albums, eh? Or memorabilia? Friend of mine sold a Beatles jigsaw puzzle a while back for four hundred and fifty bucks."

Leo did in fact still have his mother's boxes of Beatles stuff. Somewhere. He hadn't thought about that stuff in a while. Were they in his storage room in the basement of his building? Did Aunt Rose have them? All he could remember was that he'd promised his mom he wouldn't sell them until he was old and gray. He had been tempted to sell them when he needed cash to open the bar, but a promise was a promise and it was the only thing his mother had ever asked of him.

Leo didn't answer McDonaugh as he was called away to attend to one of the college students who'd been hired to recite the poetry for the night but refused to put on the kilt that Leo had rented. The kid was just finally agreeing to put on the kilt and read the damn poetry, when there was a ruckus at the bar. McDonaugh had fallen off his barstool again. Jules was helping him up. Leo ran over and took him by the arm. He walked him to the door. "See you next week, Mr. McDonaugh."

"Maybe ya will and maybe ya won't," he said.

Leo didn't see him the next week, or the week after that, or the week after that. But the week after that, while he and Veronica were lying in bed at her apartment Sunday morning, watching the news on WGN, Leo saw McDonaugh's face flash on the screen.

"What the hell!" Leo said, turning up the volume.

"...Seventy-year old was found at the corner of Addison and N. Wilton Avenue beaten and bloodied. Police report that this is the third incidence of a beating of an elderly man in the area, the first being on Christmas Eve, and the second on New Year's Day morning. The victim, Brody Lennox, is a resident of Beloit, Wisconsin, and told police he was in Chicago on business. He was treated for lacerations at Thorek Memorial Hospital and released."

"Wait a minute," Leo said to Veronica. "What did they say his name was?"

"Brody Lennox?" Veronica said.

"No, that's Brody McDonaugh."

The clip continued, showing another man helping Brody Whoever-He-Was walking out of the hospital. The newscaster continued: "Mr. Lennox's brother said, 'What kind of world do we live in, aye, that an old man gets beaten up for no reason at all?'"

"Holy crap!" Leo said.

"What?" Veronica said.

"I think that other guy is my father!"

17.
leo & merricat

"I'M SURE IT *was* him!" Merricat said, when Leo called after the news report. She had seen the news, too. "And that old guy is your uncle."

"It all makes sense now," Leo said. "He must be after the Beatles stuff. He asked me if I had any albums or memorabilia."

"And remember, the one and only time you talked to your dad on the phone, he asked you about the Beatles stuff. The absolute nerve!" Merricat said. "If he ever shows his face again, Leo, tell him you sold all the stuff and you have no interest in seeing him or his brother. You still have that stuff, don't you?"

"Somewhere. Maybe at Veronica's"

"It must be really valuable if he wants it that badly."

"Maybe. I don't know."

"What a loser. A bottom-feeder. This is as low as it gets. Listen, I gotta go. I have a doctor's appointment. They're doing an ultrasound and I think we're going to find out the sex. Brice is still wavering, but you know me, I can't stand the suspense."

Veronica was packing. She was leaving later that morning for Amsterdam and Leo was already feeling lonely. Sometimes when Veronica was off flying around the world, Leo would sink into despair. He didn't like to admit it, but he seemed to be the kind of man who needed a woman in his life. So, when he was alone, he often felt unmoored. The shock of seeing his father on TV got to him.

The bar was closed on Mondays and if Veronica were home, they would go exploring. Since neither was a Chicago native, they could spend the rest of their lives finding cool and interesting things to do and see in the city. After Veronica left for the airport, Leo paid some bills, watched some TV, and then grew restless. He thought about Veronica flying to Amsterdam, which made him think of the line from the Ballad of John and Yoko about driving to the Amsterdam Hilton, which made him think of the Beatles, which made him wonder where the hell that Beatles stuff was anyway. He took a trip down to the basement and unlocked the lock on Veronica's storage cubicle (he had no storage space at his apartment). He rummaged around his and Veronica's stuff and found the boxes of albums and then the boxes of memorabilia. "Phew!" he said out loud. He hadn't thought about that stuff until Brody Lennox came into the bar, and he'd had a sick feeling he'd lost it all and let his mother down. He was glad it was intact.

Bored, he went for a walk. Veronica lived a couple blocks from the bar, on West Cornelia Avenue. He cursed the temperature, which was a balmy nine degrees. Damn lake effect. Sometimes he seriously thought about moving to a warmer climate, where a person's face wouldn't freeze off in the winter. He blew air into his fists—he'd forgotten gloves—and then jammed them into his pockets. The area was quiet, typical for a January Monday in Wrigleyville. He walked north for a couple of blocks but decided it was just too darn cold and was headed back toward the apartment when he realized he was starving. He ducked into the Thai restaurant next door to Veronica's building, a funky little place, called Cozy Noodle and Rice, whose bright yellow walls were lined with shelves displaying hundreds of vintage tin toys—animals, trains, trucks, boats—that the owner had collected as a boy in Bangkok. He sat down at a table by the life-size statue of Elvis and across from Mo-Mo, a German Shepherd therapy dog, who sat on the floor next to his blind owner, Charlie Karem. Leo and Veronica had gotten to know the pair over the last year.

Charlie said, "Hello Leo," before Leo could greet him. Leo once asked Charlie how he could identify people without seeing them. He explained it was a combination of the sound of footsteps, the smell of a person, and also the way Mo-Mo reacted. "Plus, you always clear your throat when you walk in." Charlie was a piano-tuner by trade. "The Good Lord blessed me with good ears."

Leo had some Thai Vietnamese soup and it warmed him up. Charlie cheered him up. So did Mo-Mo. Maybe what Leo needed was a dog. They'd never had one growing up. Rosie didn't want one and what Rosie didn't want the family didn't get. Obviously, he couldn't really get a dog. He was rarely home, and it wouldn't be fair to the animal.

"Get a cat," Merricat said, when he called her after he walked back to his own place.

"You know I'm not a cat person."

"Leo, I thought you called for a more important reason!"

"What?"

"To find out if it's a boy or a girl?"

"Indeed! That is why I called."

"Liar. Anyway, I can't tell you."

"You didn't find out?"

"No, I did, but Brice wants to be surprised so the doctor wrote it down on a piece of paper and gave it to me. Brice made me swear I wouldn't tell anyone, especially not you."

"*Especially* not me? But I'm the person who couldn't care less."

"Leo!"

"I mean I couldn't care less about the sex, just so it's healthy and all that."

"I know. At least since I'm not biologically related to the Quinlaynes, I won't have to worry about the baby having big feet."

Leo thought, *but you do have big feet,* but he said, "So, it's a girl! That's wonderful!"

"Leo, I didn't—"

"Who am I going to tell?"

A month later, Merricat invited Leo over for dinner, and even though he wasn't all that keen on seeing Brice, he missed Merricat, so he accepted. As he drove up to their place in Andersonville, he realized he hadn't seen Merricat since New Year's Eve. She'd looked then as though she were about to "pop" any minute, so he was worried about seeing her now. Like his father before him, Leo didn't like "lady shit." Pregnant women had always made him uneasy, although he couldn't say why. He usually found himself blurting out something inappropriate: "Was it planned?" or "Are you sure you're not having twins?" or—completely and absolutely jokingly to Merricat—"Do you know who the father is?" which Brice did not find the least bit funny.

It was worse than he could have imagined! Gone was his beautiful cousin and in her place was this big, swollen blob. She lay on the sofa with a pillow under her knees, her stomach protruding like a giant mound of mashed potatoes. He hated Brice for doing this to her.

"I could have picked it up on the way," he told Merricat when she said Brice had run out to get the pizza.

"But then you would have paid for it and you wouldn't have let me pay you back."

"How are you fairing?"

"Put it this way: next time I will be smarter. Next time I will *not* gain sixty-three pounds and get gestational diabetes. It's as if this baby activated a "hunger" button inside me! I can't stop eating!"

Brice brought the pizza, and true to her word, Merricat ate slice after slice as if her stomach were a bottomless pit. After dinner, she waddled to the nursery, dragging Leo behind her to show off her decorating skills. The small bedroom was filled with all the things that said, "Baby, we can't wait to meet you!" Brice joined them and proudly pointed out the shelving he had built. He held up some vintage tin toys, just like what they had at the Cozy Noodle—a train, a navy airplane, a motorcycle, a robot—that had been his treasured playthings as a child.

Leo blurted out: "But I thought it was a girl!"

"Leo!" Merricat exclaimed. "You just spilled the damn beans."

"You *told* him?" Brice asked.

The next morning Merricat woke up Leo with a six a.m. phone call. "It's a girl," she said.

"I know," Leo said.

"No, you dummy! She was *born*. Just now! I'm holding her in my arms. Brice is holding the phone for me. I called Mom and then you! She's a doll. Her name is Camilla Rose Davinsky. Seven pounds even!"

"You named her after Mom?"

"Both moms."

"Wow! Congratulations! Are you okay?"

"I ended up having a C-section, but I'll spare you the details. Come on up and meet her. Room seven twelve."

She looked like Yoda. Good thing he didn't blurt that out. But he did think it. Merricat demanded that he sit in the chair next to her and hold her. "I want her to know her uncle immediately."

Leo did as he was told. Maybe it would be hard for some people to believe this, but he had never held a baby in his life—newborn or otherwise. The only babies he had ever encountered were those that belonged to the mothers at the safe house, and those babies seemed always to be whisked away from their distraught mothers. Holding the baby felt like holding a giant tamale. A little Yoda tamale! She was amazing and before Leo knew what was happening, he was crying.

"Oh, Leo," Merricat said. "That's absolutely the most wonderful reaction you could have. I love you!"

Now here was a big surprise: Merricat and Brice had Camilla baptized. Brice, a semi-practicing Methodist, insisted on it. Leo was just glad they didn't ask him to be the godfather; he couldn't be the *father* of anything. Brice's sister and brother-in-law did the honors.

After church, there was a luncheon at Merricat's. Leo hadn't expected the crowd, so many people milling about. Veronica abandoned him almost immediately, seeking out the baby, so Leo found his way to the kitchen to see if he could be of use.

"Yes, get that bowl from the top shelf," Aunt Rose said.

He did and then he sat on a stool at the island.

"Already hiding?" Merricat said when she came in the kitchen.

"I didn't know you had so many friends," Leo told her.

"That's what happens when you're nice to people. They're nice back and then the result is something called *friendship*.

"Very funny," Leo said. "I'm nice." Merricat and Aunt Rose gave him a look. "I'm nice to Veronica."

"Yeah? When are you going to get married?" Aunt Rose asked.

"When you do," Leo said.

"Very funny."

After lunch, Leo went in search of Veronica, who had abandoned him again. He found her in a club chair in the baby's room with Camilla asleep in her arms. He asked if she was getting close to "take-off" (he often teased her with airline jargon and puns, even during sex—coming in for a landing, about to de-board, connecting flights...

"Departure may be delayed," she whispered, this time playing along with him. "I'm in seventh heaven," she said, smiling up at him.

Uh-oh. Leo knew he was in trouble.

Veronica didn't say much on the ride home. Neither of them had to work the next day and they usually would stay at her place and then go exploring on Monday, but Veronica said she needed to clean her apartment and catch up on laundry and why didn't he just come over tomorrow night. Leo knew if Veronica had an entire day to think about things...well, he knew where this was going. He'd been through it with Alondra, Poppy Li, and Angie. Leo was beginning to wonder if he was only good at beginnings. Beginnings were exciting and new. Middles grew mundane, and endings—for he was sure there was one brewing—were pure torture.

"I decided I do want children after all," Veronica said over dinner the next night. Leo had just stuffed his mouth with a huge sushi roll dipped in a dab of wasabi. Even though he knew these words were coming, he choked on the food. Veronica got up to get him a glass of water. He tried to compose himself, knowing that when she returned with the water, she would also tell him about her biological clock and the current state of her uterus.

"I'm not getting any younger, Leo, and holding that baby awakened something inside me. I can't describe it, maybe it's hormones, but I know what I want: I want you and I want a baby. Just one. I'll be happy with just one wee little bairn."

"Vee."

"I know it's not fair. I know we both thought that wasn't what we wanted, but I've changed my mind. I can't see myself in the same place twenty years from now. I think it would be lonely and pathetic."

Leo didn't know what to say. Maybe he should tell her about Angie. How she had moved on and found someone new and had a baby. Or about Poppy Li. How she had tried to pressure him into getting married and starting a family when he was only twenty-two. She'd even picked out names for the two sons they would have: Adam Chang Lin and Lee Chin-Chin. He had told his mother that with Poppy Li, it was her way or no way, but maybe it was he who was so inflexible. Maybe it was his way or no way. He didn't mean to say it out loud.

"My way or no way," he said.

"You really didn't just say that, did you?"

At that moment, who knows why, Mo-Mo, the therapy dog popped into his head and he said, "I know, why don't we get a dog?"

Christopher looked like hell. And he was in a foul mood besides. His eight-week-old baby still wasn't sleeping through the night. And his wife wasn't nursing, so he had to take his turn bottle-feeding the baby at all hours of the night. "The baby's got to have this special formula that costs like a million dollars a case or something," Christopher told Leo as they sat in the back office, discussing whether they should fire one of the day servers. "Good thing Dad's paying for it." As far as Leo was concerned, Christopher's problems never seemed like real problems. Every day he would come in complaining about something: "The Jag needs a new transmission." "The hot tub is broken." "The contractor installed the wrong marble countertops." But he always followed up his complaints with, "Good thing Dad's paying for it."

Christopher and Leo had been butting heads since the beginning of their partnership, but lately they seemed to disagree on everything. Part of the problem was that Silver Darlings was really two different businesses: by day, more restaurant, by night, more bar. Christopher's focus was on the quality of the food and the skill of the wait staff. Leo cared more about the quality of the beverages and about the charisma of the bar staff. Christopher was the numbers guy, but Leo thought he spent too much on outside marketing instead of four walls marketing (inside-the-venue-promotion focused on regulars and repeat customers). Christopher was focused on quick service for the lunch crowd; turn the tables around, get them in and out. Leo wanted customers to stay, languish, have fun, and eat and drink as much as they could. Christopher couldn't care less about details that created a great customer experience: lighting, acoustics, music, technology. Leo tried to explain that in the hospitality business you were as good as your last week, but his partner, engrossed with his wife and kids, was just going through the motions.

Christopher told Leo they needed to cut back on the expensive Scotches. Leo told him to piss off. Christopher said it was basically an order. Leo got so angry he threw a stapler at him. Thankfully, it missed. In retaliation, Christopher kicked the wastebasket at Leo. It missed.

"You are going to run this place into the ground!" Leo yelled.

"And you are going to bankrupt us. I do the books, Leo. We're losing money. We're losing customers. They're not going for the high-end stuff. Face it, our customers are more beer drinkers."

"But that's not who we are!"

"We *are* who our customers say we are."

"Let me see the numbers," Leo said, holding out his hand.

Christopher handed him the computer print-out. Damn, it was hard for Leo to see that while the daytime numbers were steady, the nighttime numbers were down. Way down. "I don't get it!" Leo said. "We've been busy. Every night! We've got our regulars, our base."

"Yeah, but they're drinking *more* beer and *less* hard stuff. And they're not coming for dinner. And the bands are too expensive."

"So, what are you saying?" Leo said.

"Dad thinks we should think about switching things up…maybe do breakfast and lunch. Open at night only for home games. There aren't a lot of good breakfast places around here…"

"What are you talking about? We opened a bar, not a fricking I-Hop. I didn't invest my life savings to flip flap-jacks."

"Leo…reality."

"Here's the reality, Chris," Leo said, pointing his finger. "This is just a job to you. But this is my life. We go under and Daddy saves your ass. You have no skin in the game."

"My Dad's giving us a couple of months to turn things around."

Leo had a pow-wow with his staff. Push the food, push the hard stuff. Smile more. Converse more. Be your best. Do your best. Get your friends and family to come in. "We've got to turn things around," he told them. He didn't say it, but the "or else" in his voice was clear.

Christopher and his so-called problems. Leo had problems of his own. Problems of the heart…like maybe he didn't have one. Veronica had ended it and the worst thing about the whole breakup was that he was fine. He was just fine. It had been a month and he didn't even miss her. How could that be? They'd been together over a year. He thought he loved her. At the very least he *liked* her a lot. Wouldn't a person miss even someone he liked? Why wasn't he sad? Why wasn't he grieving? Devastated? Unable to get out of bed? He hadn't even told Merricat yet. He'd been avoiding her, but Merricat could sniff these things out. She called him to invite him over for dinner. "Mom's coming in with Eleanor and I'm making hippie food!"

"I'll be there," he told her.

"Veronica, too."

He paused for one second and Merricat knew. "You broke up."

"We broke up."

"Oh, Leo, I'm sorry. I won't ask you for any details. I promise. Who broke it off, you or her?"

"You just said—"

"Don't be ridiculous. I absolutely want the details."

"She wanted a baby. And I don't."

"Oh."

"And her alarm clock is going off and her vagina is getting old."

"Leo! When?"

"It's been a month. The day after the christening. I blame your baby. She was too adorable. She seduced my girlfriend."

"You don't really blame Camilla! That would break my heart!"

"I'm just giving you the business."

"Are you okay?"

"I am okay, which is why I think I'm *not* okay. I must have some kind of defect because I don't even miss her. It's been a month and I've kind of adapted. I'm catching up on my sleep, which is nice."

"Well, you just come on Monday and have some nice hippie food. That will make you feel better."

Leo hung up. Hadn't she been listening? He didn't need to feel better because he was feeling just fine.

In late February, the temperature rose to sixty-one degrees melting the dirty snow that covered the ground, transforming the city into one big slushie. The bar took in water and Leo and Christopher had to deal with the mess resulting from the flooding. Leo sat in his desk chair and swiveled while Christopher read off the charges on the bill. He prayed that at the end, Christopher would say, "Good thing Dad's paying for it," but of course, that's not how things worked. And more bad news, a new bar was set to open one block up on the Cubs' opening day and rumor had it that they were going to have five eighty-five-inch flat screen TVs. And their "Cubby Beer" was going to be blue.

"Sounds gimmicky to me," Leo said.

"We need something big that day to draw people here," Christopher said. "Work your magic."

"Yeah, let me think about it," Leo said, and swiveled around in his chair a couple of times. "I got it!" he said. "We get a celebrity to come to the bar that day. We get a celebrity who is a big Cubs' fan. The number one Cubs' fan! We get…drumroll…Bill Murray!"

"Bill Murray. The actor."

"Yes!"

"He's Irish, not Scottish."

"It doesn't matter. He loves the Cubs and he's known for doing eccentric, random things like crashing karaoke parties and snatching people's French fries at restaurants." Leo had read stories that were urban legend in size and scope—Murray reading poetry to construction workers, sending Christmas cards to random people, showing up to a Los Angeles ice cream social, crashing weddings, and photobombing people. He often left the scene saying: "No one will ever believe you."

Christopher repeated, "Bill Murray."

"Yeah! It'll be like the movie 'Big Night' only instead of Louis Prima, Bill Murray shows up and the bar is saved."

"How are you going to get him?"

"I have no idea."

Opening game was March 31st, which meant Leo had a little over a month to work his magic and get Bill Murray to come to the bar. He made some calls. He knew this guy who was friends with the Cubs' manager, Lou Piniella. He also had dated a girl whose uncle went to school at Loyola Academy with Bill Murray's brother Brian Doyle-Murray. Also, if memory served, Murray's sister was a nun and maybe he could just say a prayer. What he needed was a miracle. In the end, he called Calvin and asked if he could have his people look into it. They did and reported back that they were warned: any attempts to *force* an encounter with Bill Murray could result in "ill-tempered disaster."

On to Plan B. Plan B was bloody brilliant—a Scottish actor. Ewan McGregor, Gerard Butler, Sean Connery, or James McAvoy. But getting them seemed even more challenging than getting Bill Murray. Other celebrity Cubs' fans? John Cusack, Bob Newhart, Eddie Vedder? How about actress Bonnie Hunt? He'd read that she hadn't missed an opening day at Wrigley Field since 1977. A girl he knew in college said her mother worked with Hunt when she was an oncology nurse at Northwestern Memorial Hospital in Chicago. Leo made call after call. He exhausted all his resources and got nowhere.

Maybe they could have some kind of contest, do something with the score: add up the two scores of the game and that's what you'd pay for a beer: a score of 9-6 would get you a fifteen-cent beer. (Even if they beat the highest-scoring game record of 1922 when the Cubs beat the Phillies 26-23, they would still only pay forty-nine cents for a beer.)

Calvin came in for a pow-wow. He had spies—a plumber and an electrician he knew—get inside the new bar and bring back intelligence. "It's a thing of beauty, all hip and slick."

"Don't you think true fans are going to get tired of the ever-modernizing Wrigleyville?" Christopher said.

Ignoring him, Calvin said, "Their cover is outrageous but people will pay it. The place is huge, too. It can hold eight hundred. Plus, because they created an 'apartment' above the bar they'll be taxed at the residential rate instead of the commercial rate. They'll save thousands in taxes." (Years ago, Cook County had passed a law to give property-tax breaks to "mom-and-pop businesses, but the law had been exploited by area businesses, particularly in Wrigleyville.)

Finally, they decided on the "Pay the Score" gimmick, keeping their fingers crossed that drunk patrons would understand the math. Oh, the ins and outs, the ups and downs, the highs and lows of owning a bar. And by the way, Christopher's wife was expecting their third baby.

On the day before opening day, Leo got a hankering for some Pad Khee Mao from Cozy Noodle and Rice. He walked over, hands in pockets, hoping the rain would hold off for the game tomorrow. The Cozy was busy. He sat down with Charlie Karem and Mo-Mo. Before he could say anything, Charlie said, "LL. It's been weeks."

"Been busy," Leo said, giving Mo-Mo a head massage.

"Getting ready for the big game then?"

"All ready. Just waiting for the fans."

"What about the new place? You worried?"

"Oh, yeah. What have you heard?"

"You know. Bigger, better, cheaper. A novelty. It'll wear off."

"That's what I'm afraid of," Leo said. "We were a novelty once ourselves. How's the piano-tuning business?"

"Meh. People buy these gorgeous Steinways and Bosendorfers and then they don't even play them! They're for decoration. I ask, then why do you need it tuned? 'Just in case someone comes who can play.'"

"Do you play?"

"I do. For a fact, I used to play in clubs. Back in the day."

"Why'd you stop?"

"Drunks love to hassle the blind guy."

"Oh, Charlie, that sucks."

"Well, that was before Mo-Mo. Wasn't it, Mo? You wouldn't let someone pour a beer over my head, would you, boy?"

"What kind of music?

"I'm pretty versatile. (He pronounced it 'ver-sa-tie-ul.')

"If you know the Cubs' song and Take Me Out to the Ballgame you're hired."

"Be careful what you wish for."

"I'm serious. What's your fee?"

"We'd play for tips and a nice doggy bone, wouldn't we Mo?"

"I'd pay you. Only one problem. Don't have a piano."

"That's not a problem. I have two."

"Charlie, let's give it a whirl. Weekends and Cubs' games?"

Leo extended his hand for a shake but then felt like an idiot because Charlie couldn't see the gesture. "High five," he said, and Charlie held up his hand for a slap.

As Leo bent down to knead Mo-Mo's head, he heard the manager call out, "Thanks for coming Mr. Murray!"

It couldn't be. He turned in his chair and watched the back of a man exit the café. Leo jumped from his seat and started for the door. Ah, it couldn't be. He turned around and sat back down. Charlie said, "No one will ever believe you."

"A piano player," Christopher said, running his hand through his intractable head of thick, blond hair.

"A *blind* piano player," Leo corrected him. "And a cool dog."

"And that's going to attract people."

"Bill Murray was at the Cozy, but I just missed him."

"Sure, you did," Christopher said.

Early afternoon on opening day, a burly guy delivered an upright piano and shortly after Charlie and Mo-Mo pulled up in a cab.

Leo went out to greet them. "You found the place."

Charlie said, "My wife put the Cub's sweater on poor Mo-Mo. Does he look like an idiot?"

"He looks great."

Leo took Charlie's arm and led him inside. "They just delivered your piano five minutes ago."

While Charlie warmed up, Leo gathered the staff to review the menu and the way the "Pay the Score" beers worked. Damn, he needed this night to be a success.

The Cubs won 4-3 but the night was anything but a success. Turned out that the new bar's five ginormous flat screen TVs were a bigger pull than seven cent beers and a blind piano player. Some regulars filtered in and out. A lot of people said they liked the guy on the piano and others were enthralled with the dog. Merricat and Brice came with the baby, as did Calvin, and Christopher's wife and kids. But the rest of the world was at the new place—Cisco's. (Ironic, since *Cisco* was the type of lake herring that Silver Darlings was named after.)

Christopher sent Brice over to Cisco's to spy. He came back and tried to say the place was no big deal, but his eyes said otherwise. Leo got a pain in his stomach.

Three weeks later, he sat on a stool at his own bar. Jules fixed him a Seven and Seven. He'd just fired a server who showed up drunk. He sat stooped over his drink and wondered how he got here. He'd never been ambitious. He'd fallen into this venture. Merricat… She pushed him into it. And Brice. Suddenly, he remembered that night after his mother died and Aunt Rose had come into his room, crying about controlling his mother's life. Overshadowing her. It was just starting to dawn on him that Aunt Rose and Merricat had in fact controlled, or at least steered, his life, too. Well, this time he would take the steering wheel. He'd had ten good years with the bar.

He didn't want to own a pancake shop. He took his drink and walked over to Charlie's piano. He sat on the stool and took out his phone and called Calvin.

The fact that Calvin wasn't surprised by Leo's call led him to believe it had been the plan all along—to push him out.

"I'll have the lawyers take care of everything, Leo. They'll call you to meet. It will be an uncontested dissolution, so you'll come out okay. You and Christopher decide on the timing."

That was it. No thanks for doing a great job for ten years. No thanks for never missing one damn day of work in ten years. No thanks for all your good ideas. (Except for Charlie and Mo-Mo. So that wasn't the best idea. Most of the regulars thought Charlie and Mo-Mo were corny. Corny! Leo wasn't looking forward to telling Charlie that it wasn't going to work out.) Thanks for nothing. No big deal.

He walked back to the bar. "Jules, listen," Leo said. "This is crap news, but Christopher is going to turn this place into a breakfast and lunch joint. Open at night only for home games."

"What?"

"I'm dissolving the partnership."

"That sucks, Leo."

"You're telling me. I'll give you a great reference. I'd start looking now. I know Christopher will keep Pete on, but all the night staff will be let go."

The bell on the front door rang, and Leo turned to see Charlie and Mo-Mo coming through the door. Charlie was whistling.

18.
leo & brice

IN THE END, Calvin and Christopher closed Silver Darlings altogether and dissolved the business and the partnership completely. Maybe it was for the best. Leo didn't have the stomach to see *his* bar adulterated. At least he left with his dignity.

"But what will you do?" Merricat asked, her brow furrowed.

Leo sat across from her in her living room. She was nursing the baby, trying to be discreet with a blanket covering her, but it was the suckling sound Camilla made that was causing the hair on Leo's arms to stand up straight.

"She's almost done," Merricat said, sensing his discomfort.

"How do you know?" Leo asked.

"I just know. Back to you. What are your plans?"

"I might just get a bartender gig."

"Oh. That might be just the thing. For a while anyway. Low stress. But what about after that?"

"Cat, I don't know. I'm going to take one day at a time. I'm not like you with your long-term planning."

"I know. I know. We're so different that way, aren't we?"

Leo smiled. "I'm sure you've mapped out the next ten years."

"I just know I want more kids. This little girl is the best thing that ever happened to me." She fidgeted around under the blanket and then removed it to reveal a pink face. "Would you like to burp her?"

"Why would you think I would like to burp her?"

"Just for the experience."

Before he left Merricat's he got himself talked into babysitting Saturday night so she and Brice could go out for dinner to celebrate Brice's birthday. "She'll be fed and diapered, and she'll sleep the whole time. I promise. You can eat pizza and watch a movie. But don't drink beer, okay?" Leo had never been able to say no to Merricat.

A couple days later, the owner of L & L Tavern on N. Clark Street called Leo. He'd heard about Silver Darlings closing and was looking for a bartender. Could he recommend someone? Leo said, "What about me?" and—snap—he had an interview. L & L was just a half mile south of Silver Darlings in Lakeview and was legendary in its own right. Known as one of the best dive bars in Chicago, you could get a can of PBR Light for a couple of bucks and the jukebox was free. The place "boasted" that it was the "creepiest bar in the USA," partly due to rumors that a couple of serial killers, John Wayne Gacey and Jeffrey Dahmer, used to frequent the place in the seventies. Leo hadn't been there since college, but he remembered the high tin ceilings, cash-only cheap drinks, dirty bathrooms, and people coming in to watch "Jeopardy" every day at three-thirty. L & L's could not have been more different than Silver Darlings, and that would be a good thing.

Merricat was happy to hear the news when Leo showed up for babysitting duty on Saturday. "Oh my gosh, remember when that tamale guy would show up?" L & L, like many dive bars in the city, didn't serve food. Twenty years ago, this guy started bringing in a cooler filled with homemade tamales and sold them to the starving bar crowd.

"Those were some good tamales," Leo said, averting his eyes as Merricat situated Camilla at her breast. "Again, with the nursing," Leo teased. "Seems all this kid does is eat and poop."

"You want her fed so she will sleep, right?"

"Oh, well, yes. Drink up, little girl."

After Camilla was burped, Merricat made Leo hold her for a bit. He was crap with holding babies, but as long as he was sitting and she was sleeping, he could deal with it. After a bit, he followed Merricat into the nursery. "She has to sleep on her back," Merricat whispered. "SIDS prevention and all."

"What if she rolls over?" Leo whispered, as he lay Camilla gently down.

"She's not rolling over yet, but if she does, then that means her brain is mature enough to alert her to breathing dangers."

"So much to know."

"And to worry about."

Merricat changed into a black dress, ecstatic that she fit into it, and she and Brice left for dinner. "Call us anytime. We will both have our cell phones on the table."

"We'll be fine," Leo said, trying to convince himself.

One hour later and three bites into the ham sandwich Merricat had made for him (he was expecting pizza) the baby started crying. At first Leo thought it was the TV. He hit the mute button. It was the baby all right. When he checked on her, she was mad as a hornet, her little fists clenched, her face flushed red. Then he caught a whiff of her. "Lordy!" he said out loud. He was going to have to change her! He had hardly paid attention to Merricat's instructions. He picked her up and lay her on the table. She shrieked even louder. "Give a guy a break, huh?" Leo said. He unsnapped her pajamas and pulled her legs out. Oh! The smell. What if he puked? Could he do this? (It was so cliché—a stupid man with a baby.) He held his breath and pulled the tabs on the diaper, revealing a smeary mess. Gagging, he managed to wipe Camilla clean. He put on a fresh diaper, snapped her back up, and was genuinely surprised when she didn't stop crying.

He had to wash his hands. He picked her up and—she stopped crying. Just like that! "Now that's more like it," Leo told her. He brought her back to her room and slowly lowered her into the crib. She started bawling before her head even touched the mattress. "Aww, come on little darling, don't get so bent out of shape." He picked her up and she stopped crying. He walked around the room with her, patting her on the back. He tried laying her in the crib again, but she was having none of that. His hands...he had to wash them.

He picked her up and walked down the hall to the bathroom, but now what? Merricat would probably have a conniption, but he set her on the floor—on the rug—for a few seconds so he could wash his hands. This royally ticked her off.

When he picked her up, she stopped crying immediately. "Okay, I see where this is going." He tried the crib a few more times and then gave up. He walked her around the house. When he passed the big mirror in the dining room, he saw that she was asleep, her little head on his shoulder. He stared at the reflection for a few seconds. It was hard to believe it was him—Leo Lennox holding a baby.

He didn't dare put her back in that crib, so there she stayed, nestled against him like a tree frog, causing no problem at all while he sat on the sofa, finished his sandwich, and watched the movie Merricat had left him, some dumb romantic comedy. The only casualty of the evening was the little blob of mayo that dribbled on Camilla's sleeper.

When Merricat and Brice returned, Merricat said, "Oh no, she woke up! Why didn't you call?"

Leo smiled sheepishly. "We managed just fine."

That night Leo couldn't sleep. He kept thinking about that darn niece of his. She was so tiny and innocent. So new and unadulterated. It made him miss Veronica. Maybe he had blown it with Veronica. Maybe he did want a kid. He punched his pillow down. Who was he kidding, he wasn't father material. He took account of his losses: his mother, his women, his business. Things seemed to slip through his fingers.

On Monday, he met with Murphy, the owner at L & L's. The place was just as he remembered it. Time had left it untouched. On the outside, the place looked kind of classy. A stone façade, two windows framed in block glass, a dark green door with a diamond-shaped window, and a brown wooden sign done in elaborate script all belied what was inside. Inside was the definition of seedy—green, peeling linoleum floors that hadn't seen a broom in a while; a scratched and battered bar that ran the length of the south wall; ancient bar stools with stickers affixed, some even duct-taped together; forest green painted interior with classic silver-painted tin ceiling; and cool vintage Pabst Blue Ribbon beer posters and neon signs on the walls. A couple of TVs. A blackboard over the bar with a comprehensive list of Irish whiskies, and that cool jukebox that played anything from punk to Johnny Cash. All with a unique odor that you couldn't quite place but suspected it had something to do with piss.

"We're one of the last shot-and-a-beer joints on the North Side," Murphy said proudly.

Leo followed Murphy on a tour. The bathrooms were cleaner than he had remembered, and that was a good thing. The bar was just one room, plus the bathrooms, and a storeroom that was separated from the main room by a lattice partition. The tour was brief. Behind the bar, well it was like kindergarten. Nothing on tap. No bar food. Some twenty different beers and some nice whiskies—Jameson, Michael Collins, Bushmill, Knappouge Castle. Hand-written signs that said "Cash Only" were taped around the bar in a way that made you think people probably still asked if you took plastic. The bar looked like a place that was full of stories; the perfect place to land for a while.

"We get a mix of clientele," Murphy told him. "Neighborhood barflies, wayward Cubs fans, Lakeview professionals, and lately, these young kids in their skinny jeans and hipster satchels. TV is either WGN Channel 9 news or Jeopardy, otherwise it's off."

Murphy got a phone call, so Leo browsed. A glass wall case that in a normal place would hold community events instead held a typed sign that said, "When I die, I want to go peacefully, like my grandfather did, in his sleep. Not screaming like the other passengers in his car." The case also had a yellowed newspaper cover from The Weekly Heckler with the headline: "FOOLISH OLD MAN WITH GOAT ATTEMPTS TO HEX MIGHTY CUBS." There was a sign from the surgeon general about the dangers of drinking while pregnant and another about proof of age. Leo's favorite though was the one that said, "NO BITING."

Murphy finished his phone call and they talked about hours and pay. "You know about the serial killers, right?"

"Yeah, I've heard."

"You're not creeped out?"

"Hell no… Actually, kind of, but that's neither here nor there."

"Job's yours if you want it."

"I want it."

Did it feel like a demotion? Yes, because it was. When he showed up for his first day, he was nervous. He knew who he was at the Silver Darlings. He was the cool guy—one of the owners of a unique place. A skilled bartender who knew his whiskies and scotches inside and out. He knew people's names, where they were from, their signature drink. A good guy. A good boss. He liked that. He wanted low stress but now he was second-guessing the decision. Silver Darlings gleamed; this place dulled your soul when you walked through the door.

The first thing he did was clean the bar. He wiped down the counter of the front bar which was sticky to the touch. He cleaned the under bar where the glasses and supplies were kept. He scrubbed the well and the sink and had just started to clean the bottles of booze on the shelves of the back bar with a wet bar towel when Murphy arrived. He looked at Leo as if he'd knocked down his sandcastle. Leo could tell he was insulted. "Sorry," he said. "Just habit."

"I get it. But we're a *dive* bar. The grit is part of the charm."

"Of course," Leo said, setting down the bar towel.

The tavern's hours were from five p.m. to two a.m. Easy-peasy. The pace was much, much, much slower than at Silver Darlings. People came in to drink, talk, and complain. Not for food or ambiance. He got to know the regulars right away. They were wary of the new guy at first. But when he started dressing a little grungier and shaving every other day, they embraced him as one of them. Maybe he *was* one of them.

"You are not one of them!" Merricat said.

He'd begun having a late lunch/early dinner with Merricat and the baby every day at her house before heading to work. Merricat would take advantage of the visits and often run out for quick errands. Today she made a diaper run and Leo sat on the floor with Camilla. She was five months old now and with the help of some propping pillows, she could sit up. That alone seemed to make her come alive to him. He could interact with her. She was giggling now and blowing raspberries. These were all new discoveries to

Leo. He never knew babies were so smart and funny. All he had to do was stack some toys up and then knock them down and she went wild with laughter. She was looking more and more like Merricat every day, except for her hair which was getting a red tint.

He heard the door and thought Merricat had returned but it was Brice. "Oh, you're here," he said, leaving the silent "again" hanging in the air.

"You're home early, honey," Leo said.

"Where's my wife?"

"Diaper run."

"How's my sweetheart?" He bent down and swooped up Camilla. She smiled and drooled on her dad. "She's something, isn't she?"

"She's something," Leo agreed, standing up.

"I was at a conference today. That's why I'm home early."

"Ahhh," Leo said, feeling awkward that Brice felt the need to explain.

Thankfully, Merricat returned with the diapers and a couple of shopping bags. "Diapers, wet wipes, and baby food," she said. "We're starting Camilla on solids next month. How was the conference, hon?" She pecked Brice on the lips.

"Fine, good. You staying for dinner, Leo?"

"No thanks, I just had breakfast an hour ago." He patted his stomach. "I'll head over to the tavern now. Arrive a bit early. Brown-nose the boss a little."

"Is it true about the serial killers?" Brice asked.

"I guess. Why?"

"Don't see how you could work there. They killed so many people."

"Yeah, well, hospitals kill people too and you work there."

"Touché!" Merricat said, a bit too loudly. She startled Camilla, who jumped in her arms.

Brice gave his wife a dirty look.

She said, "I just read the other day that something like a hundred thousand people a year die because of mistakes in hospitals."

"Geez, Merricat," Brice said, "whose side are you on?"

Merricat scrunched up her face. "I'm not on anyone's side."

Leo scrammed, but not before hearing Brice say, "Is he coming here every day now?"

Carless, since he'd had to return the Silver Darlings van, Leo walked everywhere. Once he got used to it; it wasn't bad at all. He walked to work, to Merricat's, to the corner market, to Cozy Noodle. He'd also been learning the ropes of public transportation, the city bus to be exact. Lots of interesting people! His life had become an exercise in studying human nature in all its manifestations. Silver Darlings had attracted a higher-end crowd. Now he was getting to know the underbelly of the city.

Today, the Jackson Browne song *These Days* was running through his head as he walked to work. Leo had read somewhere that Browne wrote that classic when he was just sixteen. This blew Leo's mind. The song described melancholy and angst so precisely—how could he have known these things at such a young age?

Merricat and Aunt Rose worried that Leo might slip into a depression when he lost the bar. (He'd heard them whispering.) But Leo was fine. Good, even. His daily lunches with Merricat and the baby were the highlight of his life. For months now, he would bring lunch to them and when the weather got nicer, they would venture out with the stroller and eat at neighborhood places. Camilla was a good sport. Leo complimented her "portability." And she really took to him, often preferring him over Merricat.

Sometimes Murphy had him open up. At the Silver Darlings there was a lot of prep to be done before they opened and then again for the night shift. At L & L, you basically showed up and opened the doors. Today he arrived at four-fifty, unlocked the door at four-fifty-nine, and eight or ten people straggled in within minutes. Regulars like Old Pete and Ugly Tony. Seemed the old guys all had adjectives before their names. (If you didn't call Tony *Ugly Tony*, he wouldn't answer.)

A twenty-something girl named Trinny had a crush on Leo. She showed up for a beer every day after her shift at the legendary punk/goth clothier, *The Alley*, up the street from the bar. Like many from the punk/goth contingency, Trinny was pale-complected and dressed in black from head to toe. She was all leather, piercings, and tats. "Leo the Lion!" she sang as she climbed up onto a barstool.

"Where's your sidekick?" Leo asked, popping open a cold can of PBR Light and setting it in front of her.

"Adam? He thought he should give us some alone time." She smiled and batted her lashes.

Leo smiled. He'd never been flirted with so blatantly and shamelessly. He didn't think she was serious, but you never knew. Two sips into her beer and her co-worker Adam waltzed through the door, all black leather, crossbones, and chains. "Hey," he greeted.

Trinny scowled at him. "I thought you were giving Leo and me some alone time."

"Too thirsty," he said, climbing up onto the stool next to her.

Leo popped open another can of PBR and left the two to serve some other customers. When the bell on the door rang, he looked up and was surprised to see Brice walking in. Brice nodded to Leo and took a seat at the end of the bar.

"To what do I owe the honor?" Leo asked as he walked over.

"Thought I'd get a look at the serial killer incubator."

"Here it is. Jeffrey Dahmer used to sit right there by that window, scoping out victims. They say John Wayne Gacey showed up once in a complete clown costume."

"Creepy."

"What can I get you?"

"What's on tap?"

"No tap. Just bottles and cans. Nice and cold."

"Bottle of Bud."

While Leo went to grab the Bud, Trinny put on Al Green's *Let's Stay Together* on the jukebox.

Leo uncapped the bottle and set it in front of Brice. He was suspicious of this surprise visit. Brice's crisp white button down dress shirt made Leo self-conscious of his somewhat wrinkled tee shirt. The fact that the shirt was imprinted with the words *You look like I need a beer* didn't help. Brice had done it; he had made something of himself and Leo was still a toddler. Except...look at this guy with his bushy red hair and freckles. What in holy heck did his cousin see in him?

"So," he said to Brice, "tell me why you're really here. Merricat is worried about me? About my future?"

He was interrupted by Trinny. Still at the jukebox, she called out Leo's name and then sang the lyrics to the Al Green song: *"I'm so in love with you."*

Brice gave him a look. Leo shrugged.

"So," Brice said. "Mary Catherine—"

"Why the hell do you call her that? Nobody has *ever* called her that. Not family. Not friends. Not teachers. It's Merricat or Cat."

"So... Mary Catherine asked me to talk to you. She doesn't want to 'do lunch' with you anymore." He put 'do lunch' in air quotes.

"What are you talking about?"

"She said it's getting awkward."

"Awkward? What's awkward about having lunch?"

"Leo, it's too much! You're spending too much time with my wife and kid."

"So, what you're really saying is YOU don't want me 'doing lunch' with your wife and kid."

"This isn't coming from me."

"Come on. I've known Merricat all my life and she wouldn't say 'it's getting awkward.' What is wrong with you?"

"I'll tell you what's wrong with me." Now his voice was raised, and his face was flushing. People were staring. "My baby saw a picture of you yesterday and said, "DaDa.""

"She's talking?!" Leo said. "That's fantastic!"

"I'm not fooling around, Leo. Once a week and no more."

"You cannot tell me how often I can see my cousin. These people are my family!"

"She promised me. Once a week."

"We'll see about that."

Brice got up from his stool and threw some bills on the bar. "Oh, and did Mary Catherine tell you the good news? I'm interviewing for a position at Mayo Clinic. That's in Minnesota."

Leo couldn't think of a pithy reply, so he just grabbed the money and watched Brice walk out. "Ignoramus," he said out loud. As Brice exited, seven or eight people entered, and Leo got so busy he couldn't call Merricat. He'd have to call her in the morning.

Murphy was closing up tonight, so Leo punched out at midnight. He walked home with his hands in his pockets and that Al Green song in his head. He was one hundred percent sure that Merricat had not promised Brice she would only see him once a week. That was impossible. They were closer than close. Closer than cousins, closer than siblings, they used to call each other *cuz-lings*. And even though Leo was three weeks older, Merricat had always assumed the role of big sister. She was Leo's protector. Leo remembered once when they were playing hide and seek with some neighbor kids, nobody found him. He stayed put, hunched under a neighbor's deck for the longest time. It scared him. He was young enough to know that you could get lost; you could get forgotten. That night, as they lay in their twin beds, Leo and Merricat made a pact: if one of them got lost, the other would find him. "Good St. Anthony, turn around, someone's lost and must be found."

Leo slept fitfully. He dreamed that he lost Camilla when he was babysitting her. He'd put her in her crib and when he went to check on her, she was gone. He woke with a start. He couldn't get back to sleep; his mind roiled with dark thoughts. What if Merricat did promise Brice?

Merricat called him at nine in the morning, a minute after his alarm went off. "Brice told me he came to the bar."

"Yes, he did."

"Now, before you explode into a million pieces, let me explain."

Leo sighed. So, it must be true. He sat up in bed.

Merricat told him about Camilla calling him "DaDa." "Brice is feeling left out because you get to spend more quality time with me and Camilla than he does."

"So basically, he's jealous."

"Yeah," Merricat said.

"But you didn't really promise him we could only see each other once a week."

"Leo, I did. Because he threatened to move us out of state!"

"He said he has an interview with Mayo."

"He does not!" Merricat said. "It's a scare tactic."

"Merricat, this guy is your husband. He's jealous and small. Not to mention a pretty good liar."

"Hold on, Leo. Hold on. Don't go there. He's my husband and I love him. And I love you too, but my husband and daughter are my priority. I have to do what's right for my marriage."

"I can't believe it. This is stupid! Does your mom know?"

"Of course not."

"But we promised always to take care of each other. To find each other if one of us got lost. I'm lost, Cat." Leo started crying. "I'm really lost." He hung up. He lay back down in bed and covered his head with his pillow. His phone buzzed, but he was done talking to her. He felt betrayed by a red-headed, humorless, buffoon.

He watched TV in bed until noon. He ate an over-ripe banana for lunch and then walked to the laundromat, his canvas sack slung over his shoulder like Santa Claus. Laundry was the last thing he wanted to do but he had no clean clothes, and even though he was dressing grungier for the L & L, he at least had to have *clean* grungy clothes.

At the bar, he went through the motions. Pop a top, pour a shot, pop a top, pour a shot. Throw some bills in the register. Act interested in the antics of the customers. Cringe when the jukebox played a nerve-splitting punk song. Someone gave him a couple aspirin for his headache, but nobody had anything for his heartache.

When he got home, he started drinking some good whisky. He thought about calling Aunt Rose, then realized how depressing it was, the fact that he had no friends to lean on. His only intimates in life were Merricat and Aunt Rose. Why hadn't he made more connections? There had been all those girlfriends but no guy friends. Was this because he never had a father in his life? Maybe he didn't know how to be a guy friend. Here he was almost thirty-three years old and what did he have to show for his life? Suddenly he felt rootless and branchless. The only thing he was good at was losing.

The next day, Merricat called. He didn't answer. She called every fifteen minutes for four hours—sixteen times. Left no messages, just kept calling. Then she texted: *How about twice a week?* Well, that really pissed him off.

At work, he was getting some notoriety for his bar tricks. Most had to do with beer bottles, rock glasses, dollar bills, and quarters. He executed a sneaky one tonight for a group of guys where you take an unopened wine bottle and you bet somebody that you can drink out of it without uncorking it and without breaking the bottle. When someone takes the bet, you then ceremoniously turn the bottle over, pour a shot of whisky into the "punt" of the bottle—that little indentation at the bottom of a wine bottle—and then you drink and collect your bet. Actually, Leo never took anyone's money. It was all for fun. He'd become an expert at appearing to be fun and entertaining.

Over the next week, Merricat called and texted dozens of times. Then on Friday she showed up at his door. Usually when someone knocked at his door, he asked who it was before opening it, but he was distracted because his cell phone was buzzing at the same time as the knock. When he opened the door, Merricat stood with her cell phone in her hand—she was the one calling—and Camilla in her stroller.

"Leo," she said, and started to cry.

He opened the door wider to let her in and then he unbuckled Camilla and pulled her gently out of the stroller. How she'd changed in just a week's time! She smiled at him and he breathed a sigh of relief that she had not forgotten him.

While Merricat paced around the flat, wiping her eyes with a tissue, Leo sat on the sofa with Camilla on his lap, facing him. If you would have told him a year ago that he would be this crazy about a baby, he would have told you that you were the one who was crazy, but here he was goo-ing and gah-ing. Camilla touched his chin, not used to his scrubble. The Beatles song, *Ain't She Sweet* ran through his head.

Merricat came and sat next to them on the sofa. "I screwed up!"

Leo couldn't look at her.

"Leo, you have got to understand. Things have not been easy with Brice. Ever since the baby…he's…difficult."

Leo raised his eyebrows.

"But he means well. He's just insecure. Kind of needy."

Leo shook his head. Where was this going?

"I only promised because I was scared he would move us to Rochester or Cleveland or somewhere, and I'd rather see you once a week than once a year!"

Camilla burped loudly and it broke the ice a bit. Leo laughed.

"There!" Merricat said. "A smile."

"For her," Leo said.

"Come on, Leo."

"Listen, I'm sorry, but I can't stand the guy. I know that's a terrible thing to say but I couldn't stand him the day I met him, and it's only gotten worse. Often, I have an urge to dunk his head in the toilet."

"Well, that's just mean."

"What has happened to you? You never took crap from anybody. If I recall, you specifically took the word "obey" out of your hippie marriage vows. Why are you letting him control you now?"

"I can't explain it. It's different when you're married. You compromise."

"No, compromise is: he will eat chicken more because you like it, or you will watch football more because he likes it. Compromise is not telling your wife how often she can see a family member."

They sat quiet for a few moments. Camilla tried to suck on his shirt button.

"It's ridiculous, isn't it?" Merricat said. "I'll tell him tonight. I'm breaking my promise."

Leo finally looked at her. "Are you sure?"

"Yes, I'm sure. Now, can we go get some lunch? I'm starving."

They walked to Cozy Noodle. Leo was pleased to see Charlie and Mo-Mo. He hadn't seen them since Silver Darlings closed. Camilla was enthralled with the dog and they enjoyed some noodles and conversation. Leo felt better. Things seemed back to normal.

Except they weren't.

A few weeks later, after he and Merricat and Camilla had returned to their normal lunch rendezvous, the bell on the door at L & L rang and Leo looked up to see Brice enter and take a seat at the bar. They weren't busy. Leo was doing a card trick for Old Pete and Ugly Tony. Leo headed to the other end of the bar.

"Bottle of Bud?" he said to Brice.

"I don't want your beer."

Leo threw up his hands. "How about a shot?"

"Yeah, Jameson. Bring the bottle."

Leo poured a shot and slid it across the bar.

Brice downed it and said, "I thought we had a deal."

"No, you and your wife had a deal. I made no deal with you."

"You've been sneaking around behind my back for weeks now."

"Merricat didn't tell you?"

"Tell me what?"

"Never mind."

"Tell me what?" He pointed to his glass for another shot.

"Brice, this doesn't make sense. Why are you so worked up? It can't be because the baby called me Daddy. What's the real problem?"

He downed the second shot. "Listen, I'm not stupid."

"Well, I don't know about that…"

"I know what's going on."

"Tell me, please, what is going on?" Leo stared Brice in the eyes.

"You are in love with my wife."

Leo threw his head back and laughed. "That's what you think? You're a sick bastard. She's my sister, you idiot!"

"She is not your sister. She is not even your cousin."

"We were raised like brother and sister. We love each other like brother and sister. God, you have two sisters."

"Yeah, and I'm not in love with either one of them. I don't spend every day with them and talk on the phone with them and worry about them and stroll around the city pushing a stroller."

"Is that it?" Leo asked. "I'm working, you know."

"We had a deal."

"No deal. We have no deal."

Brice took a twenty out of his wallet and threw it on the bar. He walked to the door, but then turned and said, "Wish me luck on my interview with Mayo."

Leo waved him off. Ugly Tony called him back to finish the card trick. Leo pretended to be engaged, but he was wondering why Merricat had never talked to Brice; she'd just been going behind his back. This wasn't good. This changed everything. Now he had a weird feeling…like he was caught having an affair. He shook off the thought.

Leo texted Merricat: "Brice was here. You never talked to him?"

Merricat didn't text back.

19.
leo & merricat & rosie & camilla

SUMMERTIME BROUGHT MORE Cubs fans and it made Leo miss Silver Darlings. The excitement, the hope for a win, the playoffs, a longed-for championship. Pop a top, pour a shot, unscrew a cap. Pop a top, pour a shot, unscrew a cap. The bar was booming and more than once, Murphy had to man the door to keep people out so as not to exceed the forty-person occupancy rule. Murphy was pleased that Leo had brought in a lot of business. "You're a chick magnet," he told him. Word had gotten around that the new bartender at the L & L was a stud with great bar tricks. The place had never been busier.

Leo functioned on cruise control. Like his fellow Generation X-ers, he often felt disaffected and directionless. He decided to change his attitude about being alone so much (he and Merricat had not spoken for weeks) and take advantage of it. He saw a movie every week, enjoying a full tub of popcorn for dinner. No sharing with Merricat like he usually had to. No sticky fingers since Merricat wasn't there to drown the popcorn in movie theater butter. He took in concerts and Cubs games. He took guitar lessons on Wednesday afternoons and voice lessons on Thursday afternoons. He filled his Friday slot with library time. He had started reading again and discovered John Irving, Richard Russo, and Michael Crichton. On Sundays, he would take the bus to Rockford and treat Aunt Rose and Grandpa Barry to brunch. (Leo knew that Aunt Rose knew about Merricat and him, but neither brought it up.) Barry's Parkinson's was progressing and, in addition, he was having memory problems. He repeated to Leo, "I'd give anything for your head of hair."

Maybe most helpful was the running. Leo had never been any kind of athlete, but on his walk to work one day he counted eight joggers. I can do that, he thought. That would be a great filler of time. Before he knew it, he was hooked and made sure to get a run in, weather-permitting, nearly every day.

Leo promised himself, before his one-year anniversary at the L & L, he would be employed elsewhere. There was no meaning in what he was doing: getting people drunk every night. Amusing them. Maybe he could manage a restaurant. Or, since he was good with kegs, lines, and soda systems, he could be a line tech for a distributor. He was a good salesman, thanks to Homer at the bike shop, so he could sell liquor. Also, he had become interested in wine and even considered starting an import business. For one split second he entertained the romantic idea of becoming a *sommelier*, but it would require a lot of training and, well, maybe he wasn't smart enough. Furthermore, he was starting to feel his age. He was thirty-four now and tempting fate as he had no medical insurance, after leaving Silver Darlings. Luckily, he was never sick. A cold here and there, and that was it.

One night, out of the blue, he got a call from Veronica. When her name popped up on his phone his heart beat a little faster. Was she in town? Did she miss him? Could they patch things up?

"Are you missing something?" she said provocatively when he answered.

Without missing a beat, he said, "A piece of my heart."

"I'm talking about a box. I accidentally took a box of yours. It's got Beatles' stuff in it. Bobble Head figures, mugs. That's yours, right?"

"Yes, oh, wow."

"I thought about selling it all and keeping the money, but then I remembered that stuff was your mom's, wasn't it?"

"Yes, she hoped it would be worth a bit of money someday."

"Okay. I'm going to ship it to you. Same address?"

"Or, I can come and pick it up…"

She laughed. "Leo, I'm in New York."

"I'll reimburse you for the shipping. Let me know what it comes to. Maybe you should insure it. Yes, please insure it."

"Fine. How's Merricat? And that sweet baby."

"Great. Awesome. Great."

"You sound lonely. Are you okay?" (She was an emotions psychic. Her special gift.)

"I'm fine."

"I'm not. I just broke it off with the guy I've been with. He's quite a bit older—doesn't want kids either."

"I'm sorry, Vee."

"I know."

"Maybe we can—"

"No, no, no. That's not why I called, Leo. No way, no!"

"Okay. Okay."

"I don't have an ulterior motive. I really called about your stuff. I'll ship out the box tomorrow. Be good, Leo." She hung up before Leo could even say goodbye.

As impossible as it seemed, he moved Merricat and Camilla to a place way in the back of his brain and at the far-right corner of his heart. Did he miss them? Yes, he did. If they popped into his head, like a bubble, he popped them right out. "Pop! Pop!" he said to himself, enjoying the onomatopoeia. He had no desire to wallow. Move on, keep busy. Wait for something wonderful to happen.

But then something terrible happened. Leo was walking home from work on a humid August night. The Supertramp song, *Take the Long Way Home*, was running through his head. He had just learned it on the guitar. Cm7…Bb…F…C. Lost in his own musical musings, he didn't see the yellow cab swerve to avoid a speeding black Jeep. The Jeep hit Leo and sent him flying. He felt the impact and then the sensation of being airborne and then everything went black.

In the blackness, he could feel the pain. It spread slowly through and around his head, as if someone had broken an egg on it and the goo was running slowly down. Was it possible for a person to feel his brain collide against the internal hard bone of his skull? Because Leo thought he felt his brain reposition itself. He felt his hip ignite as if on fire. And his elbow felt as if someone had taken a hammer to it. Then he melted completely into unconsciousness. Or so he thought. He felt himself moving, flying, twirling, doing somersaults in mid-air. Then it was as if he was going through a tunnel and down a slide, but he was sliding up, not down. The tunnel widened, and he was able to lay on his stomach and glide along, like Superman. He put his arms straight out in front of him and found he could steer. What was this? Then the pain was gone. He felt warm and effervescent. His blood streamed through his body all bubbly, like seltzer water. He vibrated like a purring kitten.

And then—oddly—somehow, he was watching himself from above. He saw his crumbled body lying on the asphalt, his arm bent at an unnatural angle, the streetlight shining on him like a spotlight, onlookers gathering around. A man started performing chest compressions. Leo floating above could feel the pressure from the man working on his chest. What was happening? How could this be? Time was flowing differently. The ambulance came and he saw the EMTs lift his body onto a stretcher and into the ambulance. There was a lot of blood. They gave him oxygen. The red lights flashed; the siren whined. Leo thought, "Wait for me!" He glided along above the ambulance, but somehow, he could see inside. "He's crashing!" somebody said. This was too much! He couldn't watch himself die! He levitated himself higher above the ambulance until he saw a light. A bright, prism-like radiance, the likes of which he had never seen before. And then the light expanded and engulfed him. He felt more soul than body. Maybe he was the light? But then the light took form and he saw Camille! She looked bright and almost transparent! His mother was smiling, and she said, "Not yet, honey! Go back!"

In a snap he was back. Now he was above his body in an operating room. He saw a flurry of people all dressed in green scrubs scurrying around him. "BP is coming back," someone said. A lady with a red polka dot skullcap was holding his hand. "Atta boy," she said. And then somehow, he zipped back into his body and into a cotton ball of semi-consciousness. The last thought he had before fading out was Bill Murray's favorite line: "*They'll never believe you.*"

"Broken pelvis, broken elbow, cracked rib, concussion, contusions," some doctor was telling him when he finally came to. "You are a very lucky man, Mr. Lennox. Or, if you are a believer, then you are a very *blessed* man. We lost you for a while there."

Leo tried to say something, but his throat was dry as stale bread.

"The police recovered your cell phone, but it was smashed and it took a while for us to locate your family. We just called someone named Mary Catherine Davinsky to let her know you're here."

"Where?" he squeaked out.

"Illinois Masonic."

It figured, Leo thought. Brice's hospital. The evil thought ran through his head that Brice likely knew he was here but had not told Merricat. "How long?"

"How long do you have to live or how long have you been here? I'm just joking," the doctor said.

If Leo wasn't broken, he would have punched the guy's face!

"You'll make a good recovery with a lot of physical therapy. You've been here three days. They brought you in at—" He looked down at the chart. "Two-o-nine a.m. Wednesday. A hit and run, I am sorry to say. Police are still looking for the driver. You were in surgery for three hours. How's the pain? This little thing here is your new best friend. A morphine pump. Hit that button as much as you want. It's programmed so you can't overdose. Are you following everything I'm saying, Mr. Lennox?"

Leo hit the button three times. He drifted off.

When he woke up Merricat and Aunt Rose were standing over him, brows furrowed, eyes red and swollen.

"Leo!" they both said at the same time.

He tried to talk but he was morphined-up and he drifted back into a thick, fuzzy, sleep.

When he woke up later, he was alone. He couldn't remember if Aunt Rose and Merricat had really been there or if he had dreamed it. He pressed his pain button five times. Every inch of him hurt.

An older heavy set nurse with short gray hair, false eyelashes, and broad shoulders came in and checked his wristband. "Hello, Mr. Leo, my name is Gayle. I am going to change your IV bag. How are we doing today?"

He swallowed and snarkily said, "*We're* fantastic."

"Well, look at that," she said. "A sarcastic one. That's good. Means you're a fighter. You'll heal faster."

He asked if he could eat.

"Whoa, Mama. Hold your horses there, mister. You are not ready for food. This is your food," she said, holding up an IV bag. "How about we start with some gourmet ice-chips. I made them myself just this morning." Leo liked her no-nonsense manner. She had huge hands, but they were warm to the touch. "So, I guess you feel like Humpty Dumpty, huh? But don't you worry, we'll put you back together again."

Leo was weepy. He had been through something he couldn't explain.

"Go ahead and cry, honey," Gayle told him. "It's good for you. Gets your juices flowing. Very common. Especially in big, strong men like you. I understand you are a bit of a Lazarus. You know about Lazarus, don't you?"

Leo nodded, but he wasn't sure.

She leaned in to spoon some ice chips into his mouth. "Well you just brace yourself, honey," she whispered. "In my experience—forty-one years now in nursing—this is where grace begins. You know about grace, don't you?"

Leo nodded. But did he? Did he really?

The ice chips felt like rain on his desert tongue. He cried some more. It seemed everything made him cry. What the heck was this?

When Aunt Rose and Merricat returned Leo found himself crying again. All his pent-up anger for Merricat had evaporated. He was lost and now he was found. That's all that mattered.

The police found the driver. He was a drunk twenty-two-year-old kid who panicked when he hit Leo. His dad was filthy rich, some prominent

Chicagoan, so he was generous with a settlement. Leo's medical bills and therapy would be paid for. And then some. A true miracle, since he had no insurance of his own.

Leo slept more than anything. Coming in and out, he saw Merricat, and Aunt Rose, and maybe even Brice. Murphy from L & L had come to visit. And even Christopher stopped by to check on him. Then again, he might have dreamed all of that. Dreams and reality overlapped. He kept trying to remember something important that had happened. It was there at the corner of his brain, but he couldn't reach it. But this he knew for sure: we were meant to fly.

Recovery would be long, he heard the doctor say. The Beatles song *The Long and Winding Road* went through his head. He can't be alone, the doctor said. Rosie being Rosie took control of everything. She was taking Leo home with her. She had just put Barry in a nursing home as the Parkinson's was worsening and he had been suffering hallucinations. "Grandpa's room is all ready for you, Leo. You can move right in. We'll get your stuff later. Your boss knows you won't be back to work. Everything is going to be fine."

Leo nodded but the tears flowed. His damn leaky eyes.

He had an entourage to ferry him to Rockford. Merricat rented a huge van and put Leo in the way back with pillows and blankets. Rosie sat in the middle with Camilla in her car seat, and Merricat drove.

Leo cried as Merricat wheeled him into Aunt Rose's condo. With the place filled with pieces from Mifflin Street, he felt connected to his mother. It was home.

Rosie put him to bed. He was exhausted from the ninety-minute car ride. In a way, he wished he was still in the hospital with his best friend, the pain pump. He lay in bed, certain he could not do this. Turned out, he was a wimp; something he didn't know about himself until now because he was never sick. Now every part of him was sick. He woke up in a sweat remembering what he'd been trying so hard to remember. He had heard about the phenomenon before, but he never put much thought into it; he'd always attributed a near-death experience to be nothing more than a dying brain, until he had one of his own. It all came back to him now. The tunnel. The light. His mom telling him to go back. It hurt his head to cry but cry he did.

315

In the morning, he woke up to the sound of a baby crying. Confused he thought it was his own wailing, but then he realized it was Camilla. Hadn't they gone back to the city? Rosie being Rosie had given him a call bell. "Use it to summons me day or night, kiddo."

He felt silly using it, but he gave it a little tap. Merricat was at his door in seconds. "The baby woke you. I'm sorry."

"No, I was already awake."

"What can I get you?"

"Bring Camilla in. I miss her."

"Hold on, Mom's changing her."

"I didn't know you guys were staying the night."

"Actually, we're staying the week. We had a guy pack up your apartment. He'll come tomorrow with your stuff and I've got to rent you a storage unit today. And get you a new phone."

"What about Brice?"

"Brice will survive for a week."

"I refuse to eat lunch with you so I can say I didn't."

"To hell with him," Merricat said.

Leo waited to see if she would elaborate but she didn't. She shook some pills from four prescription bottles into her hand and then dropped them into his palm. "Now," she said pointing her finger at him, "you've got to stay strong and positive. Mom and I have been reading up on traumatic brain injuries. Good that you only had a contusion and not a hemorrhage. Sleep now." He slept. He slept a lot.

In the hospital, he had had one day of bed rest post-surgery before the torturers started therapy. The torturers explained that prolonged immobilization could lead to other complications such as circulatory and respiratory problems. The therapist had started with small movements and exercises repeated four times a day in his hospital bed: pointing his toes, moving his leg back and forth, tightening his thigh muscles, raising and lowering his legs. Movements that would have been so simple but now were excruciating. But Leo was determined to recover as quickly as possible and so he was diligent with the therapy. At Rosie's he zipped around the condo in his wheelchair anxious for the day he would be back on his feet. Once weight-bearing was resumed, Rosie took him to the ortho clinic for more intense therapy: gait training and resistive exercises for his trunk and extremities. After five weeks he started walking between parallel bars and he was elated when over time he graduated to a walker and then to a cane.

Disability had a way of making one gain perspective. Leo had nothing but time to reflect on what was important in life. When all was said and done it was just four people: Barry, Rosie, Merricat, and Camilla. Four people. That was it. That was all. It was enough. But was it? In his mind's eye, he pictured his life as a circle, inside of which were his four loved ones, rendered in childish stick figures. He himself was half-in, half-out. He was a halfway-man, hard to classify, hard to know.

Merricat and Camilla visited every week, driving in on Wednesday morning and returning home by dinner time on Thursday. Leo lived for Wednesdays and Thursdays. It was when he felt connected to the world again and gave him strength to endure the physical therapy.

The therapy was brutal. And it did not end at the rehab center—Merricat made him get out for short walks. He would just as soon lie on the sofa and watch game shows. Lying there, still as a throw pillow, he could pretend his body was his pre-accident body. When he was upright and walking, there was no pretending. He was sick of all the pain. He had missed his last two therapy sessions. "I know what to do now," he told Rosie. "I can do the exercises myself at home." But he didn't do the exercises at home. He resigned himself that he would walk with a painful limp the rest of his life. He would live out his days as a lonely, crippled man. Did anyone even use that word—*cripple*—anymore?

But Merricat pushed him to walk…so he walked, leaning on Camilla's stroller with Merricat walking alongside him. The October air did feel good. "I miss your mom," Merricat said, out of the blue.

"Oh, yeah," Leo said.

"She was quite possibly the sweetest woman that walked the earth."

"She was like water. She went with the flow."

"I know. But she had my mom to help her steer the boat."

"True," Leo said. "Very true."

Then Merricat said something surprising: "Leo, now is the time to be more like your dad than your mom."

"An asshole?"

"Yes! An angry asshole. Harness that asshole-ness!"

Leo stopped walking, shook his head.

"I'm just saying, your dad was an asshole, but he was resilient. He never gave up being an asshole. How else do you explain six wives and surviving colon cancer? How else do—"

"Wait. What? How do you know?"

Merricat grabbed the handle of the stroller and resumed walking. Leo grabbed her arm. "Cat! How do you know?"

"He came to see my mom."

"When? Why?"

"Last year. Said he was looking for you but he was really looking for the Beatles stuff. My goodness! Have you ever had that stuff appraised? He must think it's worth millions."

"Why didn't you tell me?"

"It would've just hurt you. He only cares about himself."

"And you want me to be more like him."

"Just in the never-giving-up-resilience area."

Later, he asked Rosie about the encounter. "I was still in Madison," she told him. "A knock on the door and there he was. Idiot was still good looking, but he was scruffy. Full head of salt and pepper hair, those royal cheekbones, green eyes, and that accent. I let him in, and he had a cup of tea. Told me he still lived in Beloit, had worked at just about every bar in town. He was married to his fifth wife."

"Merricat said sixth."

"Fifth, sixth, I can't remember. He asked about you... I told him we knew what he had been up to, sending his brother to do his dirty work. Then he just point-blank asked about the Beatles stuff. He could really use the money. It belonged to him after all. Had the nerve to tell me Camille stole the stuff."

"Did she?"

"Of course not. Well, sort of. Actually, yes, but only because she knew she would never get a cent out of him. It was an insurance policy." Leo exhaled deeply. Rosie said, "I told him we burned it all. You should have seen his face! I said after he broke your heart by never calling you back, we had ourselves a bonfire in the backyard. He said we had no right. I just laughed and told him he would soon be old enough for Social Security and Medicare—he's sixty-three now, though he looks older."

Leo didn't know what to say. So much pent up emotion. "Does he know you moved to Rockford?"

"No," Rosie said.

"But he found me before."

"Put him out of your mind. He doesn't deserve a second thought. And the Beatles stuff is safely stored in a climate-controlled storage unit. So there."

The news about his father didn't sit well. Leo couldn't shrug it off. He grew melancholy again. He'd stopped physical therapy all together and made a permanent indentation in Rosie's sofa. Rosie was never home much anymore, having started a new business with Eleanor, who had retired from the safe house. A letter service business with a feminist bent. "We're calling it *Fe-mail Letter Service*" Rosie said. "A one-stop source for printing, mailing, and marketing services. Naturally, we won't leave men out, but we'll focus on women entrepreneurs."

So, Friday through Tuesday, Leo was alone in the house. He got hooked on a stupid soap opera. Late afternoon he brushed up on his Jeopardy skills. "What would you like for dinner?" Rosie would ask. He would answer: "Dating back to the eighteenth century, this dish jumped from the Mexican silver mines to become a fast food staple." Rosie would answer, "What is a taco?" Leo would say, "Ding. Ding. Ding."

The way Leo saw it: he didn't just have an "infrastructure" problem. It was more than that. It wasn't just tissue and bones. Something had happened to his soul. Whenever he thought about his near-death experience, his heart would race. He wanted to talk to Merricat about it, but he couldn't. He started to think about life in a different way. Was there more? Was that really his mom? He remembered the way he felt—so peaceful and loved and at one with everything. Was he crazy? Did he really in the deepest part of him believe in all that?

Then they went and staged a damned intervention. Leo on the sofa; Rosie and Merricat standing above him, lecturing, pleading, begging. Leo promising to do better and to think about getting a job.

"You are not an invalid," Merricat said.

Leo responded: "Originating from eighteenth century Latin, this word describes a person who is unduly anxious about his health...What is a valetudinarian."

"You're incorrigible."

When she returned the following week for her Wednesday to Thursday visit, Merricat showed up with suitcases. "We're staying for a month. Until you get back on your feet."

There was no arguing with Merricat. But Leo felt bad. The condo was small. There were only two bedrooms and Merricat had to sleep with Rosie. The baby slept in a portable crib thingy.

Merricat knew how to manage Leo. She had been doing it since they were small. She made sure she ran "errands" every day and left Camilla with Leo. She was a full-fledged toddler now, her specialty being eating inedible things. You couldn't take your eye off her for a second. (Leo never told Merricat, but once, Camilla "taste-tested" the potting soil from the fig tree in the living room. She didn't seem any worse for the wear.) Watching Camilla kept him on his feet and alert.

Leo was smitten with the kid. She was saying a few words now, her favorite being "Nah." (She was too sweet for "No.") "Camilla, are you ready for your nap?" "Nah." She could say a bunch of words, but the best one of all was "Lee-Lo."

They fell into a nice routine and Leo got some of his pep back. You couldn't help it when you were in the company of a toddler. He counted the days until the month was over, dreading the day when Merricat and Camilla would return to Chicago.

But the day came and went. And another day. And then Rosie and Merricat were arguing in Rosie's bedroom, right next to his, and he could hear Merricat crying. The next day, while he was making pancakes, Merricat told him, "It's over. I'm leaving him."

"Cat, I'm sorry. Is he pissed that you're here with me?"

"Oh, Leo, it's so much more than that. He works non-stop. He is not all that interested in his own daughter. He's jealous of anyone I interact with— man or woman. I'm friends with my neighbor, Andy. He's a stay at home dad. We walk the kids in the stroller and once we stopped for ice cream. He thinks we're having an affair. He thinks you and I have an unhealthy relationship. He wants me home—barefoot, but not pregnant. Doesn't want any more kids. He got weird. And mean."

"If he laid a hand on you, I'll—"

"No, no, nothing physical but scary just the same. He would scream and throw things. The veins on his face would bulge."

"Merricat!" Leo breathed heavily, anger coming off him like sweat. He accidentally burned a pancake while listening. He shoveled it up and tossed it in the sink. Camilla was eating her pancake with her hands, saying, "Mmmmmm, Mmmmmmm." Naturally, Leo was sad for Merricat, but he was human after all…inside he was pleased. It would be just like old times when they were Rosie, Merricat, Leo, and Camille, except now they would be Rosie, Merricat, Leo, and Camilla. But maybe that's not what Merricat wanted at all. Maybe she wanted to stay in Chicago.

"So, what are your plans?" Leo asked.

"Well, Mom and I were thinking…maybe we could sell the condo and get a house where we all could live in and help each other out."

"Like we used to."

"Like we used to."

Camilla stuffed a pad of pancake into her mouth and said, "Mmmmmmm."

They found a big, red-brick, four-bed/three-bath house on Clinton Boulevard, where old historic homes were treasured and rehabbed by crazy people who were not afraid of stripping woodwork, replacing steam radiators, and throwing money out the window. The house needed some work but Leo was quite the handyman. After taking care of the apartments on Mifflin, student housing at UIC, and his bar, there wasn't much he couldn't do.

Rosie's business had taken off and she and Eleanor worked at the shop Monday through Saturday. At sixty, Rosie was still a tornado and a mentor to many young women in the community. She hired Leo and Merricat, and they split up the week: Merricat worked Monday, Tuesday, and Wednesday while Leo stayed with Camilla, and Leo worked Thursday, Friday, and Saturday. In between, Merricat painted the interior of the house and Leo repaired windows, stripped and stained the crown molding in the living room and dining room, and installed new toilets in the bathrooms.

Leo was glad to be working on the weekends because he could avoid seeing Brice when he came to visit Camilla every other weekend. Brice did not want to take her overnight so he would spend a few hours with her at the house. This was the extent of his "joint custody." Two or three hours every other week. Merricat would usually go to the grocery store or the mall during the visits.

Once when Leo left his cell phone at home and went back to get it, Brice's car was in the driveway. (He had forgotten it was *his* Saturday.) Leo almost turned around, but he needed an address a customer had texted him. Reluctantly, he walked in the front door. He found Brice sitting on the floor with Camilla in the living room, playing with some blocks. It had been months since Leo had seen him.

"Brice," he said, hands in his pockets.

"Lee-Lo!" Camilla said, jumping up and running into his arms.

"I'm sure she thinks you're her father now," Brice said, getting to his feet.

"She thinks I'm her *uncle*," Leo said. "Her Uncle Lee-Lo." He kissed Camilla on her cheek and bounced her a bit.

"Well, you got what you wanted. Your childhood recreated. The women who always took care of you to continue taking care of you. I'll bet you ran out in front of that car on purpose just so they would have to take care of you."

"You've lost your mind."

"Have I?"

"I just came home for my cell phone." He tried to hand off Camilla to her dad, but she wasn't having it. "Nah. Nah. Lee-Lo!" Camilla said, turning her face away from Brice.

"Honey, Uncle Leo has to go back to work. Go to your daddy and play blocks." He tried to set her on the floor, but she clung on to his neck like a little tree frog. "Come on, honey."

Brice was ticked. "You are loving this, aren't you? You knew I was here. You staged this."

"You really have a problem," Leo said, gently uncurling Camilla's fingers from his neck. "Look what I have for you!" he told her as he set her down. He pulled a deck of playing cards from the desk drawer. This satisfied her and she shook the cards from their box and spread them on the floor. "Hearts!" she sang. "Hearts!"

Leo grabbed his phone from the desk and took his leave.

Their neighborhood association held an annual "Luminaria Night" in mid-December, where, at dusk, homeowners lined their sidewalks with white candle-lit bags weighted with sand. Camilla stood on the sofa to peek out the picture window. "Pretty lights!" she exclaimed. Rosie had invited some neighbors over for drinks and nibbles. When the last neighbor left, Leo could tell Merricat was beat. "Let me put Camilla down," he told her, scooping up his best girl from the sofa. "Nah!" Camilla said in protest. "Pretty Lights!" She settled down when he got her into the bathtub. The kid loved bath time.

Merricat came into the bathroom. "Leo!"

"What's wrong?"

"Brice called me. He's getting married."

"What?"

"The ink on the divorce papers is barely dry."

"Who the hell is it?"

"Another doctor. They've been having an affair for months."

"I'm so sorry."

She shook her head. "It's weird, isn't it? All that faux jealousy."

Leo kept his mouth shut.

"My poor baby," Merricat said, watching Camilla splash happily in the tub. "To have a lout for a daddy."

"She'll be okay. Look at me. I had a lout for a dad and I'm fine."

"But that's just it, Leo, you are not fine!"

Leo waited for her to elaborate, but she just turned and left.

After he got Camilla to bed, Leo found Merricat in the kitchen drinking straight from a wine bottle. "Can I get you a glass?" he asked.

"I'm fine."

"Let me quote your own words back to you: 'you are not fine.'" He climbed up on the counter. "What is it? What's really changed with this news?"

Merricat took a long swig from the wine bottle. "Yesterday, I was the divorcee of an OCD, Type A, workaholic; today I am a divorcee of a lousy cheater. I don't know why it's different, but it's is." She downed the rest of the bottle.

The tables were turned. Now it was Leo who had to give Merricat pep talks. He had never seen her like this before. She was always up, always go-going, always optimistic. Now, she was Merricat in slow motion. "Who *am* I?" she would ask Leo, out of the blue. "Where did I go wrong?" She stopped working. Leo, feeling much better, took her hours, happy to be employed full time. But not happy that Merricat and Camilla stayed in their pajamas all that snowy winter, venturing out only when necessary.

One night, after Camilla was in bed, Rosie, Merricat, and Leo sat in the living room and enjoyed a crackling fire in the fireplace. Rosie had opened a nice bottle of wine. Merricat held hers up and said, "Here's to continuing the tradition of misfit families."

Rosie said, "Now, Merricat."

"But it's true, Mom. Think about it. You and Aunt Camille had only one parent who really loved you—Grandpa Barry. Leo had only one parent who loved him—Aunt Camille. I had only you. And now Camilla is really going to have only me. Wouldn't it have been nice to get a traditional family in the mix?"

They never were a traditional family, but they always seemed to make things work. "We did okay," Leo said.

"Nothing against you, Mom," Merricat said, "or the way you and Aunt Camille did family, but I just wanted ordinary—Brice and me, kids, dog, school, church, ballet, soccer. Chicken pox, teenagers. Tra-di-shun-al!"

"Geez, Merricat," Rosie said. "It wasn't that bad."

"Not bad. Just not traditional," Merricat said. "No offense."

Rosie just shook her head. Leo kept his mouth shut.

When Barry died on April Fool's Day, Merricat sank into an even deeper depression. Poor Barry had died sitting in his recliner. The nursing home staff thought he was just napping, but he had been dead for a couple of hours. Stella Maris did not even have the decency to attend the funeral. It was a touching event, attended by hundreds of teachers and former students. "Grandpa was loved," Merricat said. Leo wondered how many people would show up at his funeral if he died today. Bloody hell, he could probably count them on two hands (one hand?). Was this any way to live? So unconnected?

Merricat started seeing a counselor. Leo saw a glimmer of improvement. But the counselor also dug up buried wounds. "My counselor thinks I should do DNA testing to figure out my ethnicity. I only know that my mother was German and Swiss. I would like to know more," she told Leo, one night while they were cleaning up the kitchen.

"That's a good idea," he told her.

"Here's the weird thing, Leo. When we were little, it was all about you finding your dad. Why didn't I want to find my dad?"

Leo thought about it. "Because no one knew who your dad was."

"Yeah, because my birth mother was a skank."

"I remember the term *free-spirit* being used."

"Anyway, I want to find out who my dad is and what my ethnic background is. For me and for Camilla." Merricat became obsessed with the mission. She met with a genealogist who recommended testing with as many DNA-testing companies as she could afford. The lady explained that this would give her the best chance of finding her father. Tests came back that she was seventy-two percent Italian/Greek, twelve percent Scandinavian, and sixteen percent Swiss.

"*Mamma Mia!*" Merricat said when she got her results. "I'm Italian! Let's go out and celebrate with some spaghetti and meatballs."

Just as Leo had embraced his Scottish heritage after one telephone conversation with his father, Merricat soon became obsessed with all things Italian. She took out books from the library, made friends with owners of local Italian restaurants, and set on a mission to learn the language. Post-it notes could be found all over the house with Italian words written on them. By the light switch: *interruttore della luce*. On the refrigerator: *frigorifero*. On the bathroom mirror: *specchio*. She tried to speak Italian whenever she could and was even teaching Camilla some words: *mangia*, and *grazie*, and *prego*. But words were one thing; she needed help with pronunciation and usage. She found a teacher, Massimo Reggio, and started taking classes on Thursday nights at St. Anthony of Padua Catholic Church, south of town. On those nights, Leo would take Camilla on little excursions. They would ride bikes on the bike path, watch the Rockford Ski Broncs perform on the Rock River, and sometimes take in a movie.

"Are you my daddy now, Lee-Lo?" Camilla, now four years old asked him one night as they were feeding the ducks at the lagoon.

"No honey, you have a daddy."

"But you're a better daddy."

"I'm a better *uncle*."

"Can I pretend you're my daddy?"

"Sure, kiddo, why not?"

Merricat greeted Leo and Rosie with news when they returned home from work one night: Brice's wife was pregnant, and he got a job at the Cleveland Clinic. Camilla, thinking her mother was trying out a new Italian phrase, mimicked her, but with the cutest, attempted Italian accent: "Cleveland-a Clinic-a." Leo was surprised Merricat would even bring this up with Camilla in the room. She was usually so careful to shield her daughter from anything negative about Brice.

"Cleveland Clinic," Merricat spat, waiting for someone other than Camilla to comment. "That's in Ohio!"

On any other day, Leo would have said, "I know where Cleveland is, Merricat," but today he said, "How will that work?" He went over to the sink to wash his hands; he was starving and the kitchen smelled wonderful. Part of Merricat's Italian immersion was cooking Italian food.

"I'll tell you how it will work," Merricat said, donning huge oven mitts and bending to retrieve something wonderful from the oven. "It means he's giving me sole custody and more money."

Rosie said, "He's buying you off then."

"Yep," Merricat said.

"Good," Rosie said. Leo was glad she said it first. Merricat set a perfect pan of lasagna (lasagna in July?) on the table. She cut huge squares and slid them onto their plates. Leo's mouth watered. One delicious bite into the lasagna and Rosie made her own surprising announcement: "I've been offered a job in the Obama administration."

"In Washington, D.C.?" Merricat asked.

"Yes, honey. That's where the Obama administration works. But of course, I wouldn't even consider it."

"Why not?" Leo asked.

"Because," Rosie said. "Because of us. We're here, together, doing great. We're a family. Plus, *Fe-Mail* is doing well."

"What's the position?" Merricat asked.

"Ambassador-at-Large for Global Women's Issues."

"Mom! You have to take it. Leo and Camilla and I will be fine. With grandpa gone now, it's a good time to go."

"You'd let me go so easily?" Rosie said.

"You know we'll miss you terribly, but you're young and you have so much to offer! I'm so happy for you!"

"Then why are you crying?" Rosie said, smiling and reaching out for Merricat's hand. When Leo asked his aunt if she really thought she could survive the man-eaters in D.C. again, Rosie said, "For pete's sake, Leo, I skinny-dipped at f-ing Woodstock!"

Rosie sold *Fe-Mail* to Eleanor who decided she would move the business to Madison by the first of the year. At least Leo could count on keeping his job for several more months. Rosie tied up all her loose ends and the day after Camilla started pre-school in August, she took a bus to O'Hare and then flew out to D.C. where she would share an apartment with some fellow feminist friends. "I'll be home for Thanksgiving and Christmas!" she promised.

Camilla cried in Leo's arms as she watched her grandmother board the bus. "It will be okay, honey. Nana will be back real soon."

Camilla took Leo's cheeks in her hands. "That's not why I'm crying, Lee-Lo," she wailed. "I just really want to ride on a bus!"

Merricat smiled. She put up a good front, but she was devastated. "I didn't think she'd really do it," she told Leo. She walked around for a few weeks in a daze, not knowing how to absorb all the change—Barry was gone, Rosie was far away, her baby was in full-day preschool, the search for her father had dead-ended, and Brice had moved on, not even offering plans about seeing Camilla.

Rosie's departure shifted their world, affecting their very health: Camilla had to have her tonsils and adenoids removed; Leo had an appendectomy; and Merricat had a hysterectomy, all in the span of five months. "Spring cleaning," Leo called it. "Getting rid of parts we don't need," Merricat said, which made Leo a little sad. Merricat was still young, and he knew she wanted more children.

"My counselor thinks I should embrace my spiritual side," Merricat said one day out of the blue. It was October. Camilla was at their neighbor's house while Leo and Merricat took an after-dinner walk. They both had put on some weight due to all the Italian dinners.

"Oh?" Leo said.

"Can I ask you something personal, Leo?"

"Shoot."

"Do you believe in God?"

"I guess so. I don't know. Do you?"

"I want to!" Merricat said. "With grandpa's death, the divorce, and Mom leaving, I'm just thinking about life and what it is, and I think it has to be more than just this."

The perfect opening for Leo to share his extraordinary experience with Merricat. He just couldn't. He didn't know why he couldn't, he just couldn't. Maybe, like Merricat, he should get counseling. Actually, he did get counseling, though in less traditional places: bars. Leo started to miss the bar scene that had been such a big part of his life, so he began seeking out dive bars in the area both for "therapy" and possible employment when his job at *Fe-Mail* ran out. Merricat had her Thursday night Italian lessons and now Leo had his Friday night bar nights. He started checking out the neighborhood bars—North End Tap, Latham Tap, Mary's Place, J-Bears Place, Rural on Tap. He felt at home at these places. Just a stranger stopping in for a drink. Each week, a different bar. A couple of beers, a couple of jokes, a ball game on TV. It eased the constant pain in his broken body and numbed his worried thoughts. For the accident had jolted something in his brain and he had begun regretting the past and worrying about the future. A new phenomenon for a man who was accustomed to living day to day, going with the flow, taking whatever life dished out. Like Merricat, Leo found himself searching for meaning and purpose.

Sometimes he took comfort elsewhere. A few times he hooked up with a woman he met at a bar. Afterward, he never felt good about it. Especially facing Merricat the next day, although he reminded himself that he was a free agent and answered to no one. Still, he couldn't shake the feeling that he was betraying Merricat and Camilla in some way when he spent the night with a woman. Once, Camilla found a condom packet in his pocket. "What's this Lee-Lo?" Leo could not grab it out of her hands before Merricat saw it. She pretended she didn't see it but Leo knew she did.

20.
leo & merricat

WHENEVER LEO THOUGHT of his near-death experience, he always heard Paul McCartney's voice in his head, singing, *Let It Be*. Wasn't Camille speaking words of wisdom to him?

Merricat began to cry when he finally told her the story one night on an after-dinner walk. "Leo," she whispered, "this changes everything!"

"How so?"

"Don't you see? It's a gift, for us doubters."

"Oh, well, I don't know."

Although she honored his request to keep the experience between just them, Merricat became obsessed and starting researching near-death experiences (NDEs). She borrowed books from the library, sharing with Leo mind-exploding stories that were eerily similar to his. Merricat helped Leo confirm that his extraordinary experience was real, and not what medical science poo-pooed as just what happened to a dying brain.

A few weeks before Christmas, while they were decorating their tree, Merricat announced that she was joining St. Anthony of Padua Catholic Church. Her Italian teacher, Massimo, a member, had invited her. She'd taken Camilla and attended mass the week before.

"Something is pulling me in, Leo. And it's not just the church… but you should see this place! It's like something out of Rome with this great big mural in the front and all the stained-glass windows. There are dozens of old statues that were purchased by early parishioners. And the priest! Leo, I never met a sweeter guy! Father Mike. He's a Franciscan friar. You know, like St. Francis of Assisi; they wear gray robes tied with a rope at the waist and sandals."

"Sandals," Leo repeated, to show he was paying attention.

"And he's not intimidating. He's a Columbo type…with that rumpled, who-cares look."

Leo hung an ornament he had made for his mother—a tin foil bell. "Colombo type," he repeated.

"Will you come with us on Christmas Eve? They have a midnight mass. I promised Camilla she could stay up late and go."

"Oh, I don't know. We'll see," he said to be nice. Leo never felt comfortable in churches. Didn't see the need.

What Leo needed was a damn job. On his Friday bar nights, he would casually inquire about openings, but as was his experience, these small, neighborhood places had little turnover. But also, as was his experience, Merricat came through for him. Apparently, her Italian teacher's cousin owned a little place not far from St. Anthony's Church, a hundred-year old restaurant called *Caffé Greco*.

"Call this guy," Merricat said, handing Leo a Post-It note.

The next morning Leo drove to the café. Located in southwest Rockford, the city's version of "Little Italy," Caffé Greco was housed in a tiny one-story, red brick building with a gray shingled roof, and was uniquely situated on a hill between separate sets of railroad tracks. Leo parked in a gravel lot across the street and made his way to the entrance, smiling when he read the sign that said, "Hard to find…Hard to forget."

The owner, Zeke Abruzzi, asked him to come in early, before the lunch crowd. When Leo entered, he saw a giant of a man. Zeke Abruzzi stood a head taller than Leo, had a full head of thick gray hair and, bushy eyebrows. He shook Leo's hand. "Have a seat," he said, gesturing toward the bar. "I'll get you a cup of coffee." Leo looked around and was surprised at how small the place was, as if it had been shoehorned into the building. A cozy hole-in-the-wall. Like a little gem you find in Europe. Small tables with fruit and floral plastic tablecloths were set with paper placemats featuring local businesses. Yellow-gold sponged-painted walls stenciled with vines and grapes and framed Italian posters were the only attempt at decorating.

Zeke explained that the place was built in the late eighteen hundreds and originally was called *Villa Venice*, although the locals had called it *Spaghetti House on the Hill*. Leo liked the place—and Zeke—right away. After working at the L & L, he had become partial to places with a history and people who were real. Leo sipped his coffee and listened while Zeke gave him the low down. When Leo shared his work history, Zeke whistled and said, "Well, you're overqualified, but if you want the job, it's just part-time. Four to ten, Monday through Saturday."

"I'll take it," Leo said without hesitation.

Over coffee, the two men shared bar stories. Leo told him about the infamous L & L Tavern with its serial-killer taint. Zeke shared that in the old days, during the Depression, moonshine was made in a huge clay vat in the basement of the café. "Right under where you are sitting, now," he said. "Three tunnels led to several different railroad tracks. They used to roll the barrels to be shipped out on waiting trains. The infamous patron was Al Capone. So, the story goes."

Merricat was thrilled that the job was just part-time. She didn't want Leo to get something else during the day. "We don't need the money," she said. "Between both of our settlements, we're fine." Well, Merricat would know since she handled all their finances. "And we always have the Beatles stuff to fall back on. (This had become a family joke—the answer to all possible financial calamities!)

"I like our routine," she told Leo. He liked it too. What was not to like? They woke up and had a nice breakfast together. Leo drove Camilla to school. Then Merricat and Leo had three hours at home to do chores and laundry and prepare meals and continue to renovate the old house (they had recently torn down the wall between the kitchen and the dining room). They took walks, exercised, and sometimes just laid around. From noon to three Merricat would go to her job in the Adoption Services Department at

Catholic Charities. Leo would pick up Camilla from school at two-thirty and the three of them would reunite at home for an hour until Leo had to leave for Caffe Greco.

"At least I divorced a rich man," Merricat would often say. Leo would reply with: "At least I was run over by a kid with a rich dad."

What surprised Leo most about Caffe Greco was not just the variety and caliber of the customers (he was expecting regular, work-a-day guys, but the place attracted professionals, politicians, business people and laborers alike) but also how friendly and upbeat most people were. Just like at L & L, customers were wary at first of the new guy, but Leo soon won them over with his charm, Chicago stories, and bar tricks. Naturally, there were a set of regulars who provided Leo with the local gossip and helped him ease into the job. Maybe bartending was what he was meant to do. Was it really such a dishonorable job? He felt at home here. He hoped it would lead to a full-time job.

As Camilla got older her hair got redder, her freckles more pronounced, and her eyes turned from a light blue to a deep periwinkle. She was her father's daughter. She wasn't bossy like her grandma Rose had been as a girl, and she wasn't as adventurous as her mom had been, but she was smart and sassy, and really sweet. She possessed a level of empathy for people that Leo never knew possible in someone so young. Leo felt like his best self when he was with his niece. She was just about the only thing that could make him smile.

Sometimes, most of the time, Leo forgot that he wasn't her dad. In the reality of their lives, for all intents and purposes, he was her dad...until she reminded him that he wasn't.

"Leo, I have a boyfriend. His name is Alexander," Camille announced. Leo told her she wasn't allowed to have boyfriends. "I'm your only boyfriend."

"Leo! You're not even really my daddy."

Well, that stung. But it also made him think. Who was he? What was he doing here? Was his presence helping Merricat and Camilla or holding them back? What would happen if Merricat met someone? (Even though she swore off men forever, Leo was sure that kind of thinking would wear off.) Or, what if he met someone? They were a family, yet they weren't. They were free agents, yet they weren't. Maybe Merricat was right to yearn for a traditional family. Even Camilla wished they were a "real" family. "Lee-Lo, wouldn't it be nice to have a sister or brother or even a dog. Let's get us a baby, Leo. Can't you and Mom have a baby?"

"Honey, we're not married."

"Julie's not married and she has a baby."

"But honey, your mom and I are cousins."

"So?"

"So, let's get us a dog instead," Leo said.

"Let's name him Chopped Liver and call him Choppy for short!"

Spring came early. Merricat wanted to plant a big vegetable garden this year. Leo was good at a lot of things, but he had never been a gardener. Merricat knew someone from church who could help. Nicky Russo, a man she extolled as a guy who could do anything, showed up just before noon on the Saturday before Mother's Day with his rototiller. Nicky was in his early thirties and his olive coloring, dark hair and eyes, and strong features signposted his Italian heritage. His big belly was a giveaway for his love of food. His easy laugh and smile reminded Leo of a boy in his grade school that everyone liked, and not because he was smartest, or richest, or the most athletic, but because he was the nicest.

Leo and Camilla sat on the back patio and watched Nicky work; there was a certain pleasure one took when observing a job well done, though the tiller was loud, and Camilla had to cover her ears. When the job was finished, Nicky wouldn't accept the money Leo offered him. "Don't insult me," he said. "It got me out of the house. My daughter had a sleepover last night. Eight eight-year-olds. Need I say more?"

"Let me at least feed you then." Leo made ham and Swiss sandwiches. He and Nicky sat out on the patio and ate theirs while Camilla ate hers sitting in the glider of her swing-set. "That child needs a dog," Nicky said looking at Camilla sitting all alone.

Leo looked at Camilla. It would be good for her.

"That, or a brother or sister," Nicky said winking.

"Well, that's not going to happen," Leo said.

"You and Merricat don't want any more kids?"

"Nick, Merricat and I aren't married. She's my cousin. We were raised as siblings."

"Oh, sorry, man, I didn't know. That's cool."

"It's a long story, but I was in a bad car accident and Merricat got divorced and so we help each other out."

"I get it, I get it. It's good when families help each other."

Leo wasn't surprised when people thought he and Merricat were a couple. It sure looked that way from the outside. He was reminded of his childhood when people thought Camille and Rosie were lesbians. Who cared, really? People could think what they wanted.

"Hey, Leo," Nicky said. "Merricat said you're just working part time right now."

"Yeah. Hoping to get full time soon."

"Merricat also said you're handy."

"She did, did she?"

"St. Anthony Church is doing some renovating. I'm doing all the carpentry, but an extra pair of hands could really help. You got some time the next few Saturdays? You aren't afraid of heights, are you?"

Was this Merricat's back way to get him to go to church? What could Leo say? Nicky had just helped him out. "No problem," he said.

The next day, when Merricat and Camille returned home from church, Nicky was right behind them, with his wife Trina, and four daughters. "They're going to help us plant the garden!" Merricat announced. Before Leo knew what hit him, he was kneeling in the dirt and laughing at Nicky's lame jokes. Merricat and Trina made lunch while the girls played on the swing set. Nicky whistled while he worked, and Leo realized the man was one of the most cheerful humans he had ever known. "Guess what?" Nicky said. "My wife is pregnant again!"

"Number five?"

"Last time. If we don't get a boy this time, we'll be happy with five girls."

"God bless you!" Leo said.

"He has, my man, he has."

Leo smiled. A thought crossed his mind: *I think I may have a friend.*

He was certain of it when Nicky started to show up after work a couple nights a week at Caffe Greco to have a beer. "I used to come here with my mom and dad," he told Leo as he climbed up onto a barstool. "It's been forever." He looked around at the stenciled walls and the ceramic-tiled bar top. "Hasn't changed much, has it?"

"So, I hear," Leo said.

"And every other customer is named, Tony, Joe, or Nick."

"Just about."

"Watch this," Nicky said with mischief in his voice. He turned to the diners and said, "Hey, Joe, your wife's on the phone." Immediately, three guys got up and headed for the bar.

"Sorry, guys," Leo said, "wrong number."

Nicky sipped his beer and feigned innocence, averting his eyes. "You play cards?" he asked Leo.

"I do card *tricks*."

"No, you play poker?"

"Not since college."

"I was thinking of getting some guys together. Zeke said we could play here after they close on Wednesday nights. You in?"

Leo set a fresh bottle of beer in front of Nicky. "I'm in."

Nicky said, "About your sister, Leo. I have a cousin…"

"Thanks, Nicky, but Merricat isn't interested in dating."

"Oh, too soon? Well, keep my cousin in mind. He's a good guy."

Merricat had friends over. When Leo got home from the bar, six neighbor women, all in an assortment of swimsuits sat at the kitchen table. Music was blaring. They were drunk.

"Lee-o! Lee-o! Lee-o!" they chanted as he entered. Leo shuffled back a step, pretending surprise.

Patricia Lewis, fifty-something and fabulous-looking, poured some red wine into a glass and pushed it into Leo's hand.

"Camilla's sleeping over Susie's!" Merricat told him. "Her first sleepover."

Leo wondered if that was wise. Susie was two years older than Camilla and very bossy. Plus, they had an in-ground swimming pool.

"Don't worry, Leo, Jake is watching them," Susie's mom said.

"Show us some card tricks, Leo," somebody said.

They chanted, "Card tricks! Card tricks! Card tricks!"

Leo wondered how long they'd been at it. He laughed, glad to see Merricat enjoying herself. Maybe she was getting her "traditional" family life after all.

Leo performed six card tricks and then excused himself, citing a headache. The ladies protested. "Stay!" He put his hand to his forehead and said, "But my head! I need sleep."

He wasn't lying; his head did ache. But it wasn't a physical headache per se; it was more of this indescribable yearning that he couldn't name. He beat himself up about it—life was good, things were better all around. Still, he felt like a street with potholes in it. He knew he had to fill those potholes, but what with? That's where he came up blank. Would friends fill the void? A woman? A different job? Religion? Maybe some world traveling. Or become a big brother. These were the kinds of thoughts that made his head hurt.

As he put on a fresh undershirt and a pair of boxers for bed, he found himself worrying about Camilla. She had never spent the night away from them, ever. What if she woke up in the middle of the night and didn't know where she was? Did Jake and Bonnie have guns in the house? Had Merricat even thought to ask? And they wouldn't forget to lock the pool gate, right? Merricat would call him a "worrywart" and tell him to calm the hell down. He smiled. He had been "pretending" to be Camilla's daddy now for so long that he really felt like he was her dad.

On a hell-hot Wednesday night, Leo sat at a round poker table at Caffe Greco. Nicky sat to his right, Nicky's cousin Dominic sat on his left, and Zeke, a guy named Pete, and a new guy named Mike (a sit-in for Dave who had to take his kid to college) sat across from him. Earlier in the day, one of the window air conditioners had gone out causing some crankiness among the crew. Zeke had set up an oscillating fan and each time the fan blew a blast of air in Nicky's direction he said, "Ahhhhh." The fact that cigars were banned after diners started complaining about the lingering smell also added to the crankiness. Plus, Pete was winning; and nobody liked when Pete was winning.

Leo had been a little nervous when the group first got together since he hadn't played in a while, but, like riding a bike, it all came back to him after a couple of hands. He was pretty good at poker tells. He had learned that poker was a game of information availability as much as a game of deception. Betting patterns were the main tells, of course, but physical tells were important too. You had to make observation your habit; something Leo had been good at all his life.

Like now, a few games in and he knew that Nicky bit his lips when he had bad cards and flexed his cheek muscles when he had good ones. Dominic got nervous legs when he had a good hand. Zeke was a hard read; he was steady either way. The new guy—Mike—wasn't a very good player but he was a friendly guy. He looked to be in his early thirties. He wore jeans, a black Beatles T-shirt, and sandals, and looked slightly disheveled. He drank Coors beer, ate most of the mixed nuts, and made an effort to get to know everyone. "You got family, Leo?" Mike asked him.

"Yeah, I do."

"I hear you got a nice sister," Dominic said, after throwing in some chips.

"She's actually my cousin," Leo said, "but we were raised together by our mothers, who were sisters."

"Divorced, eh?" Dominic said.

"Yeah," Leo said. "But she's not interested in dating."

"Who said anything about dating?" Dominic said.

"Oh, sorry, I thought…"

"Wrong cousin," Nicky said, smiling. "Dominic's married with three kids."

"Ahhh," Leo said.

When Pete laid his royal flush on the table, Leo said, "You lucky bastard!"

"Hey," Zeke said. "Don't be swearing in front of the priest."

Leo looked around. "What priest?" he said, lifting his hands in the air. Nicky thumbed in the direction of Mike.

"Mike?" Leo asked.

"*Father* Mike," Nicky said. "I thought you knew."

"I didn't know. Sorry, Father."

Father Mike smiled. "No worries, Leo. Pete *is* a lucky bastard!"

Leo wondered if he was turning red. The only time he had ever been around a priest was at his mom and grandfather's funerals. Priests didn't wear Beatles T-shirts and jeans and play poker and drink and swear, did they?

"We're not required to wear the garb all the time," Father Mike said, reading Leo's mind. "Especially when it's so god damn hot."

Leo did a double take. Father Mike smiled a mischievous grin. Then it dawned on Leo that Father Mike was Merricat's Father Mike.

"Hey, I hear you're a handy guy," Father Mike said to Leo as the men were breaking up and beginning to leave. "Did Nick tell you about our renovation?"

Nicky cut in. "Yes, and he's in, Padre."

He didn't really know how it happened, but Leo found himself in a pew in the third row of St. Anthony of Padua Church on Sunday. Didn't he agree to help out on Saturdays? Merricat couldn't stop smiling, but Leo felt out of place, like a cowboy in a ballroom. He stood, he sat, he kneeled, he listened, but mostly he stared. There was so much to look at in the century-old church. Merricat was right in saying that it looked like a great church in Rome. Situated between the colorful stained-glass windows, statues of saints perched on pedestals seemed to keep watch over the congregation. The mural at the front of the church was so beautiful it made Leo's knees go weak.

After Mass, Father Mike grabbed Leo by the arm. "Come on, let's get a doughnut before those damn kids eat 'em all." Down in the Parish Hall,

Camilla and her friends zigzagged through the rows of tables, red-faced and giggly. Father Mike insisted Leo get a doughnut. Only three were left, all jelly rolls. Leo placed one on a paper plate, while Father Mike poured coffee into two Styrofoam cups and asked, "Cream or sugar?" Merricat pulled a chair out for Leo and Father Mike grabbed one across from them next to Nicky. Leo took a bite of his doughnut and was humiliated when a glob of jelly fell on his shirt. Merricat made the blob worse with her napkin.

"Damn it!" Father Mike said. Leo looked up and saw that Father Mike had a big blob of jelly on his robe, too. Silence at the table.

"My apologies, kind ladies and gentlemen," Father Mike said as he scooped the jelly blob off his robe with his index finger and then popped it into his mouth. "My dear, sweet mother always told me my mouth would get me in trouble! The kids didn't hear me, did they?" he asked with an impish grin. Who was this guy? Leo thought. And did he do that on purpose—spill jelly on himself—to help mitigate Leo's embarrassment? Leo ate the rest of his doughnut very carefully.

On Saturday, Leo found himself on a ladder at St. Anthony's washing the feet of Jesus...on a stained-glass window. The windows were so massive, he could only get through one in a day. It was something being up high on the ladder and watching the sun streaming through that colored glass. He looked over at Nicky. "I know!" Nicky said, smiling. At the end of the day, when Leo climbed down from the ladder, muscles he didn't know he had ached. "Man, I'm out of shape."

"You run?" Nicky asked, as they put supplies away.

"From responsibility. Ha. Ha."

"Father Mike and I run on Monday, Wednesday, and Friday mornings. Join us."

"I'd hold you back."

"We're slow. We usually end up walking and talking. I'll pick you up."

On Monday, instead of picking Leo up, Nicky dropped off his four daughters. Trina's water broke and she was in labor. Camilla was ecstatic to have her friends over. There were shrieks, and twirls, and cartwheels. "This is a mess of estrogen," Leo said to Merricat, sheepishly looking up from the floor where five little girls pummeled him with throw pillows. Merricat fed the kids pizza and ice cream on the back porch, and then they caught lightning bugs and had baths. Merricat finally got everyone settled down in Millie's room when the phone rang. It was Nicky. "It's a girl!" he cried. "Her name is Francesca. Trina did great." More shrieks, twirls, and dancing.

The next morning, Camilla woke up and decided she wanted everyone to call her "Millie" from now on. One of Nicky's kids couldn't say "Camilla." First, Gia called her "Milla" and then it morphed into "Millie."

"Millie Rose Davinsky," Leo said out loud when Merricat informed him of the name change. "Sounds like an eighty-year-old in a babushka."

"Nevertheless," Merricat said.

The doorbell rang. Father Mike, dressed in a T-shirt and shorts, smiled at Leo, and said, "The new dad is otherwise occupied this morning, so it looks like it's you and me."

Leo was confused. "I thought you ran on Mondays, Wednesdays, and Fridays."

"No," Father Mike said. "Tuesdays, Thursdays, and Saturdays."

Leo was sure Nicky had said...oh well, he was here. He asked Father to come in while he changed into his gym shoes. He felt a little guilty about leaving Merricat with a houseful of little girls, but she waved him off.

"Haven't run since my accident," Leo told Father as they started up the street.

"We'll take it slow," he said.

At first they didn't talk; Leo was feeling out his body parts, making sure the titanium inside him held. But soon he got into a groove and remembered the wonder of it.

"I want to thank you for all your help, Leo. Especially the windows. That's a tough job," Father said.

"You're welcome. Nicky's one persuasive guy."

"Nicky's got charisma."

"Wish I had it..."

"Oh, but you got something else, Leo."

"What do I got, Father, please tell me."

"You got some kinda cool, my friend. A kind of quiet, steady cool. And that accent!"

"What accent?"

"Why, that Scottish lilt you have!"

"I thought the accent was gone. It was a put-on anyway."

"Oh, no, I can detect it. My mother's side were Scots. Listen, can I ask you something?"

Here we go, Leo thought. He's going to ask me if I believe in God, if my soul is saved, if I pray, if I'm baptized...

"Gotta call from my friend Father Larson up in South Beloit. He visits people in nursing homes who don't have visitors. There's this Scottish guy. No family. No friends. Hospice is in so he doesn't have long. Father asked me if I knew anybody Scottish who could visit him. Could I talk you into it? I think he would be comforted by your voice."

"I don't know, Father—"

"No pressure, if you're not comfortable."

"I'm not really a big conversationalist."

"Don't think that really matters."

They ran a few blocks in silence. Back at the house, Father Mike stretched a little and then got into his car. "It's called Fair Oaks, it's on Blackhawk Boulevard in South Beloit, and the old geezer's name is Brody," Father Mike said and sped off.

Leo stood in the driveway. What the hell? He found Merricat in the kitchen. "The darndest thing just happened. With Father Mike."

"Huh?" Merricat said. She was loading the dishwasher and Leo could tell her mind was elsewhere.

"Merricat, listen."

"I'm listening. I can do two things at once you know."

"Father Mike asked me to go visit some guy in a nursing home. Said the guy is on his way out. Hospice. No friends or family. He's Scottish and might like to talk to someone with a Scottish accent."

"That would be nice."

"Maybe... If the guy's name wasn't Brody." Merricat's face went white. "Cat, what did you do?"

She sat down on the stool. "Wow. Wow. This is weird."

"This can't be a coincidence."

"Maybe it's a miracle!"

"Out with it."

"Maybe it will lead to your dad. Then you can get some closure."

"Who says I need closure?"

"Father Mike."

Merricat was always loose in the lips and she couldn't keep a secret if her life depended on it. She would pantomime zipping her lips, she would "swear on the Bible," she would even "go to her grave," but invariably she would end up spilling the beans. He could just picture her telling Father Mike his whole life story.

"Geez, Merricat." Leo shook his head and walked out back. He joined *Millie* on the swing set. She was pouting now that the Russo girls had gone to their grandma's.

"What'd you do, Leo?" she asked.

Leo sat down in a swing. "I did nothing. Why?"

"Cuz Mom's staring at you with that face she gets."

Leo looked at the kitchen window. Sure enough, Merricat was looking out, wearing that "face she gets."

"Leo, can we go out for lunch?"

"If your mom gives the green light."

"Who made her in charge?"

Leo laughed. "Story of my life, kid. Story of my life."

Leo had made no promises to Father Mike. So why did he feel guilty about not going to see his uncle Brody? And how the heck did he track him down anyway? What was the story behind that? And, did Father Mike just make up the story about his priest friend visiting family-less nursing home residents? Was it normal for priests to swear and lie and have poor hygiene and magical powers of manipulation? Merricat and her big mouth. Closure my foot. Why did she think contact with his uncle would be a good thing? How the heck could it bring closure? He tried to get inside Merricat's mind, to follow her thought process, but despite being surrounded by nothing but women his entire life, darn if he could ever figure them out.

A week or so later, Father Mike sat himself down on a barstool at Caffe Greco. "A glass of your finest Chianti, my good man," he said to Leo. By the looks of his shirt, it appeared he'd already had a glass, or maybe it was a ketchup stain. "How's things?"

"Things are good," Leo said, not making eye contact.

"I was going to ask you—"

Leo cut him off. "I haven't had a chance to go to the nursing home."

"No, not that. It's just that Nicky and Trina are finding it hard to get all the girls up and dressed for the 9:00 Mass and so they're going to start coming to the 11:30 Mass, which means I'm short an usher at the 9:00 and I wondered if you could help me out. No pressure."

Leo cocked his head a little. Oh, this guy was good. "Sure, Padre, no problem."

Father Mike swigged down the rest of his Chianti and said, "God damn, that's good stuff." He set his glass down and left his money on the bar. "See you Sunday!" he called without even looking back.

The guy sitting at the bar said to Leo, "Isn't that guy a priest?"

Leo smiled. "That or a wizard."

Merricat and Millie were thrilled that Leo was coming to church with them again. "I wish I could be an usher," Millie said.

"Are you wearing high heels, Mil?" Leo asked her as they walked out the back door to the garage.

"Yes, I am," she said, holding her foot out for admiration. "Designed them myself." Leo took a closer look. It seemed to him she had glued two wooden blocks to a pair of ballerina slippers. "I re-fashionized some old slippers," she said proudly. She could barely walk.

Ushering made Leo feel old. The other ushers weren't old, it just seemed like an old man's job. He recognized several people from Caffe Greco's. He felt as if a spotlight were on him. At the end of Mass, Father Mike said, "Let's give our new usher, Leo Lennox, a hand." The congregation clapped and Leo bowed slightly. He regretted it the moment he did. Geez, it was probably a sin or something.

Downstairs, Father Mike insisted on bringing Leo around table to table to introduce him to some of the parishioners. Leo noticed that most of the people were older Italian-Americans. Most people seemed friendly and polite, but Leo couldn't help but feel he was the subject of gossip. Was he being paranoid?

When Leo said goodbye to Father Mike, he said, "See you next Sunday, right?"

What could Leo say?

21.

merricat & leo & millie

THEIR BLOCK OF Clinton Boulevard hosted an annual block party the first Saturday in September. This year, Merricat and Leo and Jake and Bonnie were hosts. Merricat, who usually hated the heat, was glad the temperature was in the nineties because it meant all the kids could swim in Jake and Bonnie's pool after lunch.

Merricat covered the buffet tables with plastic coverings while Leo and Jake set up the street barricades. In a flash, the boulevard was filled with little ones on bikes decorated with streamers and balloons. Millie had been practicing all summer to be able to remove her training wheels before the block party, but, in the end, decided she could wait another year. She and her best bud Susie swished past Leo and Jake. Merricat saw Leo do a double take. "Wait just a minute, Missy," he called after her. "Are you wearing lipstick?"

The girls did a U-turn and pedaled past Leo and Jake with big, lipsticked-smiles.

"Mom said," Millie sang.

"Mom didn't say," Susie said and laughed her head off.

For lunch, Merricat and Leo sat at a folding table with Jake and Bonnie and the girls. Millie and Susie squirmed and begged to be excused so they could resume riding bikes. "We can eat anytime," Millie said, "but we can only ride bikes in the street once a year."

Merricat said, "Eat two more bites."

Millie took two more bites of her hot dog and said to Jake and Bonnie with her mouthful, "I can't wait to swim!" and ran off.

"That girl is something else," Jake said.

They heard a crash and a scream and Jake sprang up and ran over to help Susie who had fallen. "No casualties," he reported back. Everyone headed to the center of the street for the egg toss. Millie was naughty and purposely threw her egg at a neighbor boy instead of tossing it to Susie. Merricat almost didn't let her go swimming after that, but Leo said, "Aww, let her go." Merricat stood with Leo at the edge of Bonnie and Jake's pool, watching Millie like a hawk. Too many splashing, screaming kids! Millie was a good little swimmer though, proud that she could go underwater with the purple goggles Leo bought her. But Leo wouldn't let her use the goggles today. "Too many kids in the pool to go underwater, Mil. Just splash around today."

She said, "Man!" and looked to her mom.

"You heard him," Merricat said.

"Man!" she said again, setting the goggles on the pool's edge.

After swimming, the mandatory annual block party photo had to be taken. Dr. Singh had the fancy camera with the timer. He set it up on the tripod and told everyone to say "Stinky Blue Cheese" on his countdown. Ice-cream sundaes were next before the night would end with a bonfire and S'mores. The day was pure heaven for the kids; pure exhaustion for the adults.

Merricat helped Bonnie scoop ice cream into plastic bowls. Leo looked like a kid holding out his bowl for a scoop of vanilla and a scoop of strawberry. "Did Millie get ice cream?" Merricat asked.

Leo said, "I thought she did. I don't know."

"Where is she, anyway?" Merricat asked, looking around.

"She was on her bike," Leo said, stretching his neck to scan the street. He looked for her in the bike parade and over in the field where Jake was stacking the wood for the bonfire.

"I don't see her," Merricat said.

"I'll find her," Leo said, taking his ice cream with him.

Merricat handed her ice cream scoop to Bonnie and followed Leo. Susie said she last saw her riding bikes. Patricia Lewis saw her playing with the Arnolds' dog. Dr. Singh had showed her how his tripod folded up.

Suddenly, like a flash, like a sword to her heart, Merricat knew where she was. She ran with Leo close behind her to Jake's backyard, to the pool. And then, stopping in her tracks, before her, a sight she would see in her nightmares for the rest of her life, her little Millie, face down, floating in the pool. She and Leo screamed in unison, "Help! Help! Call 911!" Leo dropped his ice cream and jumped in. When he pulled Millie out someone's arms were there to help him. He lay her gently on the ground, turned her on her tummy, and pounded on her back. Some water spilled from her mouth. Merricat could hear the buzz of the whole neighborhood surrounding her. Leo turned Millie over on her back and Merricat gasped when she saw that her lips were blue; those lips that were ruby red only a while ago. Leo was calm and deliberate. He started mouth-to-mouth, but Dr. Singh pushed his way through, and said, "Please. Let me." Dr. Singh delivered chest compressions as Merricat held Millie's hand. Suddenly, Millie moved and coughed. Thank goodness the sirens grew closer. Next thing Merricat knew she was at Millie's side in the back of the ambulance. Leo followed in his car.

The memories are in vignettes. A triptych: the discovery and ambulance ride; the hospital stay; the aftermath. A blur of sirens and beeps and machines and commands. Merricat's eyes dripped like faucets so everything was a literal blur as well. Leo beat them to the emergency room and was waiting to meet her. She crumbled into his arms. And then they waited. Leo made phones calls: to Rosie, who said she would get on a plane as soon as she could; to Father Mike, who said he could be there in minutes.

When Merricat was finally able to see her, it was devastating. Hooked up to machines and tubes, Millie looked like a robot, not her beautiful little girl. When the doctor came in, she said, "I can't tell you much right now. We have no way of knowing how long she was underwater. And everything depends on how long her little brain was deprived of oxygen. Anything more than five minutes can result in severe brain injury. We'll do a bunch of tests."

She checked some readings on one of the machines and then took Merricat's hand in hers. "These cases are all over the board. Some kiddos don't make it through the night. Some do, but then there's significant brain damage, and some are little miracles—they wake up as if nothing happened. Your little one looks like a spitfire with that red hair. I'll bet she's a fighter. Brace yourself—the waiting is torture. But only time will tell." She squeezed Merricat's hand. "Stay strong. We'll do everything we can."

The nurse brought in another chair so Merricat and Leo could sit at Millie's side. "How can my baby be on a ventilator?" Merricat cried. It was horrifying. Only two people were allowed in the intensive care unit at once, so when Leo got a text from Father Mike, he sent him in so he could spend some time with Merricat. He already had tears in his eyes when he entered the room. Merricat cried on his shoulder. "Father, they don't know if she's going to make it, and if she does, she might be…"

Father Mike said. "We're going to just sit here and pray for a miracle. God's will be done, but we can always ask him for a miracle." He laid his hands upon Millie's forehead and prayed over her. "Do you believe in miracles, Merricat?"

"I do. But then I wonder why they seem so selective. This person gets a miracle cure but that person dies."

"Heck if I know," Father Mike said. "I wonder that myself. But there's a quote I love about miracles from the mystic George Gurdjieff. It goes— I'm paraphrasing—A miracle is not the breaking of a natural law or a phenomenon occurring outside of the law. Miracles only seem to break laws because the laws are unknown and incomprehensible to us in the first place, and therefore seem miraculous."

Merricat rubbed her eyes, "Sorry Father, I'm not following."

"All I mean, my sweet friend, is that a miracle is not something out of *God's* ordinary. It's just a less common way of God working in the world. What I'm getting at is this: be bold with God. By asking him for a miracle, you are not over-asking. It seems such a big thing for us that God could intervene. Pray, Merricat," he whispered. "And be bold in your prayer." Father Mike leaned over and kissed Millie on the head. "And, Merricat, because we can't predict God's will, may I anoint her?"

Merricat nodded and Father produced a small bottle of oil from his pocket. Using his thumb, he rubbed oil on her forehead and palms while saying prayers. When Father Mike left, he hugged Merricat and reminded her to pray boldly.

She prayed with her entire being and then dozed off in her chair. When she opened her eyes, Father Mike was gone and Leo sat next to her. "Jake and Bonnie are here. They're devastated."

"You told them it's not their fault."

"Of course."

"It's no one's fault," Merricat repeated.

Leo said, "Cat, Brice needs to know."

"Oh, Leo! This whole time, I didn't even think about Brice. It's like you're her father. I can't do it. Will you do it?"

"Of course."

The nurse came in to tell them that only one of them was allowed to stay with Millie overnight. Merricat felt bad, but told Leo to go home and get some sleep.

"I'll sleep in the waiting room and wait for your mom. She gets in tomorrow at ten. And I'll give Brice a call, too."

Merricat prepared for a long restless night. She thought she never slept, but in fact she did, but so lightly she still heard the beeps and whirs of the machines and the voices of the nurses and hospital staff. The good news was that Millie made it through the night.

Merricat, Leo, and Rosie took turns spending time at Millie's side, praying for a miracle. "Lord," Merricat whispered when she was alone with Millie, "I've never asked for anything before. I'm being bold here. Please save her. Please."

When Leo joined her later in the morning, he told her that he had talked to Brice. "He can't come. His wife is due with their second child any day. He said to give Millie a hug and to keep him in the loop."

"Good," Merricat said. "We don't want him here."

"Go get something to eat," Leo suggested.

"I'm not hungry."

"Too bad. I want some alone time with her."

Merricat did as he said and she and Rosie headed to the cafeteria. They had just paid for their coffees when Merricat's phone buzzed. It was Leo: "Come quick."

Well, of course, you think the worst. The sprint down the hall to the elevator, up three floors, another hallway, and past the nurses' station was torture. But Leo was smiling. "It's all good!" Millie had regained consciousness and they were going to do a short trial to remove the ventilator to see if she could breathe on her own.

"My baby!" Merricat said, gently caressing Millie. One look at Millie and Merricat knew, as only a mother could, that she was going to be okay.

All in all, Millie spent four days in the Pediatric ICU. She won over all the nurses' hearts and made them smile when her first words off the ventilator were: "Get me outta here!" The doctor told Merricat they would monitor Millie closely over the next couple of years. The doctor said, "We are so glad for a good outcome. I knew Millie was a spitfire."

With Millie home and tucked into bed, Merricat sat with Leo and Rosie in the sun room. "More wine, Aunt Rose?" Leo asked.

"Just a little," Rosie said. "It's making me sleepy."

They were all sleepy. Merricat said, "I think I could sleep for a straight week."

A light knock on the door and Leo jumped up to get it. Millie had always been a sound sleeper. But for a week now, everyone was tip-toeing around the house.

Merricat looked up to see Nicky. He had a friend with him.

"His name is Larry," he said, holding a little butter-colored dog. "My neighbor just got him and her husband got laid off. They can't keep him. I think this little guy would be great for Millie. Please take him or my kids are going to beg me to keep him and there is just no way!"

Well, Larry was adorable and Merricat, who had been reluctant to get a dog, said, "Nicky, he's perfect!" Nicky transferred him to Merricat's arms and he licked every inch of her face and then some.

"Somebody!" Millie called from her room.

"Darn!" Merricat said, "She woke up. I'd rather she meet Larry tomorrow. She'll never get to sleep otherwise."

"I'll go," Leo said.

Nicky told Merricat he would get the paperwork for the dog in the morning and Rosie ran to the store to buy dog food and the paraphernalia they would need. Merricat took the dog into the kitchen, hoping to keep him quiet until Millie was asleep. She carried him around like a baby. When Leo came into the kitchen, his face was pale and his eyes glistened with tears.

"What?" Merricat said.

"You better sit down," Leo said, taking the dog.

Merricat sat on a stool at the kitchen island.

"She had had a bad dream about an octopus, only he wasn't an eight-armed octopus; he had twenty-three arms, and she wanted to know what a creature with twenty-three arms would be called. I didn't know what she meant. She said, 'You know Leo, like tri is three and penta is five and octo is eight. What would you call a something-pus with twenty-three arms?' I teased her and said, 'Let me think…pentagon, hexagon, octagon…I know how about *Oregon*?' She didn't think that was funny."

"I do!"

"Thanks. Anyway, I looked it up on my phone and the Latin word for twenty-three is *Viginti Tres*, so that's what she called her scary twenty-three-armed octopus. She was satisfied and yawned and said, 'I'm tired again. Thank you, Leo.' Just as I was walking out she said, 'Oh, and your mom says *hi*.'"

"She dreamed about your mom?" Merricat said.

"This was more than a dream; this was like what happened to me…" He lowered his voice to a whisper. "A near-death experience."

Merricat slapped her hand to her mouth.

"I went back and sat on her bed." Leo began to cry. "She said, 'Leo, I just went to find my googles, that's all. I didn't mean to fall in. Then I kept saying in my head, *Somebody! Somebody*! But nobody heard me. Then I just flew up like a bird. I could see me in the water. It was weird. And I saw you trying to help me. Thank you, Leo. I learned about CPR in school. And then I was flying over the ambulance and I saw those people trying to help me but then I saw a tunnel. It was like a water slide! And I slid through it, way up in the sky. And then a nice lady came up to me and said, 'It's okay, sweetie. You can go back. And tell your Uncle Leo hi for me. I'm his mommy.'"

"Oh, Leo," Merricat said, squeezing his hand. "God is so good."

"We'll have to have Father Mike talk to her about this."

The puppy was a hit. Millie woke up the next morning, rubbing her eyes, saying she thought she heard a dog bark. "You did," said Leo, not looking up from his phone.

Right on cue, Larry scampered in to meet Millie.

"What?" Millie said. "When did Choppy get here? Hello, Choppy!"

Merricat said, "His name is Larry."

"No, it's not," Millie said. "It's Choppy. Short for Chopped Liver."

Merricat had read all about near death experiences after Leo had told her about his own. Now she sought out information about NDEs in children. There were many. Over time, Millie shared more memories about her experience. They would seem just to pop in her head from out of nowhere. "Did I tell you that there were colored lights in the tunnel?" "Did I mention I saw Susie's sister kissing Kevin O'Malley when I was flying over the yard?" (Susie's sister did confess to kissing Kevin the day of the block party.) "And, oh, there really is a stairway to heaven like the song, but it's called a stair*case*." Millie was always precocious as a child; now she was over the top. Father Mike counseled her that it might be best to talk about her experience only with her family and him. "There will be people who won't understand."

"Is it a secret?" she asked, whispering.

"Yes, it's our secret. You've been given a very special gift, Millie. Very special, indeed."

Leo's runs with Father Mike continued, but without Nicky. The poor guy just could not find the time anymore due to his ever-expanding family. While Leo missed seeing his friend (they still had poker night) he was glad to have one-on-one time with Father Mike. It was like having a friend, a counselor, a priest, and a work-out buddy all in one. Today, on their run,

Father Mike shared his talk with Millie about her NDE. "I explained that some people simply won't understand."

Leo said without thinking, "Right, that's why I never told anyone about mine."

"Yours?"

"I had one, too, when I was run down by a car."

"Similar to Millie's?"

"Eerily similar. The out-of-body stuff, the tunnel, the light, seeing my mom…"

"You lucky son-of-a-bitch," Father Mike said. Leo laughed. He could never get used to this swearing priest. "Does Millie know about your experience?"

"No," Leo said.

"Maybe you should tell her. It might help her to process it. And in the meantime, will you tell me about it? I want to hear everything!"

That night, at bedtime Leo shared his story with Millie. She clapped her hands. "So now we both have a secret with God," she said, her eyes sparkling. "And with Father Mike, too, who is kinda like God's vice president." Leo chuckled. "Well, I know one thing, Leo. I'll never be afraid to die. It will be wonderful!"

"Yes," Leo said, squeezing her tight. "It will be."

22.
leo & company

LEO WAS NEVER one to open up. He was the listener. Always listening to the women in his life. He had been in awe how easily women shared intimate parts of their lives with each other. Men just didn't do that. Well, he had never done that. Until Father Mike came along.

"So, what are your plans?" Father Mike asked Leo on their morning run. They had added to their route and were up to three miles.

"For what?"

"For what? For life."

"You're looking at it."

"Leo."

"You should be happy. You got me to come to church!"

"I'm concerned about your living situation. I'm only thinking of Millie."

"Millie's great!"

"Leo, Merricat met someone."

Leo stopped in his tracks. "What? When? This is news to me."

"Well, she didn't *just* meet him. It's her Italian teacher, Massimo Reggio. You've met him."

"Of course," Leo said. "We went to his wife's funeral last year." Leo resumed running. He wondered why Merricat hadn't told him.

"I'm not saying it's anything. They've stopped for a glass of wine after class."

"Merricat told you about him?"

"She's confused."

"Does she know you're talking to me about this?"

"Leo, she *asked* me to talk to you about this."

Suddenly Leo's chest hurt. He had to stop running. He panted a bit and then bent over, holding his knees, to catch his breath.

"Mike," Leo said, "what's this all about?"

"It might be a good idea if you started apartment hunting."

Leo said, "I gotta go." He left Father behind and turned toward home. He couldn't believe Merricat could be such a coward, not to discuss this with him herself! But then he remembered the whole incident in Chicago with Brice and how cowardly she had been back then. Did she really want him to leave? Why now when Millie needed him and the new puppy needed training? He just couldn't believe it and he started to cry. He didn't want to go home—how could he go home? But he had to pick up Millie from school and get ready for work.

He managed to avoid Merricat by sneaking in through the backdoor and prowling up the stairs to change for work. He escaped without being noticed. He got in his car and drove over to St. Peter's to pick up Millie. He feigned cheerfulness, listening to her daily report, and then dropped her off home, saying he had to go to work early today. Millie leaned over the seat to kiss Leo's cheek, and said, "Lo! Scratchy. Why didn't you shave today?"

"Growing a beard, kiddo. See you tonight." He watched her as she skipped her way to the front door. But then she turned around and ran back. Leo rolled down the window.

"I forgot to tell you," she said. "I broke up with Alexander. He's a male chauvinist pig!"

Leo waited until she got in the house. Usually, he would be smiling at the absolute cuteness of Millie's announcement, but today, his mouth remained paralyzed in a frown. Instead of driving to the café, he drove over to Nicky's office to see if he knew of any cheap apartments to rent. Nicky knew a guy (of course he did). Not an apartment, but a tiny house over by the church. "Perfect," Leo said.

"What's going on?" Nicky asked.

"Looks like Merricat has a boyfriend and wants me out."

"Hmmmm."

"Hmmmm, what?"

"Well, you gotta admit, buddy, it's been an odd set-up."

"I know that, but it worked."

"But you and Merricat aren't married. You aren't Millie's dad. It's like you've been playing house, bud. You guys need to need to live your own lives."

"But Millie needs me!"

"Who says she won't have you? You'll just be a couple miles away."

"Says the man with the perfect life."

"Perfect life? Leo, we just found out my daughter Sophia has Type 1 Diabetes. And one of my employees has been stealing money from me. Don't know if I can make payroll this month."

Leo felt like an idiot. "I'm sorry, Nick. Damn, am I a narcissist or something? It's always all about me, isn't it?"

"Nah," Nicky said, slapping him on the back. "Life throws a lot of tricky shit at us."

"What can I do, Nick. You need money? I have a little."

"Bud, you're going to need your money. Uh, you've been a little spoiled all these years."

Only two people sat at the bar at Caffe Greco tonight so Leo had too much time to think. Is that what everyone thought? That Leo was a freeloader? Did they think he mooched off his cousin and didn't contribute? He could see how it might look that way. He only worked part time as a bartender. He drove Rosie's car. He lived in Rosie's house. But he contributed. Even though Rosie still owned the house, Leo paid half the mortgage payment each month. He paid the property taxes each year and covered all the home repairs. He and Merricat had a joint checking account they used for food and household expenses. Merricat paid for Millie's tuition, clothes, and doctor's bills. He wasn't a freeloader, but he could see how it might look that way to an outsider.

Nicky's words stung. "Spoiled?" He never thought of himself as spoiled. His old partner Christopher was spoiled. Leo was happy with just the basics. He had no fancy clothes, no fancy cars or high-powered job, no status symbols at all. Leo was easy. Like his mother he just went with the flow. Maybe that was the problem.

After work, he did not go straight home. He stopped downtown for a drink at the Rue Marche. He uncharacteristically flirted with a woman way too young for him with hopes of going home with her. But she ended up getting a call from her babysitter and had to get home to her kids. He knew he dodged a bullet, still he ached for some comfort. He sat in his car for two hours and played Solitaire on his phone. Finally, he drove home and climbed into bed. He even slept.

At about nine o'clock, Merricat knocked on his door and let herself in. "You didn't die, did you? You never sleep this late."

Leo rolled over, so she couldn't see his face. "Little bit of a hangover, if you must know."

"Geez, sorry. I just wanted to remind you that Millie has her Halloween play at school today at one. I'll meet you there, okay?"

"Okay."

"Leo, what?"

He turned over. "Merricat, what the hell?"

She leaned against the doorframe. "What the hell, what?"

"What the hell, I got a talking-to from Father Mike. Said you want me to move out."

"Wait, that's not what I said."

"What did you say then? He said you asked him to talk to me."

"I did, but just to tell you about Massimo."

"Oh, right, Massimo."

"It's not a big deal or anything with Massimo, but it got me thinking about our futures. And it reminded me of what went wrong with Brice. Massimo doesn't understand our arrangement. I think a lot of people don't."

"We're family, Merricat. What's not to understand?"

"Leo, I don't want you to move out—"

"Too late, I already am. I'm going to rent a house by St. Anthony's. Nicky's setting it up."

"You're really moving out?"

"On Saturday."

"Leo, that's not what I want."

"Well, it's what *I* want. I didn't realize I'm notorious for being the town mooch. I'm moving out and I'm going to get a full-time job."

"What about picking up Millie from school?"

"Maybe Massimo can pick her up," Leo said and rolled over.

How could he break Millie's heart? She had a huge part in the Halloween play. She was a magic pumpkin who saved the school from a giant black cat that was eating everyone's homework. He sat in the parking lot arguing with himself about going in. At 12:59 he made his way into the gym and stood at the back door just in case he needed to make a quick escape. He spotted Merricat sitting by Jake and Bonnie. She pointed to the chair she had saved next to her. Leo shook his head. He was staying put. He thought about *Massimo* and his charming accent. Merricat was probably making the same mistake his mother had made, falling for a man with a sexy accent. He thought Merricat was smarter than that. But then again, she fell in love with Brice. He was sorry to think that his cousin had such rotten taste in men. Hadn't she carried this Italian obsession a bit too far?

The play was clever and Millie stole the show. The only glitch was when one little boy fell and said, "Oh shit!" That was hilarious and Leo couldn't help but smile, but as soon as the play was over, he was out of there. Walking to his car, one of the mothers stopped him and said, "Your daughter was adorable."

"Thanks," Leo said, and climbed quickly into his car.

While Merricat was at work, he packed up his room, and then headed down the basement for his summer clothes. Rummaging through (neither he nor Merricat were organizational freaks) all the crap, he came upon the boxes of Beatles albums and memorabilia. For some reason, the boxes pissed him off. He took several trips and carried them upstairs and loaded them into his trunk and the backseat of his car. He looked at his watch. He had some time before he had to be to work. He decided to do something he should have done a long, long time ago.

He got on I-90 and drove north to South Beloit. He put the address of the nursing home into his phone and arrived at Fair Oaks twenty minutes later. At the front desk, he asked for Brody Lennox's room. The receptionist, a young girl with pink hair, looked up. "Oh, sir, please hold on one moment." Soon the girl returned with a woman.

"Sir, I am terribly sorry to inform you, but Mr. Lennox is no longer with us. Are you a relative?"

"Yes, I'm his nephew. Where is he?"

"Oh dear, he died, oh, I think it's been five weeks now."

"Oh, that's sad."

"Very sad, especially since no one came to claim him. There was no funeral or anything. We called his brother," she looked down at a notepad, "Mackinney Lennox, but he told us he couldn't come. We still have his things in storage. Would you like to have them?"

"Oh," Leo said, shifting his weight from one leg to the other. "I don't think so. I'm moving soon and trying to lighten up myself."

"There's not much really, but there is a really nice photo album with wonderful old pictures. Surely, you'll want that."

Surely, he would not but what kind of louse would say no? The woman gave the pink-haired girl a set of keys and told her where to find the photo album. She returned shortly and handed a black album to Leo.

"Thanks," he said. "I, er, I think his brother would like to have this. I live out of town so I'm out of the loop. Would you happen to have Mackinney's address?" With HIPAA and all the privacy laws, Leo was surprised when she looked at her notebook and said, "Sure, it's 3909 Blane Avenue, in Janesville. That's just about twenty minutes north of here. The pink-haired girl wrote the address on a scrap of paper and Leo thanked them. Twenty minutes later Leo pulled up in front of his father's house, a drab beige bungalow with moldy moss growing out of the gutters. Leo cut the engine. What a dump! He paused. Did he really want to do this? He didn't have much time; he'd have to leave in fifteen minutes max to make it to work on time. It was now or never.

Leo rang the bell, but realized it was broken when it didn't depress. He knocked on the door and then pounded. His heart raced and he wanted this over ASAP. He waited. He bit on his thumbnail. The dirty lace curtain in the window moved. The door opened and there before him stood his father. There was no mistake about that.

"Well, god damn! It's like looking in a mirror!" Mackinney said, fully opening the door. He grinned, displaying a set of straight but yellowed teeth. Hardly like looking in a mirror. Yes, the likeness was there and Leo could tell how his mother and aunt had said he was the spitting image, but not now.

"So, you're Mackinney," Leo said, wishing he hadn't come. It was one thing to know he was out there; it was quite another to actually see him. And there wasn't much to see. Mackinney Lennox was skin on bones. Yellowed skin, from alcoholism, surely.

"Call me Dah. Come on in my boy."

"No, sorry, I can't. I just came for one thing. Hold on just a minute." Leo walked to the car and retrieved a box. He carried it over and set it down at his father's feet. "There's a few more," he said.

Mackinney watched in awe as Leo carried the boxes of his long-lost treasure.

Leo said, "It's all there and it's all yours, on one condition."

Mackinney looked up. Leo thought he would probably agree to just about anything to have his stupid stuff back. "That this visit is a one and only. I don't want to see you again. Don't try to find me. I forgive you and I release you, but I don't want to know you."

"Have it your way, then," Mackinney said. "Can ya help your Dah and carry the boxes in for me?"

Leo sighed. "I'll be late for work."

"Please."

Leo picked up a box and followed Mackinney into the house. It was dark but surprisingly clean. To Leo's astonishment, there was a picture of his mother holding a baby (him!) on a side table. He shook his head and went out to retrieve the other boxes.

"Your aunt said you burned it all."

"She was lying."

Mackinney rummaged around in one of the boxes. "I dunna really know what to say. Thank you?"

"It's okay. Uh, I have to go." Leo opened the door.

"Leo!" Mackinney said. "I think about her... Sometimes I wish I could get a re-do."

"Don't we all," Leo said. He walked to his car and didn't look back, but there were tears. What did he expect? That his Dad would do a jig? Haul out the champagne? It felt good to get rid of that stuff; he hadn't realized it had been an albatross around his neck. Maybe it was time to quit playing house and grow up. Maybe he had needed closure.

On the drive home he got a call from Aunt Rose. "Wow. Did Merricat sic you on me?"

"Nobody's siccing anybody on anybody. I'm calling to see if you'd be interested in a job."

"What? What are you talking about?"

"Eleanor is moving to D.C. She's got to sell Fe-Mail. You loved working there; wouldn't it be nice to own your own business again? Move back home to Madison?"

"Wow," Leo said. "Merricat must have it bad for this Massimo guy. Everyone I know—Father Mike, Nicky, you, Merricat—everybody's trying to get rid of me."

"Cut it out, Leo. It's not that at all. And Massimo is just a friend. But you and Merricat have always had a strange relationship."

"And whose fault is that, Aunt Rose? Yours and my Mom's. You guys could have gone and lived on your own. Maybe my mom would have remarried; maybe you would have, well not married, but been with someone. But you guys, you and mom, you did this to us. You cemented our families together."

"I know. And I'm seeing now that it was a disservice. You must know that it partly contributed to Merricat's divorce."

"Asshole Brice is what contributed to Merricat's divorce."

"Sheesh, he was an asshole."

"Aunt Rose, here's the long and short of it. I'm moving out. I'll get a full-time job. I'll buy your car."

"Don't be ridiculous. The car is yours."

"But I'm not moving out of town. I couldn't do that to Millie."

"I know you want what's best for Millie. So, think about it good and hard, Leo. What would be best for Millie?"

"Thanks for thinking of me, Aunt Rose. Gotta get in to work."

Leo had a talk with his boss about full time employment. "When does Julia finish nursing school so I can take her hours?"

"You got good timing, Leo. She just gave her notice. You can have her hours."

At home, Leo had been making himself scarce, breezing in and out, pretending to be busy-busy. He promised Merricat he would stay until he could have a talk with Millie and explain his move. Millie wasn't stupid; she knew something was going on.

He needed a new mattress anyway, so he bought one and a cheap sofa and had them delivered to the house on Ferguson. Nicky brought over some dishes and pots and pans, discards from Trina. Father Mike, who was thrilled they would be neighbors, brought over an old TV. Leo arranged for Nicky to pick up some stuff from the house while he took Millie out for lunch to explain the move.

He decided to make it a special day. He took her up to Madison to Ella's Deli, which had been his mother's favorite restaurant as a child. Millie was so excited. They ate grilled cheese sandwiches and fries, while taking in all the wonderful animated displays. Then, even though it was November, and the lakes brought in a chill effect, they got ice cream from The Chocolate Shoppe. Leo shared stories from his childhood and Millie was so sweet and happy and funny. On the way up, that is. It was cowardly of him, but he planned on breaking the bad news in the car on the way home. That way, she'd be in the back seat and he wouldn't have to make eye contact. Yeah, cowardly.

How do explain such things to a child? Aunt Rose said to try to think what was best for Millie. He decided what was best for Millie would be to present this whole thing as his idea. That way, she would be angry with him, and not her mother.

"Mill?

"Yes, Lee. When you call me Mill, I call you Lee."

"I know. Listen, honey. I got to tell you something important and it might make you sad but it's actually going to be a good thing."

"What?"

"I'm going to get my own apartment."

"What? Why?"

"Well, it's time, honey. I moved in with your grandma after my accident so she could help me and then we all moved in together to help each other. And then Nana Rose moved out and now I'll move out. You've got your mom and Choppy…"

"No!' Millie said and started to cry. "No, I don't want you to go. Lee-Lo, no!" She wailed. She couldn't catch her breath and Leo worried she would hyperventilate so he exited on the next off-ramp in Stoughton. He pulled over on a side road. Millie unbuckled her seat belt and climbed up and tried to sit on his lap. "You're too big, aren't you?" He pushed the button below the seat and moved it back to make room.

"I'm not big, I'm small. Too small to leave me. Where are you going? To D.C.? Like Nana?"

"I'd never move far from you. I'm just going to be in a little house a block from church. Father Mike will be my neighbor. You can visit and sleep over sometimes."

"Can I bring Choppy?"

"Of course."

"I don't like this idea, Leo. I'm used to you!" She held his face between her two little hands. "I've had you since I was a baby!"

Leo tried but he couldn't hold the tears back. "I know. This is just a small change. Really, it's just a change in where I sleep. Everything will stay the same for you and mommy. I can even still take you to school every morning, I just won't be able to pick you up."

"Who will pick me up? Mommy works."

"Maybe Bonnie can take you home."

"Susie goes straight to ballet after school."

"Well, your mom will work that out, okay?"

"Not okay!" she said, and then she did something very strange. She slapped Leo across the face. Not hard, but still. She hopped over the seat and lay down on the back seat, crying her little heart out. She wouldn't sit up and buckle her seat belt, so Leo had to get out of the car and open the door, but she stiffened her body and wouldn't bend. Leo was afraid he would hurt her, so he got back in the car and drove home with her spread out on the back seat. She cried until she fell asleep.

He carried her into the house and lay her on her bed. Merricat followed with a worried look on her face.

"This is on you," he said, and left.

The next day, Leo moved out. He got a text from Merricat saying he didn't need to pick up Millie and take her to school anymore—she would be car-pooling with Bonnie. And Rosie was coming home for Thanksgiving. They were going to eat at two. Why didn't he come and invite Father Mike as well?

He texted back, "Thanks, I have other plans. Why don't you invite Father Mike yourself?"

She texted back, "What am I supposed to tell Millie?"

He texted back, "You'll think of something."

She texted back, "Is this how it's going to be?"

"What do you mean by *this*?"

"Our lives, Leo."

Millie called and texted him from Merricat's phone at all hours of the day and night. It wasn't hard to know it was her and not Merricat since her texts were usually one- or two-word messages: "*SAD.*" "*Choppy. Tricks.*" "*Hate shrimp.*" Sometimes she dictated long messages: "Leo, I don't know if you know about this but we learned about octopuses today at school, and it's octopuses, not octopi. But it's hippopotami and not hippopotamuses. Remember *Viginti Tres*? My twenty-three-armed octopus? I dreamed about him again. He was strangling me."

Leo texted Merricat to say he hoped she was getting Millie some counseling.

Millie spent the night one Saturday and they invited Father Mike for pizza. Millie said, "I am so glad I'm not a *bedge-a-tarian* anymore. I love sausage and pepperoni. I never knew what I was missing. Mom's not a *bedge-a-tarian* anymore either. Do you think Jesus was a *bedge-a-tarian*, Father Mike?"

"No, he wasn't. We know he ate fish and he might have eaten lamb, though the Bible only mentions fish."

"I hate fish. Gag! Father, remember when you told me to keep my NBE a secret?"

"NDE," Leo corrected her.

"Well, I had to break my promise. Alexander was trying to tell our class today that animals don't go to Heaven. And Caroline Givens' dog had just died and she just started bawling like a baby. So, I stood up and said, "Listen, people, animals do go to Heaven and I am one-hundred percent sure of it because the day I drownded, I went to Heaven and saw my great aunt and a dog. So, don't you worry, Caroline, Peabody is in Heaven."

"Did you tell your mom about this?" Leo asked.

"Oh, she knows. My teacher called her and there was yelling."

"Merricat will handle it, Leo," Father said.

But Merricat couldn't handle it. Word got all around school and the Rockford Register Star sent a reporter over to see if she could interview Millie. Merricat closed the door on the reporter. But things got challenging for Millie. Kids started to tease her. "Hey Guardian Angel, how's St. Peter?" One kid asked Millie if she would come over and hold a séance at his house because he wanted to talk to his deceased cat. Oh, Millie was a tough cookie, but everyone had a breaking point.

Leo felt guilty that he wasn't there to help. Texting and talking on the phone and sharing a night here and there was not the same as when he had been a co-parent. To self-protect, Millie developed a little attitude and it horrified Leo to see his sweet little girl morph into a kid with a chip on her shoulder. How did they get to this?

Merricat texted him that Millie got in trouble at school for telling her classmate Ben to go to "Hell-ven."

Leo texted back: What's Hell-ven?

Merricat texted: Her word for purgatory, a cross between hell and heaven. The teacher thought she said, "Go to hell, *Ben*."

Thanksgiving Day came and went and Leo just stayed in bed and ate a salami sandwich to celebrate the harvest and blessings of the year. He flipped through his Uncle Brody's photo album (he had no idea why he didn't give it to his father), and even though he found picture after picture of what looked like a normal, happy family, it made him sad. These were his blood relatives and he never knew them. At about seven o'clock a persistent knock on his door forced him to throw on some clothes and get up and answer it. Father Mike stood there balancing a plate covered in foil.

"Thank God they're not *bedge-a-tarians* anymore, right?" Father Mike said as he watched Leo remove the foil.

Leo dug into the plate, heaped with his Thanksgiving favorites, plus the new item: real turkey. Aunt Rose had made her famous sweet potato casserole. He sighed with each bite. It was home.

"Leo," Father said, "I owe you an apology and I hope you can forgive me."

"What? Why?"

"I get too involved sometimes. The Minster General, my superior, told me it would be my biggest challenge. I'm a bit of a buttinsky."

"Go on," Leo said.

"Well, when you started ushering and more people got to know you at church, there was talk and I did not like it. Talk about you and Merricat. The talk went along the lines that you were siblings in an incestuous relationship. I tried to quell that kind of nonsense."

"Mike, you think Merricat and I care about what people say or think? We've lived our whole lives with people mumbling under their breaths. People always thought our moms were lesbians. No one wanted to believe they were sisters. We don't care what people think."

"I know that. You two can handle it. But I was thinking about Millie. One day after Mass, I heard a little girl tell Millie that her mom and dad were sinners. "We're all sinners," Millie shot back. The dig had gone right over her head, this time. But she will be the one to get hurt."

"Merricat and I have talked to her about different kinds of families. You know Merricat, she researched the hell out of the subject. Did you know,

Father, there are seven different family types? There's the traditional, two-parent nuclear family, the single-parent family, the extended family, the childless family, the step family, the gay family, and the grandparent family. We explained to Millie that she lives in an extended family. It's not a big deal."

"Leo, I'm not arguing."

"Furthermore, the traditional two-parent nuclear family really only existed for a short time in history, from 1950 to 1965. It was the exception rather than the rule. Merricat read that before that time, extended families were the norm, for tens of thousands of years, and after that, it's been a mix of all types. Sociologists say those fifteen years that the traditional family was thought to be the norm was really a freakish historical moment. This one sociologist explained that nowadays people 'buy' an extended family. At least affluent people. Think about all the help people buy nowadays: professional child care, babysitting, tutoring, coaching, therapy. These were things extended families used to provide."

"Wow, Merricat really does do her research. But back to me being a buttinsky. I was worried about you guys, especially Millie. And I may have overstated things."

"What do you mean?"

"When I implied Merricat was *seeing* Massimo, I guess I was exaggerating. They just had a friendly glass of wine after class once. He may have been interested in Merricat but she wasn't interested in him."

"How do you know?"

Father Mike looked down at his hands. "She told me. Leo…Merricat is in love with you."

Leo's jaw nearly unhinged. "Father Mike!"

"Well, when she told me that, I thought maybe it would be best if you got your own place. Like I said, a buttinsky."

Leo had no words. He set down his fork. The food he'd just eaten was stuck right in the middle of his chest, putting pressure on his heart. Merricat, in love with him? *When*? *How*? *WHAT*?

Caffe Greco was closed the day after Thanksgiving through Sunday, so Leo had a mini vacation. He took Millie to the Discovery Center Children's Museum and the Burpee Museum of Natural History. At lunch downtown, Millie, said, "Leo, can't you come back? It stinks without you. Mom's sad all the time. I'm sad all the time. Even Choppy looks sad all the time, but that's just his face, he always looks sad all the time."

"Millie, I can't. It's not going to happen."

"I don't understand. Everything was perfect. Now Mom lays on the couch a lot. She's turning into a sofa spud. Get it, Leo? Sofa spud?"

Back at work on Monday, Leo went through the motions. Pour a shot, pop a top. Mix a little of this with a little of that. It seemed that all joy had drained from his life. People noticed, asking him if he felt okay, had he lost weight?

A week before Christmas, Rosie came to town and announced to Merricat that she was moving back to Madison to help Eleanor run Fe-mail. Eleanor didn't want to move to D.C. after all, and although Rosie loved her job with the Obama administration, she hated D.C. and missed Merricat and Millie. Merricat texted Leo: I think they're a couple. Are Eleanor and my mom a couple?

Leo texted back: Of course, they're a couple. Have you been blind?

Christmas approached and he received text after text from Millie and Merricat and Rosie to please come for Christmas dinner, so he said yes, he would come. Merricat had invited Father Mike but he was going home to Chicago for the holiday, so it would be the four of them, just like old times.

At the last minute, Leo chickened out and bailed. How could he go? He wasn't sure he could keep it together. It would be too weird to be a guest in the house that used to be home. He wished he had never said yes in the first place. He texted Merricat that he'd come down with a sore throat and didn't want to infect anyone.

She texted back: Liar.

And a merry effing Christmas to you! he texted.

You're breaking Millie's heart, she texted.

You broke mine. A heart for a heart.

You're an asshole.

And a merry effing Christmas to you!

He had bought gifts. They were a book family. Books for birthdays, Christmas, Valentine's Day. He'd found some pop-up books for Millie that he knew she would flip over. One on the suffragettes for Rosie and two Italian cookbooks for Merricat. He would drop them on the doorstep in the morning.

Christmas dinner was a can of Campbell's Chicken Noodle. He knew it was pathetic. He wanted it to be pathetic. He could have grilled a steak; there was steak in the freezer. He could have even thrown a frozen pizza in the oven, but he knew there could be nothing more pathetic than a can of cold soup for Christmas dinner, so he pulled back the lid and dug in with a spoon.

Millie texted on Merricat's phone around six o'clock. "This is me, Millie. Santa came, but he didn't bring me what I wanted the most: *you*." Leo texted back: I'll be by tomorrow!

Leo rambled around the house. It couldn't really be Christmas. For Leo, Christmas was always his mom. The candy-caned-shaped cookies she made. The stockings filled with healthy food—raisins and nuts; and practical treats—pencils and glue sticks. Gifts that came wrapped in newspaper: books about the Beatles, sheet music, guitar picks, socks. For some reason Leo and Merricat always got socks for Christmas, which invariably led to jokes about the Quinlayne big feet. Christmas was Camille's quiet smile, the way she went about her business with the sole intention of making things nice for everybody. When Leo had his near-death experience and saw his mother, he did not want to turn back, he wanted to keep swimming through the dark velvety air until he found himself folded in her arms. He lay on the couch, closed his eyes, and tried to bring back the experience and the feeling of great love. Leo needed to feel some love.

He awoke to a knock on the door. Nicky stood on the steps with a pumpkin pie in hand. It was snowing and he did not know why, but it was one of the most beautiful scenes he had ever seen in his life: a friend, on his snowy doorstep, with pie. Nicky smiled and said, "Friends don't let friends go through Christmas without pie." He came in and said he would have a slice himself. Leo made coffee.

"I like what you've done with the place," Nicky said looking around at the card table and microwave oven sitting on the counter.

"Thank you. HGTV is a beautiful thing."

"Dang, I forgot the whipping cream."

"Hey, this looks delicious. Did Trina make it?"

"My mother-in-law. She hates me so it might be poisoned."

"Then we'll die together," Leo said, handing Nicky a fork. "How was your day? Why are you here? Shouldn't you be home?"

"We had a good day, but we're having a hard time managing Sophia's diet and insulin. I feel guilty eating pie because she couldn't have any. Trina made her a special pie and apparently it tasted like shit."

"Poor kid," Leo said.

"So…"

"So…"

Nicky smiled. "Got any New Year's Resolutions?"

"As a matter of fact, I've been thinking I might move back home, to Madison. I miss it. Haven't been back since high school, but I'm itching to get my own place again. A little neighborhood bar."

"Sounds like a good plan. And you wouldn't be too far away from Millie."

"Yeah, Millie," Leo said wistfully. And then, very uncharacteristically, for Leo never really had a best friend before, Leo blurted out to Nicky: "Merricat's in love with me!" There, he'd said it out loud to another human being.

"What?"

"She told Father Mike, the self-proclaimed buttinsky."

Nicky shook his head. "His superior told him his nose was going to get him into trouble. Does Merricat know you know?"

"Who knows?"

"The big question is, how do you feel about it?"

"Who knows. It's complicated, Nick. We were raised like siblings, but we are cousins, but we aren't even really cousins because she was adopted."

"Merricat was adopted?"

"Yeah, as a baby."

"So, you're not really related?"

"Not by blood."

"Do you love her, Leo?"

"Yes, but not like that. I've never once in my life felt anything romantic or sexual for her. Too weird!"

Leo got up to grab the coffee pot to refill Nicky's cup, when there was a knock on the door. Leo said, "Who the hell could that be? Father Mike's in Chicago."

Nicky stuffed the last bite of pie in his mouth and said, "Well, I was just leaving." They walked to the door and when Leo opened it, Merricat was standing alone in the moonlight, holding a pumpkin pie and a can of whipped cream. "Merry Christmas, beautiful!" Nicky said and gave her a hug. Then he hurried off to his car.

"Come in," Leo said, holding the door open.

"Oh, you've already had pie," Merricat said, noticing it on the kitchen table.

"But it wasn't your mom's pie and Nicky didn't bring whipped cream." Leo took the pie and whipped cream from Merricat and set it on the counter. "Welcome to the humble abode. I just made coffee."

Merricat peeled off her coat and draped it over the chair.

"Pie or pie?" Leo asked, holding up both pie plates.

"No, thank you. Just coffee. How's your throat?"

"Fine, why? Oh, yeah." Leo had already forgotten his sore throat excuse. He cleared his throat. "Much better, thanks. How's my girl?"

"A sad sack. We had an early Christmas dinner and then Mom took her up to Madison to spend some time with Eleanor and the Femmys. She refused to go without Choppy, so Choppy went, too."

"But it's snowing. I hate to see them on the road."

"I-90's always clear. Besides, Millie's dying to meet the infamous Femmys."

"You know she'll come back and burn all her training bras."

"She doesn't have training bras."

"It was a joke. I know she's been begging for one."

"Oh, right."

Leo looked at Merricat. It's funny but when you've known someone all your life, and you look at their face, you don't just see them as they are now, at this particular moment in time. When Leo looked at Merricat, he saw her at age four with thick loose curls; at age seven, with missing front teeth; and at ten, with pudgy, rosy cheeks; at thirteen with braces; and at sixteen with zits. And he saw her in love with Brice, and he saw her pregnant with Camilla, and he saw the love in her eyes as a new mother, and he saw her at her lowest when she was going through the divorce, and then he saw her shattered when her sweet little girl nearly drowned.

Leo brought Merricat a cup of coffee with cream, or as he always teased a cup of "cream with coffee."

"Leo, how did we get so screwed up?"

"A certain buttinsky who wears a collar?"

"Choppy?"

"Not Choppy, Father Mike!"

"Oh, yeah. He tries too hard. I guess his superior warned him that his nose was going to get him in trouble."

"So, I've heard," Leo said, chuckling.

"Leo, no one understands us, but us."

"True that."

Now she was crying. "Leo, I love you."

"I love you, too. You know I do."

"No, Leo. I love you…I'm in love with you."

Leo didn't know what to say. Seeing his hesitation, Merricat cried harder and lay her head down on the table. Leo sprang up from his chair and came around and squeezed her shoulder. He bent over and hugged her. "Cat, come on. It's okay. Don't cry."

Merricat raised her head. Leo grabbed a napkin from the table and handed it to her. She wiped her eyes and blew her nose. She stood up and said, "Where's your garbage?"

"I don't have one."

"You don't have a garbage can?"

"I use the disposal or the toilet."

"Men," she said.

"Women," he said.

She grabbed her coat and put her arm through but struggled with the other arm because she had stuffed her hat and scarf inside and forgot about it. "Here," Leo said, "let me help."

Merricat pulled her arm away. "I can do it myself, thank you." At that moment, she sounded exactly like Millie.

Leo watched her struggle. He put his hands in his pockets and looked down at the floor to keep from laughing. But then the zipper on her jacket was stuck, something that happened all the time to Millie, and without thinking, he moved in closer and grabbed the pull tab and jiggled it a little. Before he knew what hit him, Merricat was kissing him...on the lips! For a split second, he thought about pulling back. Was it weird? Was it like kissing your sister? No, actually, it wasn't. Was it wrong? But then—how wonderfully strange—something inside him clicked and he felt an overflowing, powerful love overcome him. He kissed Merricat back. How can a person cry and kiss at the same time? When they broke for air, Merricat looked up and said, "Then you do love me...that way."

Leo laughed and wiped a little snot from her nose with his sleeve. "I honestly didn't know until this very moment. I mean, honestly, never in my life have I ever had romantic or sexual feelings for you—"

"Shut up, you idiot, you're breaking the spell."

"Until now," Leo said. And just like in the movies, he kissed Merricat while walking backwards to his bedroom. "I just bought a new mattress," he said, playfully pushing her down on it.

When Leo woke up the next morning, he had a flash of regret. What did we do? Now what? What does this mean? What about Mille? But then Merricat woke up and they made love again and everything was right with the world.

"I have an idea," Merricat said.

"Hmmmmm?"

"Let's get in the car and drive to Madison."

"And do what? I think it's snowing again."

"See Mom and Millie and the Femmys and share our good news."

"What good news?" Leo teased.

"That we are in love and we are going to get married and we're moving to Madison and we could give a rat's ass about what anyone thinks. We'll be a traditional family!"

"But Cat, can we actually get married? Aren't there laws?"

Merricat waved her hand. "Oh, I researched all that. As long as one of the cousins is sterile, first cousins or adopted cousins can get married in Illinois or Wisconsin. And I've had a hysterectomy."

"As usual, you've done your homework."

"Oh my god, Leo, you wouldn't believe what I found out. There's something called the *Westermarck* effect, or reverse sexual imprinting. This is where siblings or kids who grow up in close proximity—sharing bed and bathrooms, wrestling around, hugging and kissing—develop a strong sexual aversion to each other as puberty sets in.

"That was us! We were never incestuous!"

"Never! I also found that cousin couples aren't that rare. Albert Einstein's parents were cousins, and he married his cousin. FDR and Eleanor Roosevelt were second cousins."

"Weren't Queen Victoria and Prince Albert second cousins?"

"Yes. I found quite a few famous cousin marriages: Thomas Jefferson, Edgar Allan Poe, Johann Sebastian Bach, H.G. Wells, Charles Darwin, Oliver Wendell Holmes. Plus, get this, Kevin Bacon and Kyra Sedgwick are actually ninth cousins once removed which they found out after they were married, and they appeared on one of those ancestry shows."

"I'll marry you on one condition," Leo said, kissing Merricat's neck.

"And what is that?"

"That I can adopt Millie."

"Oh, I researched all that, too. We just need Brice's consent and he has proven that he wants nothing to do with us. What kind of father doesn't even come to see his daughter when she almost drowned? All he has to do is legally terminate his parental rights, which I know he will do."

"Oh, I thought of one more condition."

"What now?

"That I get to be the one to tell Brice we're getting married."

23.
leo & merricat & millie & rosie
& eleanor & paul & nicky
& father mike

MILLIE MADE HER first communion in the same church in Madison where Leo and Merricat were married. Rosie said Millie looked more like a bride in her elaborate, "re-fashionized," full-length, sparkling and bejeweled white dress and veil than Merricat did; Merricat had worn an ivory, below-the-knee fitted suit for her small wedding.

After the communion Mass they gathered at Leo's new bar *Caffe Milli*. Merricat came up with the name. *Milli* for Millie, but also, in Italian, *milli* meant thousand, and the address just happened to be 1000 East Washington Street, so the name fit perfectly. "Also," Merricat said, "because it's going to bring us *milli* blessings."

The bar had not even opened yet. The grand opening was scheduled for this coming Saturday. Millie felt very special that she got to have her communion luncheon there. With their little family, plus Rosie, Father Mike, the Russo family, the Femmys, Leo's new business partners, and Paul Soglin and his second wife Sarah (the love of his life), they totaled twenty. The guests gathered around the candlelit table and oooohed and ahhhhhed about the beautiful centerpieces Merricat had laid out.

Using all the knowledge he had acquired from opening and running Silver Darlings, Leo had decided what Madison needed was a cool Italian caffe/bar. Merricat, in her research found *the* coolest Italian caffe/bar in all of America in Greenwich Village, New York, called *Caffe Dante*, and they took a belated honeymoon to the city and visited Dante and some other wonderful cafes and bars. They "borrowed" many of the cool features of Dante to achieve the desired mix of New York cool and Italian classic: white subway tile on the bar, white brick walls, brown and cream checker-board tile flooring, banquettes, small tables with bentwood chairs, and lots of greenery. Cuisine would be simple classic Italian with classic cocktails like Negroni, Aperol Spritz, Bellini, Rossini, Puccini, just to name a few.

Leo and Merricat knew they needed a partner, both for financial reasons and to help run the place, as they planned on being open from eleven a.m. to two a.m. Jules Freeman, Leo's bartender from Silver Darlings, jumped at the opportunity to relocate to Madison from Chicago. Jule's wife, Luna, was Italian-American and a great cook. She and Merricat would do all the cooking. As they did today, only today's meal was not restaurant fare, it was "Millie fare." Millie requested Quiche Lorraine, Pigs in a Blanket, fruit salad but with only grapes and kiwi fruit, bacon, fresh-squeezed orange juice, champagne for the adults, and cannoli cake for "my holy communion feast."

Rosie looked a little ragged as last night she and Eleanor hosted three of Nicky and Trina's five girls at their home, since Leo and Merricat didn't have room for the whole family in their place above the caffe. Rosie, nearly seventy, hadn't slowed down even a smidgen. At home now back in Madison, she was gearing up to manage Paul Soglin's next run for mayor. Paul had served from 1973 to 1979 and then again from 1989 to 1997. He took time off to teach at Harvard and to practice law, and had run in and lost the mayoral election in 2003, but he was ready and raring to go for a seventh term in office. He had asked Rosie to manage his 2011 campaign and she had accepted, already canvassing the room and recruiting volunteers. Vintage Rosie.

After Father Mike said grace, Merricat served Millie her orange juice in a champagne glass and Leo made a toast: "To our beautiful little Millie, on this holy day."

"*Very* holy day," Millie added.

"*Very* holy day," Leo repeated.

"Thank you for being a joy in our lives and for keeping us on our toes. To Millie!"

"To Millie," the guests joined in, clinking glasses.

"Millie," Merricat said, "would you like to say a few words?"

Millie, never one to shy away from the spotlight, scooted her chair out, stood up, and cleared her throat. "I would like to take this opportunity to thank you for coming today to celebrate me. It is a very important day in my life. And, I just want you to know, that I found the body of Christ to taste very delicious, and I'm glad I'm not a bedge-a-tarian anymore!"

One of the Femmys gasped but everyone else laughed, including Father Mike, who seemed to get the biggest kick out of Millie's declaration.

"Thank you, Millie," Merricat said, gently pushing her back down in her chair.

Merricat turned to Leo. "Only Millie," she said.

Leo smiled. "Only Millie."

Leo looked around and took it all in. The beautiful people, the beautiful place. He had to pinch himself each and every morning to confirm that this was his life: married to the love of his life, legal father to the little girl of his life, true friends, sweet dog, and now a new caffe/bar to boot. He knew in his bones, his mother was here, in the room. Was it her saying, "Behold! Look at your blessings. Be thankful! Be glad!" And he was.

Merricat once told Leo that Father Mike didn't think miracles were extraordinary happenings. "Father Mike says we just think miracles break natural laws," Merricat explained, "but earth's miracles are just Heaven's laws."

Leo teased, "Oh, what does he know, he's just a buttinsky." But really, Leo knew he was surrounded by miracles. Like the miracle that happened to Leo a month ago. He had opened up his mailbox to find a rather formal-looking envelope from Green & Grayson Attorneys at Law. He thought it must have something to do with the new business, but when he opened it, he was hit with a swirl of emotions. A check from the estate of Mackinney B. Lennox in the amount of $6,328.51 was enclosed with a letter from the attorney explaining his father's last wish: that upon his death, his Beatles albums and memorabilia would be sold and the proceeds awarded to his only legitimate son, Leo Mackinney Lennox. Leo was sure poor Mackinney thought his treasure was worth a lot more, but Leo was touched and grateful and he used the money to build the beautiful bar in the caffe. He thought his dad would have liked that.

Leo popped a Pig-in-a-Blanket into his mouth and looked around. The sun streamed in through the freshly washed windows and the faces of all the people he loved were aglow. It could bring a guy to tears.

Oh, the wonder of it all. The pure wonder of it all.

acknowledgments

Special thanks to Mr. Mayor Paul Soglin, who in his generosity, allowed his real persona to be used in my fictional story. As I researched mayors and mayoral elections in Madison, Wisconsin, I came across the story of the young, hippie mayor. Paul's real life story was so compelling—so much more interesting than anything I could create—I knew I had to reach out to him to see if he would let me put him in my novel. He was game! In 2020, during the pandemic, we zoomed and I was able to interview him. What stories! Of course, I have taken liberties with some of the names and places, but all the historical events about Paul Soglin are true! Thank you, Your Honor, for the honor!

a note about the author

Acclaimed picture book author Karla Clark began her writing career with women's fiction. She returns to women's fiction with her fourth novel, *The Wonder of It All*, a family story following four generations trying to navigate what family really means. Clark lives in Rockford, Illinois, with her husband, son, and Shih-Poo. To stay creative, she creates paper collages and digital art which she sells at art fairs.

connect with the author

Facebook: @karlajclark
Instagram: @karlaclark123
X: @karlaclark
Email: karla.clark@comcast.net
Website: karlaclarkauthor.com

www.ingramcontent.com/pod-product-compliance
Lightning Source LLC
Chambersburg PA
CBHW020509020726
47493CB00001B/245